HEAD OVER HOOVES

BOYS OF THE BAYOU GONE WILD

ERIN NICHOLAS

Head Over Hooves ISBN: 978-1-952280-26-9

Editor: Lindsey Faber

Cover photo: Wander Aguiar

Cover design: Najla Qamber, Qamber Designs

THE SERIES

Boys of the Bayou-Gone Wild
Things are going to get wild when the next batch of bayou boys falls in love!

Otterly Irresistible
Heavy Petting
Flipping Love You
Sealed With A Kiss
Head Over Hooves
Say It Like You Mane It

Connected series...

The Hot Cakes Series
Appleby, Iowa

One small Iowa town.
Two rival baking companies.
A three-generation old family feud.

And six guys who are going to be heating up a lot more than the kitchen.

Sugar Rush (prequel)
Sugarcoated
Forking Around
Making Whoopie
Semi-Sweet On You
Oh, Fudge
Gimme S'more

HEAD OVER HOOVES

You know in movies where the big city girl lands in a small town for the holidays and falls for the hunky guy who saves Christmas?

This isn't that story.

But this guy does look fantastic in flannel. And out of flannel...

Finding true love with his one-and-only soul mate? Drew Ryan's given up on that.

But a hot holiday fling in Louisiana, far from his responsibilities and good guy image back home, is now on the top of his list for Santa.

So when he's knocked on his ass—literally—by a Christmas elf who's stealing a sleigh full of gifts and using his reindeer to commit the crime, he definitely doesn't expect to fall head over heels.

This holiday couldn't get any worse for Rory Robins.

First, her hair wasn't supposed to turn green. It's not even Christmas green.

And the elf costume wasn't supposed to be two sizes too small.

And her con-man father wasn't supposed to show up and go all real-life-Grinch on her beloved new hometown.

And she definitely wasn't supposed to run into anyone while trying to fix the problem. Especially not the hunky guy who already seems too good to be true.

But he does have a way of making her "cocoa" even hotter and a whole lot sweeter...

Still, he lives in Iowa. The only good thing her father ever gave her was a healthy distrust of men who are never around. She's *not* doing a long-distance thing.

This little fling is only going to last as long as the temporary color of her hair.

Only nothing seems to be fading. And she might be asking Santa for just one more thing...

1

Autre, Louisiana was a little less *merry and bright* and a lot more *crazy and garish*. But there was no doubt this was where Drew Ryan was supposed to be.

There was fake snow, *lots* of red and green and white, an instrumental version of "Santa Clause Is Comin' To Town" blaring over the loudspeakers, and a giant wooden cutout of a cartoon alligator wearing a red Santa hat and holding a sign that read, "Santa's Village".

And if that wasn't enough to convince him, the elf chasing the eight tiny reindeer with the person-sized candy cane would have.

After all, eight tiny reindeer came right out of the poem *'Twas the Night Before Christmas*.

But the poem left out the gorgeous elf in the skimpy red dress, thigh-high black boots with candy cane striped stockings peeking out of the tops, and bright green hair.

It was a good thing she wasn't working at the North Pole. She'd freeze very important body parts in that dress.

Not that it was *hot* in Louisiana in December, but Drew appreciated not needing his heavy winter coat right now and definitely appreciated that the elf wasn't feeling chilly enough to cover up.

The entire scene was the very definition of chaos, and he had no idea what to do. So, he just leaned his arms on the top of the fence that surrounded the barnyard/Santa's Village—which he assumed was the Boys of the Bayou Gone Wild petting zoo under normal circumstances—and watched.

The "reindeer" were actually baby goats wearing reindeer antlers and the elf was trying to herd them toward the barn using the giant plastic candy cane as a shepherdess hook. But they seemed to think they were playing tag and scattered in eight different directions.

Clearly fed up, she tossed the candy cane and lunged to try to grab one with her bare hands.

She missed.

"You little bastards!" she exclaimed.

Just as the music abruptly shut off.

"Bastards is a bad word."

The woman turned and Drew looked to his left. There was a little boy standing there eating a red and white snow cone.

A snow cone. In December.

For an Iowa-born-and-raised boy like Drew, that was weird. But at least the red and white was festive.

"Oh, hey, Samuel," the woman said, pushing her neon green hair back from her face. "Didn't see you there."

"I know. You probably wouldn't have used that word if you did."

The woman didn't look entirely convinced of that. "Are you *sure* it's a bad word?" she asked him.

He nodded. "Very sure."

"Maybe not in... elvish."

"You weren't speaking in elvish."

"Do *you* speak elvish?" she asked.

"Well..."

"Exactly," she said with a nod. "So what I said sounded bad in *English* but in elvish I was saying, 'You guys are so cute!'"

She and Samuel stood there looking at each other for a long moment.

Neither blinked.

"Say 'have a Merry Christmas' in elvish," Samuel finally replied.

"Oh. Um." She scratched her neck, clearly trying to come up with something.

Drew pushed away from the fence and walked toward the gate that would let him into the main yard of the petting zoo. "I'm going to need your name and date of birth."

Samuel and the woman both swung to face him.

Drew stepped through the gate and looked at Samuel expectantly.

"What for?" the kid asked.

"For the Rudeness Report I'm filing with Santa, of course."

"Rudeness Report?" Samuel asked. "What's that?"

"When a kid is being rude to one of the hard-working elves who are just trying to make Christmas nice and festive and happy for everyone, we file a report with Santa. He doesn't like his helpers being treated badly."

Samuel looked him up and down. "What about what she said? Santa is okay with that?"

"You mean when she called the goats cute?" Drew asked. "I don't understand the problem."

Drew glanced at the woman. She had her arms crossed and was watching, amused. Samuel looked suspicious.

"Who are you?" Samuel asked.

"Santa's nephew," the women interjected before Drew could respond. "He's here to inspect the village."

Just then there was a loud crash somewhere behind the little shack with the wide front porch where Drew assumed Santa would sit with the kids.

3

The elf closed her eyes and took a deep breath. "Little bastards," she muttered as she let it back out.

"They really are cute," Samuel said.

Drew fought a grin.

Clearly bored with all of this—and not actually buying that he was being written up for anything—Samuel started toward the other end of the petting zoo, but after just a few steps, he stopped and turned back.

"When I call my sister a little bastard later and tell my mom that Rory told me it means cute, we're all going to be in trouble, you know."

So, the elf's name was Rory, huh?

Rory sighed. "Or you could just...not do that."

"I could." Samuel took a bite of his snow cone, considering that.

"I can file more than one report," Drew said.

Samuel nodded. "Yeah, but Santa probably already knows I'm impotent."

Drew managed to disguise his laugh as a cough at the last minute. Surely the kid meant impertinent, right? "I don't think that's the word, man."

"Do you know my grandma?"

"No."

"Then I probably know better than you what she calls me."

Yeah, he definitely meant impertinent.

That kid was *destined* for the naughty list, Drew decided.

Drew watched the boy disappear around the snow cone stand several yards away. "What are the chances he calls his little sister a bastard and you get in trouble?" Drew asked the elf.

"About eighty-seven percent. That kid is kind of a button pusher."

Drew chuckled as another crash came from around the back of the Santa shack. "Like the goats?"

"You mean the *reindeer*?" Her lips twitched.

Just then one of the goat-reindeer came barreling around the corner, his antlers hanging under his chin. "Yeah, that's what I meant."

Another goat came trotting after the first. He stopped when he saw Rory and gave her a quick, "*Behhhh!*" Then started toward the snow cone stand.

Drew took a single step to the left and leaned over to scoop the little animal up. The goat bleated again, but Drew held him firmly.

Rory's eyebrows rose. "You're a goat wrangler?"

"Goats, alpacas, even actual reindeer." He shifted the goat so he could extend one hand. "I'm Drew Ryan."

"Oh, you're the guy from Iowa. You're bringing us real reindeer."

Rory took his hand, and Drew noticed that they both more or less just held on instead of actually shaking.

"I am. You've heard of me."

"This is obviously a Boys of the Bayou Gone Wild thing, but I'm in charge of putting Santa's Village and all of the activities together," Rory said. They were still holding hands. "Jordan told me they had a friend who had actual reindeer and he was going to loan us a few. Pretty cool."

Another goat darted by and Drew reluctantly let go of her to lean over and scoop that animal up as well. They were squirming and Rory immediately led him toward the barn and opened the pen for him. He put the two animals down and closed them inside.

"So you work for the Landrys and the petting zoo?" he asked as they headed back out to the yard.

She shook her head. "No. I—" She closed her eyes and sighed. "Actually, I shouldn't tell you what I do for living. But no, I don't work here. I'm volunteering my time. I think this is a really cool thing they're doing and since it's the first time, I thought it was a great chance to jump in and get involved."

He was intrigued.

He knew the petting zoo hadn't been around for long and that this was the first time they'd had a big holiday event. But he didn't care about Santa's Village. He was intrigued by Rory.

And he really shouldn't be. Any woman who was into sweet things like baby goats in reindeer antlers and making children's holiday wishes come true and cartoon alligators wearing Santa hats was not what he was looking for. He could have all of that back in Iowa. Well, maybe not the alligator. There weren't a lot of those that far north. But a cow in a reindeer hat? Or a pig? Sure, definitely.

And he didn't want sweet and cute. He was here for... not that.

The other six goats were still darting around the yard and he managed to reach out and snag another one. "Why don't you want me to know what you do for living?" he asked as he carried it to the pen and lifted it over the gate to set it inside with its friends.

She narrowed her eyes. "Because my hair is green."

Drew chuckled. Even though he wasn't sure what they were talking about. "Okay."

"It wasn't supposed to turn *green*. I mean, it's not even Christmas green."

He nodded. "More of a..."

"Neon lime green," she filled in. She laughed. "You can say it. I have a mirror."

Drew grinned. "It's still festive."

"How very polite of you to find such a nice word to use. Yeah, this hair is exactly why I should not tell you that I own the hair salon in town and am in charge of making other people's hair look good."

He laughed again. "Yeah, you probably shouldn't tell me that."

She nodded, smiling widely.

He pulled his gaze away from that smile and leaned over as another goat darted by. He grabbed it and carried it to the pen as well.

Rory scooped one up as well and put it in the pen with the others.

He was impressed by how easily she handled the animal. He also appreciated the way handling the goat made the short skirt of her elf dress pull up on her thighs. Her very nice thighs.

Now see if *those* were attached to a just-here-for-a-good-time girl who wasn't into making Christmas magical for a sweet little town, he'd be a very happy guy.

"I suppose we should tell Jordan that you're here," Rory said.

"Oh, is Jordan around?"

"She's just over with all the people on the other end of the petting zoo. Where the snow cones and face painting and story time is going on today. We're trying to keep things festive in the zoo while also keeping this area open so we—I"—She sighed—"can get it all set up."

Don't react to that sigh. Don't offer to help. You do not *need to be Santa's handyman.*

Drew shook his head. "I didn't notice any other people. Except for the kid."

Rory put a hand on her hip and tipped her head. "Because of the dress, right?"

Without thinking about doing it—or specifically why he *shouldn't* do it—Drew let his gaze travel over her from the top of her neon green head to the tips of her black leather boots. It was a good dress. And the body inside it was giving him a few thoughts about *unwrapping* things and yes, activities that might land him on the naughty list.

He cleared his throat. "What about the dress?"

"It's maybe the reason you didn't notice there were other people around?"

"I don't know what you're insinuating," he said with mock insult.

She laughed and plucked the front of the dress away from her breasts. "This dress is supposed to be two sizes bigger than it is."

She sighed again as she let go of the fabric and the dress went back to clinging affectionately to those breasts. Understandably.

"It's not appropriate for wearing here with kids around," she said. "Or really with *anyone* around. Which I realized *after* I put it on in the back stall of the barn and didn't have a choice. And then Lionel Benoit, Jordan's grandpa, about tripped and fell, and Nancy Howell gave me one of her looks. It's just one more way I'm blowing this whole Santa's Village thing."

Drew decided not to comment on the fact that he was definitely pro tiny dress. "What do you mean, you're blowing this whole thing?"

She lifted a shoulder. "I just really want this to go well. I only moved here three years ago and I really want to fit into the community. I want them to know that I love being here, and I want to be a part of the town, and this is the first time I've headed up a big project. And nothing is going right."

Drew felt a very familiar urge rise up in his chest, but he fought it. *Don't worry, I'll help. We'll fix this. It will all be okay.* All of that was right on the tip of his tongue.

That was who he was. Always. The quintessential good guy. The guy who would be putting together Santa's Village if he was back home in Appleby, Iowa at this moment and they actually needed a Santa's Village.

And it was exactly that reputation that he was trying to forget about for the week or so that he planned to spend in

Louisiana. He just wanted to let loose and have fun. The only thing he wanted to be responsible about was condom use.

So, his first instinct to jump in and help this woman set up a sweet Christmas village for the children of a new small town seemed like exactly the kind of thing he should be resisting.

"Just three more to go?" he asked as another goat got close enough for him to grab.

She looked around. "Yep." She lunged for one, but she didn't even touch fur as he scampered away.

She did, however, give Drew a flash of red panties under the very short skirt. He wondered if those had come with the dress or if she'd already had them.

Then told himself *firmly* to stop wondering about her.

She's not the one, bro. No sweethearts. You can have a dozen of those back home. Focus.

He needed to grab some names from Santa's naughty list. He wondered if Samuel could hook him up with that. Seemed the kid was well acquainted with that particular spreadsheet.

Drew stuck his leg out and got one goat nudged up against the side of the barn. Rory quickly picked the animal up and they headed for the pen.

"And now that we have real reindeer, we can take these antlers off." She undid the antlers from the goat she held before setting her down. "I really thought those were going to work." She held the antlers up, turning them back and forth.

He looked at the antlers on the goat he was holding in one arm. "Did you make these?"

She nodded. "I did a DIY tutorial on YouTube."

Good guess, Drew thought dryly. See, that was really sweet. She was a crafter. On top of being a Christmas elf volunteer. She'd even tried to die her hair for the occasion. Okay, so it hadn't turned out. It was still an indication of how seriously she took the small-town event.

He knew all about small-town events. Appleby wasn't any

bigger than Autre. And it had more than its share of everyone-pitch-in-and-come-together-as-a-community festivities.

He should definitely help her get the goats back into the barn and then make a plan to head to the local bar and pick up a hot bayou girl tonight. Sooner rather than later. The sooner he got reacquainted with his dirty side, the easier it would be to suppress his save-the-day side.

He started herding a goat that was still on the ground with one foot until Rory could scoop it up.

Once she had the goat in the pen, she leaned over and pulled the antlers from its mouth. "Not edible, Jafar."

"Did you say his name is Jafar?"

She nodded. "The older goats, including these guys' moms and dads, are named after the seven dwarves—yes, even the girls. So these guys and gals all have fairytale names too. This guy is Jafar. We also have Maleficent, Gaston, Cruella, Facilier, Gothel, Flotsam, and Jetsam." She frowned. "Now that I say them all out loud, they're all villains, aren't they?"

Drew huffed out a laugh. He was no expert, but many of those sounded vaguely familiar. They'd shown a lot of children's movies at his farm for various events over the years. Kids loved farm animals. Especially baby farm animals. "I think you might be right."

She narrowed her eyes at the goats. "Though I have to admit, it kind of makes sense."

Drew laughed as he helped her collect the rest of the antlers and ignored the goats begging to be released from their pen to run amok.

"Well, you've been replaced," Rory told them. "I'm sorry, but you were not able to fulfill the job requirements satisfactorily." Rory turned her back on them. "Please tell me that real reindeer are better behaved."

"Well..."

She groaned.

He laughed. "The ones I brought will be fine. Three girls and a boy. And the boy is a young one. So he's not a full-grown bull. *Those* can be a big pain in the ass."

"Awesome." She stood looking at him for a long moment.

Drew felt a distinct *something* crackle between them.

It was awareness. And attraction. Chemistry.

Dammit. There was no question she was gorgeous. And funny. And clearly a good person, at least as far as wanting to help her little town have a Santa's Village for the kids.

If he was looking for someone who was sweet and kind and generous and funny and a little awkward, he'd be thrilled right now.

But he'd been in town for less than an hour. He couldn't *already* get side-tracked. He couldn't let his natural tendencies screw this up *already*. He was looking for hot and sexy and a little adventurous and... yeah, those were about it.

He needed to focus here. He had a very short to do list. One —bring the reindeer to his friends. Two—have a hot fling. Three—remind himself that he didn't always have to be the guy who did the right thing. *Other people* could step up and do the right thing.

He knew Mitch Landry lived here. He'd heard a lot of stories about the Landry family from Mitch's girlfriend, Paige, who was originally from Appleby. He'd heard all about the Landrys and their friends from the rest of the Appleby gang who'd spent a couple weeks down here just this past summer too.

They'd all headed to Alabama to help out after a hurricane hit the coast. They'd literally gone out in boats and rescued people from their flooded homes, for fuck's sake. They'd helped set up temporary shelters. They'd helped with medical triage. They'd rescued animals.

And then there was this whole "petting zoo". It was really part of a bigger animal park that was also a sanctuary for abandoned and abused animals. They had alpacas and donkeys and camels. They also had a sloth, red pandas, lemurs, a zebra, a tiger, and a colony of *penguins*.

This was not just a bunch of fun guys and girls he thought could show him a good time during his week-long vacation from the cold up north. These were *good* people. People who made the shit Drew did back home seem like nothing.

And the idea of hanging out with people who would step up and jump in before he could, sounded *great* to him. This trip to Louisiana could actually be just a fun vacation. He didn't need to help Rory with this Santa's Village. There was a huge, rowdy, big-hearted Cajun family who would be here in two minutes to do whatever she needed done.

This wasn't his circus.

He didn't need to be a good guy here.

"Thanks for helping with the goats," Rory finally said.

"Sure. No problem." He started to take a step back.

But just then her eyes flickered to something past him and she frowned.

"Oh...*crap*." She suddenly looked upset.

Drew reacted by stepping forward again, closer to her.

Her eyes were still focused past him though. "Rory?" He glanced behind him but didn't see anything, but the barnyard and the line of trucks parked along the fence and a couple of guys walking toward the gate.

"What is he doing here? Oh no. No, no, *no*. This is terrible," she muttered.

It seemed that she was talking to herself, but it was clear that something—or someone—had her worried.

Drew frowned. "Are you okay?"

He glanced back again. Both men had now started in the direction of the barn. Okay, so one of them was worrying her. But it was impossible to tell which one it was.

"He might be here to ask me out," she said, again sounding like she was talking to herself. "*No.* I can't believe this."

If the guy was here to ask her out, he was *probably* the younger of the two. One of the men looked to be in his mid-50s, and was wearing khakis and a button-up shirt. Not that he couldn't be the one who wanted to take Rory out. But the other guy wasn't much older than thirty. He was in blue jeans and a t-shirt with a baseball cap on his head. He had dark hair and a beard and was built like he did construction or something. In other words, he was in great shape. And drove a nice truck.

But hey, Rory didn't want him to ask her out. That was all Drew needed to know.

"You don't want to see him?" Drew asked, focusing on her.

Rory shook her head, not looking at him. "Definitely not. Like *ever.*"

Okay then, he might not want to jump into saving the day by building a Santa Village, and fixing *all* of this woman's problems, but he wasn't about to make her face some guy that she didn't feel comfortable with.

"Crap. He's coming in here," Rory said, looking around as if for an escape.

Drew thought fast. He grasped to her upper arms, pulled her close, turned her so her back was to the open barn door where the two men were approaching and, just as the younger man's boot hit the wooden floor, Drew covered her mouth with his.

2

Rory would've gasped, except that Drew Ryan's lips were against hers. And he was kissing her. Like seriously kissing her. This was not a peck on the lips. It was not an oh-look-there's-mistletoe-overhead kiss. This was a full on I-*really*-mean-to-kiss-you kiss.

And she responded.

Drew was a good-looking guy. And he had not only swept in and helped her with the goats—which maybe on a good day would've seemed like a small thing, but today was *not* a good day—but he'd also made her laugh. And *that* was something that hadn't happened in too many days.

Everything about the Santa's Village project had been a mess. But now Drew Ryan was here and she not only had real reindeer, but she had a hot guy helping out without even being asked. And kissing her.

Kissing her *very well.*

Yeah, there was just nothing wrong with any of this.

His lips were demanding yet gentle and after a few seconds, he reached up to cup the back of her head with one hand in a sexy move that made her stomach swoop. His fingers slid into her hair and he tipped her head to fit their mouths together more fully.

Her lips opened on a swoony sigh, and he deepened the kiss, pressing closer and bringing her body up against his so they were thigh to thigh and belly to belly. The denim of his jeans against the bare skin between the tops of her boots and the bottom of her skirt was soft in that way only well-worn denim could be, and her palms itched to run over it. And the hard muscles under it.

And then there was the other hardness behind that denim that was a bit higher and more toward the front of his jeans. And made her palms even itchier.

Well, hello Iowa farm boy.

Rory went up on tiptoe to get closer, her breasts pressing into his chest. Her nipples beaded and she was very aware her girls were encased in only a black bra and the bit of red velvet she'd managed to tug up and over them when she'd pulled the dress on. She'd sacrificed coverage of her thighs to make her top half more kid-friendly. But she needed a new dress ASAP.

Though she might not toss this one out right away. Maybe Drew would want to play Santa's-hot-nephew-and-the-naughty-elf sometime while he was in town...

Drew lifted his head just then.

Rory stood staring up at him, breathing hard.

He stared back. His breathing was a little fast too.

She pressed her lips together, wanting to seal in the heat and tingles that he'd evoked.

"They both headed off toward where Jordan and everyone is," Drew said, his voice a little rough.

Rory frowned. Then a second later, it all came back to her. Oh, yeah. There had been a *reason* for the kiss.

Beau Hebert and her father—what the fuck was he doing here?—had been coming toward the barn.

Drew let go of her and they stepped apart. Rory ran a hand

through her hair and pried her hot, tingly lips apart. "How do you know?"

"I waved them in that direction," Drew said.

He must have done that behind her back—literally—while she'd been totally absorbed in the kiss.

Were they going to talk about the kissing? She'd like to.

Then she frowned. Beau Hebert, possibly the most perfect man for her, had seen her kissing Drew.

That might complicate her plans to marry the guy. Beau, that was. Not Drew.

Not the guy from Iowa. Which was somewhere way north of here. North enough that she didn't even know exactly how far it was.

"They both went?" she asked.

He nodded.

So he'd gotten rid of her father too. That was a good thing at least.

Roger Robins was the *last* person on earth she wanted to see. She could say that with confidence. And that included Camille Jackson, her nemesis from high school, and Susan what's-her-name, the one of her father's mistresses who'd thought it might be a good idea for her to get to know Roger's eighteen-year-old daughter. Stupid didn't even begin to cover *that*.

"He must not have recognized me from behind with my hair green," she said, wincing. This may be the first time she was happy about the mishap with her hair dye.

"Sorry. I was trying to think fast and give him a reason to definitely not ask you out."

She focused on Drew's face again and thought about what he'd just said. She frowned. "What?"

"You said that he was coming to ask you out and you didn't want him to. I figured the fastest way to get that message across was for you to be kissing another guy when he came in."

Right. She had said that. Kind of.

She shook her head. "I was actually talking about not wanting to see *my dad.* I definitely wanted Beau to ask me out. Although it *was* in the same sentence, and I can see why that was confusing."

"Um...huh?"

"The older guy is my dad. I do *not* want to see him. But Beau, the younger guy who is here to drop off the donated toys for Santa's Village, is the one I thought might ask me out. Something I've been hoping he would do for a while now." She watched Drew's face as she made that confession.

There was just a flicker that crossed his face, first of understanding, then maybe just a hint of jealousy.

She liked that more than she should.

Beau Hebert was one of the few guys in Autre, Louisiana who wasn't already taken, who also checked off all of the boxes on her checklist. And being from Autre, Louisiana was one of those boxes. The first one, incidentally.

Drew took a second to process that. "Oh. Shit. Um...sorry." He gave a little shrug.

She gave him a grin. "Did I act like I was upset while you were kissing me?"

He looked at her for a few beats. "As a matter of fact, you did not."

She nodded. "Because I wasn't. I mean, it's not ideal for the guy I want to ask me out to see me kissing another guy," she said. "But Beau and I aren't actually dating. And you just got to town, so it's not like he can think anything too serious is going on with us."

Drew nodded. "Absolutely. I'll tell him so, if you'd like."

Her eyebrows shot up. "Well, I mean, you don't have to rush out and tell everybody that now that we've kissed, you can't wait to not be associated with me."

He gave her a grin. "Not what I meant. It was a good kiss."

She agreed. Wholeheartedly. In fact, it was too good of a kiss.

The number one thing on her list of things she was looking for in a guy was that he be from Autre. Drew Ryan was very much not that. He was from...far away. She didn't even know how far away. She might Google it later out of curiosity now, but it still wouldn't matter.

Him being a good kisser did not matter to her at all. And knowing it for sure was kind of like knowing there was a layered carrot cake with homemade cream cheese frosting in the pantry and having had a small taste of it, but knowing it was now off limits.

"So you're mad at your dad?" Drew asked.

Rory appreciated the change of topic. She figured it was going to be hard enough to forget about the kiss. Especially if she kept comparing it to favorite desserts. Delicious, decadent, addictive desserts...

"Rory?"

Was she staring at his mouth? Oh, God, she was.

"Oh well, no. I mean yes. Definitely. I've been mad at him for about..." She did the math quickly. "Nine years. We're... estranged," she told him.

Estranged was a nice word for it. Her dad was a con man who had always been in and out of her life, but since she was sixteen and she'd found out just what a scumbag he really was, he'd been mostly *out*.

"He was an over-the-road-trucker all my life. When I was sixteen I found out that he'd been having affairs with women all over the country for years. For some reason, he'd finally decided to confess. It shattered my mother. She's *still* not over it. They divorced. And I cut him out of my life. As much as I could anyway. Fortunately for me, he really didn't want to be around me either. Until I got old enough to have money. Now he shows up every once in awhile when he needs some quick cash. He really liked it when I was dating a guy whose daddy owned a jewelry store. Of course, that ended when my dad tried to rob them."

Drew was staring at her.

She could understand why. What the hell was she doing telling him all of that? She tried to keep her past, especially her family ties, to herself. She didn't need people in Autre knowing that her dad had done prison time. And likely would again.

Rory ran a hand through her hair. "Sorry. I don't know why I spilled all of that." She winced. "Is there any chance you could maybe *not* tell Paige or Jordan or Charlie or any of the other Landrys about that?"

Rory knew that Paige was from the same town Drew was. That was how he'd gotten to know Jordan and Charlie and had gotten roped into bringing reindeer to Louisiana.

She still didn't know why the guy was willing to drive this far just so they'd have reindeer for their Christmas village, but it was really nice. He seemed like a good guy.

Wow, she should probably leave him alone if Roger was in town. Roger had a way of making good things, and good people, not so good.

Drew nodded. "I can do that. Though I doubt anyone would blame *you* for things your dad did."

"I'd just rather not be associated with him at all."

Drew tucked his hands into his front pockets. "Okay. And I can understand why you don't want to see him."

Yeah, see, he *was* a good guy.

"Well, I'm sure he's here for money. And I don't have any. Not that I ever really do, but he knows that I'm usually happy to give him what I do have just to get rid of him." She held up a hand. "And yes, I know that's enabling him."

"I'm not going to judge your relationship with your dad, Rory."

There was something about the way he said her name that made her stomach dip in a weird, not-unpleasant way.

She believed him. "Well, this time I really can't give him anything. I bought the salon here three years ago and I'm working to pay off that loan, so I don't have a lot of extra money. I live in the apartment over it, so I don't have any additional assets beyond that building. So Daddy Dearest is gonna have to hit the road without any pocket change from his favorite—and as far as I know, only—daughter."

And again, what the hell was she doing spilling all of that? Her financial situation was none of Drew Ryan's business. Nor was her relationship with her dad. Or her crush on Beau Hebert. Why was she suddenly doing a tell-all here? Maybe because he wasn't from Autre and there was no way she was going to get involved with him.

"Oh, hey, Drew!"

Thank God, Rory thought as a voice called out.

They both turned to find Jordan Landry stepping into the barn, interrupting them before Drew could respond to the further info dump about her life.

"I didn't know you'd made it! I'm so glad to see you!" Jordan said, coming forward with a huge grin.

"Hey, Jordan!"

Drew gave the other woman a big smile that made Rory's breath catch for a second. God, he was good-looking.

Jordan Landry was the education director for the Boys of the Bayou Gone Wild, and had been Rory's primary contact, along with Charlie Landry, Jordan's cousin-in-law, in getting the Santa's Village set up. Rory loved Jordan and Charlie. In fact, she wanted to be like them when she grew up.

Which was kind of funny, and kind of pathetic, considering she was their age.

But they definitely had their crap more together than she did and, as pathetic as it may seem, she wanted to impress these two women. She wanted to be their friend and she wanted to do more community projects with them.

They were both a part of the Landry family, which was a bit like being royalty in Autre anyway, but they were also very well-liked and respected for their own contributions to the town.

Drew met Jordan halfway and caught her up in a hug. "It's so nice to finally meet you in person."

"Same. Thank you so much for coming!"

Drew set Jordan back on her feet and they grinned at each other as if they were old friends.

"Beau just dropped off a huge donation of toys for Santa to give out to the kids," Jordan said, including both Rory and Drew in the explanation. "I'm sure he'd be happy to help you unload the reindeer after we get everything into the storage area."

"Absolutely happy to," Beau said, stepping into the barn. He glanced over. "Hey, Rory."

Damn, he was good-looking too. And he had a drawl. Drew didn't. And through his mom's side of the family, Beau was related to one branch of the Landry family tree. Everyone here was just one big, connected family, whether it was by blood or friendship. Every time Rory was around them, she was filled with happiness, along with an ache to be included in it all.

Beau Hebert checked all of her boxes. He was a hard-working, blue-collar, small-town guy who was hot, had a Louisiana drawl, and had roots here in Autre.

But her lips were still tingling from the Iowa farmer standing just two feet away from him.

Crap.

"Hey, Beau," she said, giving him a big, bright, I'm-happy-to-see-you-and-you-should-ask-me-out-don't-mind-the-earlier-kissing-another-guy-thing smile.

"Actually, that's okay," Drew said. "Rory can help me."

Rory looked at Drew. He was scowling. At Beau.

What were they talking about? She was going to help him with what?

"Oh," Jordan said. "Are you sure?" The last question was directed at Rory.

Rory looked at Drew. She wasn't sure what he meant, exactly. "Well, I could—"

But Drew grabbed her hand. "Yep, we're good. We've already covered everything we needed to," he said, tugging her through the bar. "So we're just going to go...take care of...the stuff," he finished as he pulled her through the back door and around the corner of the barn.

They were several yards across the dirt before she asked, "What is 'everything' we covered?"

"That you didn't want to see your dad," he said.

"Oh." She glanced back.

"I saw him coming toward the barn again. I figured it was just easier to get you out of there. But you don't mind helping unload the reindeer, do you?"

Oh, the reindeer. Right. Jordan had offered Beau's help and Drew had said Rory could help him instead. To save her from her dad apparently. For a second, she'd thought maybe it was to keep her with him a little longer. Or to keep her away from Beau. But if Beau had gone to help with the reindeer that would have done the same. So, keeping her away from her dad made more sense.

See? That was good guy stuff right there.

Sure, maybe Beau would have chivalrously run interference with Roger as well, but Beau didn't know about her dad. Because she'd never told him. They'd never really talked like that. She'd cut his hair a couple of times—the guy had really great hair—and they'd hung out at Ellie's bar a couple of times. Not together. Just at the same time. With lots of other people around. They'd also been to several crawfish boils and other such events together. They'd flirted a little and danced, but they hadn't talked about anything personal.

She glanced up at Drew Ryan.

Of course, she'd known this guy for less than an hour and had spilled her guts in a thirty-second monologue to *him* in the middle of a barn, so it wasn't like time constraints or setting were a great excuse for *not* telling Beau anything personal.

"Well...thanks for that," she finally said.

Drew glanced at her. "Of course."

Definitely a good guy response.

She knew she couldn't avoid her dad indefinitely and she knew that Roger would stay in town until he found her. But for right now she was very happy to be whisked off by her new accidental knight in faded blue jeans.

A guy who was very comfortable in blue jeans was also on her checklist.

Drew *did* check that box.

He was also wearing a flannel shirt and scuffed brown leather work boots that were clearly not new.

He fit right in here with the blue-collar, get-their-hands-dirty guys who made a living down here on the bayou. He was a farmer, after all. She knew that he had livestock back in Iowa. According to Jordan, the reindeer he'd brought to be a part of the petting zoo for Christmas were actually his.

For some reason, she'd been picturing Drew Ryan, the Iowa farmer, as older, a little overweight, and a whole lot paler.

But this version was not much older than her, was lean and muscular, clearly from the manual work he did every day, and had tanned skin that was no doubt from working outside on a regular basis. He also had big, rough hands, a bit of scruff on his jaw, and... they stopped across the fence from a big black pickup with a huge trailer hooked on the back...reindeer.

He checked a lot of her boxes. And he had reindeer. And he was a great kisser.

She didn't know if Beau was a good kisser or not.

She did know he didn't have reindeer.

So...there was that.

Drew is not from Autre. That's number ONE on the list.

Right. Exactly. It was. Definitely.

Maybe she needed to print her list off and keep it tucked in her bra or something so she could refer back to it while Drew Ryan was in town.

He climbed over the fence, those faded blue jeans cupping his fine ass right in front of her face.

Yeah, you should definitely print that list off.

Then he turned, gave her a grin, and reached out his arms. "Come on." He wiggled his fingers.

She cocked a brow. "Come on?"

"Gotta get you over the fence."

"You don't think I can get over on my own?"

"In that dress? You're gonna get a splinter where you really don't want one."

Did he get just a bit of a drawl in his voice? Surely not. He was a *Yankee*. But the way his gaze drifted over her and the roughness in his voice made her ears perk up the way they did when the bayou boys got flirty.

What. The. Hell. Was. That?

She smoothed the front of her skirt and told the parts underneath it to calm the hell down. *He's a Yankee*, she repeated, specifically to them.

They didn't care. Because when she put her hand in his and propped her foot up on the bottom plank of the fence and he pulled her up, grasped her by the waist, and lifted her up over the fence like she was a princess and he was the dashing prince sweeping out of her carriage, *all* of her parts swooned and got a little warmer.

More like you're a bale of hay he's tossing into the back of his truck.

24

But dammit, her girl parts focused only on *tossing into the back of his truck.*

Iowa boys had truck beds just like Louisiana boys did.

And Rory thought it was very possible Drew Ryan knew just what to do with his.

She needed to get that list printed off and *laminated.* Stat.

3

Drew hadn't liked the way Beau had smiled at Rory. Or the way the other man's eyes had taken in the sight of her in that tiny red dress and the sexy black boots.

Great. Just great.

She was sweet. She was putting together a toy drive for kids, for fuck's sake. She'd had a tough childhood with an asshole dad.

He didn't want that. He wanted hot and easy and...superficial. And short term.

But he wanted to fix all the things for this woman within an hour of meeting her.

Fuuuuuuck.

He should have left her in the barn. She *wanted* Beau to ask her out.

But no, Drew had whisked her away. And now he was letting his hands linger at her waist and was taking a deep breath of the scent of peppermint ice cream that drifted up from and surrounded him and made him...hungry.

He'd noticed it when he'd kissed her, of course. But he'd ignored it.

Or had he? Maybe that was why they were now standing next to his truck when she should be back in the barn with Beau the bayou boy she was making heart eyes over.

But she hadn't been.

No, she fucking hadn't been. She'd given Beau a big old bright grin for sure, but she'd kept looking at Drew. And her lips had still been a little pink from his kiss and her hair had been a little mussed from his hand and her nipples had been hard. From *him*.

Drew had been ignoring that too.

Rory's eyes suddenly widened slightly. "Are you okay?"

He cleared his throat and leaned back slightly, finally taking his hands off of her. "Yeah. Why?"

"I think you just growled."

He frowned. "What?"

She nodded. "I think you growled. It was soft, but—"

"You smell like peppermint ice cream."

He wasn't going to argue about the growling. He might have. He *probably* had. Fuck if he knew. He was trying like hell to resist grabbing her by her green hair and kissing her again.

While also trying like hell to resist the urge to build this woman an entire winter wonderland for the Christmas event she was trying to pull off.

And trying like hell to resist marching over to find her father and get in the guy's face to tell him to leave her the fuck alone.

He honestly had come to Louisiana for a hot fling. And some gumbo.

"Oh, that." She gave him a little smile. Then a frown. "I smell like peppermint. I used peppermint shampoo and body wash. I thought it would be festive. But...ice cream? Does peppermint ice cream smell different from just peppermint anything else?"

He lifted a shoulder. "That's what I think of when I smell you."

"Oh."

"It's probably the licking thing."

Her eyes widened. "The licking thing?"

"Yeah. You lick ice cream."

"And you're thinking about...licking...with me?"

Her gaze dropped to his mouth.

Fuck yeah, he was.

He should not answer her question though. At least not honestly. But, like everything else since coming to Autre, he did the opposite of what he should do and said, "Apparently."

"That's...unexpected." Her gaze lifted to his. Then dropped right back to his lips.

He gave a soft bark of laughter. "Yeah, I'd say that's accurate."

"It's also kind of inconvenient."

He couldn't disagree but he was curious about why she thought so. "Is it? You said you and Beau aren't dating. I'm here, you're here. I was thinking about having a little fun while I'm in Autre."

She didn't need to know that she was the opposite of what he was looking for. He wasn't going to pursue anything with her, he just wanted to know what she was thinking.

"But you live really far away," she said. "And I assume you have plans to go back to Iowa."

He nodded. "I do have plans to go back. I'm only here for about a week or so."

"Yeah. So it would be crazy for me to get involved with you. I'm staying here. I want to settle down here. I am interested in guys who feel the same. And if I get involved with you, not only do I potentially get my heart broken, but it will basically signal to all the other guys who I might want to get involved with that I'm not interested."

"Like kissing me when Beau walked into the barn?"

She nodded. "I was thinking we needed to come up with a story about that. Maybe hang some mistletoe and pretend we were underneath it. Or..." Her eyes widened. "I don't suppose you'd be willing to act like you're really into me and kind of stalk me, so that he would maybe feel the need to come to my rescue?"

"You want me to play your stalker?" Drew asked. "To get another guy to pay attention to you?"

"It's an idea." Then she tipped her head, studying him. "But you couldn't pull off the creepy stalker thing, could you?"

Well, maybe he could. With her. He definitely wasn't the stalker type. He hadn't even shown up to surprise a girlfriend for a date or with a gift or anything since high school. He hadn't been jealous of a woman in probably just as long.

But he'd swept Rory out of the barn away from Beau without a hesitation. Yeah, he'd used her dad as an excuse, but the older man hadn't been anywhere in sight.

"How do you know that? We just met." But he had an idea. He'd been told that he gave off a vibe. People could just tell that he was a good guy.

"It's just a vibe I get from you."

Yep, nailed it.

"Yeah, I probably can't," he agreed. "But the next time I see Beau I can tell him you're a really good kisser."

Again, her gaze dropped to his mouth, and Drew felt a streak of heat arc through his gut.

"I appreciate that," she told him. "But how about we don't?"

"Okay." He grinned. "But I'm around if you need a reference."

She laughed. "I'll keep that in mind." Then she narrowed her eyes slightly. "And ditto. If you're looking for a hot fling while you're here, I could make some suggestions."

"Oh yeah?" He wasn't sure how he felt about that. It might be helpful. She would know a lot of the women their age. But she didn't feel even the tiniest little flicker of jealousy? Because he sure as hell had when Beau had checked her out in her tiny elf dress.

"Yeah, you should go to Ellie's tonight. There will be a lot of really beautiful, smart, funny, sexy women up there tonight. I bet they'll love you."

Which was convenient. Ellie's was the bar owned by Mitch Landry's grandmother. Jordan and Paige had already told him that was where they were all meeting for dinner. He had to appreciate one-stop shopping. A hot fling and amazing gumbo all in one place sounded perfect.

"But I really will help you with the reindeer while I'm here," Rory said.

He didn't need her help. There were only four reindeer, and he could easily unload them alone. But he wanted her to hang out a little longer. "Great. I'd appreciate that."

They moved around to the back of the trailer, and as he opened it, four sweet, brown faces turned to look at them.

He smiled. "Rory, meet the gang. Everyone, this is Rory."

She was grinning brightly when he looked over at her.

"Oh my gosh, they're so cute," she said. "The kids are going to love having real reindeer."

He nodded and stepped up into the trailer. "These four are going to be great. I have them around kids quite a bit, so they won't be too skittish, and they're used to being hand fed and led."

"Do you have more than these four?"

He nodded. "Six more reindeer. And of course, all the others."

"Jordan said that some of the other animals we have here came from you originally."

"Tori Kramer—Tori Landry now—is originally from back home," he said. "Another little town, but nearby. She was my veterinarian before she moved down here, and whenever I had an animal that needed a little extra attention, it went to live with Tori. She's always had a big heart for the ones that need just a little extra love. When she came to Louisiana, she brought all those animals with her and since then she's come home and taken a few more. Some of the goats, a pig, a cow, and a few of the alpacas all started out in Iowa."

"Extra attention like what?" Rory asked, seemingly truly interested.

"Some of the runts, animals that need bottle fed, and the alpaca that loved to be sung to, the pig that was afraid of thunder." He grinned at Rory. "That kind of stuff."

She looked delighted. "I've met Alpacapella and Hermione. I know about their issues. And Chewpaca came from you too, right?"

"He's one of the more recent ones she's taken in," he said with a nod. "He was orphaned."

Rory suddenly looked sad. "Oh."

"Mitch and Paige met when Tori, Josh, and Mitch came back to Iowa to pick Chewpaca up," Drew said.

Rory had a hand on the back of one of the reindeer and was stroking her fur softly. "Well, that turned out well."

Yeah, Mitch and Paige had fallen madly in love over the back end of that alpaca right in the middle of Drew's farm. Just like that.

It seemed so simple. But Drew didn't want to think about how many women he'd had out to his farm. Who had stroked his alpacas—literally. And had never fallen in love with him.

Hell, even Paige had been out to his farm and stroked his alpacas prior to Mitch Landry showing up.

Shaking off those frustrating thoughts, Drew took one of the halters from the hook hanging on the inside of the trailer and slid it over the first reindeer's head, then attached it to a lead. He backed the animal down the slight ramp and turned her to face Rory. "Where are we putting these guys?"

She pointed. "They cleared out that end of the barn. It should work for temporary housing since they won't be here for too long."

He nodded. "Sounds good. You want to take this one?" He held out the lead.

But she shook her head and stepped up into the trailer grabbing another of the halters. "I can bring this one." She slipped the harness over the animal's head and attached the lead, then backed the reindeer down the ramp and out of the trailer the way Drew had just demonstrated.

He was impressed. "You know how to harness and lead?"

"I've helped Jordan with the alpacas several times, and we've even tried to harness and lead a couple of the goats."

He liked that she was comfortable around animals. She'd picked up the goats without much fuss and now she was easily leading his second reindeer next to him. Of course, it didn't matter if she was good with animals. Yes, that was something he would probably look for in a girlfriend, but Rory wasn't even going to be his fling. As they had just established. Even if he didn't think she was too sweet for how he wanted to spend his week in Louisiana, she wasn't interested in something short term with a guy who lived so far away.

"So your farm," she said, "is it a pretty big operation?"

"We have a lot of animals. We primarily raise the alpacas for their wool and have a nice business going with that. But that's something my brother and I started just a few years ago. The whole farm's been in my family for three generations now. I run it with my brother and my cousin."

She sighed. "Wow."

"What?"

They led the animals down the fence line toward the gate.

Drew was happy to see that the two trucks that Beau and Rory's father had pulled up in were both gone now.

"I know there are a lot of families like that around here too. They've been here for generations, and really put roots down. I'm envious of that. It's one of the things I like best about Autre. The roots and traditions and the way the big families just keep growing and incorporating more people into them. It's really lovely."

"You didn't have that? Are you from Louisiana?"

She nodded. "I grew up in New Orleans. All my grandparents are gone. And my dad... I told you about him. After he and my mom divorced, I stayed with her, and we did our best. But we moved a few times into different places we could afford. She worked a variety of jobs. She tried to date for a little while, but it just wasn't her thing. They're both from small families, so I don't have a lot of extended family and no one really close. That's why I came to Autre."

"What do you mean?"

They stepped through the gate and led the reindeer across the yard toward the barn.

"My dad ruined my idea of what a home and family was like. I spent sixteen years thinking that, even if my dad wasn't around as much as my friends' dads were, at least I had a family and we had a home that meant a lot to all of us. Then he just totally destroyed all of that. I realized that my family had been a lie and our home hadn't meant what I thought it meant. So, I decided as an adult, I was going to find all of that for myself. I definitely wanted to put down roots and find a place that could really be a home. A place I could settle and that would mean all the things I thought a home should be growing up."

They led the reindeer into the barn and to four empty, clean stalls sitting ready for his animals.

Both reindeer went easily into the stalls.

"So has that happened?" he asked Rory, wanting to hear more.

He busied himself with spreading the hay from the corners out over the floor and filling the feed and water.

"Yeah, Autre is everything Gabe said it would be and more."

"Gabe?" Drew couldn't help asking, shooting her a glance.

She was leaning against the side of the stall, watching him. "Gabe was my boss. I was bartending in New Orleans at this great bar in the French quarter that Gabe and his brother own. They had become really good friends with the Landry boys. When I started to talk about opening my own salon, he suggested Autre. He said it would be a lot easier to build the business and less expensive to get started in a small town than in New Orleans, and Gabe knew I was looking for a community connection. He knew that it would happen faster and probably deeper in a place like Autre. You can definitely get that experience in some of the neighborhoods, but a small town is different."

"A community connection is important to you?" Drew wanted to just stand and watch her as she talked, but knew that was ridiculous. He kept acting busy, stirring the feed, brushing the reindeer, filling the water to the very top of the container.

"I chose cosmetology because I wanted to do a job that can be really important to a community and where I could build up return customers. I wanted it to be something where I could get involved in their lives and get to know them over time. And where I could be a part of bigger events. You know, weddings and prom and family photo sessions. If I can help people feel good and really celebrate important events, I knew I would feel like I was more a part of their lives and a part of whatever community I was living in. And I told Gabe all of that while I was going to school." She shrugged. "He got it. His bar has been that for a long time. They have lots of tourists, of course, but they have regulars and they have tourists who come back to the city over and over and always stop at Trahans because of the experience they have there. That matters to Gabe and his brother. So he understood what I wanted from my salon."

"And has that all happened here?" Drew finally gave in and turned to fully face her. He tucked his hands in his back pockets and just watched her.

She nodded with a happy smile. "They've completely welcomed me here, business is great, I really feel like I'm getting to know people and really providing an important service." She sighed, her smile dimming. "That's actually part of the problem. I'm really booked up this week and last, and it's put me behind getting Santa's Village put together. People are getting their hair done and wanting to get colors and highlights and trims before they have Christmas parties and programs at school and church and before the taking of Christmas photos." She smiled. "Don't get me wrong. I love it. And I'm so happy to work overtime to get all that done for them. It's basically my dream come true. But I offered to do this village clear back in July and it's just been a bigger project than I expected."

"They'll all understand. Just let them know and I'm sure somebody will help you out."

She shook her head quickly. "I can't do that. I want them to know I can handle this, and to love having me be a part of it. I want them to know I'm somebody they can depend on. So I have to pull this off on my own. I can't let them know that I'm in over my head."

He shut the stall doors behind the two reindeer and they stepped back out into the yard, heading back for his truck for the other two animals. "But you *are* in over your head?"

She nodded.

Dammit. Everything about this woman, from her crazy green hair to her peppermint-scented skin to her desire to be a part of this community to the way she lit up talking about her business to the way she sighed into his mouth when he kissed her, was tying him up in knots.

He just wanted gumbo.

Okay, maybe a naked bayou girl for a couple of nights too.

But he really was just here for vacation.

This was supposed to be an escape. This was supposed to be just fun and frivolous. A get away from his own little town that was sounding more and more like Autre all the time. Everyone back home had deep roots and big families and long histories. Including him.

"I'm just gonna have to work harder and longer," she said. "So far, I've resisted coming down here at night because I didn't want them to see all the lights blazing and wonder what was going on and then have to confess that I was behind and try to make up time. But I don't really see any way around it. That or I'll have to come in early before the salon opens. But I have to be careful not to run into any of the Landrys doing that. They come down to the docks for the swamp boat tours really early. And Donovan and Griffin come in early to check on all of the animals before anything opens up. They're all early birds." She said it with an annoyed eye roll as if everyone else's daily routine was very inconvenient.

They got back to the truck and Drew put the halter and lead on another reindeer, then stood back and watched as Rory did the same.

"Do these guys have names?" she asked, reaching out to stroke the nose of the reindeer she was leading.

Drew nodded. "Of course. That's Donna and this is Jim."

"It's nice to meet you, Donna," Rory said with a little laugh. "Donna and Jim are interesting reindeer names."

"They're named after a couple people back home."

She looked up at him. "People that are special to you or people you don't like?"

He laughed. "I love all of my animals, so I would never name any of them after people I don't like."

"So, it's an honor for your reindeer to be named after them?"

"I hope they feel that way."

She looked at him for a longer moment but didn't say anything.

"The two that are already up at the barn are Lucy and Ethel."

Rory laughed. "Are they named after people you know?"

"After my grandmother's favorite TV show."

She nodded, but her smile remained. "So three girls and a boy?"

Drew had been holding his breath for her to say *oh, you're such a nice guy* or *that's so sweet*. And he supposed that it was sweet that he was naming animals after people he cared about or, in the case of his grandmother's favorite television show, something to make her smile.

But it was just one more example of how he was having a very hard time staying focused on the I-want-to-talk-dirty-to-you guy he wanted to be for this week, rather than the I-want-to-tell-you-about-my-grandmother guy he was already showing to Rory. But he did want to tell her about his Grandma Molly. And that she was absolutely kickass at *Jeopardy*. And that she made the best pumpkin pie in the world. And that about every three months she pretended her knee arthritis flared up so she could go to PT for a couple of weeks and flirt with the therapist, Blake, who was fifty years her junior.

"Yeah. Most people don't realize that reindeer with antlers are typically females."

"Really?"

"Yep. All of Santa's reindeer have to be girls," he said with a grin. "Adult males lose their antlers well before Christmas, but the females don't lose them till spring."

"What about Jim?" Rory asked.

"Well, he's still kind of a baby. He's a juvenile so it will take longer for him to lose his. So this year he gets to be a Christmas reindeer."

Rory looked intrigued, and Drew couldn't help but like that.

"What else?" she asked. "Tell me another interesting reindeer fact."

"Reindeer hooves expand in the summer when the ground is softer and shrink in the winter when the ground is harder."

Her eyes went a little rounder in interest.

It was not sexy, but he could talk about his animals all day. He'd learned the hard way that not all women were fascinated with alpacas—no matter how cute they were—or reindeer, even at Christmas time.

"That's pretty cool," Rory said as they put Donna and Jim into their stalls and got them settled. "Could you come up with a bunch of trivia facts about the reindeer that we could incorporate into some games for the kids?"

He grinned at her. "Reindeer games?"

She laughed. "Of course."

"Absolutely."

They stepped back out of the barn into the yard. Things were quieting down as the sun was starting to set and families were leaving the petting zoo to go home for dinner.

"So what all still needs to be done?" he asked, looking around.

Santa's shack was fully put together, including the porch, though the front was not painted. The sign with the alligator was up and pointing the right direction. They had gifts as of today, thanks to the "fabulous" Beau Hebert, and they now had reindeer.

"I need to finish painting the shack and pave the front walk with the sparkly red bricks," she said, pointing to the side of the shack where, sure enough, there was a pile of sparkly red bricks. "Then I need to wrap all the toys for the kids."

"You have to wrap them all yourself?"

She lifted a shoulder. "I volunteered."

Do not offer to help, do not offer to help, do not offer to help.

It was right on the tip of his tongue to say, "Let's get some cocoa, or better yet peppermint ice cream, and wrap those gifts together in front of the fire."

But he didn't need to help her. She *wanted* to do this herself. He could respect that. Plus, the more time he was spending with her, the more he wanted to know about her work, her plans for the Christmas party with the kids, and, God help him, even her childhood.

And the more he wanted to know if she smelled like peppermint *all over*.

She was so damned beautiful. The dress showed off delicious curves and creamy skin—which was probably where the 'ice cream' part of his fantasy was coming from—and he definitely loved that dress. But more, her smiles and the way her eyes showed every emotion—from her earnestness about making the Santa Village perfect to her pride in her business to how much she wanted him even if he knew too much about reindeer and didn't have an ounce of Cajun blood in him—made her absolutely gorgeous.

"Okay then." He clapped his hands together. "Uh, thanks for the help with the reindeer. I think I'm gonna head up to Paige and Mitch's. It was...really nice to meet you."

And with that he turned on his heel and started across the barnyard.

He knew he'd startled her. That was a very abrupt exit. Downright rude, actually.

Drew from Appleby would never have done something like that. His mother and grandmother—the one who loved *I Love*

Lucy and the one who loved true crime and unsolved mystery documentaries—would both be appalled.

But he honestly didn't know how else to go about pulling himself away from Rory. Or to resist her.

Getting away from her seem like the only option.

"Merry Christmas, Drew!" he heard her call behind him a few seconds later.

For some reason that made his gut clench and something in his chest feel a little tight. But he resisted turning around and instead just lifted a hand and waved to her over his shoulder. He even resisted looking over at the barn as he drove his truck past on his way out to Mitch and Paige's house a few blocks down the same road that ran in front of the petting zoo.

Well, almost. He glanced in his rearview mirror just before the petting zoo's barnyard slipped out of view.

But he couldn't see her.

Which should have been fortunate.

Instead, he had to consciously shove away thoughts of her going back inside and grabbing buckets of paint to start painting Santa's cabin all alone.

He needed to get up to Ellie's ASAP. He needed to find a hot girl with normal-colored hair, wearing blue jeans, who'd had a perfectly normal childhood, thought reindeer smelled bad, and had no aspirations for giving her new hometown a magical Christmas.

And he definitely did not need any peppermint ice cream, no matter how much his subconscious told him otherwise.

4

"So now you're Santa's little helper, huh?"

Rory jerked and screamed at the sound of the male voice behind her.

She slapped her hand over her thundering heart and sucked in a deep breath. "You scared the shit out of me!"

Roger Robins gave her one of his classic I-don't-really-care grins. "Sorry."

She'd known that he'd eventually find her. She hoped it would take him another day or so, but that was one drawback to the small-town thing. It would've taken him a single stop at any of the major businesses, including the gas station, grocery store, and even Ellie's bar, to find out where she was. Especially if he told them he was her father.

An icy coldness slipped through her. "How did you find me?"

"The guy at the gas station on the corner. Asked if he knew where Rory was. Didn't even need your last name. Pointed me in this direction."

"Did you tell them who you are?"

Roger grinned. "Didn't need to. Probably thought I was

some bigwig in town to donate to your fancy Christmas party." He ran a hand down the front of his shirt.

Rory took in his appearance. Roger did look different than usual. She was used to her dad wearing jeans and t-shirts and ball caps. He usually sported a medium length beard and often went months without a haircut. Now he was dressed in a button-down shirt, khaki pants, and was clean-shaven with short hair.

She'd seen him when he got out of his truck earlier, but she hadn't taken in the details with her brain screaming, *oh my God, what's he doing here?*

"What are you up to?"

"Nice to see you too."

"You know I don't think it's nice to see you. You only show up when you want something. What is it this time?"

"I have a new job. Starts in a couple weeks."

Rory's eyebrows rose. "New job? Where?"

Roger had been an over-the-road trucker as long as she'd known him. It had worked out well with his preferred lifestyle of meeting and sleeping with multiple women in several different towns, as well as pulling off cons in places no one knew him, and where he could avoid returning.

"One of the casinos in New Orleans."

Oh, the idea of Roger working in a casino was a terrible one. Kind of like him getting cozy with a family that owned a big jewelry store. But honestly, Rory didn't care. That was the casino's problem. If they weren't vetting their employees any better than that, it wasn't her job to fill them in.

"And what does that have to do with me?"

"The guy who's getting me the job wants me to pay him back before I start."

"A guy at one of the casinos is getting you a job but you owe him money?"

"We met across the Blackjack table."

"He was the dealer and you were the loser so he figured you were an easy mark?"

"He was the dealer and I was the guy he was helping win."

"So that was the con. Using a guy on the inside and splitting the win. That's almost too simple for you, isn't it?"

"Sometimes the beauty is in the simplicity." Roger grinned proudly.

Rory just rolled her eyes. She didn't want to know anything more. She learned a long time ago, from her mother, ways to avoid becoming a potential accomplice.

"So he's bringing you in as a dealer now?"

"Yep. But I have to pay him the three grand back first."

Rory closed her eyes and groaned. "You got into debt to him before you even started the job?"

"Yeah, but that's small potatoes compared to what I'll be making."

"So just tell him you'll pay him back after this job starts."

"That's not how it works. This is a good faith thing. He needs to know that I'm good for it upfront."

"But you're not."

"But I am. Because I have you."

Rory sighed. She already knew more than she wanted to. She crossed her arms. "Sorry. I don't have three thousand dollars."

"You sure about that, baby girl?"

"Oh, very sure. I mean, three thousand dollars would've been a little hard for me to come up with anyway, but since you haven't been around, let me fill you in. I have a life now. A real life. I own a business and I've invested in that business. That means doing things the way *normal* grown-ups do, by taking out a bank loan and slowly paying it back month by month. Not a loan shark, not a buddy who got out of prison two weeks ago, not some dude I met on a barstool last weekend. I'm doing this the legit way. So no, I don't have money just laying around in my bank account waiting for *you* to waltz into town and need a favor."

"So sell something."

She gaped at him. She didn't know why. She should have expected something like that. "No. Actually, *hell no*. First of all, I need everything that I have. Second of all, all my stuff is *mine*. Get your own stuff to sell off."

Roger's eyes glinted at that and Rory had the very familiar and very unwelcome feeling in the pit of her stomach.

"Well, that's an interesting suggestion." He held up a box. It was about the size of a box of cookies or crackers.

Rory frowned as she looked at it. She had no idea what she was looking at. "What's that?"

"You don't even know what you have," he said with a chuckle. It was definitely more of a statement that question. "You telling me I could have just walked off with the stuff and you wouldn't have even noticed?"

"What are you talking about, Roger?" She hadn't called him dad since the day she found out that he'd been cheating on her mother and faking the whole happy-family-home-and-hearth thing with her for sixteen years. She actually preferred not calling him anything at all, but once in a while it was unavoidable.

"You have fifty of these in that little storage space. The good-looking guy, not the one you were kissing, but the other one, brought these up earlier."

So these were some of the toys that Beau had brought for the gift donation. She didn't know what exactly this all meant. But if Roger knew anything about any of this it could only be trouble for her.

"So what?"

"These are new edition game controllers from a company called Fluke Inc. They're a very elite gaming company out of Chicago."

Actually, Rory knew about Fluke Inc. It was indeed a gaming company and happened to be owned by friends of Paige's, but it was now based out of Appleby, Iowa. Which was where Drew was from too. It was very likely that Drew knew the Fluke guys, actually, now that she thought about it.

She narrowed her eyes, not wanting to give Roger any information he could use as ammunition, and kept her arms crossed. "And?"

"These aren't due to be released until the spring," Roger said. "That makes them not only the most coveted toy of next year, but incredibly valuable right now. These fifty had to have been specially manufactured early. You can't get these anywhere. You can't order them. You can't even reserve them for purchase later yet. So the fact that you have fifty of them sitting right here in this little town means something. Somebody has an in and made a huge donation."

The little hairs on the back of her neck were standing up and she wanted to rush at Roger. The urge to slap him, claw his face, and scream at him was nearly overpowering. This man had been messing with her in her life for years. He'd ruined everything that was important to her from her childhood. All the memories of a happy, stable family. All of the I-love-you-baby-girls. All of the I-miss-you postcards he'd sent. He'd devastated her mother, who still wasn't over him. And since then, he'd kept Rory's life from being peaceful because he would pop in unexpectedly and stir things up and make her crazy. She felt like she'd been constantly looking over her shoulder and hiding a huge part of her life from friends. She'd never talked about her father to anyone.

Until Drew Ryan.

Which was still so weird, she couldn't think about it.

And now Roger knew she was living in Autre, and about the Christmas party and Santa's Village and, while he may not know everything Rory had to do with it, it was clear he knew enough. There was something about his expression and the tone in his voice that made it clear he knew this was the way to get to her.

"What are you saying, Roger?"

"I'm saying that these game controllers could be sold for huge money."

And there it was. Her dad's new con. Hell, it wasn't even a con. He wanted to steal these toys and resell them. For huge money.

"Those are donated. For kids. For Christmas."

Though she wasn't sure why she was even trying. Roger hadn't even cared about Christmas for her, his own kid, so the chances of him caring about Christmas for a stranger was pretty much zero. Especially if the alternative was money for himself.

"And that's pretty important to you?" Roger asked.

Rory knew that admitting that would be giving him power over her. But he already knew the answer. He wouldn't be here if not. He would have just taken the controllers and gotten the hell out of Autre if he didn't *want* to involve her somehow.

She probably wouldn't have even put two and two together right away. Oh eventually, she would've put together the fact that Roger had breathed air in Autre and that something bad had happened and so of course the two things are connected, but it would've given him time to get away. The fact that he was explaining all of this to her meant that he wanted to hurt her somehow.

"What do you want?"

"Three thousand dollars."

"You think these controllers are worth three thousand?"

Roger laughed. "Oh, they're worth far more than that. But that's what I need. I'm such a good guy, that I will return these controllers to you when you give me three thousand dollars

46

and I won't even think about the fact that I could be selling these for five times that."

"You're going to hold them for ransom?"

"Think of it as my backup plan. I'm asking my daughter for three thousand dollars. If she can't or won't help me out with that, the controllers are my plan B."

"I really have no way of getting three thousand dollars, Roger."

Rory felt her throat start tightening and the back of her eyes began stinging. She didn't want to give Roger money. But in the past, she had because it was easier than anything else. When he showed up, she wanted back out of her life as quickly as possible and she had very few resources to truly fight him with.

"You've got this whole amazing community now. And a new guy. You'll come up with something."

Oh, fantastic. Now Drew was a part of this in Roger's eyes. "He's not my new guy. I just met him."

Roger gave her a sleazy smile. "Well, turn that new guy into your piggy bank. Women have been doing that for decades."

More like centuries, actually. But that was certainly not Rory's plan for any guy, particularly Drew Ryan.

Her heart gave a little thump in her chest. Because now thinking about not getting involved with Drew was not about the fact that he lived so far away. Or that he wasn't sticking around for long. Or because he didn't check the very first box on her checklist.

It was because she couldn't.

For a brief moment while they'd been flirting and teasing and talking about reindeer, she'd thought that maybe a week-long fling with him while he was in town was better than nothing.

He was a great guy and she felt more sparks with him than she had with a guy in almost forever. She'd been very, very tempted. Of course, then he'd turned on his heel and practically run out of the barnyard, so there was that.

But now Roger was here and just reinforcing all of the ways he made her life complicated and terrible and chaotic and that she had actually tricked herself into thinking that she could have this sweet, calm, small-town life in Autre and could get away from all that.

This was Roger's first trip to Autre, but she should have known he'd eventually come. And he wasn't here just to harass her. He was going to ruin the Christmas party. Of course he was. Everything important to her that was sweet and good and just *nice* was ruined by Roger Robins. Autre would definitely be one of those things. And if she got involved with Drew or, hell, anyone else in this town, Roger would somehow ruin that too.

"I have no way of doing this, Roger. And if you take the controllers, they're going to figure out someone stole them and they're going to come after you."

He laughed. Just flat-out laughed in her face. And she had to admit that he had a reason. It wasn't like the petting zoo had security cameras. It wasn't like the storage area in the barn was being monitored by law enforcement. The only way they would find out that Roger was the one who'd stolen the controllers was if she turned him in. And that would lead to one very terrible thing.

She'd have to admit how she knew him.

She'd really hoped to keep Roger Robins out of her life in Autre and now, not only was he here and ruining everything, but she was going to have to confess who he was, that he was here because of her, he'd stolen the gifts because she wouldn't give him money, and that he'd probably be back to do something similar in the future.

This was all her fault. She never should have gotten involved with this project. If she'd just let someone else take care of Santa's Village, Roger wouldn't have come to the petting zoo to find her, found out about the controllers, and realized this was the perfect way to manipulate her.

Roger tossed the box with the controller up in the air and caught in one hand. "Well, I've got forty-nine others of these in my truck right now. I don't have to pay this debt off until this weekend. That gives you a few days to think about what you're gonna do about this. You'll find the phone number to my burner phone on the sticky note in the storage unit where these controllers used to be."

And for the second time that night, a man turned on his heel and walked away from her.

Yeah, this *was* her fault. So she needed to take care of this. That was one thing she'd learned from the Landrys—you owned your shit and you cleaned up your messes.

Now she just needed to figure out how to do that.

5

It only took Drew about five minutes inside Ellie's bar to realize that he was not going to meet his hot, sexy, up-for-a-good-time bayou girl in here tonight.

And that Rory had known that.

He grinned. Maybe she had felt just a flicker of I-don't-want-him-hooking-up-with-anyone-else after all.

Oh, the place was *full* of gorgeous, funny, sassy women. It only took about five minutes to realize that as well.

But they were all taken. Very taken.

And not just obviously in love. But were in love with men who had the last name Landry. Or the women had the last name Landry themselves.

In other words, the sexy, funny women who were thrilled he was at Ellie's tonight were all completely off limits.

At least the ones his age. The sweetest of the bunch was Cora, who had pretty blue eyes, a bright smile, and immediately brought him a tall glass of sweet tea and a big bowl of sausage and shrimp gumbo. But Cora was old enough to be his grandmother. Literally.

"I'm so glad you're here!" Paige Asher told him for the third time as he took his first bite of the gumbo.

Wow. That was good.

"Me too. It's about time."

"It *really* is."

Paige was from Appleby and Drew had known her forever. She was quite a bit younger than him, but he knew her sister Jocelyn well.

Mitch was a great guy. Easy-going, funny, quick with a grin, and no filter when it came to giving his family a hard time. A trait that seemed to be genetic.

Drew was seated at a table toward the back of the bar and was surrounded by the Landry family and their significant others.

The table was actually one of a group of about three tables that were needed to hold all of the people that now comprised this side of Paige's family. She and Mitch weren't married yet, but it was clear this was where Paige was staying and that she loved these people with all her heart. And vice versa.

It was also clear that the Landry clan gathering in Ellie's bar was a daily occurrence. They'd all settled into chairs as if they had usual spots and Ellie—the owner of the establishment and the matriarch of the family—along with her husband, Leo, and her best friend, Cora, started serving up platters, plates, and bowls of food to the group without even asking what everyone wanted.

It was every bit a family dinner around their grandmother's table—except that "grandma's house" was a bar and the rest of the room was filled with a bunch of other people. Many apparently lived here in Autre, but some were obviously tourists.

The room was definitely not a typical grandmotherly kitchen either. The bar/restaurant was one big, rectangular building with a long, scarred wooden bar running along the length of one wall.

A swinging door that led to the kitchen was the only thing that cut into the wall behind the bar. The rest of the room was filled with mismatched tables and chairs and the walls were covered in a plethora of items from posters to banners to photographs. The photos ran the gamut from old photographs of the town and bayou to pictures of people doing things like fishing, dancing, playing ball, or just grinning for the camera. Every person in the group gathered around the tables with Drew right now was represented in those photos. Multiple times. Even Paige.

Ellie's flock was loud and rowdy, but they spent most of their time laughing. Everyone had greeted and welcomed him as Paige made the introductions one by one, but no one seemed to give much thought to minding their manners or toning things down for the dinner guest. He felt like one of the gang immediately.

He was sitting between Paige and Mitch's cousin Kennedy, the mayor of Autre. Kennedy couldn't have been more than twenty-seven or twenty-eight, if that, but she apparently ran the town. It also became fairly clear fairly quickly that she ran this group of people. As much as anyone did, anyway.

"Well, I made my decision about who's going to be Santa at Santa's Village," Kennedy announced to the table at large.

It was miraculous that anyone could hear her over everyone else talking but it seemed that her announcement was important enough that they all immediately quieted and turned to look at her.

"We haven't even given you our pitches yet," Zeke, one of the cousins, protested.

He sat forward in his chair quickly and the baby he held propped on his shoulder squirmed and grunted. Zeke patted the tiny back reassuringly. How a baby could sleep through all the noise in this place, Drew didn't know, but he supposed this one, and her twin, were used to it. Jill sat next to Zeke, holding the other baby. Drew didn't know which was which, but Paige had told him during introductions the twins were Poppy and Allie and were just a couple of months old.

Drew was grateful that he was naturally very good with names and faces. When Paige had done the introductions, most of them had stuck.

"Pitches?" Kennedy said. "All y'all had to do was tell me that you were interested. I know you all well enough to pick the best Santa."

"No way," Owen said. "We've been talking about this for the last three days over breakfast."

"You've all been *arguin'*," Ellie corrected, as she leaned in to set a basket of what looked like sweet potato fries on the table. "They've all got their ideas about why they'd be best, as usual," she told Kennedy.

Kennedy rolled her eyes. "I'm sure." Then she narrowed her eyes at Owen. "I don't remember seeing your name on the list of potential candidates."

"Like I needed to sign up." Owen scoffed. "I'd be the best damn Santa ever."

"You are *not* a candidate for Santa," Kennedy informed him.

"Why not?"

"You've been disqualified."

"Since when?"

"Since December 25th at 3 a.m. when I was ten."

Owen's eyes widened. Then narrowed. Then he gave a heavy sigh. "Why do *you* get to decide?"

Okay, so there was a story there. Drew looked around. Did everyone else know the story? Because he wanted to know it. With a stupid amount of curiosity considering he'd just met these people.

"Because I'm the mayor," Kennedy said.

"This is a Boys of the Bayou Gone Wild thing, not a town thing. You shouldn't get to decide."

Kennedy looked at Charlie, who was in charge of marketing

at Boys of the Bayou Gone Wild, then at Sawyer, who Drew knew was not just the majority owner in the company but also Kennedy's older brother.

"Can I pick the Santa?" she asked.

Sawyer nodded. "Sure."

"You bet," Charlie agreed.

Owen frowned. "Seriously?" he asked Sawyer.

Sawyer shrugged. "She's my baby sister. There's only one woman who gets what she wants more often with me than Kennedy." He gave Juliet, his wife, a little squeeze.

Ellie cleared her throat. "Excuse me?"

Sawyer grinned at his grandmother. "*Two* other women. And don't tell my mom I said that."

"Oh your mama knows that Kennedy's had you wrapped around her pinky finger since she came home from the hospital, grinned at you, then spit up all over your favorite shoes," Ellie said. She gave her oldest grandson a smile. "And you'd throw me off an airboat without a second thought if it came down to me or her."

Sawyer didn't deny it. No one did.

"Only because he knows I'd be jumpin' right in after ya," Leo told Ellie, wrapping his arms around her from behind.

"Sure," Ellie said. "As soon as you were certain Sawyer had Miss Kennedy safe and sound."

Kennedy gave her grandfather a dazzling smile and he winked at her from behind Ellie, where her grandma couldn't see it.

"Yeah, well, she's using this as revenge against me," Owen protested.

"You deserve it," Sawyer informed him.

"It was *fifteen years* ago."

"It was seventeen years ago," Kennedy told him.

"Not that you're keeping track," Owen muttered, with an eyeroll.

"Oh, I am most definitely keeping track."

Owen slumped back in his chair. "You're a brat."

Kennedy's husband, Bennett, simply snorted at that.

Kennedy leaned in, resting one arm on the table. With the other, she pointed an index finger at Owen. "I'm completely serious. I have not forgotten, nor have I forgiven, and since I have a position of some authority around here, I refuse to reward you with a chance to be Santa. Ever."

"I've grown up! I've changed!" Owen said.

Kennedy gave him a look. "As long as I have breath in my body, you will not be putting on red and white fur and potentially terrorizing children."

Paige leaned in. "My God. What did you do?"

Drew blew out a relieved breath. Yes. He needed this story. And maybe a dozen more about these people growing up together down here.

"Seventeen years ago you were a kid too," Paige said to Owen.

Owen shifted on his chair. "It was just a dumb prank."

"It was a mean, horrible, gruesome *lie*," Kennedy declared.

"Gruesome?" Paige repeated.

"It's not my fault Kennedy's always had a crazy imagination," Owen said.

"That imagination is exactly why you did it!" Kennedy exclaimed.

"But it only took him about three minutes to realize he'd fucked up," Josh interjected. "He did feel bad when he realized you were *actually* freaking out and he'd gone too far."

"What did you *do*?" It was Maddie that asked now. Her eyes were wide as she looked at her husband. "I don't know this story."

Owen shifted uncomfortably again.

"Tell her," Sawyer said, crossing his arms.

"It doesn't matter that Sawyer and Josh beat my ass for it?" Owen asked Kennedy.

"Nope."

Owen looked at Bennett. "Dude. You'd better never cross her. This girl can hold a *grudge*."

Bennett nodded. "Good thing her mean side turns me on."

Kennedy gave him a grin.

Owen just shook his head.

Maddie pinched his side. "What. Did. You. *Do*?"

Drew barely resisted adding, "Yeah, come on, man."

"I might have thought it would be funny to..." Owen shifted and cleared his throat. "Change up...the Santa story a little."

Maddie's eyebrows rose. "Oh no. What did you tell her?"

Kennedy wasn't done though. "Oh, it wasn't just *telling* of the story, was it Owen?" Kennedy asked. "There was *showing* too."

"Fine." Owen sighed. "You know the story of Papa Noël and how he drives a boat on the bayou pulled by eight alligators instead of a sleigh with reindeer..."

"Of course," Maddie said.

Owen nodded. "Well, so that year Kennedy made alligator shaped cookies for Santa. Like frosted sugar cookies."

"They were *really* cute," Kennedy said. "Cora and I worked hard on those."

Owen rolled his eyes. "Well, I told her that the alligators were gonna be pissed. They weren't gonna eat cookies that looked like them 'cuz that was just wrong and they were gonna have to go hungry at our house and were probably gonna leave us crappy presents."

"Uh-huh. And?" Maddie had narrowed her eyes.

Sawyer and Josh were sitting back, clearly enjoying Owen having to relive whatever trouble he'd gotten into. Kennedy looked like she was just as mad seventeen years later.

Drew kept eating. Dinner and a show. Ellie's place was

great, even if he wasn't going to hook-up with a hot Cajun girl tonight.

"So...she wouldn't make anymore cookies," Owen went on, clearly realizing he wasn't getting out of telling this story.

"And *you* wanted more cookies?" Maddie asked.

"Well, yeah. She made *sugar cookies* for Santa. Everyone knows her hazelnut thingies are the best. Even back then."

"Oh my God, you did all of that because I didn't make *you* the cookies you wanted?" Kennedy demanded.

Owen shrugged.

"He dragged me out of bed at three a.m. telling me there'd been a terrible accident," Kennedy told the table, her cheeks pink, clearly with anger. "He took me down to the old wooden dock off the bayou where we fished and swam and showed me a single black boot that was all covered in mud and a ripped piece of red and white fur, like from Santa's coat."

"Owen told her that the alligators hadn't liked the cookies, so they'd eaten Papa Noel instead," Sawyer said. "Said it happened every so many years on the bayou and that Papa Noel got replaced so not to worry, but that next year she should make better cookies."

Everyone at the table sat in silence for three full seconds. Then they all pivoted to look at Owen as one.

He held up his hands in surrender. "Let us just remember for a moment that I was *twelve*. And a little shit. Until I was like...thirty-five. Just ask Ellie." He pointed at his grandmother.

"Absolutely true," Ellie confirmed with a nod.

"You're not thirty-five even now," Sawyer pointed out.

"Exactly," Owen said. "I'm a dumbass. Still. But definitely seventeen years ago."

"Owen. Landry. You're. Such. A. Jerk." Maddie punctuated each word with a punch to his arm.

He rubbed the spot when she was done. "I know. Okay? I *know*. I've apologized a million times."

"Twice. You've apologized twice," Kennedy said.

"But I *have* apologized."

"And you are *out* of the running for Santa in this case. And if anyone ever lets you do it in the future, I will picket in front of where you're sitting with the little kids with big signs calling you a Santa murderer with photos of Santa's boot covered in blood," Kennedy told him.

"See." Owen pointed at her. "*That* is all her imagination. There was no blood!"

"I was *ten*. It was the middle of the night! I thought *Santa had been eaten by alligators practically in my backyard*. And I never put sugar cookies out for Santa again after that!"

Owen made the mistake of smiling when he said, "I know."

Maddie punched him again. "You're not getting *any* 'cookies' from me tonight. If you know what I mean."

Owen looked at her. Then sighed. "Yeah, I know what you mean."

Kennedy looked very smug at that.

"Well, okay then. Owen is out of the running," Zeke said, raising his voice slightly as he rubbed the baby's back. "But the rest of us have good cases to make."

"You really have been talking about this?" Kennedy asked. "You all want to do this?"

Zeke looked at his older brother, Fletcher, who was sitting across the table from him. "Well, yeah. Like, Fletcher would be an awesome Santa. He's a teacher and is amazing with little kids. They all love him. He'd probably be the best at it."

Kennedy nodded. "I actually was thinking about Fletcher."

Zeke sat up straighter. "Oh, come on. Fletcher's too obvious."

Kennedy laughed and shook her head. "You were just telling me he'd be perfect."

"Well, he'd make a great Santa, but all the kids would guess it was him. They all know him too well. Don't let Fletcher ruin the magic of Christmas for all the kids in this town."

"So why were you making the case *for* him?" Kennedy asked.

"It was an *example*. We've been talking about all of our pros and cons for days. Come on, you have to at least listen to us."

Kennedy sat back in her chair and crossed her arms. She looked at the people gathered around the tables.

"Okay, fine. You can each make your case. Who wants to go first?"

Drew finished off his gumbo and sweet tea and sat back to watch this, feeling a strange sense of amusement and satisfaction that he couldn't explain. He didn't know these people, yet he was already drawn in by their camaraderie and the fun-loving spirit that seemed palpable in the air. Even when they were bickering and talking about Santa being eaten by alligators and reminiscing about terrorizing one another as children. Maybe *because* of that. A family that could endear themselves to a near-stranger with stories like that, had a special *something*.

Zeke spoke up first and Drew got the impression that was common. He could tell he would know all of these people much better when he walked out of here tonight.

"I think I would be the best Santa." Zeke rubbed his hand up and down his baby's back as the little one fussed. "Santa is all about the kids. Childlike wonder. The fun and magic of Christmas. And let's be honest, no one is more childlike than I am."

Everyone around the table laughed and Jill nodded. "Very good point."

Zeke gave her a grin. "Plus I'm a dad now," Zeke said. "I'm totally tapped into the meaning of Christmas for kids."

"Well, Josh would be awesome at it, too," Tori Kramer—well, now Landry, Drew corrected—said.

She was holding a little girl, older than the twins but not what Drew would call a toddler.

"That's true," Kennedy said. "Do you want to make a case for Josh?"

The man next to Tori, shook his head. "We all know I would be amazing at it. I'm sweet, patient, kind, charming..."

A wadded up napkin hit him in the cheek. Drew wasn't sure where it had come from.

Josh laughed. "*But* I'm all about making this Christmas special for Ella now that she's old enough to do some fun stuff." He looked at the baby in Tori's arms with a soft smile. "If you guys need any help getting it set up and stuff, I'm happy to pitch in. But I just want to hang out at home this Christmas with Ella and Tori."

Everyone nodded their understanding and Kennedy shrugged. "Okay, so no Owen and no Josh. Is it just Zeke?"

"I'd do it, of course," Mitch said.

"Oh, you would be an awesome Santa," Paige said. "You're easily the nicest."

Drew waited for someone to protest her statement. But no one did. Apparently, that was just a well-known fact.

"Mitch is kind, patient, funny, and sweet." Paige propped her chin on her hand and gazed at her boyfriend.

Drew almost laughed. Paige Asher had been one of the most eligible bachelorettes in Appleby, Iowa for a long time. She'd been proposed to five times back in Iowa. Yep, *five*. If someone had told him he would ever see Paige look at a man the way she was looking at Mitch Landry, Drew would have called bullshit.

"He would also take the job seriously and would show up on time for all of his shifts, and wouldn't be sleep deprived because of being up in the night with twins—" She gave Zeke a sympathetic look.

Kennedy was nodding. "Okay, so the sleep deprivation and

the need to be at home to help Jill with the twins is not a terrible point," she said to Zeke.

"Man, using my babies against me?" Zeke shook his head. "Not fair."

"But you *do* have a lot going on," Mitch said.

"And Josh just wants a sweet family Christmas with his girls. Fletcher might get outed by the kids since they all know him. So who else is in this 'competition'?" Kennedy put air quotes around competition.

"Well, definitely not Griffin," Zeke laughed. "We'd never keep the goats away from Santa's Village."

Paige laughed and looked at Drew. "One of the goats is madly in love with Griffin." She pointed down the table to the quiet, dark-haired man sitting next to Charlie. "Whenever he's around, she breaks out of her pen to be with him. The rest of the goats then follow her and we end up with the whole herd following him around like an entourage."

Drew chuckled. "And I've already met some of your goats. Pretty hard to ignore them."

"You have no idea," Griffin muttered.

"Plus Griffin's way too grumpy to be Santa," Charlie said, leaning in to kiss him on the cheek. "Or at least that's what he'd like for you all to believe. So let's just go with that."

The man didn't look offended nor did he dispute her comment.

"Well, if grumpy takes a guy out of the running, then Knox is definitely off the list," Kennedy said.

Paige looked at Drew again. "Knox is our city manager and Kennedy's right-hand man. Definitely grumpy, especially when it comes to chaotic events at the petting zoo. Or really anything having to do with the petting zoo at all."

"Well, obviously I would be the best one at it," Leo said as he brought a huge basket of cornbread muffins to the table and set it in the middle.

"You don't automatically get picked just because you're the old man with the gray beard," Owen said.

"No, I figure I'll get picked because I'm Kennedy's favorite," Leo said, shooting his granddaughter a grin.

"It's true. If Leo wants to do it, I'll probably give it to him," Kennedy said.

"What if *I* want to do it?" Bennett asked from her other side.

She gave him a smile. "You want to be Santa?"

"I'm just saying. Hypothetically, if you had to pick between me and Leo, who would you pick?"

Kennedy leaned over and patted Bennett's knee. "You really shouldn't ask questions you don't want the answer to."

Bennett rolled his eyes and chuckled.

"Don't worry, boy, I'm gonna die one of these days. You'll have a few good years as her favorite," Leo said.

Bennett gave the older man a grin. "You know I consider it a compliment to even be number two on the list behind you."

"And that's why you get to do my eulogy," Leo told him.

That clearly surprised, and touched, Bennett. "It would be my honor."

Paige turned wide eyes to Drew. "Welcome to my new world. Where we can talk about Santa murders, sweet babies at Christmas, and the future eulogies of our beloved older generation all over a typical weekday dinner."

Drew laughed out loud. "I'm more entertained than I've been in a very long time."

"If only we were trying to entertain the new guy and not just totally being our regular selves," Paige said.

"So, now I've got Leo, and maybe Bennett?" Kennedy asked. "We've got reasons that Owen, Josh, Zeke, Fletcher, Griffin, and Knox are nos."

"Come on, Ken, you know I'm gonna do it."

Everyone turned to look at Sawyer. Most of them looked surprised, though a couple looked amused.

Kennedy in particular had a huge smile on her face when she said, "Finally. I was going to make you do it, but I appreciate you volunteering."

The big guy nodded.

"Wait...seriously?" Owen asked. "You? You're almost as grumpy as Griffin."

Sawyer shook his head. "We all know that I'm great with kids. I can handle the schedule, no problem. And I'll take it completely seriously. These kids are coming to Santa with legitimate concerns and they need someone to hear them out."

Owen snorted. "Legitimate concerns? It's not like they're going to confession with their priest or bringing grievances to the city council. You make it sound like they're coming in for psychotherapy or something."

"Kids think Santa knows everything about them," Sawyer said. "It's important for them to think that he's been paying attention, knows them personally, and is listening. I'll have Fletcher fill me in on the kids that he knows and I'll have Ellie fill me in on the kids that Fletcher doesn't. I'll get an earpiece and Juliet will be talking in my ear, feeding me details about each kid as they come up to sit on my lap. This will be a serious, caring, and important endeavor."

They were all staring at him with wide eyes.

Josh broke the silence. "Stella and Cooper Trahan have gotten to you."

Sawyer nodded. "If Stella sits on Santa's lap, you can guarantee that guy better be ready to answer a million questions while she tries to determine if he's legit."

Drew shot a look at Paige.

"Their dad, Gabe, is a good friend. They come down from New Orleans for tours all the time. Stella is going to take over the swamp boat tour company someday. She and Cooper take everything very seriously. And Sawyer is their favorite."

Gabe. He must be the guy who owned the bar where Rory

used to work. The one who'd suggested she open her salon in Autre. So, Gabe had kids. And they were all obviously very close to the Landrys. Drew couldn't help but smile at how it all intersected.

Rory would love this big dinner and their stories from their childhood and how seriously Sawyer is going to take being Santa.

He couldn't avoid the thought. Or the pang of regret that she wasn't here right now to witness it all.

You aren't going to help her with the village and you're definitely not going to help her build relationships with this family so she feels like she belongs here. Knock it off. You're not her counselor or life coach or mother or boyfriend.

He stubbornly ignored the part that sounded something like, *but you could be* that the voice in his head tacked onto the end of all of that.

Juliet leaned over and put her head on Sawyer's shoulder. "I will absolutely help you be the best Santa this town has ever had."

Charlie leaned in. "I think that it's amazing that you want to make this a big deal and make it really special for the kids. Sawyer and Juliet, if you're willing to do that, then we will all pitch in to get information about all of the kids who are coming to the party and ask their parents and guardians some important questions so that we know something special about each of the kids and we can really make this something that they'll always remember."

Sawyer looked pleased and Kennedy looked at Leo.

"Okay with you if he does this?" she asked her grandfather.

Leo smiled at Sawyer with a look that was clearly both love and pride. "Yep, it's all his."

Kennedy banged her spoon down on the end of the table like a gavel. "Okay, it's decided. Sawyer is Santa."

"Maybe we can have an adult Christmas party up here and we can have fun Santa here at Ellie's," Owen said.

"And I suppose you think you'll be *fun* Santa?" Josh asked.

Owen grinned. "Who would be a better fun Santa?"

"Let me tell you something about who will *not* be sitting on your lap anymore if you play 'fun Santa'," Maddie told him.

He stretched his arm along the back of her chair and pulled it closer. "You are more than enough woman for my lap, Madison.

She lifted her brows. "I don't think that came out exactly the way you meant it too."

He nodded. "No, really. You fill my lap and then some."

Maddie shook her head. "You really just need to stop talking now."

Kennedy rolled her eyes. "You realize that you're going to still be saying that to him when he's ninety, right?"

Maddie sighed. But she gave her husband a look that was full of love. "Yeah, I'm aware."

"Okay so let's leave the 'fun Santa' stuff for everyone's own bedrooms," Kennedy said. She gave her husband an obvious look. "And we'll focus on the Santa's Village at the petting zoo for right now."

"Yeah, which brings something up I wanted to talk about," Jordan said, from her spot beside Fletcher.

"What's up?" Kennedy asked.

"Well—" Jordan chewed on her bottom lip for a moment. "I hate to say this, because I love Rory. I know she's working hard. But we're behind and I'm afraid we're not going to be ready."

Charlie leaned in with a little frown. "How not ready?"

Jordan lifted a shoulder. "I've tried not to step on her toes, so I haven't asked specifically. But I know there's painting that still needs done and some work around the Santa house. The whole Santa house and yard is her idea. I think she had bigger dreams than maybe she realized she could realistically do. The idea is great, but we could have done something a little smaller this first year."

"Well, we can definitely help with painting and things like that," Charlie said, glancing around the table.

There was lots of nodding.

"The gifts were dropped off today. We need to wrap those. We also need to figure out the snacks and some of the games and other activities the kids are going to do when they come sit on Santa's lap." Jordan shot Sawyer a grin.

"Okay, lay this plan out for us," Juliet said.

"There will be three days where the kids can come and sit on Santa's lap and get photos and tell him what they want for Christmas," Jordan said.

"At the same time, we're going to have goats dressed up like little elves, lots of different Christmas themed snacks, some face painting, games where they can win prizes—pin the nose on the snowman, things like that," Charlie said. "Just general festive stuff for families to do when they come up to the petting zoo. But we're going to spread the activities out so the whole park is involved. Storytime with Slothcrates will be Christmas stories. We're going to have snow cones and ice cream treats over by the penguins, and so on."

Drew shook his head. It was still odd for him to imagine Christmas involving cold ice cream treats rather than things like hot chocolate and hot apple cider like they were up north.

"But we're going to have hot chocolate and things like that too," Jill said. "Right?" She looked around. "It's really weird to have ice cream and snow cones for Christmas."

Drew shot her a grin. He didn't remember all the details but it seemed that maybe Jill wasn't a Louisiana native.

Charlie nodded. "Of course. We're not heathens. We drink hot chocolate here too."

"Hot chocolate should be by the alpacas. And we can sell those really great socks made with alpaca wool over there," Jordan said. "A general warm and cozy theme over there."

"Great idea," Charlie said. "So, yeah, those three days are

just full of lots of festive fun. General family-friendly activities along with a visit with Santa. Then on Christmas Eve the kids will come up here for the big party where they're going to get the gifts, decorate the tree with the ornaments they've made at the arts and crafts station, sing some carols, and all that good stuff."

Drew had to admit, it all sounded pretty sweet. Very Christmasy in a small town. Rory would love it.

His heart gave a little *thunk* in his chest and his next thought was, *well, hell.*

Not only was he thinking of the woman at random moments when he didn't mean to, but he actually cared that all of this came together as planned.

According to everything Jordan had explained, it really was going to be an amazing event that Rory would be very proud of. Something that she'd either dreamed of or experienced as a kid. Before her dad had ripped their family apart. Either way, it would mean a lot to her.

And the *next* next thought made him think, *well, fuck.* But it was less of a surprise. In fact, it was very in character for him.

He was going to help her pull this off.

"So what do we need to do?" Mitch asked. "I can get up there and paint. Or lay down those bricks or whatever needs done."

Fletcher nodded. "We're out of school for the holiday break as of tomorrow, so I'll have some free time."

"Yeah, I can get up there after the last tour," Sawyer agreed. "Josh and Owen too."

The other men nodded.

"No need."

They all looked over at him and Drew realized these were some of the first words he'd actually said to the group at large. Other than *Hi* and *Thanks for having me.*

"No?" Jordan asked.

"I talked to Rory today. She's got it all under control. No worries."

Rory did not have it all under control and she definitely needed some help. But it would kill her if these people came to her rescue. These were the people she wanted to impress. She wanted them to include her, to know they could depend on her, to consider her one of their group, to trust her with big projects like this. If they all came to her rescue, she'd be embarrassed and feel like a failure.

Drew wasn't going to let that happen.

Of course, he also wasn't going to leave her to try to handle this all on her own.

Jordan lifted her brows. "She has a plan? Are you sure?"

Drew nodded, working to exude confidence. "Absolutely. She said she knows it looks like things are running a little behind but everything's going to come together right on time."

Charlie smiled. "Awesome. I knew that Rory could do this. She was so happy to get involved and I know this means a lot to her. We'll let her do this her way. I'm sure she knows we're here to help if she needs us."

Drew nodded. "Oh, she definitely does. She really admires and likes all of you. She knows you all have her back."

Jordan was watching him closely. But she didn't say anything else. She simply nodded. "Okay then. It all seems like it's under control."

Drew sat back as they moved on to other topics, wondering how long he needed to hang out before he could excuse himself without stirring up any suspicion.

Because it looked like he had a couple of hours of painting ahead of him tonight.

6

"Come on, Donna," Rory coaxed. She tugged on the lead. The reindeer didn't move an inch.

In fairness, this might not be Donna. Which might explain why the animal wasn't coming with her. She also didn't have any treats or food, which might also be the reason. Personally, Rory wasn't going anywhere with anyone at two a.m. without the promise of at least a cookie.

"I just need you for a few minutes. Please just help me move this carriage and then I'll let you go back to sleep."

Rory understood the animal's reluctance to work at this time of the night—okay, morning. Rory didn't want to be at the barn right now either. But, as usual, Roger Robins showing up suddenly had turned her routine—and her common sense—upside down.

As soon as he'd left her at the barn, she'd panicked and headed to New Orleans for cardboard boxes and wrapping paper.

Of course, she hadn't realized she was panicking at the time. In fact, she'd believed she had a very solid plan. Even a very *creative*, solid plan.

And she wasn't ready to admit that the plan had its flaws. Because it truly was her only option. So, she was just going forward with it. Two a.m. or not.

Just then, she heard footsteps outside the barn.

Oh, that motherfucker was her first thought.

Roger had come back.

What now? Had he forgotten to make her life and all of her plans an even bigger mess? On his drive back to wherever he was staying, had he come up with another way of completely fucking with everything that mattered to her?

She would not put it past him to suddenly realize, even in the middle of the night, that there was one more way he could make things difficult for her and to immediately turn his car around and come back to do so. It wouldn't be unlike him to forgo sleep in order to make sure that he wreaked as much havoc as possible.

Well, that was it. He wasn't getting out of here this time without at least a little bit of a fight from her.

Rory looked around, spied the first heavy item that she thought she could lift herself, grabbed it, and ducked just inside the barn door.

For just a second, she acknowledged that her eyes were a bit blurry and her brain was foggy. She'd been working long days even before Roger had showed up and she'd been under more than a little pressure. Roger's appearance tonight had pushed her stress and I'll-do-anything-to-make-this-work levels into the red zone. She didn't remember the last time she'd eaten today and knew that the three Diet Dr. Peppers she'd had earlier this evening were not adequate sustenance. She was also just really fucking tired. But she shoved all of that away and focused on the task at hand—making Roger Robins really sorry he'd bothered to come back here tonight.

Roger stepped through the barn doors and without registering anything else, Rory heaved the bag of feed at him. Okay, half a bag of feed because she wouldn't have been able to lift a whole bag. Still, it connected with the target.

"*Oof.*"

Roger stumbled back as the bag hit him in the gut.

Rory realized it was more from surprise than her actual strength, but he took a few steps back. The heel of his boot hit the edge where the wooden floor and the dirt yard met and he tripped, falling backward onto his ass, just outside the pool of light from inside the barn.

Rory stomped to the door, planted her hands on her hips, and glowered down at him.

"What the hell are you doing back here?" she snapped. "Just get the hell out of here. You already done enough."

"Me? What the hell are *you* doing here?"

"I'm—" She snapped her mouth shut. That was not Roger's voice.

A second later, that actually sunk in. *That wasn't Roger's voice.* Then she sighed. Of course it wasn't. She'd assumed it was Roger because who else would be skulking around the barn at this time of night? But now that the shot of adrenaline from the surprise and anger was clearing, she realized she was staring down at Drew Ryan.

And of course it had to be *him.*

The man who already knew too much about her vulnerable state and background. Whose truck had been up at Ellie's tonight when she'd driven by to head to New Orleans. He'd probably been surrounded by Landrys and elbow-deep in amazing gumbo. While she was literally on the outside, in the dark, trying to clean up the mess her scumbag father had created for her. Again.

She'd wanted to cry.

Hell, she wanted to cry now.

And she kind of wanted to just take the three steps between her and Drew, drop down into his lap, and ask him to hug her.

She had the strangest feeling that he would. And that he would feel really fucking good.

God, she was *so* tired. Obviously.

"Seriously, what are you doing here?" she asked him. But she took a step forward and held out a hand.

He shoved the bag of feed that was still in his lap to the side, then reached out and took her hand, letting her help pull him to his feet.

"I was up here earlier and then couldn't sleep, so thought I'd come back and finish what I was working on." He paused and studied her face for a moment. He was still in the shadow and she was in the light. "What are *you* doing here?"

It was only then that Rory realized that to anyone but her father, this might look strange. She glanced around. There was really no explanation for what she was doing. It was two a.m., she was in the barn with a sleigh—okay, it was more of a carriage considering it had wheels, since there was no snow in Louisiana to warrant a sleigh—and a reindeer that she was trying to hook to the front of said sleigh. One of Drew's reindeer.

Oh, and the sleigh was full of wrapped boxes.

None of this had been here a few hours ago.

Honestly, her emotions had been on such a roller coaster today, and she was so tired and hungry, and she was so sure that everything sucked and nothing was going to work out, that every thought of making up a story, charming her way out of this, or even just distracting him, fled her mind and as she looked up at him. She was appalled to feel her lower lip tremble.

Drew immediately noticed and stepped closer. His expression was one of sincere concern and seemingly without thought, he reached up and cupped the side of her face. "What's wrong?"

"I'm trying to save Christmas." She sniffed. "And it's not

going to work."

His eyes widened briefly. "You're trying to save Christmas by stealing all the presents?"

Now *her* eyes widened and she gasped. "I'm not *stealing* them! I'm moving them! I'm..." Then all at once, she completely deflated. "Oh, fuck."

And the tears started.

"Dammit." He didn't even hesitate. He pulled her in and wrapped his arms around her.

The tears flowed harder.

Drew Ryan, the Iowa farmer—who didn't check off the first thing on her checklist, who didn't have a speck of southern accent, who probably cheered for a Big 10 football team, who lived so damned far away—knew who her dad was and was now here at her lowest moment, seeing her messing everything up, and hugging her.

It was the best thing that had happened to her in weeks.

It was probably because it was 2 a.m.—though her father being a complete asshole certainly factored in—but Rory gave into the urge and leaned into Drew, wrapping her arms around him and letting him hold her.

She couldn't remember the last time she'd been hugged. It wasn't as pathetic as it sounded. Her friend and partner, Lennon, hugged her. Ellie Landry hugged her. Charlie Landry hugged her, for that matter. She seemed to recall even being hugged by Donovan Foster. The Landrys and the people they hung out with tended to be kind of a huggy bunch.

She just couldn't remember the last time.

And Drew Ryan was good at it. Maybe better than all of those people.

It didn't hurt that she was already incredibly attracted to him. The hard muscles behind his flannel shirt, the biceps wrapping around her, the big hands spread on her lower back, the way her head nestled right underneath his chin, and the way he smelled, all contributed to the absolute this-is-amazing feel of the whole thing.

And she was down and out. There was no denying that. This was a very weak moment. But even in the midst of all of that, Rory could acknowledge the fact that there was not ever going to be a time, place, or situation when she would *not* enjoy being up against Drew Ryan's body.

After nearly a minute of just holding her and not saying anything, his voice rumbled under her ear. "I was kidding. I didn't really think you were stealing the gifts."

She sniffed and resolutely kept her cheek against his chest. "I can understand why you would think that I was."

There was a soft chuckle that vibrated against her cheek. "Come on, there's no reason I would think that you would do that. Obviously, this whole Christmas village thing means a lot to you. There's no way you're gonna do something to sabotage it."

And that made the tears start fresh.

"Dammit."

He muttered it softly enough that had she not been pressed up against him and right underneath his mouth she might not have heard it.

She sucked in a deep, ragged breath and made herself look up at him. She was certain that she looked pathetic.

"I'm fucking this all up," he said softly. "I really do want to make you feel better."

"You are. Honestly. By just being here and believing me and trusting me and thinking I would never do something to ruin all of this...and hugging me." She sniffed. "That was a really good move."

One corner of his mouth tipped up. "Yeah? Because it was kind of an I-have-no-idea-what-else-to-do move."

"You have good instincts."

They just stood looking at each other for another long

moment.

Then he asked, "You gonna tell me what this is about?"

She really didn't want to. But...she kind of did. She would actually really like to share this with someone. And there was something about Drew that made her want to talk.

She was still surprised by what she'd shared earlier. Drew knew more about her than anyone else in Autre. Including Lennon. Lennon knew that Rory's dad was out of the picture and that her mom was a mess. She knew that Roger had cheated and left the family and that Rory definitely had some issues with that. She knew that Rory wanted to put down roots and that being a part of the community was hugely important to her. But Lennon didn't know about Roger's arrest record or that he bopped back in and out of Rory's life periodically or that she lived with the constant fear of him coming in and ruining everything. Basically exactly what he'd done with the Santa village.

Rory sniffed again and finally made herself let go of Drew. She stepped back and pulled in a deep breath. "My dad stole the gifts."

Drew frowned. "What do you mean?" His eyes flickered to the sleigh full of gifts behind her.

She took another deep breath, then looked at this man who had shown up in her life that very day. She had literally known this guy for only a few hours. And she didn't really know him all that well. Maybe that's what made it so easy to spill her guts. She really didn't know. And she didn't care. She needed a friend. And there was something about Drew Ryan that made her think that he could be her friend.

He was a good guy. She'd had that vibe from the first moment. And maybe it was stupid, and maybe she would regret it, but she honestly was feeling so alone right now that she opened her mouth and the entire story about her dad spilled out.

"I decided to wrap fifty boxes so no one here will know those toys are missing," she finished. "Now I just need to move them outside to the display so no one else sets up the display and realizes they're empty."

Drew took it all in without much reaction.

When she finally paused and took a few deep breaths, he nodded. "And what's the plan now?"

Well, that was a great question. She honestly didn't know. She'd been in solve-this-problem-in-this-minute mode since Roger had showed up.

"This"—She waved her hand at the sleigh with the gifts —"is just my plan to buy some time to figure the rest of it out. If I can get him the money to bring the controllers back, then we'll be okay. Or..." She took a breath and shook her head. "No, I really don't have any other plan."

"You could turn him in."

She closed her eyes. "I know. I *should*. The thing is, if I do that, then they'll know something happened. And Zander has to get involved. And they'll all realize that their sweet town and their charming Santa's Village and their wonderful charitable event isn't as safe and perfect as they think. Because of *me*." She focused on Drew again. "They're going to want to know how I know him and how I know what he did. Even if I make an anonymous tip, he'll tell them who he is. Who *I* am. I just..." She sucked in a breath and worked on not crying again. "This is all my fault. I should have thought about the possibility that I was putting this project at risk by getting involved. I guess...I wanted to believe I could do something good, have something nice, without him messing it up. But I should have known better." She shook her head. "Now I need to fix it. There's no reason to stress anyone else out, or upset them, or get them involved. I need to clean up the mess I made. And keep them happily oblivious to the idea that bad things might happen to their petting zoo at Christmas time. Or any time."

Drew had tucked his hands into his pockets and Rory felt a stupid sense of loss. As if with his hands in his pockets there was no chance of him reaching out and touching her or hugging her again. She would really like him to touch and hug her again.

"Okay."

That was all he said to all of that. He just accepted her feelings about it.

"So what are you doing with Lucy right now?"

She looked at him for a long moment, trying to process what he just asked her. Then she glanced at the reindeer. Oh, this was Lucy, not Donna.

"I was going to move the carriage to the side yard with the Santa house and everything. We're doing some photos tomorrow for flyers and the website and the newspaper is going to come by and do a little story. I was thinking that if the gifts and everything are already set up, no one else will be moving stuff around and no one will notice that it's fifty empty boxes instead of boxes with game controllers in them."

"And Lucy?"

"Normally we move the carriage around using horses but the horses are way out at the other barn and Lucy was right here and I thought maybe the reindeer could pull the sleigh..." She gave a heavy sigh. "Honestly, Drew, I'm exhausted. Nothing I'm doing is making any sense. And I realize that. But I have no better plans."

He didn't say anything to that. For just a moment she thought he was actually going to reach out and hug her again and she couldn't remember wanting anything more in a very long time. But instead, he stepped past her and took a hold of Lucy's lead. Then he hooked Lucy to the front of the carriage and proceeded to pull the carriage around the side yard. Easily. Without question or argument.

"Where do you want it?"

Rory followed him. And because there is nothing better to do, she told him where she needed the sleigh positioned for the photo shoot tomorrow. Drew made sure it was all set up, then unhooked Lucy and put her back into her stall in the barn.

When he came back out, he didn't stop walking until he was standing directly in front of Rory.

"Time for bed."

Her eyes widened.

"I'm taking you home and putting you to bed. Alone," he added as he seemed to read something in her expression.

Yes, she was thinking exactly what he thought she was thinking when it came to him putting her to bed.

"I have a lot more to do."

"It's two thirty in the morning."

She shrugged. "Yeah, and this is the situation. I don't have a choice."

"Maybe you don't have a choice. But you have something else."

"What's that?"

He gave her a little smile and he finally reached out and took hold of her upper arms. "A friend."

She started crying again.

His smile fell. "Dammit," he muttered.

She smiled and shook her head, lifting a hand to dash the tears away. "No, no. That was the perfect thing to say. Thank you so much."

"What else needs to be done?"

"I can't ask you to stay here without me."

"Nope. I'm going to bed too. But we'll get this done together tomorrow."

She looked around. "The painting and the..." She trailed off as her eyes landed on the front of Santa's shack. "Oh my God." The front of the shack had been painted. It was done. And it looked amazing. Her heart sunk. "Oh crap."

Drew frowned. "What's wrong?"

"Someone finished painting the shack."

"Yeah. Does it look okay?"

"It looks awesome. But I didn't do it. And obviously whoever did do it knows that. That means one of the Landrys came up and realized they needed to pitch in. That means that they know that I got behind and over my head and they're trying to bail me out, but that's just pathetic, and—"

"Rory."

Drews firm tone stopped her and she looked up at him.

"The Landrys didn't do it."

She studied him and then the realization dawned.

She looked down at him and realized that he had streaks of red and white paint on the t-shirt he was wearing and a streak of green on one forearm.

"You did it."

He nodded. "It didn't take long and it was no big deal. But I wanted to give you a hand."

Rory had no idea what to do with that information. He'd helped without being asked. He'd helped so that she can keep the secret that she was actually failing at this entire project. He'd helped so that she wouldn't fail. And now he was up here learning about her father, her worst secret of all, and he was going to keep that secret too.

Looking into his eyes, she thought for the first time that maybe all of this could work out somehow. She had no idea how she was going to replace fifty special edition advanced game controllers, but being here with Drew, knowing he was on her side, made her feel so much better. So much less alone.

And because she really had no idea how to express all of that to him, or to even begin to help him understand what that meant to her, she did really the only thing she could to let him know that he'd absolutely come in as her knight in faded blue jeans.

She took the front of his shirt in her fist, pulled him down, and pressed her lips to his.

She'd kind of intended it to just be a thank-you-you're-awesome kiss. Not exactly a peck on the cheek, but just a quick meeting of their lips. She just needed to do something more than *say* thank you.

But the moment their lips touched Rory realized she'd been lying to herself. She didn't want anything short or sweet from this man. She wanted everything with Drew to last as long as it possibly could. And there was nothing sweet about what she was feeling. She wanted raw and emotional and deep. And not just in the sexual way, though certainly that as well. But she wanted him to wrap her up and pull her in and to...be a part of her.

Having him on her side, feeling like she had an ally and a true friend—someone who knew what a mess she was, but wanted to be there for her anyway—was such a freaking relief, she hadn't even realized how much she wanted it.

Thankfully, Drew didn't seem to be thinking short and sweet either. His hands dropped to her hips to pull her up against him firmly and she regretted that she'd changed into yoga pants from the tiny dress she'd been in earlier.

At least she wasn't wearing denim. The jeans he had on were simply too thick. The soft cotton of her yoga pants at least let the heat from his hands soak into her skin and she could feel each one of his fingers individually as they gripped her hips and then slid around to her ass, cupping her and bringing her up onto tiptoe so he could press into her.

His mouth was hungry on hers and his beard rasped deliciously against her chin and cheeks as he angled his head, deepening the kiss. Their tongues tangled and Rory felt the strokes between her legs and on her nipples. Heat swirled in her belly and she had the urge to lift a leg and hook it around his thigh so he could settle the hard bulge behind his fly against her aching center.

What the hell? It was the middle of the night, and it was just her and Drew and the reindeer. She lifted her leg, but as she was moving to wrap it around him, one of his big hands dropped, grasping her thigh and helping her. He lifted her, bringing her up more fully against him and the next thing she knew, her feet had left the floor. Carrying her with his one hand under her ass and the other wrapped around her thigh, he carried her into the barn and put her back up against the side of the first stall. Her arms went around his neck and she moaned into his mouth as his cock lined up perfectly with her pussy and he pressed into her.

His answering groan sent pleasure racing from her scalp to her toes and she arched closer.

His mouth slid from hers over her jaw to her ear. "Fuck, you feel good," he said roughly.

His gravelly voice made her body tingle as if he'd stroked a hand down her side and over her breast.

She clamped her knees more firmly around him and tipped her head back against the barn wood behind her.

"Oh my God, ditto. I didn't even know how much I needed this."

He gave a soft chuckle, which danced hotly over the skin of her neck. He followed the hot air with his lips, kissing along the column of her neck and making goosebumps chase each other down to her nipples which beaded happily behind the light green hooded sweatshirt she wore.

He was really doing most of the work when it came to holding her up, so she took the chance to move her hands down his hard chest to his abs and then under the soft cotton of the t-shirt he wore under the open flannel. As her hands met hot bare skin, his muscles tensed and she moaned again.

She wanted to see them. She wanted to lick them. She

wanted to watch them contracting and relaxing as she rode him cowgirl.

"Come home with me," she whispered hoarsely.

Drew stilled. His mouth rested just above her collarbone and his body, which had been pressing hungrily against hers, tensed.

A moment later he lifted his head, his hot gaze locked on hers.

"I can't."

Rory couldn't believe the way her stomach plummeted. She frowned. "Why not?" It was clear that he was into this.

"You're exhausted, you're stressed, and you're feeling very grateful right now."

She shook her head quickly. "I'm not doing this out of gratitude. I want you." She stroked a hand up and down over his abs and ribs. "I've wanted you since I met you."

He gave a soft chuckle. "Which was less than twenty-four hours ago. And you want a guy from Autre. You've got a thing for Beau."

"Beau who?"

Drew just smiled and shook his head.

Rory sighed. "Okay. That's all fair. But Beau and I aren't going out. We've had a few conversations. But he's never touched me. We've never kissed. He has no idea that I've thought of dating him. And...you've made everything so much better for me in the few hours I've known you, that yes, I'm being selfish. I want to know what else you can make better. I know you're not sticking around. Honestly, with the mess my life is, that is probably for the best. For your sake. But that's what makes this great. This doesn't have to be any major thing."

He held her gaze for several seconds. Then he said. "The problem is, it kind of feels like a major thing."

7

Rory sucked in a little breath and felt her heart flip over in her chest. It was the look in his eyes. Or the tone of his voice. Or...something. Maybe the fact that he wasn't stripping her naked and fucking her against the wall of the barn right now when she'd clearly given him an open invitation to do exactly that. But he thought this felt major? After just a few hours? In spite of all of the craziness and weirdness?

But looking at him right now, she understood what he meant. This definitely felt like something *different* anyway.

She pulled in a deep breath. "Okay."

They just stayed like that. They weren't looking away. They weren't talking. He wasn't letting go of her.

Finally, she said, "Now what?"

"I know I can't spend the night in your bed, but I can't seem to take my hands off of you."

She gave a little smile. "I very much like having your hands on me. Honestly, this is the first time I've felt *good*, and even a little calm in a long time." She frowned. "Which is strange, considering my hormones are jumping, my heart is racing, and I'm breathing fast. None of this actually feels *calm*, but it's like emotionally, I feel..." She wasn't sure she should say what was on the tip of her tongue. It would sound like a lot. Because it was a lot. But he was the one that had just said everything felt major.

He squeezed her ass with one hand. "Say it."

"I don't know if I should," she hedged.

He squeezed her a little harder and she felt heat twirl through her tummy.

"Say it, Rory."

She suddenly really wanted to. If he ran, then he ran. She hadn't even known him yesterday morning. She'd survive if she didn't see him again after this.

But damn, her heart ached a little at that idea.

Major. That was actually a good word for this, she decided.

She wet her lips. "Okay, this is the first time in longer than I can remember that I feel taken care of."

Something flashed in his eyes. It was definitely desire, even lust. But there was something more. It seemed like possessiveness. And satisfaction. Though that didn't totally make sense.

But then he said, "Well, I can definitely take care of you."

He let go of her then, letting her slide to the floor.

She wanted to protest. The last thing she wanted was for him to let go of her. But maybe he was just going to hug her again. That would be okay. Maybe not exactly what her body was longing for, but that had felt pretty damn good too. If he wanted to take care of her, hugging qualified.

But as soon as she was on her feet, he took her face in his hands and leaned in to kiss her. The kiss was sweet, but it had a hint of spice. The promise of more. It was deep and his scent and heat and touch surrounded her and filled all her senses. She felt almost trapped. He was caging her in against the wall, her face held in his hands, completely dominating the kiss. There was a definite feel of possessiveness and even protectiveness in it all. And yet she felt the same sense of comfort. Like he was caring for her. Like he wanted to take care of her.

When he lifted his head, he was breathing faster too.

Without a word he turned her, so she was facing the wall. He took her hands and put them up on the stall, the wood rough against her palms. His hand covered the back of her hands, flattening her palms against the wood.

His mouth was right against her ear when he said, "Don't move."

He ran his hands down her body, over her breasts to her belly where he rubbed back and forth, causing her shirt to bunch and his palms to meet her bare skin. She sucked in a breath as electricity sparkled from there to her clit. Then he slid his hands down over her hips to the front of her thighs before he came back up and cupped her through her yoga pants.

"So hot," he said roughly against her ear.

Her eyes slid shut and she gave a little shiver.

"At any point you want to stop you just say so," he said, his voice still gruff. "We don't need a safe word. You just say no."

She nodded, unable to speak. She was so turned on. He was taking over, caging her in against the wall again, yet making her feel safe and completely cared for. Nothing could get to her here. He wasn't trapping her inside, he was blocking everything else out. All that was in her sphere of awareness right now was Drew and the pleasure he could bring her.

His hands slid back up over her belly and under her shirt stroking over her skin on his way up to her breasts. His hands were slightly calloused and so hot she whimpered. His touch was gentle, but confident and intentional. He cupped her breasts, playing with her nipples through her bra for several long seconds. She pressed into him, wanting more and he gave it to her, tugging harder, then pinching lightly.

She huffed out a breath and then moaned.

He pulled the bra cups down, freeing her breasts, baring them to his touch. He again toyed with her nipples for several long, delicious moments, tugging, rolling, and pinching until she was hot and wet between her legs, restless for more, shifting foot to foot.

As if sensing what she needed, he slid one hand to her belly and pressed her back against him, his cock nudging her butt.

"You're amazing. I've been turned on since I saw you chasing a goat with a candy cane," he told her. "You're gorgeous and sweet and funny. And I've never wanted to fuck a woman in red and white striped stockings while the pom pom on her Santa hat bounces, but I now have a new fantasy because of you."

It was ridiculous that that line actually worked, but Rory felt her desire ratchet up three more notches. She desperately needed release. She needed something against her clit and filling her up. Right now.

She started to turn in his arms, but he reached up and clamped a hand around one of her wrists, pressing against her back with his big, hot body.

"Don't move," he reminded her. "I can't fuck you tonight. You're too emotionally raw. You're exhausted. But I'm going to give you the release you need, sweetheart. I can take care of you that way."

Something about his words was her undoing. She let herself lean back against him fully, giving him her weight...and her surrender. She *was* emotionally raw and exhausted. She wanted a release, but she also needed someone who knew what she was feeling and what she *really* needed right now.

She let her head drop back onto his shoulder and she pulled in a deep breath.

Maybe this is all just a dream. Maybe she was hallucinating. She didn't care. At this moment she was going to wrap herself in this fantasy and ride it out for all it was worth.

His big, hot hand stroked over her belly and then into her pants and silk panties. He ran the pad of his middle finger over her cleft a few times, gently, just teasing and tempting. Then his clearly knowledgeable fingers easily found her clit and he circled there for a moment.

She was hot and wet and already on edge, and she pressed into his hand with a ragged moan that almost sounded like a sob.

He slid his middle finger lower through the slick folds and then teased the tip of his finger into her entrance.

"Yes," she begged hoarsely.

"I've got you," he promised roughly against her ear. "I've got you. Just let me take care of you."

She moved a foot so that her thighs were further apart but that didn't feel like enough. She lifted one foot up to the wooden slat on the bottom of the stall.

"That's my girl," he praised. Then he slipped his whole finger inside her as his thumb circled over her clit.

Yes. She cried out. It'd been a long time since another human had touched her there.

His finger was thick and long, though certainly not the size of her favorite vibrator. Even when he added the second finger. Still, he could do things plastic couldn't. He thrust in and out slowly at first then picked up the pace, curling his finger just right to rub over that magical spot that made swirls of pleasure start rotating in her core and spreading out. Then he pressed harder into her clit, circling faster and said against her ear, "I've got you, Rory."

It was, stupidly, the words that sent her over the edge.

Not that his hands and fingers weren't amazing. But having someone else focused on what she needed and her pleasure was the ultimate fantasy.

He circled her clit and thrust into her one more time and

she came apart, crying out as an orgasm rolled over her. She felt tension and worry and regret flood out of her as well.

She clung to the feeling for several seconds. She absorbed the feel of the big, hot body behind her, the arms wrapped around her, the hand and fingers in that most private place, the hot breath against her neck, the heart pounding against her shoulder blade.

Then she finally sucked in a deep breath and slumped forward. Drew's hands were there on her hips to hold her up as she took a few moments to gather herself.

She wasn't even undressed. So she simply pulled her bra cups back up over her breasts and turned in his arms. His hands stayed on his hips as he studied her, waiting for her to speak first.

There was really only one thing she could say. She gave him a soft smile. "Thank you."

He gave her a sexy half smile and said, "Absolutely my pleasure."

"Are you sure that's all you want to do?"

He nodded. "It may sound strange, but that was highly satisfying."

She nodded. "That does sound a little strange."

"To me too." He gave her a grin. "But I mean it."

She pulled her bottom lip between her teeth and studied him for several more seconds. Then finally she nodded. "Okay."

"Okay. You need to get home. When you get there, you need to eat something, and take a shower, and go to bed. What time is your first appointment tomorrow?"

She looked at him with what she was sure was a puzzled expression. No one ever worried about her and her habits and routines. "I don't have anyone coming in until one."

"Okay, good. Sleep late. And have more for breakfast than coffee."

Her eyes widened. She definitely didn't have people worry

about what she ate. "How did you know that sometimes I only have coffee?"

He shook his head. "I'm not sure. But you kinda strike me as the type to worry about what you're doing for other people more than you worry about yourself."

How did he know that? She nodded. "I do that. Because it matters to me that other people are taken care of."

He lifted a brow. "I think that's probably true, but I think you're also worried about other people liking you."

"You don't think people like me?"

"I think other people like you a lot. And I don't think that you have to try to *make* them like you. But I think that *you* think you do." He lifted a hand and brushed her hair back from her face. "And I have no idea why I'm suddenly playing psychologist. It's really not like me."

Well, he was good at it. She wasn't going to tell him that, but he'd hit the nail on the head.

It came from her father and how he'd screwed her up psychologically, of course. She'd obviously spent years wondering why she hadn't been enough for him. Why their home and family hadn't been enough. Why he'd had to go out seeking more and wanting more than he could have at home with them.

"Okay, then I guess I'm heading home."

"Okay. And you'll call me when you get there." He didn't phrase that as a question.

She laughed. "Really?"

He shrugged. "Really. I want to be sure you get there and I would like to know that you really are eating something and then going straight to bed."

"Why don't you just walk me home?"

"Are you within walking distance?"

"Well, not exactly. We'd have to drive. But you can come with me and make sure that I eat and shower and get to bed."

He shook his head slowly. "See, the fact that I want to do that more than I want to do anything else, means I shouldn't. I can't sleep with you tonight, Rory."

The way he said her name, combined with the way he was looking at her, made her stomach flip. In a very good way.

"And if I come home with you, I'd like to think I'm a good enough guy to resist, but..." He brushed a hair back from her face again, but surely there wasn't another one there. "I'm not at all sure that's true."

"If we sleep together tonight, you're going to worry that it's because of everything else that's going on with me right now," she said.

He nodded. "Exactly."

That was fair. And he *was* being a really good guy. She needed to let him off the hook. "You really are a nice guy, Drew."

He actually rolled his eyes at that. And sighed. "Yes, I know."

She laughed, then lifted on tiptoe and pressed a kiss against his cheek. "That's a good thing. Since coming to Autre, I've been around a lot of good guys, but none of them are—" She abruptly stopped. Wow. She'd almost said *mine*.

None of them are mine.

No, none of the good guys in Autre were hers. But neither was Drew.

He lifted a brow.

"None of them have done *that* to me," she said, tipped her head toward the stall next to them. That was totally true.

His gaze heated. "I'm really fucking glad to hear that. And see, *that* makes me not such a great guy."

"It does?"

"I shouldn't be possessive about a woman who I just met and who deserves to have men falling at her feet and worshipping her. You deserve to feel good and have people wanting to make you feel good all the time."

She smiled. How could she not like a guy who said stuff like that? She kind of liked the idea that Drew might feel a little possessive of her.

And *that* could be trouble.

"I don't know," she told him. "Still seems like you're a good guy."

"Dammit."

She could delve into that like crazy. She wanted to know all about him. Everything about him.

So instead of going into all of that, she turned on her heel and started to step past him and head out the of barn. But one thing made her turned back. "Hey, earlier when you just turned and walked away. What was that about?"

Drew shoved his hands into his front pockets, then took a deep breath and blew it out before answering. "Because I absolutely did not want to walk away. At all. Maybe ever."

Her stomach somersaulted again, a much bigger flip this time and her brain said, *oh, hell.*

So, instead of getting into any more of that, she just nodded, then did the same thing by turning on her heel and walking away from him this time.

But as soon as she was inside her house and in her kitchen, she called him.

"I'm home and making a sandwich."

"Good. What kind?"

With some distance from him, she felt a little more rational. Like a sandwich *was* a good idea. And that staying up all night doing dirty things to Drew Ryan was maybe not the best call. Tonight. Only for *tonight*, though.

His question made her smile and feel warm now. "Peanut butter and jelly. It's fast and always good any time of day."

"Good choice. I approve."

"Where are you right now?" she asked as she pulled bread, peanut butter, and jelly together on the counter.

"In my room at Mitch and Paige's."

She knew where Mitch and Paige lived, but she'd never been inside, so the bedroom she conjured as she thought about Drew was purely made up. Not that it mattered. "What are you doing?"

She started spreading peanut butter on the bread, only half her mind on her task. Or less than half her mind. She was definitely thinking about Drew, and what they'd just done in the barn. Or what he'd just done. And what she would really like to do to him the next time she saw him.

He was right to have sent her home alone. She was not at her best mentally, emotionally, or physically. But her desire for this man hadn't started with her exhaustion in the barn and she didn't see it dissipating.

Still, it would be nice to assure him of that the next time she saw him.

"I'm just lying on the bed. Wanting to make sure you're safe and sound before I fall asleep."

"What are you wearing?" she asked with a little smile as she added jelly to her sandwich.

His soft chuckle caused goosebumps to trip down her arm even over the phone.

"Nah. We're not doing that tonight, Rory."

Something about the way he said her name filled her with happiness and lust at the same time.

She couldn't remember a guy ever doing that to her before. She'd certainly wanted guys in the past. Been turned on. Been even a little wanton, if she was honest. And she'd dated guys she liked, of course. She'd been friends with guys, for that matter. But the combination of all of those things that she felt with Drew was unique.

"Okay, then I guess I won't get frisky with this peanut butter."

He gave a little half-groan half-laugh. "No. Eat the sand-wich. Then take a hot shower."

She took a bite and chewed. "Is that your not-so-subtle way of telling me I didn't smell like peppermint ice cream a little bit ago?"

He paused, then cleared his throat, then said in a husky voice that made her whole body say *let's freaking go to Iowa!*, he told her, "I wanted to put my mouth on every single fucking inch of you. Does that answer your question?"

She sucked in a little breath and nodded. Then remembered she was on the phone. "Yeah. I guess it does."

"Good. Keep eating on your way up to the shower."

"Are we going to talk on the phone while I shower?"

"It's probably going to kill me to know that you're in the shower and to hear the water running and imagine what you're doing, but yeah, I want to keep the phone on."

"This isn't really phone sex, but it feels really intimate." She started for the stairs.

"I know."

She could have been imagining it since they were on the phone, but he sounded a little puzzled by the whole thing too.

"Why do you feel like you need to hear me shower? You think I need a babysitter?"

"Actually, I think that you take care of yourself pretty well, except when you're really stressed about a big project. And I think you've been doing it for a long time. Probably since you were about sixteen and your world fell apart. I guess I want to let you know that there's someone here for you. I want to be the one who you know cares even if you are doing nothing more than eating peanut butter and jelly and taking a quick shower before bed. I want you to feel connected with somebody." He paused. "And I want that somebody to be me."

Rory stopped at the top of her stairs.

Holy shit.

That was, no doubt about it, the best thing anyone had ever said to her.

Several seconds stretched by but Drew didn't seem to feel the need to fill the silence. Maybe he knew she needed to process all of that. Or maybe he knew that she was just letting it soak into her like the warmth from a fire when she'd come in from a cold rainy night.

Finally, she said, "Would it be okay if I called you once in a while when you're back in Iowa?"

He let out a breath. "Any time. Day or night."

She smiled. "I'm going to take you up on that."

And for the first time she thought that maybe she'd been wrong about not being able to trust people who weren't around all the time. It seemed that Drew Ryan was potentially an exception to a number of rules.

"Are you getting in the shower?"

Suddenly feeling a shot of mischief to go along with the happiness he'd sent fizzing through her veins, she smiled. "There's definitely something about your deep voice rumbling in my ear that makes me want to take my clothes off, I'll tell you that much."

He gave a little groan. "Yeah, this is going to kill me a little bit, isn't it?"

"We could hang up."

"No. I'd rather be hard as a rock and connected to you than comfortable and not."

"That probably shouldn't sound sweet, but it did."

He chuckled softly.

She hit this button for speaker and set the phone on the counter. Then she started stripping.

"We should've made this a video call," she said as she stepped out of her panties.

"Yeah, maybe we should have." His voice was especially gruff now.

"Maybe you should take your clothes off too." There was a long pause. Then she was ninety-nine percent sure she heard rustling. She grinned. "Are you doing it?"

"Yeah."

Heat swirled through her body. "Oh my God. That's hot."

"You think so?" He actually sounded slightly hesitant.

"Knowing that you're going to be touching yourself while I'm in the shower and we're on the phone together? Yeah." She took a deep breath and let it out. "You are going to touch yourself, aren't you?"

"I already am."

The heat in her belly shot straight between her legs. "I'm not going to be able to keep from touching myself. Though, I really preferred how you did it."

His groan was not as soft this time. "Rory."

"I'm just starting to think that maybe a long-distance thing with regular phone calls could be kind of fun."

"Get in the shower. Get wet."

"I'm already wet."

"Rory." Now he sounded like he was saying her name through gritted teeth.

She giggled, which a few hours ago she would not have thought possible.

She started the water, then turned on the shower and stepped into the tub. Her bathroom wasn't large, and she was sure that the phone was close enough that he could hear the water running. They didn't need to talk through this part probably.

Rory closed her eyes as the hot water ran over her body and imagined Drew lying on a big king bed on white sheets, his sun-tanned skin and hard muscles standing out in sharp contrast. She imagined one of the huge hands that touched her so expertly, wrapped around the hard cock she'd felt pressing into her back. She soaped her body, paying extra attention to her nipples and between her legs. Then she dropped the soap and let her fingers continue working over her clit. It was still sensitive from Drew's fingers and she imagined that it was his hand back in place. It didn't take her long to take herself up and over the edge again and as she thought about coming quietly, she discarded that idea immediately and cried out his name so that he could hear her over the phone.

She braced a hand on the shower wall and sucked in deep breaths as the water continued to rain over her. Then she heard his voice call out her name and she smiled even as heat cascaded through her.

She shut the water off and reached for the towel drying off and wrapping herself in the soft yellow terrycloth before reaching for the phone.

"I'm done," she said softly.

"Yeah, me too." He sounded a little breathless.

"I think the next time we do that, it's definitely a video call," she told him.

"I'm in."

Grinning, she made her way into her bedroom. She laid the phone on the bed as she pulled on her pajamas and slid between the sheets. "Okay, I'm in bed."

"Okay, good night," he said huskily.

"Wait." She couldn't stand the idea of letting him go just yet. Or maybe ever. But she quickly pushed *that* thought aside. This wasn't an "ever" situation and she needed to get a grip. Still, she didn't want to hang up yet. "Talk to me 'til I fall asleep."

"What do you want to talk about?"

"Tell me about your childhood. Tell me about Appleby. And your parents and your farm, and everything."

"You really want to know about all that?"

She really did. "You know all about me. Tell me about your mom and dad. And your brother you run the farm with."

"Really pretty normal childhood," he started. "It was just me and my brother, Dallas. But we had a bunch of cousins to grow up with that felt like siblings. Justin is just the one who wanted to go into business with us.

"We grew up climbing trees, playing outside, getting dirty, driving tractors and four wheelers. I've always loved animals and knew I wanted to work with them. I just always assumed that meant farming."

Rory smiled and snuggled into her pillow, pulling her comforter up. This was an amazing way to fall asleep. "Keep going," she told him softly.

"My mom's a teacher, so she was always home after school with us and on weekends and holidays and in the summer. My dad farmed and when we were ready to take the farm over, he and mom moved into town and he started doing ag insurance. He still comes out and drives around the farm and will get on the tractor once in a while because he misses it, but he's really left it mostly to us."

"Sounds perfect," Rory told him sleepily. Her eyes closed and she imagined his farm, and him climbing trees with a bunch of other kids, and his mom calling to him from a front porch to come in and wash up for dinner.

It sounded so completely opposite of how she'd grown up. It sounded exactly the way she'd always *wished* she could have grown up though. It also sounded a lot like she imagined the people in Autre had grown up.

"I wouldn't say *perfect*," Drew said. "But it was pretty great. I've been in Appleby all my life so I've known a lot of my friends for as long as I can remember. The new guys, the ones who came from Chicago and bought the snack cake factory..."

"Ollie and Dax and the others," Rory said. "The ones who donated the game controllers."

97

"Right. Two of those five guys are from Appleby. I've known Aiden and Cam forever. But Ollie, Dax, and Grant came to town more recently. They're the first people I've become friends with that I haven't known since I was ten." He sounded amused.

Rory just smiled. She didn't have *any* friendships that extended that far back. But it was interesting that she felt that she'd known Charlie and Paige and Jordan and the others here far longer than she had. Jordan had grown up here and Charlie had spent summers and holidays here, but none of those women had lived here permanently in the three years Rory had been here. Still, this was clearly their home, and she was the outsider. But she didn't feel that way with them.

"What was Christmas like growing up in Iowa?" she asked.

"Cold and snowy." He chuckled softly. "I don't know how you all grow up without making snowmen and sledding and having snowball fights."

"I've only seen snow a couple of times. It falls here but it's rare and doesn't stick around. I've never made a snowman," she said.

"We'll have to fix that. We've got snow in Iowa well into March."

Her stomach swooped at the implied invitation to come north, and Rory smiled, then yawned deeply, and cuddled into her pillow further.

Yeah, maybe this long-distance thing could work.

8

The next day Drew decided he should do something with the friends he had supposedly come to Autre to visit.

He took a swamp boat tour captained by Josh with Tori and their little girl Ella alongside.

He hung out at the petting zoo, learning more about Jordan's program with the alpacas, and then let Charlie take him on a tour of the other exotic and domestic animals they had brought into their park/sanctuary.

Tori and Jordan had both told him that they were looking for some additional help around the park. Especially someone with some animal handling experience, and that if he knew anyone—wink, wink, nudge, nudge—they'd love to talk about that person joining their team.

It wasn't so much that they were being openly welcoming about him potentially joining them that surprised him—after all, he ran a farm, and his love for animals and ability to handle them, made him someone who would be an obvious fit. What surprised him was that he'd been in Autre for just short of twenty-four hours and he was already thinking that that sounded like a pretty sweet deal.

And it wasn't just about Rory Robins.

At least that's what he told himself every time he thought about it. He loved alpacas. He loved goats, donkeys, and every other barnyard animal he'd ever worked with. He also thought it was amazing that they had camels and a zebra, not to mention a sloth, lemurs, red pandas, a *tiger*, and freaking penguins in this animal park.

He wasn't a veterinarian, but he definitely knew his way around hooves and wings and beaks and muzzles. If they needed a farmer with a biology degree, who was interested in learning more about zoo keeping, he could definitely be their guy.

Of course, his brother and cousin would have to be willing to run the farm back home on their own. But Drew knew Justin and Dallas would be fine with it. More than his mother would be. He would have to swear to Linda Ryan that he would come home on a regular basis and that any kids he had, would be guaranteed at least a month back home on the farm in the summers.

Kids? He was thinking about kids?

He'd been in Autre, Louisiana for *a day*.

But yeah, he was thinking about kids.

And wondering if Rory wanted to have any.

Fuck.

"Hey, good news," Fletcher Landry called as he strode toward where Drew was standing by the lemur enclosure with Jordan and Paige. "Becca's free tonight."

"Oh, great." Paige turned to Drew. "We're going to head over to Bad, a little town a few miles up the bayou. They have an amazing bar and restaurant. One of Fletcher's teaching friends is able to go along. I think you'll really like her."

Drew looked from Paige to Jordan to Fletcher and back to Paige. They were all grinning. "Don't you guys have a cool restaurant-bar right here?"

Paige laughed. "Oh, well, of course. But Ellie's is kind of like sitting around grandma's house with the whole family. When we want to get away from that a little bit, we head over to Bad."

"Bad Brews is owned by a couple friends of ours," Fletcher said. "Zeke and Mitch did some of the interior work when they were remodeling. It's really cool. They have live music and all that. And Becca is excited to meet you."

Yeah, Drew hadn't missed that part. "You're setting me up with someone?"

Paige gave him a wink. "I promised I would set you up with a hot bayou girl when you made it down this way."

She had. Drew had been lamenting the fact that all the girls in Appleby saw him as such a good guy that he hesitated to get dirty with any of them. Paige assured him that he could start off as a bad boy with the bayou girls and show them his good side later.

Which he had totally screwed up with Rory, of course.

She thought he was a great guy. Nice. Good. Decent and noble.

Hell, she'd been offering him just about everything last night and he'd still sent her home alone.

His body heated thinking about what he'd done before he'd sent her home though. She hadn't been horny so much as she'd been wound up. She'd been stressed out and exhausted, but he knew she was the type to go home and either keep working or lie in bed with her head spinning. He truly had wanted to give her some relief and release, hoping it would help her calm down.

Yeah, he'd really wanted to touch her. But more, he'd wanted to connect with her.

And they had connected. Physically, for sure, but more than that. The phone call, as she'd said, had been strangely intimate. Talking to her while she made a sandwich had been so routine it should have been boring, but it seemed like something he could do every day and never grow tired of it.

Yes, listening to her shower had been hot. And he'd definitely jerked off. And he knew he would again. And again. But also talking to her, telling her stories about growing up in Iowa, keeping his voice low and steady so that she would fall asleep and the listening to her breathing even out and grow soft until he was sure she was sleeping peacefully had been strangely satisfying too.

He was going to her house tonight. She needed to wrap fifty more gifts for Santa's Village, and he was going to help. Because she needed someone to help her out. And because she wouldn't ask anyone else. And because he really wanted to see her.

Yep, it seemed that he was exchanging a night out on the town with a hot hookup to go wrap Christmas presents with a sweet woman who really needed a friend more than anything else.

"Sorry, can't do it. I... made plans."

Fletcher glanced at Jordan then lifted a brow to Drew. "Oh yeah? With Charlie and Griffin? Or Zeke and Jill? Or maybe Zeke and Donovan and Owen offered to take you to New Orleans?"

Drew shook his head. "Uh, no."

"So what are you doing tonight?" Paige pressed. "Is it with anyone we know?"

"Uh..." Drew scratched the back of his neck.

"It's with Rory, right?" Jordan asked.

He couldn't give away that they were wrapping gifts. That might lead to questions about what else wasn't done and needed more work. "Yeah," he admitted. "We're going to watch a movie at her place." He had no idea if that was true, but he did intend to show up on her doorstep. What happened on the other side of that threshold wasn't anyone's business.

"I knew it," Jordan said, with a huge grin. She elbowed Fletcher. "Told you."

He nodded. "Not surprised. Rory's great."

"You knew it?" Drew asked.

"Of course. I saw you two talking when you first got to town and there was a spark. Then at Ellie's, when Charlie was all concerned about the village and party and everything, you jumped right in to defend Rory." Jordan smiled. "I'm glad you two met. She's so great, but she doesn't really let us get too close. It's like she doesn't quite trust us. I hope you can convince her that we're cool."

Drew smiled. "I'm positive she knows that." He hesitated, then made himself say the next thing that occurred to him. "She kind of has a thing for Beau. You should set them up."

Jordan and Paige both frowned "Beau Hebert?"

Drew shrugged. "How many Beaus are there?"

Fletcher chuckled. "You might be surprised."

"The guy who brought the toys to the petting zoo yesterday," Drew said.

"Yeah, that's Hebert," Fletcher confirmed.

"Well, we can't set her up with Beau. He and Becca are meant to be," Jordan said.

Paige just nodded.

"Wait, Becca? The one you were going to set me up with tonight?"

"Yeah," Jordan said. "Well, we weren't really setting you up. Fletcher made that up to see what you would say."

"Oh." He must have been more transparent than he'd realized. "So Becca and Beau are together?"

That's awesome.

Then he frowned. That was not awesome. Rory liked Beau. He shouldn't be pleased that Beau was spoken for. Drew was going back to Iowa. He shouldn't wish spinsterhood on her.

And he definitely didn't. But he wished for some phone sex

and a few trips back and forth between Iowa and Louisiana, he realized.

"No, they're not *together*. Not in the dating-falling-in-love sense anyway," Paige said. "But Becca and Beau have been friends forever and everyone thinks they should be together."

Jordan nodded. "The whole town tries to matchmake them."

"Tries to?" Drew asked. "It doesn't work?"

"Well...getting them to spend time together isn't hard. They see each other all the time," Jordan said. "Like we said, they're really good friends."

"We just all want them to start kissing already," Paige said with a grin.

Drew lifted a brow. "You? The woman who was so adamantly against a town trying to marry her off?"

Paige waved that away. "That was before I fell head over heels for my one and only. When you find *the one*, your whole perspective changes."

Drew thought about that. He was already starting to think that being a good guy wasn't such a bad thing when it came to Rory. She made him want to be good—to do things to show her how special she was, to make her feel good, to take care of her —and she clearly needed more of that.

A change of perspective. Huh.

"So Beau and Rory aren't going to happen?" he asked.

Paige gave him a look. "Well...why don't *you* tell *us*?"

No. Beau and Rory weren't going to happen. Because he thought he knew who the right guy for Rory was.

And that should really freak him out.

So why didn't it?

Six hours later, Drew walked up the Main Street sidewalk toward Rory's salon. As he approached the front of I'm Gonna Dye, he realized he was hoping that she'd open the door and it would hit him that wanting to be the one to take care of her forever was completely crazy.

He was hoping she would open that door and be just another girl. A beautiful girl, sure. A girl he would still want to kiss. But just a girl that he could say goodbye to in a few days when it was time to go back to Iowa.

All of the thoughts about how he never wanted another man to touch her and how he wanted to be the one who hugged her whenever she cried and how he wanted to protect her from her dad and anyone else who ever hurt her, were ridiculous. It was probably sleep deprivation. Or maybe something in Ellie's gumbo. Or the fumes from too much reindeer manure.

Then they could then wrap presents and maybe even kiss some more, but he wouldn't be thinking about taking her to his farm and teaching her to make snow angels or how cool it would be to add to the Santa Village here in Autre next year... together. Or how fucking glad he was that the entire town wanted Beau Hebert with Becca whoever-she-was.

He passed the huge front window of Rory's salon. The salon was closed, but the lights were on and he could see her inside, sweeping up. Even that sight was enough to make his heart rate kick up a notch.

Dammit.

He stopped at the door and knocked twice. She turned at the sound, clearly startled. But she immediately relaxed when she saw it was him and gave him a huge smile.

Fuck. The flip in his chest didn't feel like he was over how much he liked her and wanted to make her happy.

She put the broom to the side and came toward him quickly.

She smiled at him through the glass and twisted the lock on the door, then pushed it open.

"Hi."

That was it. One word. Two letters. And Drew realized he was totally fucked in the don't-fall-in-love-with-this-woman department.

Everything he felt for her last night was absolutely just as potent right now, if not more so.

"Hi." His voice came out gruffer than he'd intended.

"I'm glad to see you," she told him.

He fucking was too. She was dressed in black leggings and an oversized red t-shirt that said *Dear Santa, It's Actually A Funny Story*. Drew grinned.

Her green hair was pulled back into a ponytail and...then he saw her feet.

She was wearing red and white striped socks.

Just like the ones she'd worn with her elf dress. Just like the ones he'd been fantasizing about in his dirty elf daydream.

He couldn't see the tops of them under the yoga pants, of course, but he knew they were thigh highs and would just peek out of the top of her black leather boots.

His eyes met hers and he was certain he looked intense and turned on suddenly.

"I like your socks."

She blushed. And he wanted her more than he'd ever wanted anything.

"I was going to text you with a photo of them later."

"You remember what I said about those." It wasn't a question.

She pulled her lower lip between her teeth and nodded.

Drew pulled in a long breath, resisting the urge to grab her and put her up against the front window of her shop that looked out on downtown Autre. That was *not* the type of sweet, Christmasy scene they wanted displayed in their shop windows.

Except for those socks, she looked completely relaxed and casual and like she was ready to just hang out at home for the evening. Completely different from the tiny red elf dress he'd first seen her in and from the yoga pants and shirt she'd been in last night at the barn dealing with the sleigh and reindeer.

But she was just as gorgeous. Maybe more so because she was relaxed and clearly truly happy to see him.

He cleared his throat. It was probably a good thing he had his hands full.

"I brought supplies. Thought you could use some wrapping help." He held up three roles of wrapping paper in one hand and two rolls of tape and a pair of scissors in the other.

She looked surprised, then intensely pleased. "That was sweet. Come on in. I was just heading up there to start wrapping. Do you want some cocoa?" She turned and led him into the salon. She wasn't insisting that he didn't have to do this. She wasn't telling him not to worry about it. She was letting him in. Literally.

And maybe figuratively too.

He fucking liked that idea way too much.

But he turned and locked the door behind them, before following her through the salon. He was staying.

He glanced around as he walked, taking in a few details about her workspace. It looked very much like any other hair salon, but it was decorated in a multitude of bright colors and seemed welcoming and warm.

"So this is where people come to get their hair dyed green, huh?"

She gave a little gasp and spun around. "I can't believe that you said that." But she was smiling.

He laughed. "No luck washing it out?"

She lifted a hand to her hair. "No, it hasn't faded at all. But I guess it's okay. The kids keep telling me how much they like it. I guess nobody cares that neon green isn't really Christmasy."

His palm itched to touch it. Damn the wrapping paper rolls. "I really like it too."

"You've never see me without it."

"I don't think it would matter. I think you could probably have bright orange hair, purple skin, and dress in a brown paper sack, and I would still want you."

Her pupils dilated and her lips parted and Drew mentally cursed himself. So much for keeping this light and friendly and not getting sucked into all of these emotions that he was feeling so quickly for this woman.

Of course *she* was the one who'd put on the candy-cane-striped socks.

"Well this is how I normally look." She leaned over grabbed a photo off one of the shelves, holding it up for him. "This is me and Lennon, my friend and business partner."

Lennon was beautiful. She had dark hair and large almond-shaped eyes and a gorgeous smile. But Drew was having a hard time looking away from Rory. She was a blonde. A very light blonde. Her hair was nearly white, except for the last four inches or so that were dyed bright pink in this photo. She also had a bright pink gem pierced through her nose and the crop top she was wearing showed off a matching bellybutton piercing. The top also revealed the flowery tattoo that ran from her left elbow to her shoulder.

He hadn't seen any of this yet. She'd been in long sleeves and had apparently taken her nose piercing out. He looked at her. "Yup, you're gorgeous. No matter what you're wearing or what color your hair is."

She seemed pleased as she set the photo back on the shelf.

She turned and led him up a staircase at the back of the salon and through the door at the top of the landing. It opened into an apartment that smelled like chocolate and peppermint and was lit by a crazy number of multicolored twinkle lights.

"You do really love Christmas."

"I really do," she agreed as she crossed to the tiny kitchen. She started pulling mugs and spoons out of a cupboard and a drawer. "I love the way the season just seems to permeate the air. It seems to touch everything. Even grumpy Bob down at the gas station has little decorations on his countertop. I know some people complain that it's become commercialized and it isn't just religious the way it was supposed to be initially, but I kind of like that. It's bigger than that. I like that people from all walks of life, no matter what they do the rest of the year, still have little ways of celebrating this same season. It feels like it brings us all together. I mean, anybody can watch Frosty the Snowman and enjoy it, or get a peppermint hot chocolate and think it's delicious, or listen to Christmas carols and smile. Sure, we could do those things any time of the year. But there's just something special in the air in December."

He knew exactly what she meant. And it made him want to reach out and pull her in for a hug. It was interesting how this woman turned him on more than he could remember a woman turning him on in forever, but he also seemed to have the constant urge to hug her and hold her and kiss the top of her head and just make her smile too.

"I completely agree," he finally said.

There was no doubt in his mind that he would rather be here with her doing this, than on the blind date Mitch and Paige and Jordan and Fletcher had tried to set him up on. Or had pretended to set him up on, anyway.

Rory's grin indicated that she was just as happy as he was in this moment. She finished prepping the cocoa and Drew looked around her apartment.

It was small. Cozy. She had a tree in the corner near the stand that held her TV. One wall was a large window that overlooked Main Street below. There was a short divider between the living room and the kitchen, which was a narrow space with a countertop, cabinets and sink on one side, and a stove and fridge on the other. There was a small window on the far end and she had a tiny table tucked below it with two straight-backed chairs. To his right were two doors. He assumed one led to the bedroom and one to the bathroom.

Rory came into the living room area with a tray that held two mugs of hot cocoa, a little bowl of marshmallows and four frosted sugar cookies in typical Christmas shapes. She carried it to the coffee table that sat in front of the couch. It was the only piece of furniture in the room to sit on other than a wicker Papasan chair.

She dropped onto the floor in front of the coffee table where she also had rolls of wrapping paper, tape, scissors, and ribbon laid out on the carpet. Drew joined her on the floor, and she lifted her remote and pressed play. "Is *The Family Stone* okay?"

"Never seen it."

"Oh, it's so good." Then she shot him a smile. "Thanks for coming over to help me do this."

And he officially admitted that he was falling for her. He was wrapping presents, watching a Christmas movie, and drinking hot chocolate with a very sweet woman who loved Christmas, and thinking about when that woman could come visit Iowa rather than dancing and drinking at a bar with a hot woman who was all in for a short-term fling.

"No place I'd rather be," he told her honestly.

For the next hour they wrapped presents and sipped hot chocolate and watched Sarah Jessica Parker and Luke Wilson fall in love. But they finished the gifts before the movie was done. Rory put the last of the boxes onto the pile near her front door, then sat back against the couch, cradling her mug. She watched him for a moment before reaching out and hitting the stop button on her remote.

"I don't get to see how it ends?" He was actually into it. He wanted to see how all three couples ended up together.

"We can watch the rest later. But I have a question."

Yes was probably the answer he was going to give this woman, no matter what she asked of him. Drew took a long drink of his hot chocolate trying to keep from reaching over and running his hand up her leg. "Okay."

"Why don't you have a girlfriend?"

Okay, he hadn't been expecting that. "I've had some girl-friends."

She smiled. "Yeah, I'm not surprised."

"Okay." He turned so he could rest his arm on the couch cushion and face her more fully. "The truth is that I've known most of the women back home that are my age, straight, and who want to date me all of my life. I've dated the ones I thought might work out. Just haven't had the right chemistry with any of them, either before or after dating."

"Why did the chemistry change *after* you started dating?"

He took a deep breath. "I think a lot of them had an idea of what I was like, and then we got to know each other, as more than friends, and it turned out I was different than they expected."

"What did they think you were like?" she asked with a little frown.

"They thought I was the type of guy that you go out with a couple of times, then introduce to your grandmother, then start talking about engagement ring styles, and then check into when the local reception hall has an opening in the calendar."

"So they saw you as marriage material."

"Absolutely. I'm from there, have my family business, and a reputation for being a decent, upstanding guy."

She took another sip of her cocoa watching him over the

edge of her cup. "Well, that all makes sense. What was the problem? You don't want to get married?"

"I didn't want to marry someone who..." He wondered how much he should say. Then he realized that if she didn't like what he was going to say, he didn't have to see her again. And *not* being open about this was what had cost him a couple of relationships in the past.

He cleared his throat. "I'm not going to marry anyone who I've never said the word pussy to, who I've never made come on my tongue, and who I can't imagine covering my cock in chocolate sauce and licking every drop clean."

9

Rory didn't even blink. She just sat watching him. Then she ran her tongue over her lower lip.

Drew gave her a little half grin.

"I think the women back home think I'm a good guy, but they can't imagine being dirty with me. They don't realize that I've got a side that wants to bend my woman over the couch, that wants to finger her in a movie theater and make her come without making any noise, that wants to send her hot texts in the middle of a serious work meeting, that wants to do something naughty with her favorite cocktail so that even when she's out for a girl's night, when she takes a drink, her panties get a little wet for me."

Rory was watching him with wide eyes. But not the scandalized look he'd gotten from Lissa when he'd mentioned the movie-theater thing to her. No, Rory looked turned on.

"My friends think I need to start with the dirty stuff with a woman and *then* show her my nice-guy side."

"You didn't do that with me." Her voice was a little breathless.

"No. I didn't."

"And I'm super into this naughty-with-the-cocktail thing," she said. "And absolutely yes on the couch, the movie theater, and the texts."

Drew felt a grin stretch his mouth. "Well, we were dirty in the barn last night."

"You were *so* a good guy before that," she said. "I promise. But I'm still very excited to know more about your dirty side."

"That can be arranged." Like right fucking now.

"Good. You have to be with someone who you can be *satisfied* with. Someone who wants the same things you do. Whether that's a Bassett hound or to go four wheeling on the weekends or who loves Ryan Reynolds movies or who's cool with nipple clamps."

Drew felt heat arrow through him and he shifted on the floor, leaning closer to her.

"So, what? You just have good girls who want vanilla sex in the dark back in Iowa?" she asked.

"I doubt it very much," Drew said truthfully. "But I think the ones who want that stuff, didn't look at me as the guy to give them the nipple clamps and movie-theater orgasms. And the girls who did want to date me weren't into that stuff. I shocked a couple of them before I learned to shut up about role-playing and handcuffs."

"You have a bunch of dumb girls in Iowa."

He gave a short laugh. "I don't know about that. Just haven't found the right one to connect with."

Rory shifted, setting her cup on the table and then moving on to all fours and crawling toward him. She took his cup from his hand and set it on the table as well, then moved to straddle his thighs. She leaned in, took his face between her hands, and pressed her lips to his in a sweet, quick kiss. She leaned back.

"Just so you know, I love chocolate sauce. On pretty much anything."

He was already hot and hard for her, but he gave her a smile and settled his hands on her hips to keep her from wiggling closer. "You don't have to do this."

"Do what?"

"You're feeling grateful to me again."

She laughed. "I *am* feeling grateful to you. You helping me wrap gifts tonight was a really great thing to do. And the hot cocoa and cookies is to say thank you for that." She leaned in and put her lips against his again. "The sex is just going to be sex."

His cock loved that answer, and his fingers instinctively curled into her hips. "Rory," he said roughly. "Are you sure?"

"Are you kidding?" She brushed her lips over his again. "Even before you did what you did to me in the barn last night, I wanted you. But ever since I had your hands in my pants, I haven't been able to think of anything else. Yes, I needed to wrap gifts tonight, but in case you didn't know, I brought you up here to seduce you."

He laughed and then groaned as she wiggled closer, pressing against his cock. "It won't take much seducing, girl."

"Good." She reached for something on the sofa cushion behind him, then sat up and pulled a Santa hat on, flicking the white pom pom on the end and making it bounce. "Because I'd really love to hear you say the word pussy to me."

That was it. One hand went up to cup the back of her head and he brought her in for a full, deep kiss. Their lips fused, their tongues tangled, and Rory's hands gripped his shoulders as he brought her more firmly against his cock.

She ground against him and they kissed hungrily for several long seconds.

They both seemed to remember at the same moment that they were alone and in a very private space. She leaned back and they both stripped off their shirts. She was only wearing a sports bra and she quickly got rid of that as well, tossing it over her shoulder. She pulled the Santa hat back on.

Drew drank in the sight of her. Her breasts were perfect, full and round, with sweet pink centers that were already hard. He lifted both hands and cupped her, teasing her nipples with his thumbs. "For the record, these nipples were made for nipple clamps."

She shivered. "I would love that. Never done that before."

"I would love to be the first." He realized he meant that in any number of ways. He loved to be the first to do everything she'd never done before. Hell, everything *he'd* never done before.

She leaned into his touch, bending slightly to kiss him again. She ran her tongue over his lip and then nipped him gently. Fire seemed to lick through his gut to his cock and he pinched her nipples firmly, causing her to gasp and her knees to clamp around him.

"Need you naked," he told her.

She simply nodded and pushed up off of his lap. She stripped her leggings off, revealing that she wasn't wearing underwear. He paused in his unbuttoning and unzipping. "Fuck, Rory."

She stood in front of him, completely naked except for the candy-cane-striped thigh-high stockings and the Santa hat, seemingly unabashed.

"You're fucking gorgeous."

"Need your hands and mouth on me, Drew."

He quickly shucked off his jeans, underwear, shoes and socks and she lowered herself onto his lap again. She ran her hands over his shoulders, chest and abs down to grip his cock in both hands.

He sucked in a breath and made two fists as he clenched his jaw, fighting for control.

Her touch was heaven and he knew he wasn't going to last long, but she seemed intent on exploring him. He could hold on. For a little bit.

She ran her hands up and down his length, stroking and squeezing. Then she looked up at him. "I don't have chocolate syrup but we can maybe make do for tonight." She reached out for the tray on the coffee table and ran her fingers over one of the cookies, swiping up some of the frosting.

He tensed as she painted it down his length, and then leaned over to lick it clean.

His breath escaped in a long hiss. "Yesss, Rory." His hand came up to the back of her head and he grasped her ponytail as she continued licking long after the frosting was gone.

After she'd taken him nearly to the edge, she lifted her head and reached for the cookie again, swiping at more frosting and then painting it on her nipple. She climbed up his body and his hands gripped her waist, lifting her a little higher so that he could fasten his lips onto the nipple, licking and sucking.

She moved against him restlessly, his name on her lips.

"Need more of you. Need this sweet pussy," he said. Loving that he could talk to her like this.

"Oh my God, yes."

He slid to lie on his back and with only a little urging from his hands, she shifted herself so that she was above his mouth. He palmed her ass and brought her down so that he could lick over her clit.

"I don't want to smother you," she said breathlessly, bracing her hands on the couch cushions above him.

He gripped her butt and brought her down more firmly against his mouth. "Fucking smother me, please." He licked her again, then sucked.

She gasped, and pressed closer, and he ate at her for several minutes until she finally cried out, coming on his tongue exactly the way he'd described.

He slid her down his body and took her mouth in a deep kiss. He didn't know which tasted better, but he would be happy to spend the rest of his life with his mouth on all parts of this woman's body, trying to decide.

"Oh my God, I can't tell you how happy I am that you're good at that," she told him.

He ran his hands down her back and gripped her ass, grinding her against his cock. "I'm just getting started with you."

"I'm so happy to hear that." She kissed him again, then pushed herself up, bracing her hands on his chest and rocking her pussy against his cock. "I'm on birth control. And totally clean. It's been a long time, actually."

He gripped her tighter and had to relax his hold as her meaning crashed over him. "I'm clean too. But are you sure?"

She nodded. "I totally trust you, Drew. And I would love to do this without a condom."

It would be intensely intimate even with a condom, but the idea taking her bare was the hottest, most tempting thing he'd ever heard.

"I'm only asking one more time. Are you sure?"

"Hundred percent."

"Then are you ready?"

"So ready."

He gripped her hips and shifted her so his tip met the hot wetness between her legs.

They both moaned and then she took over. She slid onto him, taking him slow and deep. Drew grit his teeth, letting her set the pace, when everything in him screamed to thrust hard and fast.

When she'd taken him fully, she sat up straighter and again they both moaned.

"Oh my God, you feel so good."

"Ditto," was all he could manage.

She moved on him, circling her pelvis and then lifting and lowering herself a few times slowly as if adjusting to the feel of him. The motion caused the pom pom on her hat to bounce and, stupidly, Drew had to grit his teeth against the wave of lust that sent coursing through him. He ran his hands over the silky striped stockings and knew he'd never look at candy cane stripes again without thinking of her.

After a few minutes of moving like that, she looked up at him almost shyly. "Would you..."

"Yes," he answered before she even asked the full question.

She smiled. "Would you be on top?"

"However you want me," he told her.

She clamped her knees around him and then rolled and they flipped so she was on her back and he was on top of her. Her hat fell off as she wrapped her stockinged legs around him, and Drew felt himself sink deep.

Heaven. It was absolute heaven.

"Yes," she told him, gripping his back. "I love having you on me and around me and in me."

He started to move. Thrusting slow, deep but slow, absorbing the feel of every inch. But pretty soon her heels were digging into his ass and she was asking for more.

"Harder. Faster. Please, Drew."

He would always give this woman anything she wanted. He was certain of it. It was the strangest realization at the oddest moment, but as of that very second when Rory said *Drew* in that breathless, needy way, Drew knew that he could never be with another woman like this, and he could never let another man touch her this way.

"I've got you," he told her, sliding his hands under her ass and lifting her slightly.

It changed the angle and the depth just enough that they both moaned and then he started to move. Faster, deeper, harder until they were both gasping and he could feel her inner muscles starting to clench.

"Yes, Drew, yes," she said, nearly panting.

"I've got you," he repeated. "Whatever you need. I'm it. Always."

"Yes, right there."

He lifted her another half inch and shifted his hips and suddenly he hit the magic spot because she cried out and came apart in his arms with the sweetest sound as she clenched around him.

He drove deep five more times and then he exploded, filling her up, emptying into her in a way that seemed so much more than physical.

They lay together, gasping for air, for several long seconds after.

Finally Drew shifted to the side, keeping one arm and leg draped over her. He rested his forehead on his other arm, working on just breathing, and absorbing the moment.

"So, that was fucking amazing."

She smiled and rolled her head toward him. "Yeah, I was thinking the same thing."

"Rory."

"Yeah?" She reached out and ran her fingers through his hair.

"Ask me to stay."

Of course he meant tonight. In her bed. So they could do that again.

Of course he didn't mean stay for good. In Louisiana.

Probably.

But several emotions flashed across her face before she nodded and said, "Stay."

"Yeah."

The smile she gave him was full of desire and happiness and something more that he wasn't quite ready to label. But he was very sure he was feeling it as well.

10

The next two days were perfect.

He'd spent another night in Rory's bed. But last night, they'd just talked on the phone. For five hours. And had phone sex. Yes, even though they were in rooms only about eight blocks apart.

She'd had some late clients and he'd agreed to dinner and drinks at a restaurant and bar in New Orleans with the Landry clan.

But he'd been eager to get back to Autre. To Rory.

He'd called when he'd hit the city limits and she'd said she'd just gotten out of the shower. In that moment, he'd wanted only one thing more than to head straight over there and get her dirty all over again—he'd wanted to show her they could still connect even once he went back to Iowa.

Instead of going to her house, he'd gone to his room at Mitch and Paige's and propped on his bed. And they'd just talked. About everything. They'd shared stories about their work, their friends, and their favorite things. They'd video chatted this time, but the phone still kept them from getting distracted by kissing and touching.

Though, eventually, they'd gotten there too. They'd just had to touch themselves. They'd talked each other through one of the hottest orgasms Drew had ever had. There was something about having your partner say *all* the words out loud, the thoughts and feelings that were going through their mind, that made it seem even more intimate in a way.

The final conclusion had been...yeah, they could do this long-distance thing.

But he knew he wasn't going to last long being away from her.

Three days ago, he'd met a woman who was nothing like he'd expected to find and yet, he was planning to talk to his brother and cousin the second he got home about transitioning the farm operation to them so he could move to Louisiana.

It was crazy. But he thought that maybe the craziness in Autre needed a little bit of his steadiness.

Drew stood back, surveying Santa's Village and took a deep, satisfied breath. The Landrys didn't know that he'd painted and laid the sparkly red bricks or helped with the sleigh or anything else. But it was all finished and Rory could relax.

Well, except for, of course, the fifty empty boxes that still sat in the sleigh. But Drew was going to fix that as well.

He pulled his phone from his pocket and dialed Oliver Caprinelli's number.

"Hey, Drew, what's up?" Ollie answered on the second ring.

"Need a favor."

"Okay."

Ollie and Drew had an interesting relationship. When Oliver and his wife, Piper, had first moved to Appleby, they had not been married. They hadn't even been dating. Piper had been Oliver's assistant, and Drew had immediately been attracted to the gorgeous, sassy woman.

She was like a younger sister to the five men who had become accidental millionaires when their online video game had become an overnight worldwide sensation and it had taken Drew a little time to figure out that she was madly in love with Oliver. It had taken Oliver even longer to figure that out. And that he felt the same way about her. But prior to realizing that what he felt for Piper was love, Ollie had been jealous of Drew and Piper's friendship and flirting.

Now the men had not only called a truce but had actually turned into friends. Ollie and Piper belonged together, there was no doubt about it, and there was no way that Drew would ever get in the way of that.

Plus, Piper wasn't the one for him. Now that he'd met Rory, that was even more obvious.

"We had a little... situation here. Wondering if I could get fifty more of those game controllers from you."

"No can do, man," Oliver said.

"Oh." Drew had fully expected Ollie to agree to replace the controllers with no problem. Ollie was not only incredibly rich, he was also incredibly generous. "Seriously?"

"I mean, I would, but we don't have any more," Ollie said. "These controllers aren't releasing until May. The ones we got ahead of time were purely for charitable and promotional purposes. We sent fifty to you guys, we've got fifty here in Appleby for the kids, and we sent fifty-some to a children's hospital somewhere. The company is doing a couple of give-aways for like ten or something, but we don't have a big stash of them anywhere."

"Dammit," Drew muttered. It hadn't occurred to him that this might be a problem. He supposed he'd gotten used to having friends in high places with lots of resources.

"I mean, I could possibly talk to the manufacturers," Ollie said. He owned the company. He was the biggest name at Fluke Inc. and if they needed more controllers made and he told them to, Drew was sure they would. But there was no time.

"I need them like in two days."

"Oh yeah, that's just literally, physically not possible."

Drew shoved a hand through his hair. "Well, fuck."

"So what happened? Is there some other way we can help?"

Drew sighed. "It's just there was a little mishap with these controllers and now the Christmas party is kind of hinging on us being able to replace them."

There was a slight pause, then Ollie chuckled. "You've been there for three days."

"So?"

"So you're all worked up about the Christmas party in this other town? And talking about it in terms of *we*. You've only been there a few days and you're trying to save Christmas for Autre?"

"Well, I'm trying to help someone..."

Ollie chuckled again. "Oh my God, it's a girl."

Drew grinned despite himself. "I didn't say that."

"You're already in love?"

Well, there was no reason to deny it. "I figured you'd be the one most thrilled by that. You said you wanted me to find a girl far, far away from Appleby and Piper."

"I absolutely said that. But I didn't actually think it would happen. I was hoping you'd go down there and get laid. Now you're telling me you're falling for someone?"

Drew laughed. "Trust me, no one is more surprised than me."

"Well, man, that's amazing. So seriously, how can we help you with this?"

Drew sucked in a breath. "I suppose the only people who actually know these are game controllers that are missing— long story—are the Landrys, right?"

"I think Piper and Paige have been dealing with most of this. I don't even know if everyone down there knows what they are. Hang on a second."

Drew heard the sound of Oliver's squeaky office chair and

then the door opening. "Hey babe, who have you been talking to about the game controllers down in Autre?"

"Paige. Why? Who's on the phone?" Drew heard Piper's voice ask.

"Drew. There's some issue they need some help with."

The next thing Drew heard was Piper's voice on the phone. "Drew? What's going on?"

"It's a long story. But I need to replace the fifty controllers."

"Are they broken? Did they not make it in time?"

"No. It's not that. I can't really get into the details."

Piper paused for just a moment, but, like a true friend, she simply said, "Okay. What can we do?"

"Let's just give them some money to replace the toys," Ollie said.

"Yeah, we can totally do that. Do you want me to just send you money to your bank account?"

Drew smiled and shook his head. It was kind of amazing having friends who were millionaires and could just come up with this kind of money, but it was also amazing to have friends who were wonderful people and who were willing to do things like this. Then he sighed. "I don't know if we have time to actually go buy fifty more gifts."

"You're totally right," Piper said. "I know you all have a lot of activities and things going on. How about I buy the toys and ship them down to you. I can do that overnight so they're there tomorrow. Do you need them to be wrapped?"

Drew's grin grew. Not only did he have rich friends who were generous, wonderful people, but one of them happened to be one of the most organized humans he'd ever met. Piper could get anything done.

"Piper, that would be amazing."

"Consider it done. I'll have everything shipped to you at Paige's house."

"Uh, ship them to the petting zoo. You guys are really the best."

"We'll do anything for you, Drew. And now I can't wait to have Ollie tell me all about this girl you've fallen in love with."

Drew let out a short laugh. "You weren't in the room when he said that."

"But that's what this is, right?"

"I'd like to think that I would try to be helping these people do this amazing Santa's Village even if I hadn't met Rory."

"You are a great guy. You probably would be helping them with this even if it weren't for this girl. But you're also very resourceful and the fact that you didn't want to mess around with other potential solutions and just called in a favor like this means something."

"Taking the easy way out and calling my millionaire friends means something?" Drew asked.

"It does. You're not the type to take the easy way out. But this is obviously something that matters a lot, that you need to know is done right. And exactly on time. So you're willing to put aside the idea that you shouldn't just throw money at all the problems and actually get on the phone and ask someone else to get involved."

"I do want this to be perfect for her. She's done all the hard work, she's put the time in, and the heart in. It's not her fault it's falling apart. So yeah, I guess in this case I'm okay with using my resources to fix it easily for her."

He could hear the smile in Piper's voice when she said, "I hope she realizes what a good guy you are."

Drew rolled his eyes, but he was starting to understand that being a good guy, especially for Rory Robins, was exactly what he wanted to be.

"I think she does."

"I'm going to miss you," Piper told him.

"Miss me?"

"When you eventually moved to Louisiana."

His heart kicked hard against his rib cage. "Did I say I was moving to Louisiana?"

"No. But you're exactly the type of guy to turn your life upside down when you finally fall in love."

Drew thought about that. For about four seconds. Then realized that Piper was absolutely right. "You know what? I'm gonna miss you too."

They disconnected and Drew felt amazing. He'd just fixed the final piece of this whole Santa's Village situation for Rory.

They had the gifts replaced, the village was completely put together, and as he spoke, Sawyer was sitting on Santa's big chair with little kids in his lap telling him all their hopes and dreams.

Drew watched as a little girl beamed up at Sawyer.

"Hello, Sophia," Sawyer greeted her. "What would you like to talk about today?"

Drew smiled and shook his head. Sawyer really was taking this seriously. He wasn't asking the kids if they had been good or what they wanted for Christmas. He was inviting them to have a conversation. They could ask him anything or just chat about whatever was on their minds. It was very interesting how many of the kids actually just wanted to talk.

"I want to know what my best friend wants for Christmas," Sophia told Sawyer.

Oh, that was cute. Honestly, all of these kids had been cute. Drew had been hanging around making sure that the reindeer were mostly behaving themselves. And that the kids were behaving themselves around the animals.

Donna, Jim, Lucy, and Ethel were used to people, including children, but it didn't hurt to have someone the reindeer knew and trusted nearby, and someone that knew *them* in case any interventions were needed. He rotated between the animals, petting them, talking soothingly to them, and offering them treats as the kids came by.

"What does your friend like?" Sawyer asked.

"Grass. And being outside. And when I pet his nose. And when we talk and tell stories."

Sawyer nodded. "Is your best friend an animal?"

"He's an alpaca."

Drew perked up at that. Jordan had told him about a little girl who'd bonded with the orphaned alpaca that had come from Drew's farm to live here in Louisiana. Apparently, the little girl had lost her father to cancer and she and the alpaca had developed a unique bond that had helped her come out of her shell and start talking about her feelings again.

"Well, I mostly hang out with reindeer," Santa Sawyer told her. "But I know that reindeer and alpacas can be very good friends and my reindeer have been spending a lot of time with the alpacas here while we've been visiting. Maybe we should ask one of the reindeer if they know something special that Chewpaca would like for Christmas."

Sophia's eyes rounded and Drew could only assume it was in delight over Santa knowing which of the alpacas was her friend.

"Drew, do you think that Donna would know what Chewpaca might like for Christmas?" Sawyer called to him.

The reindeer he was standing next to was Ethel, not Donna. But Drew nodded. He was a Reindeer Wrangler, after all. His name tag even said so.

"I'll ask her," Drew told him. He leaned over. "Hey Donna"—There was no need to call Santa out on not knowing his own reindeer—"any idea what Chewie might like for Christmas?"

Ethel raised her head and blinked at him. Probably wondering why he was calling her Donna. He gave her a wink. Then he looked up at Santa and Sophia. "She said that

Chewie is hoping that Sophia will come and take him on a walk and...sing him a song." It obviously had to be something the little girl could "give" the alpaca that wouldn't cost any money.

Sawyer looked down at Sophia. "Well, there you go. What do you think?"

Sophia was frowning. "I'm going to have to work on that. I tell him lots of stories, but I don't sing to him."

Drew grimaced.

"But I can do that. I'll make up a really good song." Sophia told him.

Okay, whew.

"Is there anything else you want to talk to me about?" Sawyer asked.

"Just be sure you tell my dad I love him," Sophia said. "And I miss him."

Drew could tell that Sawyer needed a second to swallow before he answered. "I'll be sure to tell him."

"But I know he's around," Sophia said. "I met a new friend this summer. Her name's Grace. Do you know her?"

Sawyer nodded. "I know Gracie Trahan really well."

"Her daddy died too. Well, her first daddy. She has another one now. Anyway, she still talks to her first daddy and she said that our daddies come and visit us and watch over us. Even if we can't see them."

Again, it was clear that Sawyer was struggling to keep his composure.

"That's true. I'm certain that your dad will be here for Christmas."

Sophia gave him a huge grin. "I'm so glad. Maybe he can come with me to meet Chewpaca." Then she reached up and gave Sawyer a little hug before sliding off his lap and running to join her mother.

Sawyer looked over at Drew and shook his head. "Damn.

These little girls. They just get to me." He thumped his chest over his heart.

Drew understood. That had all been pretty fucking sweet.

Sweet was not what he had come here for, but it was everywhere he looked.

He glanced across the barnyard, searching for Rory, seemingly instinctually. He saw the top of her green head when she straightened from giving a little boy a candy cane.

Then something else caught his eye just beyond where she was standing.

Protectiveness and anger immediately tightened his body. *No fucking way.*

He started in that direction but remembered that he was in the middle of Santa's reindeer herd.

"Hey, Jordan," he called, trying to make his voice sound normal.

Jordan looked over. "Yeah?"

"I need you to handle the reindeer for little bit."

She came over and took her place next to Ethel. Drew handed her the tiny treat bucket.

"Everything okay?" She clearly read in his face that it wasn't.

"No. But it's going to be."

Without any further explanation. Drew started in the direction of the man he'd seen hovering by the pickups parked along the fence line.

Roger Robins was here.

He couldn't believe that fucker had showed back up here and thought he was going to just walk in and out of here as if he hadn't stolen from these good people and nearly ruined his daughter's Christmas.

Well, when he walked *out* of here—which he would be doing without saying so much as a single word to Rory—it would be for good.

This guy wasn't going to mess with Rory anymore.

Drew was here now.

And yeah, he was a good guy.

But he knew how to be a real asshole when the situation called for it.

As Roger was about to find out.

11

Rory saw Drew hand the reindeer over to Jordan and start across the barnyard with a scowl on his face. Everything had been going so well and he'd seemed to really be enjoying himself earlier. What was going on? She turned and scanned the area he was headed toward. And her heart stuttered.

No. Roger was here? What was he doing? And what was *Drew* doing?

She started in that direction as well, but was several yards behind Drew.

Her eyes widened as she saw Drew take Roger by the front of his shirt and shove him against the side of the pickup.

She didn't want to draw more attention to this—and her bright green hair and red dress with her candy cane striped thigh-high stockings likely would—but she couldn't walk away. She *had* to know what her new boyfriend—yes, she'd just called him her boyfriend—had to say to her father. So she ducked behind the truck parked three down from the one where Drew had Roger pinned.

She crept closer to where Drew and Roger were standing, stopping behind the gray Ford-150 just a few feet away. They were on the side of the truck opposite of the petting zoo was so only people on the road would be able to see them. Fortunately, none of the little kids and families who were trying to have a nice happy day at the Christmas village would likely notice them.

"You need to stay far away from her," Drew said to Roger as Rory got close enough to overhear.

"Stay away for my daughter? At the holidays? What kind of a coldhearted bastard are you?"

Drew pressed Roger harder into the truck. "Don't fuck with me. You've done enough damage to her. I'm not going to let you do anything more to hurt her."

"And what do you think you're going to do about it when you're back in Iowa, Mr. Ryan?"

Rory was surprised that Roger knew Drew's name. It was clear from the expression on Drew's face, he was as well.

Roger sneered him. "Yeah, I know who you are. I know you're from Iowa. I know you own a farm with your family. And I know that the nights you've spent in my daughter's bed were just a fun diversion while you were on vacation."

Drew thumped Roger against the side of the truck again. "You don't know what the fuck you're talking about."

"Well, I know that you and Rory didn't have a relationship before the other night and that you've been in town three days and you've spent two of those overnight at her house. As her father, I should probably be asking what your intentions are."

"You're the scumbag who has been hurting her most of her life. You don't get to have any say in what is going on between her and I."

Rory's mind was spinning. It was so damned gratifying to see someone getting in Roger's face and calling him out on his bullshit. Having someone defend her was not something she was used to. That was mostly because she didn't share this part of her life with many people, even those who cared about her.

She typically felt that she had to deal with all of this by herself. It was her mess, after all. But now, seeing Drew come to her defense was definitely making her heartbeat harder.

Still, it was clear that, as usual, she couldn't have anything nice. Everything good in her life, Roger found a way of touching and ruining. So, even though Drew had known about him prior to this moment, he hadn't been face-to-face with him. He hadn't witnessed Roger's blatant disregard for her feelings and hadn't been pulled directly into the conflict between her and her father. Now Drew was literally in the middle of it.

"You're going to leave her alone," Drew said, his tone was low and angry. "I get why she has a hard time saying no to you. You're her father and she doesn't know any different. She doesn't understand what it's like to have someone supporting her and protecting her instead of using her. The thing is, *I* happened to have been raised by a very good man who knew exactly how to be a great father so I know a dirtbag when I see one. And Roger, the good man in your daughter's life doesn't have to be her father. I know what she deserves and now that I'm here, I'm going to make sure she gets that. From everyone."

Rory's stomach swooped and warmth spread through her at Drew's words. He thought she deserved better and he was going to make sure it happened. That right there was why women watched romantic movies. That was the kind of stuff she thought guys only said when it was scripted.

"Oh, feeling a little protective, are we?" Roger's eyes narrowed.

Well, crap. Rory recognized that look. That was his calculating look. He was somehow going to use this against Drew.

She doubted the farmer from Iowa had had many dealings with soulless con men like Roger, who would happily use his own daughter to literally steal toys from kids at Christmas.

"Yeah, I'm feeling protective. Rory is mine to take care of

now and you are the major threat to her. Of course I'm going to keep you away from her."

Mine. The word bounced around in her mind. And her heart.

Rory should not like that possessive term quite so much. But she really did. Drew Ryan was staking a claim and all she really felt was...proud. If he thought she was worth claiming, in spite of everything he knew, that was amazing. He knew things she didn't even let her closest friends know. And now he was faced with one of those things and was still saying that he wanted her. Out loud. To someone else.

"What's it worth to you?" Roger asked.

Drew's jaw clenched and for just a moment Rory thought he was going to punch Roger.

Instead, he pulled air in through his nose and then pushed back from Roger.

"What do you mean?"

"Let's make a deal. What is it worth to you for me to leave Rory alone?"

"You leave her alone, no contact at all, and I won't beat the shit out of you."

Roger laughed. "I've had the shit beat out of me by bigger and better men than you. Bruises and cracked ribs can heal. And then I'm still poor on the other side of it. You'll have to do better than that."

"What do you want?"

"I know Oliver Caprinelli, the CEO of Fluke Inc. is a close, personal friend of yours."

Drew narrowed his eyes. "So?"

Roger looked over at the sleigh full of wrapped boxes, then back to Drew. "So I know you were able to replace the controllers I stole. And I want the new ones too."

Rory could practically hear Drew growl from where she stood.

But she wasn't one bit surprised by Roger's statement.

This was exactly what she'd expected.

She'd known when they did the photoshoot with the sleigh and the gifts and talked about the generous donation from Fluke, Inc. online and to the reporter, that Roger would somehow see the story and would assume they'd replaced the controllers.

She'd known he'd come back. And she'd planned to be here when he did.

She'd intended to record Roger stealing the boxes and then send the video to Zander anonymously.

She hadn't quite worked out how to do that without any kind of traceable information on the video or email. Or what Zander would be able to do since the boxes were empty. It had been a work in progress. But now...

Drew was going to ruin her plan.

No way was he going to let Roger near those boxes, empty or not.

It made her stomach turn, however, to know that Roger had looked into Drew and had figured out who he was. She was aware that Roger knew people who knew how to do all kinds of shady things. Finding out who Drew was, where he was from, and who his friends were had probably not been that difficult. Drew wouldn't have anything to hide. There was no way she'd ever believe that Roger had checked into Drew out of any kind of concern for her though. It had been strictly to try to get dirt or at least leverage.

And it looked like it had paid off.

Drew glanced over toward the sleigh that still held fifty empty wrapped boxes, then back to Roger. "Yeah, I guess it's your lucky day."

Roger nodded. "So you'll trade? The controllers in exchange for me leaving Rory alone?"

"I'm willing to do anything to keep you out of Rory's life for good."

Roger shook his head. "Oh, not for good. It's not like you're giving me a million bucks, or a private island. You get me those controllers and I'll stay away for a year."

"A year is not enough," Drew snarled.

"Well, tell you what, next year when I come back around, I'll call *you* first. You can be my Santa next year and we can leave Rory out of it."

Drew stepped closer again and glowered down at the man. He had a couple of inches on Roger and he looked like he was barely holding himself in check. "I'll be here. And you know what? You're free to talk to Rory next year."

Wait, what? Rory frowned and straightened slightly.

"Because right now, your relationship with her is built on the fact that you can manipulate her," Drew went on. "She doesn't want anybody to know who you are or about your connection with her. Because she's embarrassed by you. She would be devastated if the people that she cares about, and respects knew that she was connected to a scumbag like you."

Drew's eyes narrowed. "But I promise you that a year from now, after she's been loved by me for a year, after she's been loved by these people for a year, after she's been welcomed into their family and their town and she understands that they respect her and will lift her up and support her, no matter what, no matter who she comes from, no matter what has happened in the past, you're not going to be able to manipulate her anymore. You won't have any power over her anymore, Roger. So, yeah, you come back to town next year. You try to pull your bullshit with me and Rory. I promise you, it will not go well. So enjoy this year with your fucking game controllers. This is the last time you're going to feel lucky around here."

Rory's heart was pounding so hard in her chest she was certain that Roger and Drew could hear it where they were standing. Her mouth was dry and she actually pressed her hands to her chest trying to keep all of the emotions from bursting out of her. She couldn't believe what Drew had just said. He'd just confessed his love for her to her father. He'd not just staked a claim but had promised to be here next year, to be here for the next twelve months, loving her, supporting her. He'd put her father in his place and he'd said the most amazing things anyone had ever said about her.

Roger ran his hands down the front of his now wrinkled shirt. "So you'll bring the controllers?"

That was his only response.

Again, Drew's jaw clenched and he just shook his head for a moment as if trying to tamp down the urge to pummel Roger. "Yeah. I'll bring them. I assume since you know what Rory's been doing for the past few days that you're staying locally."

"Don't you worry about where I'm staying. I'm selling the controllers tonight. You meet me with the new ones and I'll take them all at once."

Drew nodded. "Just name the place."

Dammit.

This was definitely ruining her plan. If *Drew* took the controllers from the barn, she wouldn't be able to catch Roger on camera.

What was Drew's plan here exactly? The boxes were still empty. They did have replacement toys, but they weren't game controllers and weren't worth nearly as much.

She knew Drew had arranged for the replacement gifts, but she hadn't asked how. It didn't matter. She knew it was important to Drew that he had stepped up to help and had fixed that problem for her, so she'd just hugged him and said thank you. Because in the end, that was the important thing. It had been fixed and it gave him satisfaction to have been the one to do it. She understood that and she was happy to give that to him.

But Roger didn't want the new toys. He wanted fifty additional game controllers. Which they didn't have.

"Cypress and old Highway Six. Nine o'clock. I'll be in a 1998 blue Chevy. You pull up, we'll load them into the back with the rest, and I'll take off. And you won't see me again until next December."

"I'll be there," Drew promised, his voice low with a dark edge to it. "And I'm going to hold you to that. Because I'm going to be here every day, and if I see so much as a text from you come through on her phone, I will find you and I will make you sorry."

"Geez, and everybody here thinks you're such a good guy. Wholesome, noble farm boy from Iowa, right?" Roger taunted.

"I am all of those things. But something we do in Iowa that is very much like what people do here in Louisiana...we take care of the people we love no matter what."

With that, Drew gave Roger a final shove, then turned and walked away from him.

Fortunately, in the opposite direction from where Rory was ducked behind the truck listening.

She scooted around to the front of the truck as Roger stepped out and started down the line of trucks toward the one he'd driven into town. It was not a 1998 blue Chevy, but she wasn't surprised that he had a second vehicle lined up to make this mysterious delivery to whoever was buying these controllers. She assumed it was someone in New Orleans. That was where most of his connections were. It was probably the guy that he was going to be working with at the casino. Or a friend of a friend. She really didn't care.

She was still sitting on the front bumper of the truck, chewing her bottom lip, when the owner came out with his two little kids.

"Hi, Rory!" Olivia, the little girl, greeted.

Rory stood and forced a smile. "Oh, hey, guys. I was just taking a little break."

Brad, the father, gave her a grin. "I can see why you would need one. This is amazing." He tipped his head toward the petting zoo and Santa's village.

"We had *such* a good time," Olivia said.

"I'm really so glad," Rory said, meaning it with everything in her. Santa's Village had come together and she was really proud of it. The guests all raved about it. And, even more importantly, all of the Landrys were very pleased.

She watched the little family drive away and with them, her sense of satisfaction disappeared. Yes, Santa's Village was awesome. But because of it, Drew Ryan had come to Autre, made her fall in love with him, and was planning to meet her con man father on a dark backroad tonight. With a bunch of empty boxes. If Roger figured that out, he'd be so pissed. Who knew what he'd do?

She had to do something. Of course, she didn't want to, because it would mean confessing to someone what she knew and how, but she couldn't let Drew go out there to meet Roger alone. Roger was a wildcard. She didn't think that he would *kill* Drew or anything crazy like that, but he could hurt him. Or Roger could force Drew to go to New Orleans with him and who knew what those people might do.

A shudder went through her. This was all her fault. Drew was involved in all of this because of *her*. She had to do something to make sure he was protected. Even if it meant exposing herself.

She turned and surveyed the petting zoo. It was full of people who would know what to do. Who would definitely have Drew's back. Who could easily handle Roger. Zander was the only one missing. He was the town cop and, of course, couldn't take off duties to hang out with reindeer and elves, but he was probably her best bet.

The only problem was that he was a Landry too.

She just had a real allergy to disappointing Landrys.

But she didn't have a choice. Drew had to be safe and if that meant she had to confess about her dad and her background and the fact that she'd brought this problem to their doorstep, then so be it.

She really did want to take care of her own shit. She'd wanted to clean up this mess herself. But she was out of options. She wanted the Landrys to trust her and admitting that she was the cause of all this trouble was going to be tough, but Drew's safety was more important than her pride. If she lost the Landrys' respect, well, at least she'd have Drew.

Zander just needed to get out to Cypress and old Highway Six tonight at 9 o'clock. If he was there, nothing terrible would happen to Drew. He'd see what Roger and Drew were doing and he'd check the truck and find the stolen controllers. It would not only keep Drew safe, but it might end up with Roger in handcuffs.

Rory pulled out her phone, ready to make the call but...she didn't have Zander's number. She couldn't call 911 for this. To get a hold of him would mean asking someone else and making them wonder why she needed to know.

Drew is worth it. Drew is worth it.

She was just going to have to suck it up and take whatever consequences came. Drew loved her. That was really the bottom line. He loved her and knew all of her secrets and even if no one else did, Drew loving her was enough.

She crossed the barnyard to where Charlie was standing just inside of the barn chatting with guests and handing out alligator-shaped Christmas cookies. Rory waited until the little family moved off to step forward and say, "Hey Charlie?"

Charlie gave her a huge grin. "Hey. How's it going?"

"Everything here is great. Everything is perfect, actually," she was very happy to report. "But I was wondering...can I get Zander's phone number from you?"

Charlie lifted a brow. "Zander's?"

Rory just nodded and didn't offer any additional information.

After just a second, Charlie nodded. "Of course." She shifted the tray of cookies to one hand and pulled her phone from her pocket with the other. She swiped her finger over the screen a few times before turning the phone so that Rory could see it.

Rory put the number into her phone and then gave Charlie a smile. "Thank you."

"Absolutely."

Rory started to turn away, but Charlie said, "And Rory—"

She looked back. "Yeah?"

"For what it's worth, you've got a lot of other phone numbers in your phone that you can use anytime, you know."

Rory swallowed hard. She had Charlie's phone number, Paige's, Mitch's, Jordan's, Sawyer's, Kennedy's, and Donovan's. She nodded. "I know."

At least, she wanted to know that.

Knock it off. Why do you just assume no one will help you? Drew helped you the very first day he showed up.

Yeah, but that's Drew. He's just a good guy.

But it wasn't only Drew and Rory knew that. Charlie had just given her Zander's number without asking any other questions.

Before she could lose her courage, she walked behind the barn and dialed Zander's number. It was his personal number, so she halfway expected it to go to voicemail, assuming that he was at work. But he picked up on the third ring. "Landry."

Rory swallowed. "Hey Zander. It's Rory Robins."

"Hey, Rory," Zander sounded understandably surprised to hear from her. "What's up?"

"I need some help with something."

"Cop help or friend help?"

She sucked in a little breath. Wow. That was a really nice

question. He'd used the word *friend*. That was...yeah, nice. And he'd asked without judgement. Like he was up for whatever, but he needed to know what shoes to wear to the occasion.

She cleared her throat. "Um, both. A little. Mostly friend."

"Are you in trouble?"

"I'm...adjacent to some trouble."

"Where are you right now?"

"Santa's Village at the petting zoo."

"Okay, meet me at the corner down by the gas station. That way I won't pull up in my squad car and freak anyone out."

Air whooshed out of her body that she didn't even realize she had been holding in her lungs. "You would do that?"

"I'm on my way now."

Rory just shook her head. Maybe she did actually have more friends than she thought. That was a really nice realization. And that realization was thanks to Drew Ryan as well. She actually felt the back of her eyes stinging as she nodded. "Okay."

They disconnected and Rory took a deep breath. So maybe asking for help wasn't the most terrible thing. And maybe it was going to show her that she had more people she could count on than she'd expected. Again, she had Drew to thank for all of that. Because there was no way in hell she would've called Zander to come help her with Roger if Drew hadn't gotten involved.

She smiled. Drew Ryan had brought a lot of really nice things into her life in the last few days.

Her smile dropped a moment later. She really wanted more days with him. She really wanted him to stick around. She really hoped he'd been serious when he'd told Roger that he intended to stay. She would love to have him here, in her life, on an ongoing basis.

Which meant she really needed to keep him healthy and in one piece tonight.

Six hours later Rory was pacing her living room, chewing on her nails, and wondering why she hadn't just driven out to Cypress and old Highway Six herself.

When her phone did finally ring, she jumped nearly a foot off the ground and gasped. But she immediately dove for where it was sitting on her coffee table. *Please let it be Zander.*

It was Paige.

"Hello?"

"Hey, we're heading to the jail. Wanna come?"

Rory frowned. "Um. The jail? What do you mean?"

"Yeah, Drew's been arrested." Paige laughed. "Can you believe that he's in *jail*? I mean, we're obviously gonna get him out. He didn't do it. But Zander had to take him in. So Mitch and I are heading over there."

Rory knew her eyes were completely round. Her heart was pounding, and she felt a little dizzy. What the *fuck*?

Drew had been *arrested*. Oh, God. This was her fault. She'd sent Zander out there.

"What..." She stopped and swallowed. "What was he arrested for? Was there anyone with him?"

"Just him. He was driving a pickup that had the stolen game controllers in the back, I guess. They got a tip on the tip line about what the pickup looked like and where he'd be," Paige said. "Come on. We're going down to plead his case and keep him company while Zander does his thing."

Rory frowned. It had just been Drew? And he hadn't been in *his* pickup? And the stolen controllers had been there? Where the hell was Roger? What was going on?

"Someone called in a tip?"

"That's what Holly said."

"Who's Holly?"

"The dispatcher. Or something. I'm not sure what her official title is. She's the one who answers when someone calls and needs Zander or Michael or whoever," Paige said.

How did Rory not know about Holly? Of course, she knew very little about how emergency services worked in Autre. She kind of assumed that there weren't many emergencies in general, but she actually didn't know if that was true.

"Holly is an old friend of Ellie and Cora and all of them. She keeps track of the boys," Paige said. "And they say she knows about emergencies before they're even called in."

Oh, boy, another of the older generation who was just plugged in and *knew things*. Great.

Or maybe it was great. If a new generation was taking over protecting and serving the town and the people here, they could probably use a little mentoring and guidance from those who'd been doing it all these years.

Rory took a deep breath. Okay, so Drew had gone to meet Roger and Roger hadn't been there. But the truck had been. And apparently the controllers had been. And Zander had gotten a tip...

She closed her eyes and groaned.

Roger had set Drew up.

That was suddenly clear as day.

Roger had set it up so Drew would be out there with stolen merchandise and called in the tip so the cop would find him.

But Roger was now without the controllers. Why would he do that? Roger must have already come up with the money he needed somehow. The controllers just meant *extra* money. His greed wouldn't let him walk away or give them back. Or let him walk away from an extra chance to manipulate and torture her.

Then Drew had pissed Roger off when he'd confronted him and told him to stay away from her. This was Roger showing Drew that he was not intimidated and that messing with him was not going to be as easy as just telling him to stay away.

Rory rubbed the middle of her forehead. Dammit. Of course, this wasn't easy. Of course, Roger was still fucking things up. Of course, Drew had tried to do this amazingly protective thing and it had backfired.

"Rory?" Paige asked when several long seconds had passed without anyone speaking.

"Yeah."

"You coming to the jail?"

The jail. Where Drew was. Because of her.

If there was a guy driving around with stolen goods, of course Zander had to pick him up. Zander didn't know Drew like she did. And he didn't know the whole story. Hell, as far as Zander was concerned, Drew might've been an accomplice. Or Drew and Rory could have been making this other guy up.

No, she hadn't told Zander who Roger was. She'd chickened out at the last minute.

When was she going to stop being weak and letting Roger mess everything up?

Zander didn't know her well enough to totally trust *her* either.

And that realization settled like a lead ball in her gut.

It was time to confess. It was *past* time. She was going to have to tell everyone everything.

And possibly lose them all.

"Yeah, I'll be there," she said.

He had never gone on an airboat on the bayou, he had never made love to a woman with green hair, and he had never been arrested.

He could cross all of those things off his to do list since coming to Autre.

Drew slumped back against the wall behind the bench he was sitting on. He was technically in the jail cell in Autre, but he noticed that Zander had left the door standing open. Zander was at his desk typing up his notes from what Drew had told him about how he'd ended up driving a truck full of stolen game controllers.

Drew had also given Zander Roger's first name and a full description. He'd told him how he'd run into Roger outside the petting zoo and realized from their conversation that Roger had stolen the controllers and he was back looking for more. However, he left out the part about Rory being related to Roger and that Drew was exchanging the "additional controllers" for Roger leaving Rory alone for the next year.

"But the boxes were empty that you were giving Roger tonight," Zander said. "Is that right?"

"Yeah. My plan was to show up, load those boxes into his truck, and then follow him to wherever he was going to actually sell them. I'd planned to call you when I got there as well as record the whole transaction."

Zander looked up at him. "You know that was kind of a terrible idea, right?"

"You mean because of the fact that it didn't work?"

"Because you have no idea where he was going or who he was meeting," Zander said with a frown. "What if he'd seen you? What if the guys he was with were more violent and figured out Roger had been followed? What if I couldn't get there in time?"

"I didn't know what else to do. I didn't want him just getting away with it."

"Why didn't you tell me about meeting him out on Highway Six? I could have gone with you from the start."

Drew leaned forward on the bench, resting his forearms on his thighs. "I was hoping I could just lead you to him and you could go in without him ever knowing I was there."

"You didn't want him to know you'd turned him in."

"Right. I need him to know that when I say something, I mean it. That means if I say that I'm going to show up to meet him somewhere, I need to show to meet him. But it also means that if I tell him to fuck off, I mean *that*."

"Men like this don't have honor like that."

"Yeah, guess not."

"You make this sound like something that might be ongoing between you two."

Yeah, it was going to be. He was staying. With Rory. And that meant taking on the not-so-great parts of her life too. "Well, I'm not going anywhere and I'm afraid Roger isn't either."

"You know, we're very capable of keeping Rory safe. Not just me, but especially me. It's kind of my job. If you tell me what's really going on, I'm happy to make sure she's okay when you go back to Iowa."

"I'm not going back to Iowa. This is where I'm supposed to be."

"Because you're worried about Rory and her dad?"

"Because I want to be with her. Her dad is an unfortunate detail in her life that I am going to have to put up with to be with her, but I have no problem with that. But, I'd be staying whether Roger was a factor or not." Then Drew frowned and sat up straight. "Hang on, how did you know that Roger was connected to Rory? I didn't tell you that."

"Seriously?" Zander leaned in on his desk and gave Drew a look. "I'm offended. I'm very good at my job."

"What's that mean?"

"It means I'm a great cop because I'm naturally suspicious. A nice guy comes to town, falls in love, and helps put Santa's Village together one day and the next he's out on a dark back-road with a truck full of stolen merch? Come on. Those things had to be connected."

Zander turned his computer monitor so Drew could see it. Roger's photo filled half the screen. The other half looked like the first of many pages of information.

Drew sighed. "How'd you know I was in love?"

Zander laughed. "Because I know Rory. She's very loveable. And you're a nice guy, Drew, everybody knows that. I have no doubt if they'd asked you to help out at the petting zoo, you would've been happy to pitch in. But there are literally dozens of us. We all know how to hold a paint brush and lay bricks. We could have that place put together in half a day. But not only did you jump in, but you insisted on being the only one to do it."

"How did you know *that*?"

"What kind of cop would I be if I don't at least drive by when there are lights on some place they shouldn't be late at night? I saw you painting and laying the bricks. You wanted to be her hero. And I get it. It's cool. But a guy doesn't go from that to stealing toys from kids."

Drew shook his head. "Okay, great. But that doesn't totally explain how you knew that Roger had anything to do with Rory."

Zander chuckled. "Well, it was all pretty suspicious. But Rory also called me and told me that you were going to meet 'some guy'. It made sense she was worried, but she was more worked up than she should have been. It was like she knew more about the situation...or the guy you were going to meet... than she was letting on. I decided to see if anything came up if I put "Roger Robins" into the system. And sure enough, there he was."

Drew shook his head. Wow. "Rory called you?"

Zander nodded. "I showed up to make sure you made it back to town in one piece. And when Roger didn't show up and you were there alone, I kinda had no choice but to bring you in."

Drew narrowed his eyes. "You're talking like you believe my story though."

"I have every reason to believe your story," Zander said.

"Why? You barely know me. You've no reason to trust me."

Zander looked at him for a long moment. "Well here's the thing. Paige trusts you. Tori trusts you. Josh trusts you. Mitch trusts you. And Rory not only trusts you, but she fell in love with you. And I trust all of *them*. So that's enough for me."

"You trust Rory?"

"'Course."

"She doesn't know that. She's been trying to earn everyone's favor and prove that she's worthy of being a part of your group for three years."

"Well, we're gonna have to work on that. Having you around will be a big help."

Suddenly the door banged open, and Ellie Landry came through carrying a big, covered cooking pot, and a paper bag.

"I hear that you arrested our guest," she said to Zander.

"Didn't arrest him. Brought him in for a talk."

"Then why's he sittin' in the cell?" She set the pot and bag on Zander's desk.

"He just walked in there and sat down."

Drew looked around. He didn't need to be in the cell? He noticed there were two chairs sitting facing Zander's desk. So he could have sat over there for their chat? Well...no wonder the cell door was open.

"Are you done with him?" Ellie asked Zander.

A tantalizing aroma filled the room, and Drew felt his stomach growl.

"I think we've covered the basics." Zander shot Drew a glance. "It'd be really helpful if I had a few more details about this guy. Like maybe where he might be going or staying, but we're good for now."

Drew honestly didn't know where Roger was going or where he might be staying. And he was hesitant to send Zander after Rory. She'd already called him and told him as much as she was comfortable with apparently.

He still couldn't believe she'd called Zander. That was skating very close to telling someone some of her secrets.

His heart tripped as he realized what a huge gesture that was. She had been trying so hard to keep Roger completely separate from anything having to do with the Landrys that even giving Zander a hint that she might know about something shady going on was a big deal. She really had been worried about *him*. That had to mean something.

Like maybe that she'd be happy that he'd decided to stick around in Louisiana.

He'd talk to his brother and cousin tomorrow, but he didn't think that Dallas and Justin would have any trouble with his decision. There would be a transition, of course, and his mother wouldn't be particularly happy, but he'd make it work.

They'd all love Rory.

She not only had a lifetime ahead of her with the Landry family, but she was going to have the Ryan family back in Iowa as well.

He grinned thinking about that. She was going to have an automatic group of friends with Piper and Ollie and Dax and Jane and the rest. She might actually regret wanting to have a whole big family and community around her. She was going to get two of them practically overnight.

Ellie approached the cell and stepped through the open door, handing him a bowl of gumbo and a cornbread muffin. "I can't have you wasting away in jail. What would your mother say if I sent you home skinnier than when you got here?"

Drew patted his stomach. "That is not possible. But thank you."

Zander chuckled as he dug into his own bowl of gumbo. "You know she's up here for the gossip. The gumbo is just a cover."

"Hey, don't start without us." Paige came through the door with Mitch right behind her. "I can't believe my friend from Iowa came down here and got arrested."

"He didn't get arrested," Zander said with an eye roll.

"Did you get our toys back?" Charlie asked, as she and Griffin came in behind Mitch. "I want whoever stole them caught and punished." She turned to look at Mitch. "Do you think you could build stockades? We can put them in the town square like they used to."

Mitch grabbed a muffin from the bag and nodded. "I'm sure I could figure something out."

"We're not building stockades in the town square," Zander said.

"You can't tell me that that wouldn't be a great deterrent for crime," Charlie said. "One guy spending a day and night in the stockades and I guarantee everybody else would think twice about messing with our petting zoo."

Zander shook his head. "No one messes with the petting zoo. This is the first time anything has happened. The stockade would sit there and look stupid most of the time."

"What if this crime goes unpunished?" Charlie asked. "Who knows what will happen? Maybe people will become emboldened. Maybe more things will start to happen. Maybe we will start losing merchandise on a regular basis. Maybe they'll start stealing animals!"

Zander sighed. "I don't think anybody's going to be breaking in and stealing visors and sunglasses and, trust me, if anybody takes one of those goats, they'll be bringin' 'em back within ten minutes."

Drew was amused by the way Zander's drawl got longer when he was talking to his family and bullshitting versus when he was talking official business.

Charlie frowned at him. "That's not very nice."

"Neither are your goats."

"That seems like the perfect answer," Griffin said, dropping into one of the chairs across from Zander's desk. "Let's just keep adopting asshole animals and then nobody will mess with them."

"You do not think our animals are assholes," Charlie said to him.

Griffin's brows rose. "Don't I? I love them and I take great care of them, but that doesn't mean I don't think they're assholes."

"*Anyway,*" Paige said, coming through the cell door to join Drew on the bench. She sat down next to him, looped an arm around his shoulder and leaned her head on his upper arm. "Can I just say that I think it's hilarious that you're such a good guy, you couldn't even pull off a little middle of the night con."

"How do you know I wasn't the one stealing the toys?"

Paige started laughing. "What is this? The Farmer Who Stole Christmas?" She patted his arm. "I'm sorry the bad guy tricked you, but I love that you're the good guy."

Drew sighed. "Okay, so I wanted to be the big hero. And it didn't exactly work out."

"What you mean? We have the toys back, don't we?" Charlie said.

"Well..." Zander said.

Everyone looked over at him, including Drew. What did "well" mean?

"We have *most* of them back," Zander said.

"What?" Drew straightened. "They're not all in there?"

"Nope," Zander said. "Looks like Roger tried to set you up but couldn't bring himself to leave them all. He kept ten."

Now *that* actually made sense. "Fucker knew those things were worth five times now what they'll eventually sell for when they're released. He'll get way more than the three grand he said he needed," Drew said.

"That's what I figured," Zander said with a nod.

"Oh, he got *way* more than that," Ellie said.

Everyone swung to look at her now.

"What do you mean?" Drew asked.

She was scowling but she waved away his question. "Never mind. I'll take care of it."

"Did you—" Zander started, then he held up a hand and shook his head. "You know what? The less I know, the better sometimes."

"I got along just fine for nearly fifty years before you became a cop. I'll let you know when and if I need you," Ellie told him.

Zander nodded. "That's perfect."

Paige leaned over to Charlie and asked softly, "Does Zander seem less...*Zander-ish* lately? He's really intense about work. And he seems a lot less annoyed about it in general."

Charlie nodded. "Yep. And we all know why."

The women shared a smile.

Drew didn't know what that all meant, but before he could wonder about it much, Charlie turned to him. "Well, anyway, I don't know *everything* that went down, and I'm not sure I want to, but I have a feeling that if you hadn't gotten involved, *all* of those controllers would be long gone, right?"

He thought about that. That was true. Roger would have

just disappeared with the controllers. Or tried to steal fifty empty boxes and *then* disappeared.

Instead, he'd left the controllers—most of them anyway—with Drew. As a warning.

On his drive back to Autre with the abandoned truck full of stolen game controllers and no sign of Roger, even before Zander had turned on his flashing lights, Drew had figured out what was going on. Roger hadn't liked being pushed around and threatened. This was his way of telling Drew that if he was going to get involved in Rory's life, Roger was going to be a continual thorn in Drew's side. It was a big, obvious promise—being involved with Rory was going to be a lot of work and a big headache.

Drew was still all in.

His three days in Autre had already been crazier than his last three *years* in Appleby.

And he wanted more.

13

Rory was pacing outside the Autre jail when Ellie Landry stepped out onto the sidewalk and nearly ran into her.

"Oh, honey!" Ellie exclaimed. "What are you doin' out here?"

"Trying to decide if I should go in," Rory said honestly.

"And why wouldn't you go in?"

"I'm not sure I should be in there. I'm not sure what I can do. About anything that's going on."

Ellie stepped close with a small smile. Then she reached up and cupped Rory's face between her two hands. "Santa's Village was not a test."

Rory's eyes widened. "What?"

"You putting Santa's Village together for the petting zoo was not a test for you to pass or fail to get invited into our family."

Rory stared at her. Then she shook her head. Then she swallowed hard. "I... um... I didn't..."

But something about Ellie's eyes and the way she just watched Rory with kindness and patience and understanding, made Rory finally say softly, "How did you know I felt that way?"

Ellie gave her face a little squeeze, then let her go. She shrugged. "I've known a lot of people in my life. All kinds of people. People who want all kinds of things. The ones who want to do harm or hurt others, who want power, who are driven by greed or selfishness are harder to read. 'Cuz that's not natural. That's harder to get my mind around. But people who want companionship, friendship, home, family, and love? They're easy. Those people I understand."

Rory felt her eyes fill and she nodded. "I'm those kind of people."

Ellie gave her a smile that made the stinging in Rory's eyes grow sharper.

"Yes, you are," Ellie said. "But," she added. "You goin' inside that jail isn't about you. It's about Drew. *He* wants all of that too and you're a part of that. So get on in there."

Rory looked toward the building. "It's my fault he's in there. Getting involved with me is going to be a mess for him."

Ellie nodded. "Yeah. Probably."

Rory had kind of expected something a little more comforting. "Is that okay?"

Ellie laughed. "Have you met my family? Clearly messiness isn't a problem for me."

Rory couldn't help but grin in return.

"But one thing I *know* to be true," Ellie went on, "is that you don't really know what matters and what you care about until you're willin' to get messy for it. Be that actually messy—wadin' into flood waters or the bayou or an accident scene or a fist fight —or emotionally messy—bein' willin' to get your heart bruised or be disappointed or angry. Messy is where it all becomes clear."

Rory swallowed. "So when I walk in there, it's going to be clear how Drew feels about me."

"Yep." Ellie didn't add any additional comforting words to that.

"You really think that I should saddle Drew with all of my problems?"

"I think if Drew Ryan is the right man for you, once you lay your worries on him, they'll start to feel a lot less like problems and a lot more like simple bumps in the road. And we've all got those. That's how you test out the shocks on your relationship. The good ones give you a smooth ride the whole way, no matter what bumps you come across. The wrong ones rattle you and make it so you can't wait to get a new one."

Rory laughed softly, but she understood exactly what Ellie was saying. In the couple of days Drew had been in town she'd already felt lighter and happier having him to lean on.

Rory let out a breath. "Thank you."

"For what?"

"For...putting up with me and giving me advice."

Ellie waved that away. "Everyone needs to be loved. Some people just need stronger and more stubborn people to do it. That's where the Landrys come in."

Rory felt her eyes stinging again. Damn, that was so nice. How had she resisted just throwing herself into the middle of this family and *begging* them to adopt her?

Rory swallowed hard. "I've been a coward. I've let my dad do this to me over and over. I've enabled it every time. Now he came back around, and it got everyone else involved."

"Listen, the hardest cause to fight for is ourselves," Ellie said. "Fighting for animals and kids and our families and the climate...those are all noble and easy to get riled up about. But fighting for ourselves is a whole different thing."

Rory pressed her lips together and nodded.

"It took until now, when your dad started messin' with the petting zoo and people you loved, for you to fight back," Ellie said. She leaned in, studying Rory's eyes. "Because you were gonna fight him, weren't you? You had a plan."

Rory knew that the rumor around town was that Ellie Landry always knew everything that was going on. She shouldn't have been surprised that Ellie had figured out that Rory had come up with a way to deal with Roger once he'd started threatening the people and things that mattered to her.

She nodded. "I did. I was going to lure him in with the fake boxes and then turn him over to the cops. But Drew got there first."

"Well, it's a start," Ellie told her. "You'll get better at standing up to him with practice."

"You promise?"

"Of course. The first thing is learning that you're worth it. And we're going to teach you that."

Rory couldn't describe exactly what she was feeling. It felt like affection, and she was sure that was part of it, but there was also a sense of gratitude. She'd never had an older woman to give her advice and mentor her, and to just talk to about life. She really liked it. She also knew it would be very difficult to do better than Ellie Landry.

"I'm sorry I almost ruined everything for your family's petting zoo," Rory said.

"Nothing's ruined," Ellie said. "No one got hurt, or arrested, and the toys are back."

"But Roger only did that as a warning to Drew."

"You sure? Seems to me like he's on the run. Getting the hell away from here before Drew showed up."

Rory thought about that. They really had come out on top. If Roger had believed that Drew would end up in actual trouble with the Landrys, he hadn't done his homework.

"I don't think he's gone for good, though," Rory said. "He'll be around."

Ellie shrugged. "So are the gators. Mostly we just ignore them. Or we make a deal—we feed 'em and they show off for the tourists. We don't *like* 'em, but we tolerate 'em. Unless they become a nuisance and threaten somebody."

"Then what happens?"

"We have 'em for lunch."

Rory laughed. "I guess maybe that's a good metaphor for how things can go with Roger."

"Sure." Ellie nodded slowly. "We can call it a metaphor."

Rory felt her eyes widen. But she decided *not* to pursue that branch of the conversation—or the ingredients in Ellie's gumbo —any further.

"Alright, I'm going to tell everybody who Roger is and what he did and how I didn't stop him. Get it all out in the open." Rory pulled her phone from her back pocket and opened up her text messages. She quickly typed in a message to Paige and Charlie.

Can you guys come down to the jail? I have something I need to tell you.

Paige was the first to respond, and the message popped up almost immediately.

We're already here.

Rory looked up at Ellie. "They're already here?"

"Of course. One of us was in jail."

Rory smiled, warmth filling her. Drew was one of them. So was she. "And you'd all never leave someone sitting alone somewhere, would you?"

"Right. And it's a really good thing the family is so big. There was one night when we had two in jail, two in the hospital, one stuck at the airport, and one with his truck stuck in the bayou. We really had to spread out that night."

Wow. And now she was a part of all of that. Rory could feel it. Whether she was at the airport, stuck by the side of the road, in the hospital...or jail...the Landrys would be there for her.

"Okay." She took a deep breath and faced front of the building. "Wish me luck."

Ellie shook her head. "Nah. I'll wish you a little of what you *actually* need...some alone time with that boy of yours. There's a whole lot of people in there and he's gonna want to get you somewhere private pretty quick, I'm guessin'." Then she winked and turned and headed for her truck.

Which left Rory facing the front of the jail. She took a deep breath and marched to the door. She stepped inside and immediately everyone turned to look at her. And went silent.

Her gaze went straight to Drew. He came off up off of the bench in the cell and stalked to her. She didn't miss the fact is that the door to the cell had been standing wide open.

"Hey, are you okay?"

She smiled and shook her head. "I think I'm supposed to ask you that."

"I'm fine," he said. "A little sheepish." He ran his hand through his hair. "Your dad set me up."

"Well, he's been at this bad guy stuff a lot longer than you have."

"Yeah."

She met his gaze directly and wet her lips. "This is going to keep happening, Drew. He's not going to leave us alone. Just because you're here now, and stood up to him, doesn't mean he's going to back off. He's probably going to see it as a challenge."

"I don't care. I want you."

Those six words squeezed her heart and she had to swallow hard before she asked, "Because you want to protect me from my dad?"

"I want you *in spite* of your dad, Rory. I want you and whatever comes with you."

Relief, desire, and a love like she'd never felt or even imagined before flooded through her. "You know," she said, her voice thick. "I think maybe you can't shake this good guy thing because *I* need it. I've been waiting for a good guy all my life."

The next thing she knew, Drew had her up against him and was kissing her as if that was all that was keeping him alive.

She melted into him, her arms going around his neck, stretching her body against his as fully as she could. He palmed her ass, lifting her, angling his head to deepen the kiss.

It was only Zander clapping his hands together and his firm, "Okay. You're free to go, Ryan," that broke them apart.

Drew and Rory just stared at one another for several seconds. Drew's eyes were full of heat and wonder and love. Definitely love.

Finally, she stepped back from Drew and turned to look at Zander.

Then she took in everyone else in the room. Oh, boy.

She cleared her throat. "My dad is an ex-con. He comes in and out of my life once or twice a year, and if I don't give into whatever he needs—usually money—he wreaks havoc. He messes with my business, my relationships, whatever he can. He's mostly left me alone since I came to Autre, but obviously he knows I'm here now. He's going to keep coming back and I will totally understand if you guys want to keep your distance."

She looked at Zander. "His name is Roger Robins and he's taking a new job at one of the casinos in New Orleans. I'll be able to have the name of that casino to you later tonight. He's likely staying with one of three friends. I can give you all of their addresses. My mom probably has or can get any other information you might want. I'm happy to help however you want me to."

Zander looked at her, then at everyone else in the room, then back to her.

"Well, first of all, there's no reason to stay away from you because of this. This is kind of what we do."

"What you do?" she asked.

"Yeah...crazy," Zander said. He sighed. "We do a lot of crazy."

Everyone else in the room nodded.

"Second of all, I would love those addresses. We might not have enough evidence of a crime this time, but it wouldn't hurt to know where he might be for next time."

Rory looked at Drew, then over at Charlie. "Are you pressing charges against Drew?"

Charlie laughed. "Of course not. Even if we hadn't gotten the toys back, we would never do that. But the controllers are back and we have the extra toys that Ollie and Piper sent, so it's just going to be an even bigger Christmas party tomorrow."

Suddenly, everything that had happened—and not happened—crashed into Rory at once. She felt a little dizzy, incredibly relieved, and so full of happiness and love and hope and relief that she almost couldn't speak.

As if sensing what she was going through, Drew put his arm around her, hugged her up against his side, and said, "We should get you home."

"You can really just go?"

"Yep. I answered all Zander's questions."

"Then why are you still just sitting around up here?"

He shrugged and looked toward Zander's desk. "This is where the gumbo is."

She followed his gaze to the large takeout container that Ellie must've left behind and laughed. "Well, I have hot chocolate at my house,"

"How about frosted sugar cookies?" he asked, heat, flickering in his gaze.

"I don't have any cookies left," she said. "But...I did pick up some chocolate sauce."

Without another word, Drew scooped her up into his arms and started for the door.

"Hey, we have fifty game controllers we need to wrap for the party tomorrow," Charlie called after them, laughing.

Drew didn't even slow down. "Sorry. I need this elf's help getting me firmly on the naughty list tonight."

"Drew Ryan? On the *naughty* list? I don't believe it!" Paige called after him.

But Rory snuggled closer and grinned up at him. "I do."

EPILOGUE

One year later...

"I can't believe you thought doing a live nativity was a good idea," Rory said as she chased a goat back into the barn with her trusty giant candy cane.

Drew grinned. "Oh, come on. We had to. We already had the donkey and camels and sheep."

"Those are *not* sheep," Rory laughed, as the goat she'd just herded into the barn, darted back out. "Those are goats dressed to look kind of like sheep."

"Yeah, maybe we should get some real sheep," Drew said, coming to stand next to her.

Rory turned to see what he was looking at.

One of the goats was chewing on the side of the manger where the baby Jesus lay.

She sighed, but laughed. "Yeah, maybe."

Drew looped his arm around her waist and pulled her close. She leaned into him, absorbing his warmth.

The past year with him in Autre had been amazing. He'd, of course, fit in perfectly with the animal park, and had taken on a lot of the daily animal care activities.

He'd moved into Rory's apartment with her for the first few months, but they had decided they needed more space and were now living in a house not far from Tori and Josh.

Drew's brother and cousin were doing great back home running the farm in Iowa without him and his mom had finally gotten over him moving so far away after Rory had visited Iowa and won her over. Then Linda had taken her first trip to Autre and met the Landrys for herself. Now she, and Drew's father, were huge fans of everything having to do with Louisiana, the Landrys, and the bayou. They were on their way to Louisiana for the holiday, in fact. They'd be here tomorrow.

Rory rubbed her stomach where the butterflies were kicking up. She wanted this Christmas to be perfect. She loved the life they'd made together and something about bringing everyone they loved together for the anniversary of when everything had started seemed hugely monumental.

"So..."

She looked up at Drew. "So?"

He took a breath and met her eyes. "Your dad's getting out the day after tomorrow."

She processed that. Roger was getting out of jail on Christmas Eve.

Huh.

He'd messed up not long after starting the job at the casino. Of course. He'd been in prison for six months, so he must be getting out for good behavior. Which was hilarious.

"Well...how nice. The whole family can be together," she said dryly.

Drew squeezed her. "He's not coming down here for Christmas."

"How do you know?"

"Ellie went and visited him."

Her eyes went wide. "What?"

Drew nodded. "I actually ran into her in the parking lot."

"What parking lot?"

"The prison parking lot."

Rory pulled away so she could turn to look at him more fully. "*You* were going up to visit him?"

"Yep." Drew frowned. "I had a few things I wanted to say and figured that was the best way to make sure I'd get to say them."

She wasn't sure what to do with that information. "That's... a strange coincidence."

"Apparently she'd seen him several times. And I think she knew I was headed up there that day and made a point of getting there first."

Rory shook her head. She wondered if she'd ever get used to the way Ellie Landry was always three steps ahead of everyone else. "What did she say?"

"Neither of them would tell me exactly, but Roger is...different."

"Different how?"

"He wants to come to dinner at Ellie's. Not for Christmas. Nothing important like that. Just a regular dinner when *everyone* is around."

Rory felt her mouth drop open. "Are you serious?"

"I am. And I think it's a good idea. I want him to see the force you have behind you. The family you're a part of. What he's actually taking on if he decides to mess with you again." He paused. "But it's totally up to you."

She chewed on her bottom lip and studied Drew's face. "You think Ellie got to him? Like converted him or something?"

Drew shrugged. "If anyone could, it'd be her."

Rory wondered if Ellie had threated Roger with becoming the main part of her famous, secret-recipe gumbo. But, she'd put time into going to see Roger. That had to mean something.

"I'm not afraid of him. Or intimidated by him anymore," Rory said, reaching for Drew's hand. "Being loved by you, and the Landrys, for this past year has taken that all away. He doesn't have any power over me anymore. Just like you said."

He frowned slightly, then understanding dawned. "You heard me say that?"

She nodded and stepped close. "It was the best thing I'd ever heard."

He cupped her face. "I meant it."

"And you were right."

"I'm glad."

"And now you're being a good guy again," she said, with a smile that came from the very depths of her heart. "You want to give Roger a chance to reconcile."

He frowned. "I actually don't. I want *you* to have a choice in what happens next with him out and on the prowl. You don't have to do anything you don't want to do."

"No. I don't. But I will. Because your good guy stuff has rubbed off."

He leaned in with a little growl. "You're poking at the good guy stuff because you know that makes me get the nipple clamps and chocolate sauce out to remind you I have another side."

She grinned. "Yep."

"Well, before I do that—" He shifted back and reached into his pocket. "I have one more really sweet, good guy thing to do. And I figured this barnyard, where it all started, was the perfect place for it."

She frowned, but as soon as he dropped to his knee in front of her, her stomach swooped, her heart leapt, and her eyes filled with tears. She covered her mouth with her hands and started nodding.

He chuckled. "I haven't even asked yet."

"If you don't ask me, I'm going to ask you," she told him, dropping to the ground with him.

He popped the ring box open and the twinkle lights overhead made the diamond sparkle.

"Rory, would you—"

"*Beeehhh!*"

A goat ran past. Then another came skidding around the corner of the barn.

Through her happy tears, Rory started laughing.

"Yes." She nodded her head, making the white pom pom on the end of her red Santa hat bob. "Yes, yes, yes."

Drew slipped the ring on her finger and gathered her close, kissing her deeply.

When he lifted his head, he said, "You don't even know what you've just agreed to do. I didn't finish the question."

"Well, I'm wearing a wedding dress to it, whatever it is, so I hope that's okay."

He laughed and cupped her face. "That'll work." Then he kissed her again as goats dressed as sheep ran in circles around them.

Christmas in Autre was most definitely merry and bright... and crazy and chaotic and unexpected and fun and full of love.

Like every other day of the year.

Thank you so much for reading **Head Over Hooves**! I hope you loved Drew and Rory's holiday story down on the bayou! There's SO much more from the Landry family and Autre, Louisiana!

Next is Zander Landry's story!

What happens when a hellraiser turned hot cop is stuck with a headstrong heiress he's determined to protect...and resist?

A run-away bride, wearing a freakin' tiara, and carrying a stolen lion cub, of all things. This was *not* how rowdy, bad-boy-turned-small-town-cop, Zander Landry expected his day to go.

He *really* didn't expect his night to end with her sleeping in his bed after her near-kidnapping.

But his intense attraction to her and the feelings of protectiveness she stirs up? Oh, yeah, he knew those were coming.

She's stunning, whip-smart, and trouble with a capital T.

Which means, he needs her to head right back the way she came. ASAP.

His town is exactly the way he wants it . . . crazy and trouble free.

Well, the crazy trouble he's not related to anyway.

Stranded in a tiny town in her half-million-dollar wedding gown with no money and no place to go . . . today is going pretty much *exactly* the way Caroline Holland expected it to.

But the grumpy, tattooed, oh-my-god hot cop being the answer to all her problems isn't at all what she expected.

Now that she's turned all the criminal (and obnoxious) info

about her exotic-animal-dealing ex-fiance over to Zander, she can kick back in a hammock with some sweet tea and relax.

Or not.

Turns out Caroline's not the spoiled heiress Zander thinks she is. The gorgeous hellion wants in on the action and soon discovers just how dirty things can get in the bayou. And the bedroom.

More and more, Zander just wants her safe on the sidelines. But Caroline isn't going anywhere until justice is done.

It's a clash of wills that's gonna get hotter than a crawfish boil in July. And the most fun the Landry family has had watching sparks fly since . . . well, the last book.

Check out **Say It Like You Mane It** now!

Now read on for the special bonus holiday novella... **Oh, Fudge**, from the connected series, Hot Cakes!
Find out how Paige Asher ended up in Autre and all wrapped up with Mitch Landry!

OH, FUDGE

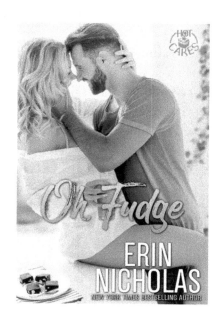

A one night stand, small town, rom com!

Paige Asher likes her men the way she likes her coffee: hot, slightly sweet, and only *to-go*.

The hot friend-of-a-friend she had a scorching single night with was just about perfect--tall, rugged, with a sexy drawl...and on the road out of town by six a.m. the next morning. Long before her mom could start picking out wedding flowers.

But now she can't stop thinking about the Louisiana boy. His texts make her smile and she suddenly has a craving for gumbo all the time...hot and spicy and far from home.

Mitch Landry had no idea Iowa would be so *hospitable* to a visitor. He knew the Midwest had a reputation for friendliness but his welcome gift--a sassy, sweet blond who is as no-strings-attached as he is--was a dream come true six months ago.

But why is he still texting her? And why did he jump at the chance to come back to Iowa? And why is he so annoyed by her obvious phobia to commitment this time around? And why is he pretty sure leaving Paige this time is going to be one of the hardest things he's ever done?

Damn, is this what falling in love feels like?

Oh, fu...fudge.

CHAPTER 1

He had the best hands. Big, hot, slightly callused, causing a delicious drag over her skin. And confident. This guy knew what he was doing when he put his hands on a woman.

His big palm slid up the side of her thigh to her hip, then under the edge of her half sweatshirt onto her bare skin. The hot touch made her suck in a quick breath and then let it out in a soft moan as he ran his hand up and down her ribs.

As his hand was moving, so was his mouth. He dragged his jaw along her neck to her collarbone, the scruff on his face abrading her skin and sending goose bumps dancing joyously down her arms and tightening her nipples.

"Paige."

She loved the way he said her name. Low and needy. The deep voice combined with the slow Louisiana drawl made heat pool in her belly and then slide lower, making her feel achy and tingly. In spite of the fact that she was wearing loose, soft, comfortable yoga clothing—a sports bra, a half sweatshirt that hung off her shoulder and had been washed so many times it felt like cashmere, satiny soft leggings, no panties so as not to pinch or restrict any motions, and nothing on her feet—she was aware of every bit of her clothing rubbing and pressing and she wanted to tear them all off. She *needed* to be naked. She needed to be free to wrap herself around him and feel every inch of him against every inch of her. She wanted his hot skin and his possessive hands and his wet mouth and—

"Paige!"

That wasn't a deep moaning sound. That was a sharp whisper.

Paige's eyes snapped open.

Piper Barry, a friend and one of the women in her afternoon yoga class, was staring at her with wide eyes.

Paige abruptly came back to the moment.

And the yoga class she was teaching. Or that she was *supposed to be* teaching.

Damn. She'd gotten caught up in dirty daydreams about Mitch Landry.

Again.

She never did that. *Never.* Guys were fun, no doubt about it. She loved guys. She loved the things she did with guys—and no, she didn't mean sex. Okay, she didn't *just* mean sex. She did love sex. But she also loved dancing and... okay, she loved men for sex and dancing. Still, that wasn't *just* sex.

But she didn't *daydream* about men when they weren't around.

She cleared her throat and straightened her spine. No more prolonged periods of meditation. She needed to kick this class up a notch. Take her mind off Mitch. And the fact that he was going to be here in two days. After not seeing him for six months. And four days.

She also *never* kept track of how long it had been since she'd seen a guy.

Of course, all the guys she typically saw for sex and dancing she could see any time. For the most part. They didn't live a thousand miles away in another state like Mitch did.

That was probably it. She just wanted what she couldn't have.

The sexy, sweet texts didn't help though. And the fact that the one night they'd had together had been the hottest she'd ever had. And the fact that—

Piper cleared her throat.

Right. Yoga. And the fourteen people facing Paige at that very moment waiting for her next instruction.

"Deep breath in. Feel your ribs rise," she said in her soothing   I've-got-your-peace-and-enlightenment-right-here voice. And as if she hadn't been having them sit and quietly center themselves for the past several minutes. And as if her heart wasn't racing and her nerve endings weren't popping and her brain wasn't full of rugged, big-handed, slow-smiling, how-about-you-bend-over-the-end-of-the-bed-so-I-can-hold-on-to-that-sweet-ass-while-I-fuck-you Louisiana-boy thoughts.

Paige shook her head and forced herself to move her class, and *herself*, through the next three poses without any thoughts of how great dirty talk was when done with a soft drawl.

Paige moved them from their beginning sitting pose to their stomachs and then into their first standing pose.

She caught Cam McCaffery eyeing Whitney Lancaster's butt appreciatively.

She could understand how it might be distracting having your girlfriend in yoga class.

If Mitch were here, bending over, or behind her watching *her* bend over... Paige wobbled as her thoughts drifted again, and she pulled in her core and forced her mind onto her practice.

She *loved* yoga. She never had trouble concentrating like this. She looked forward to her practice so she could block out all of the thoughts racing around and the distractions that grappled for a hold on her attention. She was a master at blocking it out. It was why she'd gotten into yoga in the first place.

"Pull your navel toward your spine. Roll your shoulders forward, up, and back. Hug your elbows in, and squeeze your shoulder blades in, together, and down."

Her life in tiny little Appleby probably didn't seem stressful to anyone looking at it from the outside. Appleby was a sweet Midwestern town where everyone looked out for each other. Local businesses were supported. Neighbors brought casseroles over when someone was sick or a family member died. There were town festivals—including the Apple Festival starting tomorrow—and holidays were not just family events but entire community celebrations.

Paige's family had lived in Appleby for generations. Her sister Josie lived in the house that their great-great-grandparents had built when they'd first come to Appleby.

All of that was why Paige did yoga. And collected cats. And drank vodka cranberries.

A lot of cats. And vodka cranberries.

"Now inhale, lift, and lengthen up through your spine," she coached softly and steadily.

Fred, a big, long-haired, orange cat, came strolling past her mat and stopped to have his head scratched. Which she did while still holding her pose, engaging her core, and breathing. The cats were part of the practice, and everyone who came to Cores and Catnip knew they'd be joined by feline classmates.

The cats lounged and watched. Or wound their way between participants, getting petted and cooed over. Sometimes they'd choose a mat and join one class participant for the duration. Sometimes they made their rounds. Sometimes they slept and sometimes they played.

The yoga studio was a cat café and adoption center as well. Actually, Paige's business had *started* as a cat café and adoption center. People could come in, get coffee, smoothies, and healthy treats—oatmeal, multigrain bars, cereal mixes, and low-fat muffins—and work or read with a cat curled up by their feet or in their lap. She ran a used-book swap and offered free Wi-Fi. It had been a great idea. People especially found it interesting since her sister worked at the local bakery, Buttered Up, a business that had been a part of the town for more than fifty years. Buttered Up offered all the typical treats—cupcakes, full-fat muffins, cookies, scones, and pies. Josie was a master baker and decorator. Buttered Up's offerings were absolutely delicious. And a sharp contrast to the food that Paige offered. But she and Josie had fun with it, and recently Josie had started her own side business and now made healthy muffins and bars for Paige as well.

That was just one example of how her family was interwoven into everything Paige did. She loved and hated it.

Her family was here. Everywhere. All of them. All the time. She couldn't run an errand without running into someone she was related to. She couldn't go to the doctor's office without her family knowing—her aunt was the head nurse. She couldn't even dance with a guy without her mother wondering if it was serious and telling her how nice his grandmother/sister/mother/aunt/cousin was. Or how bitchy his grandmother/sister/mother/aunt/cousin was. Sometimes a girl just wanted to *dance* and for it to have nothing to do with his female family members' dispositions.

Actually, a lot of the time a girl just wanted to dance with a guy without involving their families and the fact that his mother once hit her mother in the face with a dodgeball in PE class. On purpose. Or the fact that his aunt was the best Sunday school teacher her sister had ever had.

As if those were reasons for her to get involved, or not get involved, with a guy.

But this was what she lived with. She couldn't have the doctor check her for a rash without her mom and grandmother calling. She couldn't grab a low-fat yogurt without her dad telling her she needed to worry less about her weight and that she should just have a steak or burger once in a while. And since her apartment was upstairs from her yoga studio, heaven forbid someone park their truck along the curb overnight. She'd absolutely have family members asking about who had spent the night and picking up bridal magazines from the bookstore.

This was all absolutely why she did yoga. And collected cats. And drank.

"Keep the bright and energetic lift. Focus on your foundation. Awareness in that front foot," she encouraged, checking on the class. "Hips level. Then lift that back leg slightly."

Why was she thinking of all of this now though? She could always push all of that out of her mind.

But it was like Mitch had wedged open the door she normally shut and locked while she practiced, and that little crack was letting all kinds of thoughts sneak in.

She couldn't wait to see him. She almost wished that he *hadn't* texted to let her know he was going to be in town again. He could have just shown up and surprised her. That probably would have been better.

She wouldn't have spent the last couple of days cleaning her apartment and shopping for food that he could eat while they were holed up together—he did *not* seem like the tofu and edamame type—and juggling her schedule and coming up with lies to tell her mother and various other relatives when they wanted to know why she wouldn't be at the Apple Festival on day three.

She wasn't going to tell them that she intended to spend day three in bed. All day. Naked. Wrapped around a hot Louisiana boy who turned her insides to pudding and made her smile stupidly over his texts as if she were in high school again.

Without warning, she would have just rolled with it the way she usually did when a certain feeling or mood struck her. He could have put up with her dust bunnies and could have gotten food to go from downtown, and she could have just left him in bed to go teach a class or two.

Except leaving him would have been *very* difficult.

"Elongate from the top of your head to your tailbone," she reminded the class. "Then reach."

Bernie, the gray-and-white, short-haired cat, jumped up on the windowsill next to Paige and meowed before yawning widely.

She smiled at him and reached to scratch under his chin. She had to really stretch, pulling in her lower stomach, breathing, and challenging her balance to give him the love but that was one way the cats were such a fun part of the yoga classes. Just having them around also made people smile more, and it was scientifically proven that spending time with animals brought blood pressure and stress levels down.

Paige heard someone clear their throat and with her fingers still grazing Bernie's chin, she glanced toward the door.

Her eyes went round, both arms dropped, and her back leg dropped while her supporting leg gave out. Her brain just stopped keeping her upright. All of her mental energy was immediately focused on the man in the doorway.

She fell to the mat, and the entire room gasped and dropped their poses as well.

Piper was beside her a moment later. "Paige! Oh my God, are you all right?"

Mitch is here! He's here! Early! Already! But he's right over there! Yay! Gimme!

But she simply pushed her hair back and gave Piper a smile. "Yes, of course. Bernie threw me off-balance."

Piper eyed the cat who was still on the windowsill, now licking a paw and looking entirely unconcerned about, well, anything. Typical.

"Did you... hurt yourself?" Piper asked.

"Nope."

ERIN NICHOLAS

The rest of the class was leaning in as if to hear, and Cam and Whitney moved closer.

"I just got a little distracted," Paige said softer. She caught Whitney's eyes, then Piper's, then looked toward the doorway.

Mitch was leaning against the doorjamb. He was wearing faded blue jeans and an olive-green t-shirt that she knew matched his eyes. They wouldn't be able to tell from here but it was exactly the right shade. His hair was a little shorter than the last time she'd seen him, but he still had the short beard and, even more dangerous to her libido, that smirky half smile that said he knew she'd just fallen down because of him.

He wasn't wearing a jacket even though it was January. She assumed he had one. Though it never got all that cold in Louisiana. Not heavy-winter-coat cold anyway. And yes, she'd looked that up. She'd freaking done research about where this guy lived. That was... crazy.

He did, however, have boots on. They weren't exactly winter snow boots. More like scuffed-up work boots. But they'd keep his feet warm while tramping through the six inches of snow that blanketed Appleby currently. One booted ankle was crossed cockily over the other as he leaned against the door-frame watching her unfold herself from her yoga mat.

His arms were also crossed as if he were settled in to watch the rest of the class.

As if their thoughts were connected, his eyes traveled over her as she stretched to her feet again. A flash of heat went through her as he took in what she was wearing.

The same outfit, essentially, that he'd stripped her out of the last time he'd been here.

I love this fucking sweatshirt. The way it hangs off your shoulder, tempting me with these sweet tits right underneath. He'd hooked his finger in the neckline of the sweatshirt and pulled it down underneath her left breast. He'd pulled her bra up and then fastened his dirty-talking, hot mouth right on her nipple.

182

Now that nipple tingled with the memory and the sight of that mouth just a few feet away.

Piper and Whitney both looked in the direction that Paige was clearly looking.

She grabbed them both, forcing them to look back at *her* before the entire class swung to look at Mitch.

"Don't—"

But it was too late. The other twelve people in the room turned as if they'd choreographed it. Mitch didn't even blink. All he did was lift one hand in a little wave.

Even that made her hot.

He was laid back. God, she loved that.

She needed that.

Not that she needed *him*. Or wanted him. Not like that. She didn't want a man. Not long term for leaning on or anything like that. She shuddered. She was twenty-two, for God's sake. In spite of the fact that her mother and grandmother were convinced she was going to never love anyone the way she loved cats—a fact she hadn't disputed—she had time.

But she *appreciated* spending time with laid-back people. And if those people also said deliciously dirty things, and *did* deliciously dirty things, to her while also making her laugh, then... yeah, that was good. Really good.

Before he headed out the door and got back on the road with his truck pointed south. Very far south. Out of reach and out of you-should-bring-him-to-family-dinner-on-Sunday range.

She couldn't help but smile as everyone turned back to face her, their eyebrows up, a mix of questioning and curiosity and *oh, good for you*. That mostly came from Piper and Max—the big, burly gay man who looked the exact opposite of anyone you would see in a yoga class but who had *amazing* core control and balance.

Yeah, Mitch Landry was something to look at.

Hot. That was just the best word. Hot. Rugged. He clearly worked outside and was completely comfortable in worn denim and t-shirts that molded to his lean, hard, muscled body that could do things that she hadn't ever had done to her before.

He was older than her. Twenty-seven to her twenty-two. And his, ahem, experience showed. She also appreciated that. Along with his laid-back-ness.

She knew more about his sexual skills, of course, since 90 percent of the time they'd been together they'd been naked and doing a lot more than talking.

But when he'd asked for her number and she'd told him that she wasn't looking for anything serious he'd said, "*That* mouth, those eggs, and you don't want any strings attached? I take back everything I've said about the perfect woman not existing."

Yes, he'd complimented both her mouth—and the blow jobs it had given him—and the eggs she'd made him the next morning. Well, at 4 a.m. when they'd finally taken a break and realized they were hungry. He'd added a shit ton of hot sauce to his, but he'd said that had nothing to do with the eggs and everything to do with the fact that his Cajun roots had ruined his taste buds for anything less than a six on a zero-to-ten heat scale.

Then he'd looked her up and down and said that was why when he'd seen the blond who was a ten out of ten on the hot scale he'd had to have her.

It was corny and predictable. But even as she'd rolled her eyes, she'd laughed and maybe even blushed a little. Mostly because yeah, he'd *had her*.

"So looks like the guy is here to check... your heating system," Piper said, stepping forward onto Paige's mat and putting her hands on her shoulders, making Paige focus on

Piper's face. "I'll finish the class for you so you can go talk to him."

"Oh, um..." The guy and her heating system...

"He's not from here," someone in the class said.

"I want to get his card though," someone else—someone *female*—said.

That snapped Paige out of her stupor.

Shit. She couldn't have Appleby-ites standing around gawking at Mitch and wondering what he was doing here.

What *was* he doing here? He wasn't supposed to be here for two more days. And it was still early. Or, at least, it wasn't past closing time which was when he was supposed to come by. So she needed to hide him.

She headed for him. "Right. Yes. Mr. Landry. Thanks for coming on short notice. The heating..."

She got close to him, and those green eyes actually twinkled at her. *Twinkled.* Just like the twinkling lights in the big front window in the lobby behind him. His grin grew too. And then she was close enough to feel him. Not with her hands. She didn't reach out and grab him, though she was *itching* to. But she could just *feel* the electricity in the air as she got close. The heat. The chemistry. The magnetism that seemed to pull her body toward his.

He straightened away from the doorframe, his six feet and four inches towering over her. She wasn't as short as her sister or mom, but she needed heels to get to five seven. And she hated heels.

God, he was big. She remembered the way he could lift her and shift her, the way he could position her body *just right*. The way he could...

"The heating?" he asked.

She licked her lips. Right. She'd been talking. About something. "The heating... thing"—Fuck, what did you call the thing that heated a building—"is in here."

She grabbed his sleeve, wanting, *needing* to touch him, and pulled him with her into her office. It was a tiny space behind the front desk. She didn't really need an office except as a place to put stuff. Extra mats and foam rolls and... okay, it was more of a storage room. She did most of her bookwork on her computer while on her couch upstairs in her apartment.

She tugged him inside and shut the door behind them. The furnace... fuck, *furnace*, she hadn't been able to come up with the word *furnace?*... was not in here, but she was hopeful that the people in her class didn't know that or hadn't seen where they'd gone for sure.

"Mitch, I..."

He was right there, all of a sudden, his big body caging her in against the door, his forearms braced on either side of her head, his heat, his scent, his just-being-*him* right there. Finally. After all these months. And, well... to hell with it.

She lifted on tiptoe, put her hand at the back of his neck, and kissed him.

He gave a deep growl and returned the kiss.

And. Then. Some.

CHAPTER 2

Six months. He'd been without soft lips, soft curves, soft skin for six months. Because the only lips, curves, and skin he wanted had been in Iowa.

Of all places.

Mitch pressed Paige against the door behind her, gripping her hips, and kissing her deeply.

God, he'd thought about her every single day since he'd met her last July. Her bright, sparkling blue eyes, her silky blond hair, her sweet breasts and ass, her sassy mouth, the way she kissed him and touched him like she couldn't get enough either, the way she returned his dirty talk and her humor.

She was perfect. Fucking perfect.

Even though she lived one thousand and forty-two miles away from him.

Which just made her all the *more* perfect. Okay, a few less miles would have been good so they could have met up before six months had passed, but there had been no worries about bumping into her downtown after their hot night together, that was for sure. There'd been no chance that his grandma, Ellie, would return her bra to *her* grandma after Ellie borrowed his truck and found it tucked between the seats.

Yeah, that had happened once.

There'd been no chance of Paige bringing him a pie the next day and sitting on his porch waiting for him to get home. For two hours. And then him showing up with another girl.

That had also happened once. Or twice. The second time the woman had brought brownies, not pie. But still.

Those things wouldn't happen with Paige though. Mostly because he hadn't had even a flicker of interest in another girl since setting eyes on Paige Asher.

But also because Paige wasn't a bake-a-pie-from-scratch-and-show-up-at-a-guy's-house kind of girl. Or brownies. At least, not ones that didn't have zucchini and almond flour in them. She'd only had vegetables and yogurt in her house the next morning when he'd gotten up. No sugar. Not even syrup for the pancakes he'd offered to make. She also hadn't had any regular flour.

She'd also been pretty fine with him getting right on the road and out of town, sans pancakes. So, no, he did not think she'd show up at his house with pie. And she definitely wouldn't wait two hours on his porch swing for him.

Though she might throw the pie in his face when she saw him with another girl the very next night. That's what Abby had done, and he couldn't say he blamed her.

Paige moaned into his mouth, and her fingers slid into his hair, gripping his head and stroking her tongue against his hungrily.

Mitch slid his hands to her ass, clad in the yoga pants that molded to those curves and made him certain that yoga should be a spectator sport, and lifted her.

Her legs wrapped around his waist and he leaned in, pressing her between the door and his hard-as-wood cock. She gasped as he ground into her, wiggling her hips in response, rubbing against him wantonly.

He could easily hold her petite frame with one hand and the press of his body, so he slid a hand up under the short sweatshirt she wore.

This damned thing drove him crazy. Was it coincidence she was wearing the same shirt she'd had on in the kitchen when he'd left her spent and panting on her kitchen table in July? Maybe. Maybe she had a dozen of them. Or maybe it was fate.

She'd come into the kitchen that morning when he'd been rifling through her cupboards, trying to pull together breakfast, in yoga pants and that sweatshirt falling off one shoulder and showing flashes of the smooth skin of her stomach and low back as she moved.

He'd picked her up and pulled that sweatshirt down, sucking on her nipples, making her writhe against him almost instantly, before laying her back on the kitchen table and fucking her thoroughly.

She'd come hard, twice, before his ride pulled up at the curb.

Best. Breakfast. He'd. Ever. Had.

Now he slid his hand up to cup her breast, finding the nipple hard behind the sports bra she wore. She moaned as he plucked at it. She had fantastic nipples. Gorgeous. Sensitive. Playing with them made her pussy clench in the most delicious way.

He pulled the front of the bra down, needing bare skin. The position didn't give him a really good look, but he could feel that soft mound and the sweet, hard tip. He squeezed her nipple as he kissed her and felt her knees tighten around his waist and her press against him more insistently.

"Mitch," she rasped as he dragged his mouth from hers to kiss his way along her jaw to her ear.

"I need to be inside you. I want to talk and catch up too, I swear, but I need to feel you."

"God." She gave a soft half laugh, half moan. "Yes."

"Here? Now?" He'd take her wherever she'd let him have her. But he was aware they were just a few feet and a couple of thin walls away from her yoga studio.

"I want to say yes," she said, letting her head fall back against the door as he kissed down to her neck and then licked the satiny, sweet-smelling skin.

"So say yes."

"I have... people."

He grinned against her collarbone as he rolled her nipple and squeezed her ass. She hadn't been able to come up with the word "furnace" earlier either.

"Those people can find the door," he told her.

He didn't care if she stopped long enough to get rid of everyone. He got it. He wasn't a *complete* Neanderthal. But he also didn't really do a lot of customer service or making-nice in his job. He worked for his cousins and grandparents and was pretty behind the scenes. His cousins ran a swamp boat tour company, Boys of the Bayou, down on the bayou in Louisiana. He did general repairs and cleanup and odd jobs on the buildings and boats and other vehicles they needed for the business. His grandparents ran the local bar and he did the same for them. Basically he was the go-to guy for anything nonspecific that came up for either business and he just took care of it. No matter what it was. He loved it. He was behind the scenes, had a flexible schedule, was valuable to his family's businesses, but also the businesses weren't going to fold if he wasn't there. It was nearly perfect.

"I need to..." Paige started, but then he shifted her, hoisting her higher and put his mouth on her nipple. "Oh. My. God." The words came out on a soft breath and she arched closer to him.

He knew she was hot and wet now, and he could easily slide inside her sweet body and take them both to the peak within a matter of minutes. If he didn't move his mouth down to her clit and make her come before he fucked her.

They'd only had one night together but they'd covered a lot of bases. He knew her body pretty well and, because she was *so* willing to tell him exactly what she liked, he had a good feel for how to wring every drop of pleasure out of her tight, wonderfully flexible body.

"If you stay in here with me, I'll let you sit on my face," he said against her nipple.

She loved oral sex, but she liked to be on top, controlling the angle and the pace and telling him what to do while she held her pussy above his mouth.

God that had been hot. He'd been *very* willing to follow her directions.

She gave another little groan-laugh. "Suddenly I don't even remember why I thought I should leave this room. Ever."

"That's my girl." He sucked hard on her nipple, ignoring how great it sounded to call her his girl. That was stupid.

Just then the doorknob rattled, and the door shook slightly as someone tried to open it.

"Paige?" a woman's voice called.

Mitch's head came up and he met Paige's eyes. She put a finger to her mouth.

He glanced at the doorknob that rattled again. There was no lock on that knob. The only thing keeping the door shut was their body weight against it.

He pulled Paige's bra back up over her breast, with a touch of regret at having to cover it up, then straightened her shirt.

"Paige Elizabeth! What is going on?"

Paige took a breath and called. "Just a second, Mom!"

Mom? *Mom?* Well, shit.

Paige wiggled against him and he let her slide to the floor.

She licked her lips and smoothed her clothes as she pushed him back.

"Are you all right?" the woman asked through the door. "What is going on?"

"I'm just... rearranging the office. I've got the desk in front of the door!" Paige told her. She was frowning and sounded annoyed.

Yeah, he was annoyed too—and very uncomfortable behind his zipper. Mitch adjusted himself and then noticed the door-knob turning.

He quickly moved, leaning into the door, playing the part of a desk, preventing Paige's mom from opening the door.

Paige rolled her eyes. Then she crossed to her desk and shoved it across the floor a few inches, making the scraping noise that her mom would surely hear.

"I'm coming!" she told her mother. She faced Mitch and pointed at him, mouthing. "Hide."

He widened his eyes and shrugged, silently asking, *Where?*

She pointed behind him and he looked over his shoulder. There was a closet. A very small closet. He looked back at her, one eyebrow up. He was a big guy. All over. Something she'd not only enjoyed physically but that she'd commented on more than once when they'd been together. He'd inherited his six-four and wide frame, but he also did manual labor for a living. Working on the bayou just kind of naturally lent itself to brawn.

"Paige!" her mother snapped through the door again.

Paige came close and whispered, "Look, if you don't want to have to propose to me at family dinner on Sunday and have a spring wedding and have constant discussions about which family name we should use for our first child's middle name between now and then, you'll get your cute ass in that closet and stay quiet."

Proposals, Sunday family dinner, wedding planning and

family names used as middle names... all of that was *way* too familiar. He knew exactly what she was talking about suddenly.

He was going to learn more about her family once they were alone—seemed they had something in common besides burn-the-bed-up sex—but yeah, for now, he could hide out.

He gave her a nod and turned for the closet and slipped inside. Barely. It was definitely a tight fit.

The tiny space was filled with hoodies and coats, a couple pairs of boots on the floor, and a shovel—he assumed for the snow outside, which, he couldn't deny, made him grin. He'd never spent time in a place that got regular snow and that was going to be fun.

The door had barely closed behind him when he heard Paige open the office door.

"Good heavens!" her mother said. "I was starting to get worried."

"I'm fine. I was looking for some... files... and got to rearranging and had the desk in front of the door," Paige said.

"You look flushed. Are you feeling okay?" her mom asked.

Mitch grinned. She did look flushed. But she was feeling just fine. Well, horny, he'd bet. But not sick.

"I'm *fine*," Paige said, sounding exasperated. "What are you doing here?"

"Why aren't you doing your class?" Mrs. Asher asked.

"Because I had something to take care of in here."

Again, Mitch grinned.

"Shouldn't you take care of your business things and files and rearranging between classes?" her mother asked. "You don't have *that* many classes to start with."

Mitch could hear Paige's sigh even through the closed closet door.

"Mom, I'm handling my business just fine."

"But if you have to pay someone else to lead a class, then it's less money—"

"*Mom*, it's fine!" Paige snapped. "What are you doing here?"

Now Mitch heard her mother's sigh. The dramatic sighing was genetic. Yeah, he could understand that too. He also had very passionate women in his family.

"Your sister said that you had a headache last night and couldn't come over and help the kids with their projects. So I brought you some medicine."

There was a long pause. So long that Mitch thought maybe they'd moved out of the office into the outer lobby and he just couldn't hear them talking any longer.

But a moment later, Paige said, "You mean, you came over here to find out why I wouldn't go help Amanda's kids with their festival projects because you don't believe I had a headache. But you passive-aggressively brought me medicine to pretend to be concerned."

Mitch could have sworn she was talking through gritted teeth.

"Paige, I would never do that," Mrs. Asher said. "I was concerned. You rarely have headaches."

"That's true," Paige said. "Because I'm very good at taking care of my body, and if I *do* have a pain or ache, I have many ways of taking care of it."

"Oils and herbs," her mother said.

Mitch could practically hear the eye roll that accompanied that comment.

"Yes," Paige said. "Oils and herbs. And trigger-point work. And meditation. And rest. None of which I could have at Amanda's house."

"Well, I brought you this in case none of that worked."

"You know I'm not going to use this," Paige told her.

"You don't have to admit it. I won't ask. But you have it just in case you need it. It's your own little secret."

"If I *did* use ibuprofen secretly, don't you think that I would be able to get it myself?" Paige asked.

"Where would you get it? You wouldn't want anyone in town to know that you were using a real medicine."

"First, the things I use to deal with aches and pains *are* just as real as this," Paige said. "And secondly, I'm not trying to say that ibuprofen doesn't work, Mother. I don't judge people who use it. If I needed it and wanted to use it, I'd go buy it at the store."

"You wouldn't," her mother said. "You want people to believe that what you do is the best choice."

"It's the best choice *for me*."

"So you wouldn't go buy ibuprofen at the store."

"Because I don't use ibuprofen. Not because I'm trying to trick people into thinking that what I do works when really I'm using over-the-counter painkillers secretly."

Mitch had to squeeze his hand into a fist to keep from bursting through the door and interrupting. Paige's mother was annoying her and he wanted to intervene.

Which was absolutely ridiculous. He barely knew her, and he sincerely doubted that she needed his help. Plus it was her *mother*. That was not the right first impression to make. Probably.

It was possibly because her mother was meddling and he knew a lot about that. Meddling in the Landry family was like game night in other families. Something they all got together to do on a regular basis.

"How's your head today?" Paige's mother asked.

"Fine."

"So you could help your niece and nephew with their projects tonight?"

"No. I have plans tonight."

"Doing what?"

"Mom, we've talked about this. You don't need to know every single thing I do."

"So it's a boy."

"I'm twenty-two. I don't date boys."

"But it is a date?"

"No, it's not a date."

Mitch grinned. So wild, up-all-night sex wasn't a date in her book? He could live with that. He was hoping for some snow time though, he wouldn't lie. Snow was a novelty to a guy born and raised in Louisiana. He'd seen it twice and it had lasted for about two hours each time. It had been years. When Tori, his cousin's fiancé and the Iowa girl who had introduced him to Paige in the first place, had been preparing him for this trip north in January, she'd talked about boots and coats and gloves and when she'd told him that Appleby had about six inches of snow on the ground currently he'd admit that he'd felt a definite boyish rush of excitement. Maybe he could talk Paige into making a snowman or sledding or ice skating. He had no fucking idea how to ice skate, but he felt that was very winter wonderland-ish and that he might regret returning south without having at least *tried*.

And hot chocolate. He really wanted hot chocolate.

"But it involves a b—man?" Mrs. Asher asked.

"Mom, I said I have plans. I can't help with an art project. That's all you need to know."

"I just care."

"You're just nosy."

"I just think you could help your sister out once in a while."

"I just think my sister could have figured out how to use her birth control before she had little people she needed help with."

"Paige Elizabeth!" her mother gasped.

"You act like that's the first time I've said that," Paige said. Her tone was exasperated but also held a hint of amusement.

Mitch wished he could see her face.

"I'm always shocked when you say things like that," her mother said, definitely sounding shocked. "I keep thinking that you're going to get over this anti-marriage and family thing you have going on."

"Maybe. But I wouldn't hold your breath."

She was anti-marriage and family? Mitch felt his eyebrows rise. A part of him liked that. All the women he knew back home were very pro-marriage and family. He was twenty-seven. The girls on the bayou had been trying to tie him down—or their mamas had, at least—for five years now.

His own family had laid off on that for the most part. Or the attention had been focused on his older cousins. Until recently. His cousins had all spent the past summer falling ass over boots in love. Even his new buddy, Chase, who spent most of his time in medical school at Georgetown, had found himself smitten, somehow. Mitch had really thought Chase would be immune. They'd had a hell of a good time partying together. But Bailey Wilcox had happened and Chase was now a goner too.

Now the attention had shifted to Mitch. No one had yet said anything like, *when are you going to settle down?* But if they knew he was up here visiting a woman he'd met in July and hadn't been able to stop thinking about, they'd all be *very* interested.

There were three things the Landrys believed in with their whole hearts. One, crawfish boils were the way to fix any rift, disappointment or broken heart. Two, everyone's business was everyone else's business. And three, falling in love was the ultimate goal in life... even if you had to do it a few times to get it right.

Mitch couldn't help but wonder what his family would think of Paige. She was a yoga-doing-meditating vegetarian who clearly liked to keep her personal business personal. None of that would make sense to them.

And the Landrys would, most likely, horrify Paige.

He grinned thinking of it. His family was loud, and their idea of meditation was sitting in a boat and fishing without talking for twenty minutes straight. Other than swearing at the fish, and the fishing line, and the tree branches hidden under the surface of the water that messed with those lines.

He'd known Paige was a fling-with-no-strings girl. He'd texted her first and it had taken a couple of days for her to respond. He'd given up on hearing back from her by the time his phone had dinged with the message from her. The message that read *I can't believe you texted me.*

He'd laughed and texted back—right away, incidentally, which might have been a mistake—and said, *why can't you believe it?*

Because I'm not sending you naked photos.

I don't need photos. I got a very good look at everything and I have a VERY good memory.

It had taken a few minutes after that and he'd wondered if he'd screwed up but then she'd replied, *so what do you want?*

And he'd had to really think about that.

Clearly, she hadn't been thrilled to hear from him. She hadn't been waiting with bated breath to see if he'd text or call. She hadn't been flirtatious or encouraging in keeping the conversation going.

At first.

But as long as he was okay with twelve to twenty-four hours passing between messages from her, he did hear from her, and every damned time she made him smile.

He'd ask stupid shit like, *what did you do today?*

And she'd say, *scooped cat poop, did yoga, rinse, repeat.*

He hadn't been able to resist asking, *what about a shower? You probably took a shower right?*

She'd reply, eventually, *I did.*

That was it. Nothing flirtatious or dirty.

Until about three weeks in when, in answer to his question about what she did that day, she texted, *scooped cat poop, did yoga, got off with my vibrator while thinking of you, rinse, repeat.*

He'd almost swallowed his tongue. He'd typed three messages before finally sending, *please tell me the repeat was with the vibrator and thinking of me too.*

Her reply, *Definitely. Twice last night. Once this morning, Once just now.*

She'd texted him *right after* using her vibrator and thinking of him.

Now *that* was what he was talking about.

Strangely, from there, their conversations had gotten more in depth. She'd told him more about her cats and why she loved yoga and she'd even drunk texted him after a girls' night, and, instead of getting dirtier, she'd told him that she wished they'd had more time together and that she'd made vegetarian gumbo. Which wasn't really gumbo at all—how could it be without shrimp or sausage or at least chicken?—but he'd been stupidly touched that she'd tried something from his world and he hadn't had the heart to tell her it didn't count.

He'd told her about the bayou and what he loved about it, how he loved the outdoors, and about his family. Which now, listening to her and her mother, he realized might have been a mistake.

He came from a very big, very nosy, very involved family. If she had too much of that here, she would have very little desire to meet his intrusive relatives.

But why was he thinking about her meeting his family?

That wasn't going to happen. That was the beauty of this situation. She lived *far* away. To see her, it took him miles away from the bayou and his family, and their time together would always be temporary. It would be impossible to get serious. Even if either of them were interested in that at all. Which they clearly weren't.

Suddenly the closet door opened and Paige stood there.

He must have missed her mom leaving.

"Sorry about that."

"No problem."

She grimaced. "I'm not so sure about that."

He reached for her. "I have lots of other things for your mouth to do rather than apologize."

But she backed up before he could catch ahold of her.

"And while I would *very much* like to use my mouth in *all* of those ways and few others, we need to cool it for a little bit."

He frowned, stepping out of the closet. "What do you mean?"

"I mean, there are going to be other family members stopping by over the next few hours."

"There will be?"

"Oh, for sure." She paced away from him. "Mom's suspicious now, and I kind of admitted, stupidly, that my plans tonight involve a guy." She turned back to face him from several feet away. She was frowning. "That was really careless of me, of course. But I blame you."

"Me?"

"You scrambled my brain and then you were just *right in there.*"

"I was totally quiet," he protested around a grin about her scrambled-brain confession.

"Yeah, but you were *there.* Just a few feet away. Being all hot and stuff."

"I was being hot? From inside a closet? With the door closed?" He liked that a lot. And knew what she meant, actually. He'd been very aware of her just on the other side of the door as well.

"Yeah." She shook her head. "It must be the testosterone. You've got so much oozing out all over that it got on the floor and seeped out from under the door and soaked into me."

He laughed softly and crossed the space between them. He reached out before she could move back and caught her wrist, bringing her up against him. He bent to put his face against her neck, breathing deeply of her scent and loving the feel of her hair against his cheek and the way she shivered in his arms.

"The oozing doesn't sound particularly sexy, but I love the idea of soaking into you," he said, gruffly against her ear. "Does it make you hot?"

She sighed. "Yes."

"So you were distracted because your panties are wet, and your pussy is aching knowing that the cock you want more than anything is just a few feet away and is all ready for you."

She shivered again, and her arms went around him as she arched closer. "Yes."

"You want my cock so much you couldn't even come up with a lie for your mama?"

She huffed a soft laugh. "I guess."

"So we just have to hide out while these people stop by. We'll keep the lights off, and I'll just flip you on your stomach while I'm fucking you so you can scream into the pillow."

Paige gave a lusty sigh and then shook her head. "Won't work unless we hide my car. And change the locks."

He pulled back. "They have keys?"

"A few of them. My two sisters do. And one of my friends. She won't give it up though."

"Your sisters might?"

"You don't understand my mother's powers."

Actually, he kind of did. In his case, it was his grandmother, but he understood how manipulative a matriarch could be when she really put her mind to it.

"So what's the solution?"

"I answer the door each time and convince them that nothing is going on and that I was making the guy up and that I'm just a bitch who doesn't want to do art projects with her niece and nephew."

He squinted at her.

She laughed. "You're nice not to ask it out loud, but, yes, they will be able to believe that."

"Your family will believe that you're willing to lie to get out of family activities?"

She shrugged. "They think the fact that I like cats better than people is a huge character flaw and they mourn my lack of maternal instinct. They also think that I'm selfish when I don't want to be Super Aunt. Especially because my other sister Josie *is* a super aunt. And she's completely into romance and marriage and family. It took her until age twenty-five to find Mr. Perfect, but she was always hopeful and open to it. So they never gave her any crap about being single and nearing spinster age." Paige rolled her eyes. "They secretly hope that if I spend time around my sister's kids that it will flip the biological clock switch in me, but the truth is, I'm not that into kids. Even ones I'm related to."

He was from a family where everyone helped raise all the kids, and the kids were as close to their aunts and uncles and grandparents as they were to their own parents. In his case, he was *closer* to his relatives than to his mom and dad. His dad had been a single dad and had happily accepted the help offered from his extended family. Mitch had been an only child but had essentially grown up with a huge family with cousins that felt more like siblings.

His Aunt Hannah had absolutely been like a mother with plenty of influence from his grandmother, her best friend, and his other aunts as well.

He had to admit, as much as he related to Paige not enjoying the nosiness of her family, he didn't really understand her not wanting to be involved in their lives, at least to an extent.

But it didn't matter. He didn't need to know how Paige Asher felt about kids. He needed to know how she felt about incorporating flavored body lotion into foreplay. At most.

"So how's this going to go?" he asked, focusing on her breasts and hips and the fact that it was awesome that she wasn't looking at him as potential marriage material.

She rolled her eyes. "Various people will need to borrow something or drop something off, or they'll claim I wasn't answering my phone, and they *had* to know how I felt about something. So we can hang out and *make out*," she said with a mischievous smile. "But I'll have to stay somewhat dressed, and we won't be able to get *totally* into it until my grandpa comes and goes."

"Your grandpa?"

She nodded. "He's always the last one. Because he's the one I have the hardest time saying no to. Because he's actually sweet and sincerely concerned about me. But once he leaves, we should be good."

"So..." Mitch settled his hands on her hips and brought her close again. "Kind of like the ghosts in *A Christmas Carol*."

She looked surprised, then laughed. "How so?"

"Visitors over the course of the evening trying to teach you something."

She laughed again. "Trying to teach me what exactly?"

"About keeping secrets from your family?"

"Maybe."

"That they care and just want to be sure you're okay?"

She narrowed her eyes and shook her head. "Nope. You can't get soft. If you start to side with them, you're sleeping at Tori's tonight."

He wasn't worried. He knew she wanted him in her bed. He shook his head. "Can't. They dropped me off and left me. I'd have to hitchhike. And I don't have a winter coat," he added with a grin. "I'd freeze my nuts off. And you like my nuts."

"I might like them less if you start to sympathize with my busybody relatives."

He pressed said nuts—more or less—against her. "Nah. You're addicted."

"I've gone without them for six months."

"Ridiculous to go without them any longer," he said with a nod. "I promise not to say nice things about your family as long as you have your mouth or pussy against those nuts."

Her eyes flared with heat. "Hmm... you drive a hard bargain."

He pressed his cock against her. "Very hard." He couldn't pass that pun up.

She licked her lips and he swore that he got even harder. If that were possible.

"So you're up for this?" she asked, emphasizing *up*.

"What I heard you describe was *lots* of foreplay and creativity with prolonged release," he said. He dropped his voice. "Basically it means that you're going to be hot and dripping and desperate by the time you shut and lock that door for the last time. *That* sounds like a fucking fantastic belated Christmas present with a big old red bow around it, sweetheart."

She just looked at him for a long moment.

Sweetheart hung in the air between them.

He wondered if she'd call him on it. She didn't seem like the type to like endearments. She wasn't soft and sweet and romantic. She was sassy and sexy and fun.

And that's what he wanted.

Never mind that he had a package of the pancake mix his grandmother's best friend used in their restaurant in his bag. Just in case Paige would let him make her breakfast in the morning.

"Fine," she finally said, her voice a little husky. "Then you can stay and help me... kill time... in between visitors."

"It will be my pleasure."

CHAPTER 3

S he was playing with fire. And it was so much fun.

Paige was grinning as she stepped in front of the mirror that hung in her office and straightened her clothes and ran her fingers through her hair.

Mitch was here.

It was going to be a pain now that her mother had smelled a secret, but it was also going to be fun. He hadn't batted an eye at the idea of multiple relatives stopping by and repeatedly interrupting their naked plans.

Prolonged foreplay sounded pretty great. Frustrating, of course. But great.

They definitely hadn't done it that way the first time. They'd pretty much made some stupid excuse why they both had to leave the alpaca farm at the same time—yes, they'd met at an alpaca farm—and had barely gotten through her apartment door before they'd ripped each other's clothes off. They'd been fucking up against her door within five minutes. She hadn't *needed* any foreplay. She'd been so, so ready for him.

That had been wild. She'd never wanted a guy that much that quickly.

In spite of the fact they'd met over the back of an alpaca.

Her friend and veterinarian, Tori, had come back to Iowa to gather her menagerie of special-needs animals she'd been collecting to relocate them to Louisiana with her back in March. Her boyfriend, Josh, and his cousin Mitch had come along to help. It wasn't a small feat to move cows and pigs and a passel of cats and dogs a thousand miles to a new home.

But it wasn't until Tori had come back to visit her parents in July—and to take another few goats and another cow back with her—that Paige had met them. She'd simply gone out to Tori's place to say hi. She hadn't expected to get the hottest one-night stand of her life out of it. But she'd been more than happy with how the visit had turned out.

And now he was back. To see her. Tori didn't need his help this time. Yes, she was taking an alpaca back to Louisiana with her, but she and Josh could handle one animal. Mitch was here to see Paige. And that made her belly flutter and her chest feel warmer than it should have.

She shook that off. She needed to just focus. On getting Mitch out of here and up to her apartment before anyone planned a bridal shower and then getting him naked as soon as possible.

"Okay, we'll go out together and pretend to be talking about the heating system," she told him.

"Furnace," he told her with a grin. "It's called a furnace."

She swatted his arm. "Yeah. Okay. The furnace." So he knew that she'd lost her ability to think of the word furnace. It was okay he knew that he affected her. He did. And what would hiding that get her?

"So we're going to talk about the work I did on your furnace?" he asked, somehow making the question sound dirty.

She laughed. "Yes."

"Without any tools?" he asked, turning his empty palms up.

She shrugged. "There might not be anyone outside anyway. But I guess we can talk about the work you're *going to do*?"

He wiggled his brows. "I definitely have a lot of thoughts about what I'm going to do to your heating system."

It was the drawl. It had to be. How did that cheesy teasing make her stomach flip and her want to giggle? It was the most obvious line he could have used. *Any* other guy probably would have said the same thing. But Mitch Landry said it and her libido started dancing to "Single Ladies." And singing.

NO. No, no, no.

He was *not* going to put a ring on it.

"Yeah, so..." She cleared her throat. "Say something about..."

"Nuts?" he offered. "Or screws, maybe? I could talk about things I need to bang. Or pound. Or what a tight fit it will be."

She put her hand over his mouth, shaking her head, telling her libido to knock it off. "How about you make something up about a duct or something?"

She felt him grin behind her hand. His fingers wrapped around her wrist and he pulled her hand back. But not before kissing her palm and sending tiny electric shocks to her belly.

"I can do that," he said.

"Okay, great." Her voice was breathless. Maybe even more so than when he'd had her pinned against the door. What was that?

She didn't want to analyze it.

She took a breath and turned toward the door.

"I really think it's your blower motor," Mitch said from behind her.

She started to snort as she stepped out into the lobby.

And into a small crowd of women.

She came up short, surprised. "Uh, hi, ladies."

There were only three women left over from the earlier class, but the way they'd all swung toward the door and had wide eyes and expectant looks on their faces made them seem more numerous somehow.

Paige felt Mitch stop directly behind her. Not quite bumping into her but not with any real *space* between them.

Her blower motor. Uh-huh.

"I was hoping you could take a look at my furnace too," Linda Ritter said.

To Mitch.

Her gaze had slid right past Paige to the man over her shoulder.

"Oh," he said. "Well... yes."

Paige frowned and turned to face him. "You don't have to do that."

"He's a repairman, right?" Linda asked.

"He's just..."

"Passing through," Mitch supplied.

"But you're looking at Paige's blower motor?" Linda asked. "How long will that take?"

Mitch cleared his throat and Paige knew he was *not* thinking about her furnace. She wanted to elbow him but that would have been very obvious to their little audience here.

"I probably won't be available for anything else until tomorrow," he said.

He sounded as if he actually meant to take a look at Linda's furnace. And Linda was fifty-something, happily married, with four kids, and was a first-grade teacher. Paige thought she *actually* wanted Mitch to *actually* look at her *actual* furnace.

"Tomorrow is fine," Linda said. "We've been at my mom's for the past two days. One more night will be okay. We'd just be so grateful."

Paige frowned and focused on Linda. "Your furnace has been out for two days?"

She nodded. "And with the big storm this week, Larry and Mike have been swamped with work on a couple of roofs that had tree branches come down, so they can't get over to look at furnaces."

This was not good. Linda didn't just need her furnace filters cleaned out or something. She actually needed it repaired. And now, because of her lie about who Mitch was, Linda was going to have the hopes that she'd be back in her own warm home tomorrow night.

"Oh wow, if you're completely without heat, I'll stop by this afternoon," Mitch said.

Paige turned back to him again. She was going to have whiplash. She frowned at him. He just lifted a brow at her.

Did he actually know how to fix furnaces? Huh. That hadn't occurred to her.

"Do you know anything about gas fireplaces?" Melanie Carter asked.

Paige tipped her head, curious about the answer too.

He nodded. "I could take a look."

Paige widened her eyes at him. He widened his eyes back at her.

Damn, he knew about furnaces and fireplaces. That was... lucky. Or something.

Like hot. And not in the those-were-both-ways-people-heated-their-homes way. It was sexy that he knew how to fix things. And that he was willing to go help complete strangers like that.

"Are you in town for a few days?" Carol Lemming asked Mitch.

He nodded. "I am. I'm passing through, meeting up with some friends in a couple of days, but heard there was a great festival here and thought I might stay for a day or two."

"How did you know he works on furnaces?" Melanie asked Paige.

"Um..." Paige was distracted by the *day or two* thing. She'd thought this was a one-night thing again, like last time.

She was going to have to hide him for a day or two?

Except now he was going to be going out all over town fixing things.

Okay, he was going to go to *two* houses and help a couple of people out. But now all of these ladies knew he was here, *for a day or two*.

Her mom was so going to hear about this.

She was absolutely going to have to be *sure* her mother thought that Mitch was *just* a friend of a friend who had taken a look at her blower motor.

In a very not dirty way.

"The friends I'm meeting are mutual friends," Mitch said, when Paige had failed to answer Melanie for too long. "They mentioned that she'd been having some issues here at the studio and I offered to stop by on my way through."

"You're so sweet."

"That's so fortunate for you, Paige."

"Are you single?"

The three responses came right on top of one another, and the question about his relationship status was almost lost.

Almost.

"He's engaged," she said, before she really thought it through.

It was a great excuse for her mother *not* to think Paige should spend romantic time with Mitch for the *day or two*— why had he not mentioned that?—he was going to be in town.

Mitch gave a little choked sound behind her, but Paige covered it by saying brightly, "To Tori Kramer. Do you ladies know her? Veterinarian?"

But that made Mitch choke and cough again.

"Tori and I have been friends for a while," Paige went on, talking quickly so that no one, including Mitch, could insert anything until she'd laid the whole story out.

"She went to Mardi Gras last year and met J—Mitch, and

they kind of fell for each other, but she came back to Iowa, and they made a deal to meet up at Mardi Gras again this year if they were still interested in one another. She was, but she also happened to be down there for her best friend's wedding, and she went to find Jo—*Mitch*, she went to find Mitch again, and all the old feelings were still there and bam, they fell in love and now she's moving down there to be with him."

Paige finished the actually true story about Tori—it just happened that the guy in the story was Mitch's cousin Josh—with a bright smile. "So Mitch is just here, in Appleby, to help with my furnace because Tori told him it went out."

"Oh, how nice," Melanie said. But she sounded disappointed.

Paige frowned at that as well. Melanie was also married but had only been with her husband for a couple of years. Surely she wasn't looking for a hookup with a hot repairman? Well, stranger things had happened.

"It doesn't feel cold in here," Carol commented.

Right. The building was warm. Which was strange if the furnace was out. "Well—"

"It's not *out*," Mitch interjected. "Not exactly. The blower motor just isn't working efficiently. So the furnace is on, but the air isn't circulating as well as it should be."

Wait a second... the blower motor was a real thing? And here she'd been thinking that was a pretty great innuendo.

"So you're staying with your fiancé tonight, then?" Carol asked.

Mitch looked down at Paige. "Well, I was thinking maybe I should stick around here and offer some help with all of the trees and roofs."

Paige gaped at him. "Seriously?"

"Tori will understand," he said dryly. Then he shrugged. "Sounds like it's a town-wide issue. I'm not used to snow, but I know how to use a chainsaw."

"I bet you do," Melanie said.

When Paige glanced at her, Melanie's gaze was on Mitch's right bicep.

Stupidly, Paige found herself moving to block Melanie's line of sight. Not that she totally could, of course. Mitch was a big guy—something she *really* liked about him—but she still felt the need to insinuate herself between him and the other woman.

"But you don't have a winter coat," Paige pointed out to Mitch.

"Know anyone who would loan me one?" he asked her with a smirk that said he'd noticed her move between him and Melanie.

"I—"

"Coats and anything else you need," Carol assured him. "I was going to ask you if you knew anything about electrical wiring."

Paige looked at her. Of course they could come up with coats and hats and gloves and anything else. Everyone in town had multiples of all of those things. Carol had three adult sons herself who probably had coats that would fit Mitch. "Why do you need help with electrical wiring?"

"My booth for the festival has a glitch," the woman said, lifting her shoulder.

"But you had no idea Mitch would be here," Paige pointed out. "What was your plan?" Carol was a friend of her mother's. She would absolutely be reporting all of this back to Dee Asher.

"I was going to do without the lights," Carol told her. "Liam hooked it all up for me yesterday, but then he had to head to Dubuque for work," she said of her son. "I hated to call him back when it all went out this morning. I just thought, since Mitch was here and was obviously so capable, that I might as well ask."

Mitch was already nodding. "I can definitely take a look. No problem."

"Well..." Carol said.

Paige bit back a sigh. "There's something else?"

"It's not just my booth. Apparently, the problem is a wider electrical issue for the whole square. None of the booths have electricity."

"And normally Mike and Larry would be fixing it but they're repairing roofs," Paige filled in, letting a tiny sigh out.

"Mike and Larry work for the city. They're the general repairmen," Linda explained to Mitch. "The branches that came down were on trees in an older part of town. The houses are close together, and the four that were damaged all had older roofs."

"*Four?*" Paige interrupted. "Mike and Larry are crawling around on snowy roofs on *four* houses in this cold?"

Linda nodded. "Roof holes obviously take precedence over lights on the festival booths."

"Well, of course," Paige said. She hadn't known there were people with *holes* in their roofs or that Larry, who was easily sixty, and Mike, who wasn't much younger, were up on rooftops that had icicles dangling and snowy patches. "Why aren't they hiring a roofing company?"

"The trees should have been trimmed back before this happened," Carol said. "That was the city's responsibility, so the repairs are too."

"They're risking Mike and Larry's necks to save a few bucks?" Paige asked.

Carol just shrugged.

"The wiring won't take long, I'm bettin'," Mitch said, his drawl slow and easy, making Paige take a long, deep breath.

She felt his fingers brush against her lower back and found the gesture reassuring.

Of course, he was supposed to be engaged, so she shifted away from the touch.

"I'll get the furnace up and going," Mitch said. "I'll take a peek at the fireplace, check the wiring quick, and then go help Mike and Larry."

That was going to really cut into the naked time they could be having, Paige realized. But she'd not realized they were going to have *days* of it.

What was she going to do with him for *a couple of days* anyway? Besides the obvious. But they couldn't just have sex for forty-eight hours straight. Could they? Of course not. She had to work. For one thing. And if he was off doing other things, then it was less time they'd be together and making her mother suspicious. The Tori story was solid. Her mom knew of Tori. Paige had talked about her often enough. Dee had maybe even met Tori once when she'd been here looking at the cats.

Yeah, this wasn't a terrible plan.

"Oh, you need to go do the furnace first and then help Mike and Larry," Melanie said, waving her hand. "My fireplace can wait. It's not our main heat source."

"And our lights can wait," Carol agreed. "If you can get to it, that's wonderful, but Mike and Larry can use the help."

"Okay, then," Mitch said. "I assume Paige knows where y'all live?"

Paige could tell the drawl affected the other women as well. Their smiles all got a little bigger when he said *y'all*.

"She does, of course," Linda said. "You can stop by any time. If you want to come around dinnertime, I'd—"

"No," Paige cut in on the dinner invitation. For fuck's sake. Linda was going to, what? Adopt him as a pseudo-son? Or had she been eyeing his biceps too? Or was it the drawl?

"No," Paige said again. "Mitch will be fine. He can stop over and look at the furnace tonight and then get in touch with Mike and Larry. Then I'll be sure he's fed tonight."

"And Tori?" Melanie asked. "She'll be okay with sharing you with us?"

"She's with her family tonight," Mitch said. "I was gonna check on Paige's furnace and then head over there, but she'll completely understand if I hang out here and help y'all out."

Blatant lying for her, Paige noted. That should not be sexy. She should not condone lying. Though she had put him in the position to have to. She shouldn't have done that either. She was clearly a bad influence on a man who was turning out to be a really good guy.

This had been a lot easier on her conscience when all she'd known about him was how good he was with his hands and mouth and... other body parts.

"Oh, you'll have to invite Tori over to the festival," Carol said. "And the friends you're meeting up with. Especially after you save the entire thing by fixing the wiring."

Well, *that* was a terrible idea.

Tori would probably love to come. She was now a Louisiana girl, but she'd maybe missed Iowa and the snow and other wintery things her new home didn't offer. But that would mean she'd have to pretend to be Mitch's fiancée. How would Paige get her to do that? And then what would they do with Josh? Make him stay with Tori's family? No. He'd be a hot, single guy in town with Tori and Mitch, and Paige's mother would try to set her up with *him*. That would be more than a little awkward.

"Tori's mom has really missed her," Mitch said smoothly. "As much as she'd love the festival, I'm sure, I think they want to spend every minute together that they can. I don't want her to be even more annoyed with me for stealing her little girl to the South."

A slow, sexy smile accompanied his explanation—that totally fixed the problem *and* kept Paige from having to lie even more—and the other women visibly melted a little.

Paige almost rolled her eyes. Except that she completely

understood what they were feeling. The guy was potent. And quick on his feet. And could, apparently, fix just about anything.

Damn, she was in trouble.

"Well, you still be sure to tell her how her man saved the entire Apple Festival," Carol said.

"It's just a few lights," Paige said with a smile. "I mean, saving the entire thing is a little dramatic, isn't it?"

"It's all of the electricity," Carol said. "It's the light and the sound system for the music and the PA system. It's the outlets that will keep the cider and kettle corn warm. It's everything."

Paige stared at her. "You... didn't say that."

"I didn't want Mitch to feel bad if he couldn't fix it."

"But he might not be able to fix it," Paige said.

"Oh, he can," Carol said with conviction and a huge smile at Mitch. "I mean, I didn't know that when I first asked. It was just a hope that if he knew heating, he'd know electrical. But he's clearly very confident."

Paige agreed that he seemed sure of himself but to pin the success of the Apple Festival on him... a stranger... who had stumbled into the situation... and who she would really like to keep naked in her bed while he was in town...

But dammit, Mike and Larry shouldn't be up on those roofs. Not that they weren't able, but it was *cold*. An extra pair of hands—very capable and strong and big hands—would definitely help them out.

She felt a little pinch at the base of her spine. She looked over her shoulder at the pincher.

"It will be fine," Mitch said, meeting her eyes before looking up at the other women. "I might need to borrow some tools, but I can do whatever needs done."

"Tools aren't a problem," Carol said quickly.

"For sure," Linda added. "Someone in this town will have anything you need. More than one someone, I'm sure."

"Great," Mitch said. "Then I'm your man."

"Yeah, you are," Melanie said, not quite under her breath.

Paige frowned at her again. That was so inappropriate. "Okay, so," she said, stepping forward and gesturing toward the front door, "I'll fill Mitch in on the festival, tell him where you live, connect him with my... some tools."

Dammit. She'd almost said her dad. She was *not* going to introduce Mitch to her dad even in order for him to borrow tools. Her family was going to hear about Mitch soon enough, and she was certain the information would include that he'd been recruited at her yoga studio and that he was engaged to a friend of hers.

Fortunately, the word *engaged* would very likely be used and that would save her from having to answer questions about her interest in him.

But there was a niggle in the back of her mind that said she didn't like the idea of having to pretend she had no interest. Or that he was connected to someone else.

A really stupid niggle.

She didn't *want* them to think she was interested. She wasn't *interested*. Not in a let's-pick-out-bathroom-tile-and-maybe-a-couple-of-kids'-names way. And that's what her mom would think "interested" should mean.

The women filed past her out into the chilly afternoon with various versions of "Nice to meet you, Mitch" and "See you later."

She let the door close behind them and turned the lock. She didn't have another class for an hour, and she could do without any more people ambushing them. What had started with a simple secret visit to town for a quickie had suddenly turned into Mitch helping the entire town with fix-it projects. And saving the entire Apple Festival.

She pivoted back and said, "Come on."

She rounded the front desk and pulled open the door that revealed the staircase to the upper floor where she lived.

Paige was aware of his eyes on her ass as she climbed the steps in front of him, but he didn't touch her or say anything until they were both inside her apartment and she had that door shut and locked as well.

"I'm engaged to Tori?" he asked.

That wasn't what she'd been expecting. "It was the first thing to come to mind."

"It's really that big of a deal your mom think there's no chance anything could happen between us?"

"It really is."

He looked at her for a long moment. Then nodded. "Okay."

She blew out a relieved breath. "Really?"

"I get it."

She tipped her head. "You do?"

"I didn't tell my family about the sassy, sexy blond I was coming all the way up here to see."

She smiled softly. "Why not?"

"Because they've already noticed that I haven't been going out as much, and I haven't had a woman at my place since July."

Her eyes were totally round, she was sure, by the time he finished. Oh boy, huge, flashing, cherry-red sign. He hadn't had a woman at his place since they'd met? She had the impression that not having women over on a regular basis was very unusual. She hadn't been with anyone since she'd met him either and that was giving her a very itchy, uncomfortable, uh-oh feeling. But to know it was the same for him...

"You should definitely go look at Linda's furnace," she said. She crossed the room and grabbed her phone off the short breakfast bar between her kitchen and tiny living room.

She glanced up at him as she scrolled through to find her friend Max's phone number.

Mitch was watching her with an unreadable expression.

She blew out a breath. "You do actually know how to do all the things you told the women you could do?"

"Yes."

"You're sure you can fix all of it?"

"One hundred percent."

She dropped her arm and regarded him. "What do you do for a living?"

"Whatever my grandma's restaurant and bar, or my cousins' tour company, needs me to do. I can fix anything. Motors, electric, plumbing, brickwork, roofs, drywall. You name it."

Without meaning to, she let her gaze travel over his body. His big, hard, muscled body.

In three seconds he was in front of her, crowding close.

"What are you doing?" she asked breathlessly, feeling her body lean into his instinctively.

"You can't look at me like that without me coming over here and taking you up on what you're offering."

"Was I..." She had to stop and wet her lips. "Was I offering you something?"

"This sweet body spread out on that countertop behind you," he said with a nod.

"I was checking *you* out."

"Yeah and wanting everything you know I can do to you."

Well, that was true.

"I... you... need to go get those repairs done."

"You're throwing me out because I freaked you out."

"I..." She pressed her lips together and nodded. "Yeah."

"I haven't wanted anyone but you since we met."

"Yeah, that's... a little freaky."

"You're sorry I haven't fucked anyone else since you?"

God, when he talked like that how was she supposed to stay on topic? Especially the topic of *not* wanting him to be all hers all the time, and to hell with the fact that she was too damned young to be serious about someone.

"Not sorry," she confessed.

"Me neither."

Her heart kicked in her chest. "You're not falling in love with me," she told him softly.

"That would be ridiculous," he agreed.

"It would." But it really should have felt more ridiculous than it did.

"But," he said, "I don't want to be with anyone else. And I'm afraid I might not get over that."

Another kick against her rib cage. And a shot of fear. Because she felt the same way if she were being totally honest.

"You don't want to move to Iowa," she pointed out.

"I don't mind it so far."

She gave a soft laugh. "Give it time."

"Okay."

She sobered immediately. "Mitch—"

He lowered his head and covered her mouth with his. He kissed her long and deep, cupping her face with one hand and her hip with the other in a sweet, possessive hold.

When he broke the kiss long seconds later, he simply said, "Don't freak out."

Too late.

CHAPTER 4

An impressive fifteen minutes later, Mitch was in a bulky winter coat with a toolbox in hand—thanks to Paige's friend Max—and was walking up the front sidewalk to Linda Ritter's house.

He wasn't even sure how that had all happened. It was like Paige snapped her fingers, and everything she needed to get him out of her apartment and, most importantly, out of her personal space, had appeared.

The door had almost hit him in the ass on the way out.

You just want her because she's safe. She lives a thousand miles away and she doesn't want a relationship. It's safe to think you want more than sex with her because you barely know her.

That was all true.

Somehow, it wasn't making him wonder *less* about the men in her life since July.

He hadn't *meant* to be celibate. He hadn't met her and thought *she's the one for me forever.* But all the women he'd met since then had just been, well, *less*.

Which was crazy because he barely knew Paige.

"Mitch!"

Linda's voice calling to him from the porch of the big, two-story house, pulled his attention away from his infatuation with the blond who had practically dressed him in this coat and shoved him out the door.

"Hi, Linda." Mitch gave her a smile and climbed the steps.

"Thank you so much for coming over." The older woman gave him a bright, sincere smile.

"Of course. You don't need to go without heat if I can do something about it."

She looked genuinely touched by that. "But you don't even know us."

"Well, I don't need to know you to know you get cold when it's twenty-two degrees outside," he said with a smile.

Twenty-two fucking degrees. He'd never been in weather this cold. It was great. He certainly wouldn't want to work outside in it on a regular basis, but the air was brisk and fresh and he found it exhilarating.

And he didn't have to know Larry and Mike to know that they wouldn't use that word to describe the weather when they were up on those rooftops trying to mend the holes.

He might not feel exhilarated after he climbed up to help them out either.

"I guess you're right," Linda said. "I really didn't want to ask you, but when I heard you were looking at Paige's furnace…"

"It's completely fine," he assured her, feeling a twinge of guilt over Paige's furnace story. It hadn't even been *his* story. Thank God he did know about heating and air-conditioning. And all of the other things the ladies, and town, needed help with.

He shook his head with a grin as he followed Linda into her house. This was exactly how Autre, Louisiana worked. If someone needed something and you could do it or provide it or help with it, you did. Period. No questions. He liked that Appleby and Autre had that in common. Just with a seventy-something-degree temperature difference separating them this time of year.

It also fit that a Landry would be in town for about two hours and would already be involved in the town festival and pitching in to help. His grandparents would be so proud. His dad too. Sean Landry had always told him, "Don't be any trouble. Help out and do your part. Make 'em glad you're there."

Mitch had been doing that since he'd been a little boy.

Linda led Mitch through the house to the kitchen at the back. The entire house was decorated with an apple theme. The sofa had throw pillows with apples stitched on them and a red-and-white blanket draped over the back. The rocking chair near the window had an apple-patterned cushion. The mantel over the fireplace was decorated with a variety of ceramic apples. The entire room looked like a picture postcard.

The rest of the house was similarly decorated. The dining room table had a red runner down the center with a bowl full apples as a centerpiece. The kitchen even had a set of fat-apple canisters on the counter and a large red apple rug covering the wooden floor.

Mitch took it all in as he followed Linda to the basement door and down the steps. The house was a wonderful, old, two story that was well kept, and it was a damned shame this family hadn't been able to be here enjoying it all because their furnace had conked out. He was happy to be here to help.

He wasn't, actually, the Landry most people called for help with things. Leo, his grandfather, or Sawyer, his oldest cousin, were most often the go-tos. There were plenty of others who were always around and willing to help out, of course, and if Leo or Sawyer couldn't be found, Josh, Owen, Ellie, Cora, Maddie, Kennedy... just about any of the others could be. Mitch was the one the Landrys then called. He was in the background. The supporter. The one who had their backs. Quietly. He could always be counted on and his family knew that. He just wasn't in the town's spotlight. Or anyone's spotlight.

Being a Landry, it was pretty easy to play the wallflower, actually. The Landry clan was loud and boisterous and loved to one-up one another. They laughed and teased and loved and joked loud and often, and it was easy to just sit back and be there without adding to the noise.

"Right in here." Linda led him into the room that held the furnace, water heater, and what looked like box upon box of Christmas decorations.

"Great." He moved to the furnace and set the tools down.

"Do you need anything?" Linda asked.

Mitch could tell she was feeling a little guilty about him being here. There was no way he would have been able to let anyone go cold if there was anything he could do about it, but she didn't know him and didn't know that about him. Paige had already turned down Linda's dinner invitation, which was fine; he'd much rather spend his non-furnace-fixing time with Paige, but he also knew the dinner invite had been about repaying him somehow.

He guessed Linda would try to give him money at some point. Which he would, of course, turn down. But she needed to feel she wasn't putting him out entirely.

"I could use somebody to hold the light, actually," he said, pulling out the big work light that Max had included with the tools. That wasn't completely true. He could have found a way to set it up on boxes or something, but having Linda hold it and move it for him would be helpful.

Her face brightened. "Oh, of course." She took the light from him and plugged it into an outlet a few feet away.

"And you can entertain me while I work," he told her with a

grin as he shrugged out of the coat and tossed it over a box labeled *front yard blow ups.*

He hadn't noticed blow-up decorations in the front yard so clearly they'd been deflated. Which was too bad. He wanted to get this furnace going again so this family could get back to this house and blow those things up.

"Like singing or something?" she asked with a smile.

"That would work. Do you know any Taylor Swift?"

"You like Taylor Swift?" Linda asked, her smile growing.

"Well, and now you know one of my deepest secrets," he said. "So I'm going to have to do a really good job on this furnace so you don't spread that around."

She laughed. "I do know Taylor Swift, by the way. My oldest daughter is a fan. But you do *not* want me to sing."

"Okay, then something else," he said. "How about town stories."

"Stories about Appleby?" Linda asked. "Oh, I can do that for days."

He chuckled. "I figured." He met her gaze. "I'm from a small town too. I know how that goes."

"And you're interested in our little town?"

He lifted a shoulder. "Seems like a good place." He was supposedly engaged to another woman so he couldn't seem too interested in a certain citizen of this town, but he could hope that Linda knew Paige or at least *about* Paige. For some reason, he had the feeling that Paige didn't let a lot of people close. Of course, she'd spent her life here so people surely knew things *about* her.

"It's a very good place," Linda said with an affectionate smile.

People in Autre definitely got a similar look on their faces when asked about their little town.

He crouched next to the furnace and started pulling tools

out of Max's toolbox. "So why a festival in January instead of a holiday festival at Christmastime? Or in the fall when it's warmer?" he asked with a grin, opening the access door on the furnace.

Linda moved in, shining the light over his shoulder on what he was doing.

"Oh, in the fall we have football," she said with a grin. "And Halloween and Thanksgiving and Christmas. People are happy and full of excitement for all of that. But January," she said, shaking her head, "is a long, cold, dark month here in Iowa. We need something to look forward to."

Mitch located the problem in the furnace easily enough and set to work fixing it. "What all happens at the festival?"

"Oh goodness," Linda said.

He could hear the smile in her voice even from behind him.

"It's all about our apples. We have booths with lots of treats. Pies and cobblers and crisps and cookies and cider."

Mitch chuckled. "I'm not sure I've ever fully appreciated all you can do with apples."

"You should certainly stick around. We'll make you love apples. We also have ice skating and sledding and a snowman-building contest and karaoke and sleigh rides and even a snow-ball fight."

"An organized snowball fight?" Mitch asked. "That sounds interesting. Nobody worried about kids getting hurt, huh?"

She laughed. "It's adults doing the fighting."

He glanced over his shoulder. "No way."

She nodded. "Yep. It gets wild. It happens in the town square. It's kind of like paintball. Each team has a different color snowball—watercolor paints work great—and they have to wear white sweatpants and sweatshirts so you can see the colors show up. That's how you know who wins."

Mitch knew his eyes were wide. "That sounds awesome."

Linda nodded. "It's a lot of fun. There are rules and referees, of course."

He was nodding, thinking about his cousins and friends. They would have a blast with a colored-snowball fight. Or any snowball fight. It was really too bad a snowball would last about a minute in Louisiana.

Maybe he'd just have to haul them all along next year to Iowa...

He quickly shut that down and turned his attention back to Linda's furnace. Paige hadn't even wanted to hear how he hadn't been with another woman in six months. She definitely wouldn't want to hear about him planning to come back next winter. And bringing a bunch of his relatives with him. She clearly was up to her neck in relatives as it was.

"I'm so glad you were able to stop by and help Paige," Linda commented after he'd worked for a few minutes.

He didn't miss how his heart gave an extra *thunk* when Linda said Paige's name. Damn, that wasn't good. "Happy to," he said, trying to sound casual about the first woman he'd felt very *un*-casual about in a very long time. "She's a friend of Tori's. That makes her a friend of mine."

That was true enough. He was very fond of his cousin's fiancée. Everyone who knew Tori was fond of her. She was sweet and funny and had a huge heart and the way she loved Josh made her automatically a Landry family favorite. She'd made Josh happier than Mitch had ever seen him. And Josh was generally a pretty happy guy, actually, so that was saying something.

"Well, Paige is... a little difficult but she's wonderful," Linda said.

Mitch glanced at her before he could stop himself. "Difficult?"

Linda nodded. "I teach with her sister, Amanda, and Paige worries her."

"Her sister?"

"She has two older sisters. Amanda is the oldest."

The one with the kids, likely. So Linda was on Paige's family's side. Wanting Paige to settle down and have a family and be happy. "Paige seems to be doing okay."

She was young. He was aware they were five years apart in age and that at her age the idea of settling down and getting married had been completely laughable to him. It still was, really. His life was good. He had everything he needed. He was happy. Was he a little addicted to a woman who lived too far away to scratch his itch as often as he'd like? Well, yeah, apparently. But if that was the worst thing that ever happened to him, he'd be just fine.

"Oh yes, of course, she's doing okay. Her sister just worries about Paige's decisions."

"What decisions?" he asked. Was it okay to be talking about his fiancée's friend? Well, Linda had brought it up.

"She runs a yoga studio. It's not really an... essential business, you know? And she has cats. Lots of cats. Especially for such a young woman... that's different. Every time someone asks her when she's going to settle down or if she wants to have kids, she gets another one," Linda said. "And she's a vegetarian."

Mitch hid his smile by ducking his head to study the furnace. She got another cat anytime someone asked her about settling down. That was funny.

"I thought the cat thing was an adoption center," he commented, his face in the furnace. Tori had actually filled him in on that when she'd explained how she knew Paige. Tori had been the vet to all of Paige's foster cats.

"It's that," Linda said. "Kind of."

"Kind of?"

"Well, she calls it that, but the process to adopt a cat is

crazy," Linda said. "There's a ton of paperwork and she does a home visit and then does follow-up visits after the cat's been adopted for the first six months. Very few people make it past her process."

"Has she ever taken a cat back after letting someone adopt one?"

"She has, actually. Twice."

He couldn't fight his grin this time. That was awesome. "So she's protective of the cats."

"Oh, I think she always intends to keep most of them. That's just her way of pretending to her family that she's *not* a crazy cat lady."

Linda seemed like a nice enough lady. She really did. And he liked her decorating. But he was liking her attitude about Paige less and less all the time.

"Is it a bad thing that she likes cats?" he asked, turning the screw he was tightening a little harder than necessary.

"I suppose not. Her family just worries about some of the things she likes."

"Why?"

"They just worry," Linda said again. "Her business isn't very stable, and she clearly wants to nurture something, but she's choosing cats instead of having a family and she's a vegetarian."

Yeah, she'd mentioned that before too. "So her family worries because they think she's financially vulnerable and that she actually wants children but is filling that need with cats and they're worried she'll..." He shook his head. "I'm not sure why they're worried about the vegetarian thing."

He wasn't sure why they were worried about any of it, frankly.

"Nutrition, of course," Linda said. "They worry about her health."

Right. Well, he knew people who wouldn't understand

someone choosing not to eat meat too, but Paige was twenty-two. And clearly in good health. Smart, sassy, confident. She didn't really need people telling her what to do and questioning her decisions.

And suddenly it made sense why she'd gotten annoyed when he'd pointed out that she might have needed to learn a lesson about interacting with her family.

She clearly had a lot of people questioning how she lived her life. She didn't need a guy—especially one she barely knew—telling her that he thought she needed to give her family a break.

He pushed back from the furnace. "All done."

Linda gave a little gasp. "Really? That's it?"

"Yep. Good to go." Mitch stretched to his feet.

"Oh my goodness!" Linda threw her arms around him, nearly knocking him back into the furnace. "Mitch! Thank you so much!"

He patted her back. "Happy to do it."

She pulled back and smiled up at him. "You're a great guy. Tori's really lucky to have you."

For a second he really regretted the lie. It didn't matter in the overall scheme of things, of course. None of these people needed to know what his relationship was to Paige. Or to Tori, for that matter. But he kind of wanted them to.

Except that he and Paige didn't really have a relationship.

But he kind of wanted them to.

At least enough that it would make sense for him to tell all of Appleby to mind their own damned business and let Paige do what she wanted however she wanted to do it.

Of course, one of those things she wanted to do was to let everyone think he was Tori's fiancé so that they didn't hound her about what was going on between *them*. So he would keep playing along.

He smiled at Linda. "Thanks.'"

Linda led him out, chatting more about the festival and how he should invite Tori and how he should be sure to stop by the booth where she and her best friends would be selling caramel apples. He, apparently, gave the correct responses because she smiled and kept talking. But the whole time he was wondering what the chances were of him talking Paige into going to the festival with him and if he'd be able to keep from holding her hand or hugging her or stealing a kiss if they did go together. That would be inappropriate for a guy engaged to her friend.

The alternative was, of course, to just stay at her apartment. In bed.

But for some reason, as amazing as that would be, he suddenly wanted to go to the festival with her. Too. He definitely wanted the bed time. But he was going to be here for a couple of days. And yeah, he wanted to make her pancakes. And he wanted to walk through a winter wonderland festival and drink hot cider with her too.

Maybe showing up early had been a bad idea.

Or maybe it had been the best idea he'd had in a long time.

He drove Paige's car back to her studio and apartment. The streets were clear and dry, but he wondered what it would be like to drive on ice and snow. Might be kind of fun. Could be like driving through a downpour or thick mud, both of which he'd done plenty of.

He had thought about dropping by the houses where Mike and Larry were working and then swinging by the town square to see if he could figure out what was going on with the electrical wiring down there, but he had to see Paige first.

He'd do all of that. He was used to pulling long days. He simply put together a to-do list at the start of the day and then worked until it was done. He'd do the same here.

But first he needed to see Paige.

He let himself in the side door of the building with the key she'd given him and took the steps up to the second floor two at a time.

He knocked.

It only took a couple of minutes for her to open the door.

She was still wearing the sweatshirt that drove him crazy and those silky pants. She gave him a smile that hit him right in the gut.

He stepped in, nearly on her toes, backing her up, and swinging the door shut behind him.

"How did it—"

He cupped her face and kissed her.

She was clearly startled but only for about two seconds. Then she was gripping his biceps and going on tiptoe and arching close.

This at least made sense.

She was a gorgeous blond with delicious curves who smelled heavenly. *Of course* he wanted her. That was absolutely rational. As were her responses to him. He wasn't too full of himself, not like his cousin Owen, but he knew women found him attractive. He hadn't slept alone for the past six months because there weren't any women interested.

Their attraction was completely reasonable. The rest of it... the wanting to defend her and know her better and *date* her was all completely... unreasonable.

So they'd just focus on the part that he could explain.

He swept his tongue into her mouth as he backed her up against the nearest wall. He slid his hands down to her ass and dipped his knees to fit his cock against her softness.

She gave a quiet moan, and Mitch felt the resultant lick of fire in his belly. He pressed into her, suddenly hungry and completely focused on eliciting that same moan from her again and again.

"Mitch," she whispered raggedly against his mouth as he curled his fingers into her ass.

"Need you, Paige."

"Yes."

That's all he needed to hear. He slid his hand up under the sweatshirt that teased him with glimpses of her skin whenever she moved. He drew it up, making sure his big palm met as much of her silky skin along the way as possible. The soft cotton bunched as he dragged his hand up her rib cage, causing her to suck in a breath, and then around to her back and up to her shoulder blades.

He lifted his head, needing to see everything now. "Arms up," he commanded softly.

She met his eyes as she followed his direction. Her arms stretched up so he could whisk the sweatshirt over her head. He tossed it to the side, his gaze on the gorgeous breasts behind the pale blue sports bra.

He cupped her breasts firmly, the wide band circling her ribs, and crisscrossed over her upper back, and, honestly, he had no idea how to get it off. There were no hooks or snaps or zippers. It occurred to him that he'd never removed a woman's sports bra. He'd seen them, but now that he thought about it, those must have been in photos or something. Most of the bras he'd been up close and personal with were of the tiny, silky, lacy type. That was interesting. Kind of.

Paige must have read that he was stumped in his expression because she laughed lightly and then gripped the bottom of the spandex piece and pulled it up and over her head.

Just pull it off. Noted.

Then he was all about the naked breasts. Because he was really, like most guys, always all about the naked breasts. But Paige happened to have a pair of the best he'd ever seen.

"God, you're gorgeous," he told her gruffly as he studied her.

"Thank you." She reached for one of his hands and brought it to her breast. "Touch me, Mitch."

"Fucking gladly." He cupped her, running his thumb over her hard nipple and relishing her moan.

She leaned into him, kissing him as he played with her nipple, rolling it and plucking and squeezing just hard enough to get a quick gasp and then a louder moan.

He'd just bent his knees and taken a taste when there was a knock at her door.

CHAPTER 5

They both froze.

Then Paige's head fell back against the wall.

"I told you," she said.

Her family. Stopping by as predicted.

He pulled in a breath. Well, fuck.

He straightened. "Okay."

She stepped around him and bent to grab her sweatshirt, pulling it on sans bra. He quickly grabbed that up too. Then she was pushing him toward the bathroom. "Hide in the shower."

"What if they come look in there?"

"Josie was here while you were gone. She brought some leftovers from their dinner last night." Paige rolled her eyes. "She checked out the kitchen. You know, to see if there were two wineglasses or signs that another person was here eating with me. So *this* is Amanda and she'll fake that she needs to borrow clothes so she can check out my bedroom and see if the bed is unmade or if there are men's socks on the floor or something."

He grinned as he stepped into her tiny bathroom. "They're predictable."

"Painfully so," she said with a nod. Then shut the door on him.

He looked around, then down at the bra in his hand, then sighed. And took a seat on the edge of the tub.

"Hi, Amanda." He heard Paige greet her sister.

The apartment was tiny, and he appreciated how well that allowed eavesdropping.

"Hi! I can't stay long but wondering if I could borrow your pink sweater?"

"Oh, a sweater? Sure," Paige said.

Mitch smirked. A sister here to borrow clothes. She'd nailed it.

"Let me go grab it," Paige said.

"I can get it. No problem."

Mitch heard her move past the bathroom door on the way to Paige's bedroom.

"Sure, help yourself to anything," Paige said.

Mitch could almost picture the eye roll.

"What do you need the sweater for?" Paige asked, her voice a bit louder as if she was standing outside the bathroom and calling down the hall.

"I was going to wear it to help at Emily's Girl Scout booth at the festival."

"Oh, okay. So, like under your coat where no one would see it anyway."

Mitch didn't think Paige was buying it. He grinned.

"Well, it will be nice and warm," Amanda answered, her voice louder. Clearly she'd moved closer to the bathroom door again.

"Sure. That makes total sense," Paige said.

Mitch guessed her older sister noted the touch of sarcasm in her voice.

"So... things seem nice and warm up here," Amanda said.

"Yep."

It now sounded like they were standing right outside of the bathroom.

"I mean, you're hardly wearing any clothes."

"I'm wearing what I wear to teach yoga. Which I was just doing."

"So no problem with the heat?"

"Nope, toasty warm, thanks."

"Well, I wouldn't want you to be cold up here. All by yourself."

"I appreciate that. But I've got ways to stay warm."

"Right."

There was a pause. "Okay, so, you have the sweater."

"Yep."

No one was moving. They were definitely still standing outside the bathroom door.

"So I'll see you at the festival maybe."

"And you can't stop over tonight and help the kids?"

"Sorry. I've got stuff to do."

"You don't look like you're getting ready to go out."

"I didn't say I was going out."

Finally, Amanda sighed. "Okay. Thanks for the sweater."

"No problem."

Wow. Mitch had to admit, Paige was good at holding her ground.

He listened to them move to the apartment door and say goodbye. He heard the door shut but waited for Paige to come give him the all clear.

"You can come out," she finally called.

He pulled the door open. She was leaning against the back of the sofa facing him.

"When I came back over here, I meant to tell you that I'm sorry I tried to tell you how to handle your family earlier," he said from the doorway. He needed to tell her this before he got closer to her. Because then he'd touch her. And once he touched her, he'd kiss her. And once he kissed her, he'd be done talking except for telling her to take her clothes off and bend over.

And he really did want to tell her this.

He also really wanted to ask her on a date to the festival, but he *was* going to resist that urge, dammit. Neither of them wanted to date. Even if there wasn't a thousand miles between them making *dating* pretty much impossible.

They wanted to have a hot I'm-only-in-town-for-a-couple-of-days hookup. *Maybe* they would call it friends with benefits, if he could come up with other reasons to come to Iowa from time to time. But other than accompanying Tori on her trips home to see her family, he couldn't really think of anything. And he wasn't sure that tagging along with Josh and Tori for the next twenty years or so made a lot of sense.

Paige crossed her arms and watched him. "What do you mean?"

"Earlier I told you that you needed to maybe give your family a break because they care about you. That was not my place. I don't know your family. I don't know how things work with your family. I don't get to tell you how to act or react with them. I'm sorry about that."

Her eyebrows were up by the time he finished.

She dropped her arms. "Wow."

He stepped out of the bathroom. "I was going to go over and check in at the town square but I had to come over and tell you that first. And then..."

"You kissed me." She gave him a little smile.

He nodded. "Well, that was your fault."

"My fault? You started it."

"No. You opened the door."

"I let you in."

He took a step closer. "Yeah, but that meant you were within reach. And whenever you're within reach, I kind of forget about everything else but touching you."

She took a little breath, her smile fading. But she was still watching him intently. "Now, see, usually when guys say stuff like that, I find it pretty intense and consider it a red flag and immediately want to get some space."

He tucked his hands into his pockets and nodded.

"But with you... I don't want space."

Mitch felt his chest tighten. "You pushed me out of this apartment pretty quick when you found out I hadn't been with any other women."

She pressed her lips together and nodded.

"You didn't think that was pretty intense?"

She nodded again.

"And it made you want space, right?"

She took a breath. "I pushed you out before I could tell you that I haven't been with anyone since we were together either." She paused. "*That* made me want space."

Mitch let that sink in.

She hadn't been with anyone else either.

She hadn't been with anyone else either.

She hadn't fucking been with anyone else either.

He felt a little like beating his chest and shouting, *Yes!*

But he simply cleared his throat and said, "I'm not going to say I'm sorry."

One corner of her mouth curled up. "What would you be sorry for?"

"Ruining you for all other men."

The other corner of her mouth tipped up and she shook her head. "That's not what I said."

He nodded. "But that's what happened."

"I wouldn't put it quite that way."

"I would."

She lifted a brow. "Well, you would be wrong."

"I don't think so."

"So I ruined *you* for all other women?" she asked, crossing her arms again.

"Yeah. I'm pretty sure."

Her eyes widened. "Now *that* makes me want space."

He shook his head and stepped toward her. "You can't ruin me and then push me away."

"Oh, I think I can."

"That's just cruel."

He stopped right in front of her. He didn't touch her. But he saw her take a quick breath in. Her arms were still crossed, but she was watching him with wide eyes, her pupils dilated.

"This can't get serious," she said quietly.

"I know."

"We live too far apart."

"I know."

"And I'm... too young to be serious."

"I know."

"And I'm a vegetarian who doesn't have a real job and collects cats."

Yeah, all of those life choices that made her happy that everyone had been judging and questioning and being *concerned* about. "I know."

"I just want to do my own thing. How I want to. When I want to. I don't like explaining everything I do, and I don't like defending my choices that don't really have anything to do with anyone else and don't hurt anyone."

Mitch felt his chest tighten again. A woman had never done that to him. Well, a woman he wanted to sleep with anyway. The women he loved—his cousins and aunts and grandmother —made him feel protective and like he wanted to fix things. But he'd never felt that way over a woman he was dating. Certainly not a woman he'd had a one-night stand with. Which was what Paige Asher was essentially.

"I know," he said again. "You shouldn't have to explain yourself or defend your choices."

"So a long-distance relationship would be difficult," she said. "You'd wonder what I was doing when we weren't together. You might not like it if I went out with another guy. And I wouldn't want to explain any of that either."

No, he really fucking wouldn't like it if she went out with another guy. And no, it really wouldn't be his damned business.

He nodded. "You're right about that too."

"Which part?" she asked.

"All of it."

"You wouldn't like it?"

"Absolutely not."

Her expression was *I knew it*. "But I shouldn't have to explain that. We would be seeing each other, what? Twice a year? Maybe?"

He nodded. "You shouldn't have to explain that."

"So it would be better to just not think this was anything more than a hookup while you're in town with Tori." She actually sounded a little sad about that.

Which made sense to him. He definitely felt a little sad about it. Which was really dumb. What had he thought this could possibly be?

"We should really get on with this hookup thing, then," he said, reaching for her and catching the front of her sweatshirt in his fingers and pulling her up from the back of the couch.

She went willingly, and he whipped her shirt over her head before bringing her in to kiss her. She slipped her hands under the edge of his t-shirt, running her hands up his sides and making his skin heat instantly. She traced her fingertips over the ridges of his abs, sliding up to his chest and then his shoulders, gripping them and using them for leverage to arch closer.

Mitch let her go long enough to jerk his shirt over his head, then lifted her against him, feeling her breasts pressing into his chest.

Her arms went around his neck, molding her to his body as he gripped her ass and walked them to the breakfast bar that separated the living room from the kitchen. He set her on the edge of the counter and pulled his mouth away to kiss down to the breast he'd left wet and needy when her sister had knocked.

He sucked and licked, making her wiggle against him. Her fingers dug into his shoulders. Her pants and gasps heightening his own need.

He tucked his fingers into the top of her yoga pants and started to slide them down.

"Lift up, sweetheart."

She did, immediately—he really did love how compliant she was to his commands during sex—and he slid the pants down her legs.

She didn't wear panties with her yoga pants.

He paused, studying her completely nude body.

"Panties ride up and pinch," she said as explanation.

"I'm a huge fan of yoga, if I haven't mentioned that before," he said.

She smirked. Then spread her legs farther. "Because of yoga, I have fantastic core control. Which includes my pelvic floor," she informed him.

"That might be the hottest thing anyone's ever said to me," he told her, stepping between her knees.

She laughed. "That's maybe a little sad."

He cupped her ass—he really loved her ass—and dragged his beard against her jaw. "Well, maybe I should explain that what I *heard* you say was *Mitch, I can grip your cock and milk it with my pussy to the point it will make your eyes cross, and you might not be able to walk afterward.*"

He felt her throat work as she swallowed hard. "Well, when you put it *that way...*"

He chuckled, kissing her neck, then biting down gently on the spot where it curved into her shoulder. "I mean, you *can* grip me like a fist with that sweet pussy, right, Paige?"

"Oh... yeah," she said, breathlessly.

"Show me." He moved his hand down along her thigh, then shifted his hips so he could move his hand to cup her, sliding his middle finger over her clit.

She moaned and tipped her head back, moving her thighs even wider.

She was so sexy. So open. Not just literally opening her legs, but in this, at least, she was willing to be vulnerable. She wasn't trying to cover any part of her body or hide anything. She was bare naked on her kitchen counter with daylight spilling in through the big window across the room.

Of course, she had nothing to worry about. She was gorgeous. Tight and trim, with lots of smooth, sweet skin and curves in all the right places.

He circled her clit, loving the way she tried to get even closer to his touch. She braced one hand on the counter behind her, using it to lift and press closer. He lifted his head to watch her face as he teased her. She was so responsive. Hungry and greedy and yet had been so willing to please him in every way last time they'd been together as well.

Watching her, he moved his hand so his thumb continued to rub that sweet spot as his thick middle finger slid into her.

His knees nearly buckled. As if *she* were touching *him*. Her pussy was tight and so fucking hot. Wet. Sweet. She did, indeed, grip his finger as he pressed inside.

Her throaty *yes* made his cock ache and he pumped his finger deeper.

"Oh God, Mitch."

He added a second finger. "Show me that amazing core, girl," he told her.

Her head was back and her eyes closed, but she smiled at that. Then tightened her inner muscles around his finger.

Damn. His cock was screaming *mine*. He wanted to plunge deep and hard. Then he wanted to fuck her slow and steady. He wanted to feel all of that sweet heat gripping and clenching around him.

Just then there was a knock at the door.

They both stiffened in shock.

No. *No.* Not now. They couldn't just leave her the hell alone?

Her thighs instinctively started to close. Not that they could with him standing between them.

He put his mouth to her ear. "You're not going anywhere."

His finger was still buried inside her. He moved it in and out to remind her.

"But..."

"Shh..." he coached softly. "I can't let you go, sweetheart. I can't leave this sweet body like this. I need to feel you come apart."

Her pussy tightened around his finger. Yeah, she wanted this too.

There was another knock.

Her body stiffened but he stroked her—her back... and her pussy. "Ignore them. Concentrate on me."

Wow. That sounded pretty damned great. Certainly at this moment, but just in general. Maybe she just needed someone who could make her not think about them and their seemingly constant demands and "worry" that she was doing things wrong.

He kept his mouth against her ear. "I love your body. I could lose myself in you for days." He moved his fingers as he talked, feeling her body relax and soften around his fingers and against him.

He thought he heard another knock, then he heard, "Paige!"

"I want to make you come like this," he said in her ear,

circling her clit. He bent to take a nipple in is mouth, sucking hard as he pumped his fingers in and out. Then he said, "Then I want to turn you around, bend you over this counter, and fuck you from behind."

"Yes, I want that," she said, her pussy tightening.

Okay, good, she was with him.

He put his mouth on hers. "But you have to stay quiet," he told her. "Can you come quietly?" he asked, kissing her before letting her answer.

"I don't know," she said, teasing back, even though her voice was ragged.

"Let's try it. I don't mind if the world hears me make you come apart," he confessed.

"You can't let up on me a little? So I don't scream?"

He loved that she was teasing him even as she was on the brink of an orgasm.

"I can't let up on you," he said, shaking his head and looking into her eyes. "I need you dreaming about me when I'm not here."

She wet her lips. "I don't think you have to worry."

He liked that. Too much. He gave her a wicked grin. "Prepare yourself for some *very* dirty Zoom calls."

Her cheeks actually got pink. She was bare-assed-naked on the kitchen counter with his hand in the most intimate place it could be, but she was blushing about the idea of a dirty Zoom call? He grinned.

"That's not really having space," she pointed out.

"Nope," he agreed. He wanted zero space.

He'd worry about that later.

Then he circled her clit and she let out a lusty sigh. "Okay."

"Okay to the Zoom call? Or the quiet orgasm now?" He thrust his fingers deep.

"Both." Her eyes were shut again.

"Deal." Then he bent his knees, pulled her ass to the edge

of the counter, and put his mouth on her clit, licking and sucking as he finger fucked her.

"Oh, oh, oh..."

He looked up. She was gripping the edge of the counter, her eyes shut, her bottom lip between her teeth.

"Be quiet, sweetheart," he coached with a grin.

He had no idea if whoever had stopped by was still outside her door. And he didn't care.

He sucked on her clit again and curled his fingers and pumped in and out and suddenly her hand flew to his head, gripping his hair as her thighs tightened around him and her pussy clenched and she let out a long, but very soft, "Yessssss."

He released her clit with a gentle lick and then slowly eased his fingers from her body. He looked up at the most beautiful sight.

She was leaning back, propped on her extended arm, her chest rising and falling with her rapid breaths. Her eyes were shut, her cheeks flushed, and she had a smile on her face.

He rose and her eyes opened. She watched as he lifted his fingers to his mouth and licked the taste of her from them.

"Wow, that's dirty," she said appreciatively.

He just grinned. "You're amazing."

"I'm—"

Her phone started ringing.

She stopped. Rolled her eyes. Sighed. And then laughed. "In trouble."

"That's whoever was at the door?" he asked. Jesus, these people were relentless.

She nodded. "Or my mother wondering why that person told her I wasn't here."

She pushed him back and hopped to the floor, again grabbing her sweatshirt and pulling it on. It didn't cover much. Definitely not the sweet ass he was obsessed with.

Her phone stopped ringing.

"So the bending you over the counter..." he said.

She tossed him a mischievous look over her shoulder. "Well, you did talk about the whole delayed-satisfaction thing." Her gaze dropped to his fly. "But I guess that's more *you* than *me* at the moment."

He nodded, lowering his voice. "Maybe I should barricade the door, hide your phone, and put you on your knees."

Her breath hitched and her eyes heated. "Maybe..."

Her phone started ringing again. With a sigh she reached for it. "Hello?"

She paused, listening.

"No, I'm fine, why?"

Pause.

"I couldn't come to the door."

Pause. She looked at the ceiling.

"Because I couldn't. I don't just sit around here waiting for one of you to stop by, you know."

She frowned as she listened to the reply.

"Of course I know that."

She listened again, taking a deep breath. "Yes, I have plenty of eggs. Have him come back over."

She disconnected and gripped her phone tightly, before meeting Mitch's gaze. "You want to hide in my bedroom closet this time? Since Amanda was already in there, my Uncle Tim won't check in there when he stops by to install my new showerhead."

"You need a new shower head?" Mitch asked. "I could install—"

"No," she stopped him. "I don't need a new showerhead. But that's a good reason to check the bathroom for signs of a 'guest'. My sisters already checked the other rooms." She looked around. "I mean, everyone can see the living room."

Wow, these people would impress his family if he were being honest. All of this was Landry-level meddling.

"Well, how about I head to the town's square now?" he asked, pulling his shirt on. "That way I'm *really* not here and I have an alibi."

She smiled but sighed. "I really prefer you here without the shirt on."

"Ditto."

"But, yeah, okay."

"The square is close enough to walk to," he said. "I'll slip up the alley and won't even need to move your car."

She frowned. "It's really cold, Mitch. And you'll need the toolbox, right?"

He arched a brow. "I can carry a toolbox four blocks."

"But... it's cold. You've got Louisiana blood. You might not make it a block before you're an ice cube."

"Sweetheart—" He pulled her up against him and kissed her. "That Louisiana blood means I've got enough stubborn and cayenne in my system to keep me going for a long time in the cold."

She went on tiptoe to kiss him again, then said, "Well, maybe get *a little* cold so I can warm you up when you get back."

"I'll *never* be too warm to not need you warming me up." He squeezed her ass, then let her go, grabbing the coat he was borrowing and heading for the door. "If I swing by to see how Mike and Larry are doing too, would that give your family time to send everyone over that needs to stop by and check on you?"

She narrowed her eyes and put her hands on her hips. "It's bugging you that there's work that needs to be done and you're not helping, isn't it?"

"Well, I mean, it's *cold* out, and those boys probably haven't eaten enough gumbo in their day to counteract it."

She laughed. "Fair enough." Then she nodded. "Yeah, I think Tim will stop by and then maybe my grandpa. He'll want to check the furnace and be sure you did a good job."

Mitch paused with a hand on her doorknob. "Your grandpa can fix furnaces? Will he think it's weird you didn't just ask him in the first place?"

She shook her head. "He'll just roll his eyes and tell me that I don't have to be so damned independent all the time and that I can ask family to help out and I don't always have to hire help."

"You hire help instead of asking your family?" He immediately regretted the question and his raised eyebrows.

She frowned. "I do. It's my business and my apartment. I can handle taking care of it."

"You're an independent little thing, aren't you?"

She lifted her chin. "I am."

"Noted."

He was *not* used to that. Everyone he knew leaned on everyone else he knew. That was just the way of it. But *everyone* helped *everyone* out. Each person did their part. If someone couldn't fix a furnace, they could sure as hell make an amazing étouffée, or would help with plumbing or painting, or would do your laundry. Or they might just tell you when you needed to pull your head out of your ass when you needed it. Which was, honestly, a lot more helpful than being able to fix a furnace. Anyway, it wasn't as if anyone was a freeloader or getting away with anything.

"And don't call me a little thing," Paige added. "That sounds patronizing as hell."

Also noted. He nodded. Then gave her a little grin. "You know, with that attitude, you'd fit right in with the bayou girls."

"Oh yeah?"

"They don't take any shit from anyone."

She tipped her head. "And you respect that?"

"Completely." He shrugged. "It's what I know. Of course, if I *hadn't* respected it, my grandma would have smacked me upside the back of my head. *And* made me clean up after the crawfish boils for a month. By myself."

"Big job?"

"Very."

She smiled. "Well, with *that* attitude, I might let you stick around."

He really wanted to. *A lot.*

But as the words hung between them, and he felt that she was thinking about maybe clarifying that she meant *for a couple of days*, he quickly pulled on his coat, gave her a wink, and stepped out the door before she could.

He was in so much trouble.

CHAPTER 6

He thought about that as he walked with Max's toolbox in hand on the way to the town square. He *didn't* want Paige to point out that this was a couple-of-days-only fling? Hell, shouldn't *he* have been the one making sure that point was made and made often? That they were absolutely in agreement there? That's how it would have been with any other woman.

That's the way it *had been* with every other woman.

But this one was... different. That was the best word he could come up with and it wasn't a great word, honestly. He was intrigued by her. Intrigued enough that these few days with her didn't feel like enough.

So what did that mean?

He thought about that as he checked the wiring for the multiple small booths and the large main stage that dotted the grassy area in the center of town. The paved walkways that crisscrossed the space had been cleared of snow, and the pine trees that were scattered through the square were decorated with twinkle lights. Those along with the ones adorning the wooden booths and the front of the stage were all dark at the moment, however. As was the lighted APPLE FESTIVAL sign that hung from the archway that declared this the Appleby City Park.

Linda had said there would be music and heaters that needed to be plugged in to keep cider and other treats warm. He also noted tall standing heaters placed among the booths for people to gather around in case things got especially chilly during the festival.

Mitch shook his head. He'd fixed a few furnaces in Louisiana but couldn't say there was much call for large outdoor heaters.

"You must be Mitch."

He turned at the male voice behind him. He smiled at the older man approaching. "Yes, I am. You were warned?"

The man laughed and extended his hand as he came to stop. "I'm Phil Custer. I agreed to help set up the booths and stage and everything here. I was the one that ran into the no-power problem."

The man was in his late sixties or so and wore his long gray hair pulled back into a ponytail under his stocking cap. Even though it was early January and the ground was covered with snow, the man's skin was tanned and wrinkled in the familiar way of so many people who worked outdoors.

"I'm happy to take a look," Mitch said, shaking Phil's hand.

"Good deal. I'm good with hauling and building but not so much with electrical and such," the other man said. "I was an over-the-road trucker all my life. I can look at most motors and know what I'm doing and I thought I could maybe figure this wiring problem out, but this is a little beyond me." He looked around the square with a grin.

"Well, no guarantees that I can make it work either. I know motors and wires and plumbing and all of that," Mitch said. "But sometimes shit just breaks and you gotta start over."

Phil nodded. "That's for sure. Really hoping that's not the case here though. Not sure we've got time to rewire all of it."

Mitch looked around. There was a lot to check out. But if *nothing* was working, it had to be a pretty centralized problem.

Phil showed him around and he got to work.

And thinking.

A long-distance relationship? Was that what he wanted with Paige? Could they make that work? Did he even have the first clue how to do that?

No, he didn't have the first clue. But yes, he thought maybe he did want it. Not the distance so much, but Paige. He wanted her.

He wasn't a relationship guy, really. Short distance or long distance. But hell, maybe long distance was the way to go. He wouldn't have to be sweet and thoughtful every day that way.

By the time he'd found the wiring problem, fixed it, and had the square lit up, the sun had dropped behind the horizon. The glow of the white lights reflecting off the snow made him smile.

"Nicely done!" Phil said, joining him in front of the stage.

"Thanks. Looks good."

"It really does, thanks to you. Everyone will be so happy to know that things will be ready and working tomorrow. Thank you." Phil clapped him on the shoulder.

Mitch couldn't help his grin. This felt good. It was just some electrical wiring. It had taken him less than an hour. But this kind of work always made him feel good.

It was productive and it mattered. It was behind-the-scenes stuff. Stuff that most people attending the festival wouldn't even think about, but it made a difference. *Without* it, people would notice. They'd notice the cold cider and the lack of light and music. Fixing that wiring mattered. Just like fixing broken pipes at his grandma's restaurant and repairing tires on the bus that brought tourists to his cousins' swamp boat tours and repairing the motors on the boats all mattered.

It was stuff that the tourists, and sometimes even his family, didn't really think about but without which, things wouldn't work and wouldn't be as good as they could be.

He didn't need recognition for it. Just seeing those lights glowing and knowing that tomorrow the cider would be hot was enough for him.

"My pleasure," he told Phil.

"If you're going to keep working outside in January, you need to get yourself a good pair of gloves," Phil said, noticing Mitch's red hands.

Mitch rubbed them together and then shook them. "I'll admit I didn't come prepared to be outside in this weather."

"Well, here." Phil pulled his own gloves off. "Damn, boy, I'm sorry I didn't notice before now." He handed the gloves to Mitch.

"Oh, I couldn't have worked with those on anyway," Mitch said, holding up a hand. The bulky gloves would have gotten in the way of the fine work he'd needed to do on the wires.

"They can warm you up now, then."

"I can't take your gloves."

"I've got a dozen pairs at home," Phil said with a laugh, waggling the gloves. "These were just the first I grabbed. I'm not attached."

Mitch grinned.

"And," Phil went on, "I'm guessing you might have more need for them. Once people find out that you saved the festival, you'll have more people with things that need fixing calling you up."

Mitch wasn't so sure about that, but he had planned to stop and see how Larry and Mike were doing on the roofs about two blocks away. He took the gloves. "Okay, if you're sure."

"You bet," Phil said.

Mitch pulled the gloves on, then shook the other man's hand.

"See you at the festival tomorrow," Phil said.

Mitch just nodded. He hoped so. If Paige wanted to keep him in bed all day he wouldn't exactly object, but he was now very interested in this festival. Hell, he even kind of liked the cold weather. He wasn't sure he could live and work here, but if he had a hot, sassy blond at home to warm him up after a day in the cold, it might not be so bad.

He was actually thinking about how he could *live* here?

He was definitely in trouble.

Because as nice as this little town seemed and as charming as the snow was, he couldn't leave his family. They needed him. Sure, they could find someone else to do the things he did for them, but... he wanted to be the one doing it. He owed them everything, and he wanted to take care of them in return.

But Paige might like the heat...

Fuck. He had to stop thinking about either of them relocating. That was ridiculous.

He headed up the block, determined to focus on fixing the roofs and then going back and stripping her naked and stopping all this craziness that included words like *long term* or *committed* or *relationship*.

"Hey, guys," Mitch greeted as two older men came toward him across the snowy front yard of one of the big old houses that Max had described to him.

"You must be Mitch," one of them said with a smile.

"Yeah. Can I lend a hand?"

"Actually, we're done."

The men stopped in front of him, looking pleased.

"Already?" Mitch asked, looking up at the roof of the house behind them.

"Seems some of the ladies mentioned to their husbands

and sons about a total stranger offering to help us out and they felt guilty, and a bunch showed up to help us get things done."

Mitch grinned at that. "I didn't make the offer to guilt anyone else into helping."

One of the men laughed. "Even better. You just pricked at their consciences."

"But we appreciate your willingness," the other man said. "Decent of you."

Mitch shrugged. "If I'm able, there's no reason not to."

"Funny that you're not from the Midwest," the taller of the two said. "That's a pretty Midwestern attitude."

Mitch smiled. "Maybe Iowa and Louisiana aren't that different."

Both men nodded. "Maybe not. Nice to know."

They parted ways, also mentioning that they'd see Mitch at the festival the next day.

It seemed everyone in town showed up to the event. Mitch could understand that too. Autre, Louisiana was the same way. If there was a get-together, a party, a celebration... or just a random Friday night... nearly the whole town would turn out.

The crawfish boils at his grandma's bar was one such event. Tourists and locals alike gathered around the ramshackle building and ate fresh-caught crawfish, corn, and potatoes, drank beer and moonshine, and just generally celebrated the important things in life—friends, family, good food, good music, the great outdoors, and the roots and history of the area.

It seemed very much like Appleby. Families stayed close, friends had known each other most of their lives, the community came together in good times and bad, and people appreciated tradition and the little things. Or the things that seemed little but actually mattered a lot.

Paige would be at home in Autre. Sure, there was a huge, noisy, and nosy family to contend with, but he'd love to see her chatting with the other women in his life, charming the men, clutching the side of an airboat and laughing as he opened it up on the bayou, tipping back a mason jar of moonshine, dancing to some good old Cajun music.

Of course, he'd also love the alone time he could imagine clearly. Taking her down to the bank to lie in the bed of his truck to look at the stars. Passing a lazy Sunday afternoon, napping with her in the hammock in his backyard. Cuddling on his couch watching a movie on a Friday night. Going for breakfast at his grandma's before heading out to work. Sneaking in a quickie over his lunch break. Sitting on his front porch with sweet tea and watching the lightning bugs come out.

He was getting incredibly sappy. And too comfortable with how easy it was to picture all of that.

With a sigh, he pulled his phone from his pocket as he hit the sidewalk in front of the yoga studio. He opened Paige's car and tucked the toolbox behind the front seat. Then he slid into the driver's seat so he didn't freeze his nuts off while talking to Chase.

Because, yeah, it was time to call his buddy. The one who was just starting a long-distance relationship himself.

But Chase wouldn't be alone. No one was really ever alone in Autre unless they grabbed a boat when no one was looking, headed out on the bayou, and found a quiet nook.

City boy Chase Dawson, however, would not be able to do that. He was mostly hopeless with boats. Though if he and his stupid frat-boy friends hadn't stolen one of the Boys of the Bayou swamp tour boats and crashed it into the dock, his sister would have never met her true love, Sawyer, and Chase wouldn't have been hanging out in Autre repairing the dock and becoming smitten with the cute, nerdy alligator conservationist Bailey.

The girl he was now head over heels for.

Mitch hit the button that would call Chase, wondering if he

was going to regret this. Chase wasn't going to be able to convincingly talk Mitch *out* of trying a long-distance deal with Paige.

Chase was going to medical school at Georgetown while Bailey worked in Louisiana at her dream job. They were going to do the long-distance thing, with as-frequent-as-possible trips between DC and Autre, with the hopes for a residency in New Orleans.

Mitch expected that Chase would eventually be a small-town Southern doctor seeing everything from fish hooks stuck through thumbs to chicken pox to cancer. And he was going to love it. Which was hilarious considering the guy had gotten pretty green the first time he'd seen them cleaning fish or when Leo, Mitch's grandpa, had pulled a rusty nail out of his own foot.

The born-rich city boy was going to have to toughen up some, but Mitch was thrilled to think his friend would eventually be around for good. It was crazy how well they'd bonded. They had almost nothing in common, and Mitch was about four years older than Chase. Still, they'd quickly become friends, and Mitch missed the dumbass when he was back in DC.

"Dude," Chase greeted on the second ring. "I told you that you should never unzip your pants outdoors in Iowa in January. That's dangerous, man. But you just don't listen."

"So no sympathy at all?" Mitch asked with a grin. "No magic cure?"

"We're gonna have to chop it off," Chase said, sounding sad. Fake sad, but still. "Good thing you had so much fun with it when you did."

Mitch shuddered. "My dick is fine. But the fact that it's on your mind so much is really touching. Weird. But touching."

"Never use the word *touching* when talking about me and your dick in the same breath." Chase paused. "Actually, how about we not talk about your dick and me in the same breath at all?"

Mitch laughed. "Well, I just have to say, if I got frostbite on my dick, your phone would be the first one I'd send the photos to."

"Trust me, that would go out to all my med-school friends, and we'd talk about how guys like you will keep guys like me in business."

Mitch suddenly had a pang of homesickness. Which was strange. He hadn't been gone *that* long. And Appleby was a great place. And Paige was here.

But the thoughts of Paige down on the bayou with him and his family and friends had sunk in deep and quick. He wanted to take her down there. To have her meet everyone. To see how she reacted to cruising along the bayou. To see how much she'd love the otters. Yes, otters.

The Boys of the Bayou's main dock had been adopted by a river otter they'd named Gus. Gus had then gotten a girlfriend. And then they'd had a family. And those otters had moved into a more formal home outside of Leo's old trailer, complete with a plastic swimming pool and slides and everything. Of course, they spent time with animal-crazy Tori and Mitch's cousin Kennedy as well.

That was all temporary though. Mitch was in the process of building a bigger, better enclosure for them as a part of a new side business for the Boys of the Bayou.

Yeah, he wanted to see Paige playing with otters. Definitely. Maybe even more than he wanted to see her in short shorts. So that was... idiotic.

He scrubbed a hand over his face. "I do have a problem," he said to Chase.

"Does it involve your dick?"

"N..." Then he thought about that. It was perfectly fine to

include talk of Paige and his dick in the same breath. "I mean... kind of."

"The girl," Chase said.

Mitch huffed out a breath. He shouldn't have been surprised Chase figured that out. "Yeah. Paige."

"You *just* got there, man."

"Sounds familiar, right?" Mitch asked. He'd been shocked by how quickly Chase had been distracted and fascinated by Bailey.

Chase sighed. "Yeah."

Mitch could hear the grin in his voice. He'd fallen fast and hard for Bailey. In spite of telling himself—and Mitch—over and over that it made no sense. Chase and Bailey were total opposites. Total. Opposites. And Bailey had been pretty unimpressed with Chase's charm and good looks and money. All things that Chase was used to using to get his way with women. Well, with everyone.

Add into that the fact that Bailey and Chase hadn't even been able to execute their first kiss without almost breaking a nose and some toes, and they seemed like a total mess.

But Mitch could tell that Chase was happier than he'd ever been.

"So you're calling for love advice," Chase said.

Oh shit. Chase had just raised his voice slightly. That meant someone, or more than one someone, was close by. Which meant that someone, or more than one someone, was about to chime in.

"No worries, I'm here!" Mitch heard Owen Landry, one of his cousins, say.

"Where are you and Owen?" Mitch asked, praying they'd snuck down to the dock with a couple of beers to escape the chaos that was every Landry family get-together.

"Ellie's," Chase said.

There was a rise in noise on Chase's end of the phone, and

Mitch realized that Chase had ducked into the back room or just outside to take the call initially. And now he was back in the main room of Ellie's bar. Where *everyone* would be.

"You're a bastard," Mitch told him.

"This will just keep me from having to repeat everything later," Chase said with a laugh.

No one had a big enough house for them all to really spread out and chat and eat. They'd gather together for gift opening, practically sitting on top of one another, but for meals and hanging out, they'd all move over to the bar.

The building was really just an extension of Ellie's home in many ways. Most family meals were served there, and every member of the family stopped in at the bar at some point during the day. If Ellie and Cora, her best friend and business partner, didn't see everyone at least once a day, they got worried and sent someone to hunt the missing person down. And drag them in for some grits. Because grits were good for everything —happy, hungry, feeling sick, feeling awesome, lonely, sad, or newly in love.

"So what do you need to know?" Owen asked.

Mitch realized he was now on speakerphone. Great.

"I just..." He blew out a breath. What the hell? Owen was also madly in love. With a sassy, smart, too-good-for-him woman named Maddie. Owen might actually have some advice. "I guess I'm thinkin' about a long-distance relationship."

"They suck, man," Chase said.

"You don't even know," Mitch told him. "You *just* officially got together with Bailey."

"And I already know it's going to suck," Chase told him.

"But you're gonna do it anyway?"

"Well... yeah." Chase sounded like that was a really stupid question.

Maybe it was.

"Why's it gotta be long distance?" Owen asked.

"Because..." Well, fuck. Because it would be crazy for one of them to move to be with the other at this point.

"If you're doin' things right, she's not gonna want to live without you," Owen said. "So start doin' things right."

"If I remember correctly, Maddie was ready to move back to California even after *you* were doing things."

Owen laughed. "'Cause I wasn't doin' things *right*."

"I'm not sure I want details about what you were doing wrong," Mitch said dryly.

"Oh, nothin' like *that*," Owen said, clearly catching his meaning. "Trust me."

"So what?" Mitch asked, hoping he wasn't making a mistake.

"I just had to figure out that living anywhere *with* her was better than living at all *without* her. It just works out."

"So your advice is to move to Iowa to be with a woman I've known for like two days. Other than a few months of texting."

"What's the worst that can happen?" Owen asked. "It doesn't work out and you move back here."

"That's..." He really should have finished that thought with *crazy*. Or *ridiculous* would have fit too. But Owen had a point. Didn't he? Mitch could move to Iowa. He wasn't in medical school. He didn't own a business he couldn't move. He had a huge family that he'd miss like hell, but was this thing with Paige at least worth giving some more time to?

"I'm good," Owen said. "I know."

"She hasn't exactly asked me to stay," Mitch said.

"Well, she can't really *keep* you from moving somewhere. You're a grown man. She can't keep you out of Appleby," Chase pointed out.

"That doesn't seem a little stalkerish?"

"Why do you boys always make this all so difficult?"

There was now a new voice in the conversation. And Mitch would know that voice anywhere.

Ellie. His grandmother. The tough, no-bullshit matriarch of the Landry family.

"Tell her what you're thinkin', Mitchell," Ellie said. "Don't be weird about it. Just say, *I think I'm crazy about you, and I want to find out if this can work out.* For God's sake."

Mitch could picture her rolling her eyes at them all. He also knew she had her hands planted on her skinny hips.

"You all make this seem like some huge mysterious, magical thing. You don't have to wait for planets to line up or for some big sign like your favorite song to play just as the full moon comes up over the hill when the scent of lilacs drifts through your window."

Now she was most definitely rolling her eyes.

Owen laughed. "You and this family are the biggest fuckin' romantics in the entire universe, Ellie."

Yes, they all called their grandmother Ellie and their grand-father Leo. Because *all* of their grandparents on both sides of the family lived in town, so simply referring to them as "grandma" and "grandpa" had never been specific enough.

"Sure, we're romantic," Ellie said. "We know when it's right and we're willing to go big when that happens."

It was true that the Landrys were known for their grand, romantic gestures. It was countywide legend, actually. But he supposed that didn't mean they thought the falling-in-love part was all that complicated.

"Well, I won't tell Cora that you think her love potion is bullshit," Chase said.

Cora made all kinds of "potions". She also made balms and salves and other homemade "cures". The thing was, even skep-tical physician-to-be Chase had to admit the stuff worked. Mitch fully expected Chase to incorporate some of those things into his medical practice when he came back to Autre for good.

"Oh, she knows it's bullshit," Ellie said. "Who would believe a love potion? You can't *make* love happen."

"But... wait... what else of hers is bullshit?" Chase asked.

Mitch snorted and heard Owen laugh as well.

"Oh honey," Ellie said, and Mitch could picture her putting her hand on Chase's cheek.

"The only stuff that's bullshit is the stuff that doesn't work," Ellie told Chase placatingly.

"But..." Chase was clearly thinking on all of the things he'd tried while in Autre. "All of it worked. Didn't it?"

"Then I guess it's all real," Ellie told him.

"That's not how science works," Chase said. He sounded tired.

The Landrys had that effect on people. Chase was still getting used to them all.

Ellie laughed. "Oh well, we aren't talking about science."

"Then what are we talking about?"

"Love."

"Love isn't science?" Chase asked.

"Is it?" Ellie challenged in return. "You tellin' me that what you're feeling for that beautiful accident-waitin'-to-happen over there is all just synapses and endorphins?"

"Well..." was Chase's only response.

Mitch assumed that Bailey, who was indeed a beautiful accident-waiting-to-happen, was across the room and Chase was now gazing at her adoringly.

Mitch shook his head even though he was grinning.

"Exactly," Ellie said after a moment. "You've probably had your hormones get all stirred up before. Chemistry and what-ever. But what you feel for Bailey is different. And I don't think you can explain it with science."

"But," Chase tried again, "science is real."

"Well, of course it's real," Ellie said in her no-shit tone of voice. "Germs and stuff are real. You come out of the bathroom without washing your hands or cough on my bar without covering your mouth, and I'll slap you upside the head and cut you off from gumbo for a week."

"So..." But Chase didn't add on to that start.

"So science and things beyond science can both be true at the same time," Ellie said.

"Then Cora's potions and creams do actually work?" Chase asked.

Mitch knew his friend was rubbing his head.

Ellie blew out an exasperated breath. "I'm tellin' you that you boys are bein' nitpicky dumbasses."

"Dumbasses?" Chase repeated. "To want to prove something is true?"

"Good lord," Ellie muttered. "Do you need a research paper to tell you something is working if you can see it and feel it with your own eyes and heart?" she asked.

"If millions of people use condoms and there are fewer women gettin' knocked up, then you know that the condoms are working, right? If people start wearin' seat belts and more people walk away from car crashes, you know the seat belts are working. If you burn your hand and put a salve on it and it feels better the next day, then it worked to make your hand feel better. And if you find a woman who makes you think about turning your whole life upside down to be with her, then you're falling in love with her." Ellie's voice softened. "Nothing changes a life more than love does."

"I..." Chase trailed off. "Yeah. I guess you're right."

Ellie scoffed. "Of course I'm right. I'm old. I know a lot of shit by now."

There was a pause and the sound of shuffling on the other end of the phone.

"Well, there you go," Chase finally said to Mitch.

"She's gone?" he guessed.

"Dropped her knowledge and then went to harass someone else," Chase said. "You feel better?"

"I don't know how we got from salves to me moving to Iowa, but, yeah, I guess I do."

"So I need to pack your stuff and haul it up to Iowa?" Owen asked.

"Maybe," Mitch said, feeling a warmth in his chest. "I need to talk to Paige."

"Okay, good luck," Owen told him. "But, in all seriousness, Ellie has a point. When you find the girl that makes you feel *different*. Different from the other girls but also like you're a different person, better than you were before, then she's worth a U-Haul and a change-of-address form at the post office."

Mitch felt his smile spreading. "Yeah. You've got a point."

He and Paige hadn't been together enough for him to *be* different, but he thought maybe he *could be*.

"I'm jealous," Chase said. "Bailey and I can't really do the change-of-address-U-Haul thing. I mean, she could move to DC, I suppose, but she's happiest down here on the bayou, and I'm only in DC for a couple of years before I'll hopefully be heading back down here anyway."

Mitch grinned. His friend had already decided he wanted to be back closer to Autre. "You think you can do the long-distance thing?" he asked.

Chase paused, and again Mitch imagined he had located Bailey across the room. "Yeah," he said, his voice softer. "Fuck, yeah. We'll get together as much as we can, and the future together is worth however hard it is now."

"And with the way you two are when you're together, it's probably safer if the two of you are mostly together on Zoom or FaceTime," Mitch teased.

Just the other night, they'd disappeared down to the docks for some alone time and come back dripping wet because they'd fallen into the bayou. Bailey was definitely accident prone and she took Chase right down with her.

Chase chuckled. "Good thing I'm going to medical school, huh?"

Mitch laughed. "For sure."

"Okay, so go tell your girl that you're going to need to buy some warmer clothes, and I'm going to go try not to get my nose broken under the mistletoe."

Laughing, they disconnected. Mitch got out of the car and looked up at the light shining in the window of Paige's apartment over the yoga studio.

Here went nothing.

CHAPTER 7

Man, she was in so much trouble.

She wanted him to stick around. A lot.

The words had just hung in the air between them after she'd said them and then he'd winked at her and left before she could emphasize, "for the *next couple of days.*"

Not that she'd rushed to say that.

It wasn't like she thought there was a chance he might stay more than that.

He lived in Louisiana. He worked in Louisiana. His entire family—which was, evidently, quite large—was in Louisiana.

Plus she did *not* want him to stay. Not like *stay* stay. She was the one who got itchy when a guy wanted to go out two days in a row. Of course, around here, two dates two days in a row meant they were going to discuss honeymoon destinations.

So, no, she did not want Mitch to stay any longer. The story about him and Tori would only hold up so long anyway.

But then he walked into her apartment.

Just let himself in as if he belonged there. Shrugged out of his coat—well, Max's coat—tossed it on the chair as if that was where he always tossed his coat when he came home and stalked toward her.

Her heart started pounding. His nose was a little red from the cold but otherwise, he looked very hot. She realized she'd been imagining him with a tool belt on, even though she'd known he hadn't used a tool belt, while confidently fixing anything and everything anyone threw at him. Smiling and being charming the whole time he did it. Saving the damned Apple Festival that she honestly hadn't cared much about since she was a teenager and she and her friends would go and hope to get caught under the mistletoe.

Now she dodged that damned weed like it was poison ivy.

But the idea that Mitch had fixed the power in the town square, and everyone would know he was the big savior... like Santa, albeit a few weeks late, or maybe like the Grinch when he came blazing into town with all the decorations and gifts after finding his Christmas spirit...made tingles spread through her body. And made her wish for mistletoe.

Though the look on his face at the moment made her pretty sure she wasn't going to need it.

"Hi, how did it—" she started.

He cupped the back of her head and brought her in for a kiss. A very hot, deep, wet, backing-her-up-against-the-wall kiss.

Merry Late Christmas indeed.

She wrapped herself around him and gave a little hop to help when he scooped his hands under her ass and picked her up. He set her on the countertop next to the stove. Where she'd been stirring chocolate and marshmallow fluff together for fudge.

Shit.

She pulled back from him, breathing hard. "Welcome back."

He grinned. "Take your clothes off."

"In five minutes," she said, pushing him back and sliding to the floor.

"Now," he insisted, catching the hem of her top and slipping his hands up underneath it to her stomach as she turned to face the stove.

"I can't let this burn," she said, her inner muscles clenching hard as he dragged his palm back and forth over her stomach.

"You don't have to cook for me." He put his mouth against her neck, rubbing his beard up and down the sensitive skin.

Goose bumps broke out over her whole body making her wiggle against him. And the very prominent erection pressing into her back. She wiggled again just for good measure.

He gave a low growl. "Keep doing that and I'm tossing that whole pot in the sink, and you can just angry fuck me over it."

Her shiver was stronger this time and she sighed. He surprised her with the dirty talk and it always had a strong, immediate effect on her body.

"We need this fudge," she told him. But she had to concentrate on the stirring as his hands moved up to cup her breast.

She hadn't put her bra back on, and he teased the bare nipple making her whimper softly.

"Don't need anything but you," he said gruffly against her ear, tugging on the hard tip.

"We need it for bribery," she said, her eyes sliding closed as she gave the bubbling chocolate a half-assed stir.

"Who are we bribing?"

"Drew Ryan."

"Why does Drew need to be bribed?"

"Because he knows that you're not Tori's fiancé," she explained. "We need to ask him to play along with our story when he's out and about at the festival and hears about the fix-it guy who saved the day."

"And he won't just do it because he's a nice guy?"

"Well, the fudge won't hurt."

Mitch slipped the hand not tormenting her breast into the front of her pants. She also still did not have panties on. His finger slid over her clit making fire lick down her legs and her have to grip the counter with her free hand.

"I wouldn't have pegged you for a fudge maker," he said. "You're pretty sugar-free, gluten-free healthy."

She nodded. "I know. I'm an enigma. I happen to make the best damned fudge you've ever tasted. I started making it before I became a full 'health nut' as my father calls it. So now people beg me for it and what can I say, I'm flattered, so I give in."

Or she said something like that. There was no way she could have repeated any of it. Mitch's finger was circling her clit in lazy loops, and her whole body was melting just like the blob of marshmallow fluff in the pot.

"How much longer?" he asked, sliding his finger lower and teasing her opening.

Her knees wobbled slightly, and she had to take a second before cracking one eye—not realizing her eyes were shut—and peeking at the timer. "Just another minute."

He slid his finger into her and she gasped, clutching the counter.

"Stir, Paige," he said softly, moving his finger in and out.

"You're so mean," she said, practically whispering.

"You want me to stop?" he asked, sliding deeper. "Really?"

"No. God, no." She stirred a little faster and focused on *not* coming.

But damn, he was so good at this. She couldn't remember the last time she'd been with a guy who got her going the way he did.

She was never going to be able to make fudge without thinking of this.

The timer went off, the beeping the best sound she'd ever heard.

"I have to move," she said, picking the pot up from the burner.

He did remove his hands from her body, which she definitely regretted, but as she poured the liquid fudge from the pot into the rectangular pan to set, she heard the rustle of clothes and glanced over her shoulder to find him toeing his boots off and shrugging out of his shirt.

She stopped and stared. *Yes.* God, she loved this man naked.

Something sharp stung her foot and she jumped, looking to find that fudge was dripping from the spoon in her hand onto her foot.

Dammit!

She quickly dumped the pot and spoon in the sink and checked the cake pan. The fudge was spread evenly, and she, somehow, hadn't burned it. She carried it to the fridge and slid it onto the lowest shelf. Then she turned to Mitch, pulling her shirt up and over her head.

"Anyone else coming over?" he asked, his hot gaze on her breasts and his hands on his fly.

"Grandpa's been here and gone."

"That's great news."

She watched him unzip and shove his jeans to the floor, kicking them off. Behind the plain black boxers, he was huge and hard. And she was suddenly hotter than she'd ever been.

She slipped out of her yoga pants leaving them in the middle of the kitchen floor. Naked, she padded to him.

"Now what?" she asked, stopping right in front of him and looking up at him.

"You'll do anything I want?" he asked, his voice rough and his eyes hot.

"Definitely."

"How hot is the fudge?"

Her eyes widened. "Hot. Too hot for smearing on body parts," she said, reading his mind.

One side of his mouth curled. "Damn."

"But," she said, "I have some fudge we could heat up a little."

"You have some already made?" he asked. "Why was I waiting for you to stir that up?"

"The fudge I've already got is for you." She felt her cheeks get a little pink. She was *shy* about this? She was buck naked at the moment, and he'd done a lot of *intimate* things to her already, but admitting she'd made him fudge made her blush?

"You made me fudge?"

Dammit. He looked pleased by that. He was so going to get the wrong idea. Especially when she told him the whole story. She sighed. "Yeah. I made it around Christmas. I was going to mail it to you but then... I changed my mind."

"You were going to *send* me fudge for Christmas?" he asked, his grin growing. He lifted a hand to her cheek.

"Yes. But then I realized that you'd think it meant I liked you and was thinking about you," she said with an eye roll.

"Oh, sweetheart," he said, his voice dropping and that drawl becoming more pronounced. "I *know* you like me and have been thinking of me."

He was cocky. A little. Not overly. Not obnoxiously. But enough to be... hot. She did like confident men. "Well, you can *not* think that the fact that it's chipotle fudge means *anything*," she said.

His grin definitely grew with that. "You made me spicy fudge?"

"Spicy and sweet go together really well."

He nodded, his grin turning into an almost smirk. "They sure do."

"But it was just something I wanted to try, and since you eat all that crazy spicy food I thought you were someone I could send it to."

"But then you realized that I'd think it meant you liked me."

She blew out a breath. "Yeah."

"Do you normally make chipotle fudge?"

"No."

"Huh."

"You're thinking it, aren't you?"

"That you like me? Yeah, I'm thinking it."

"Well, if you're going to be all smug about it, I'm not going to melt it down and coat your cock with it so I can lick it off."

His smile dropped and his eyes blazed. "Oh yes you fucking are."

"What if the chili powder in it burns you?"

"I can handle that," he told her. "For sure."

The powder, especially mixed in with all the other ingredients, probably wasn't much of a risk. There was just enough in the fudge to give it some kick.

"That's pretty sensitive skin," she pointed out anyway.

"True. Guess you'll have to lick fast."

"And thoroughly," she agreed.

"Definitely."

"But I don't want to use it all up. I want you take some of it back to Louisiana with you." She gave him a grin that she was sure looked very please-fuck-me. At least that's what she was thinking. "And think of me... and what we're about to do... while you eat it."

"Yeah, we need to talk about me thinking about you from Louisiana," he said.

Oooh, that sounded like he maybe wanted to take their texting to sexting. Or maybe even phone sex. Or the Zoom sex he'd mentioned earlier. She was on board.

"Later. We can talk and... do a lot of other things... *later*." She ran her hand down his abs and stroked his cock through his boxers. "But we have other things to do right now."

She turned and reached to grab the container of spicy fudge from the counter. She was glad she'd mentioned it. She wasn't going to. She wasn't going to confess that he'd made her do something special and different. But somehow it felt right to admit that now.

Then she took his hand and led him down the hallway to her bedroom.

She pushed him toward the bed and shut the door behind her. No one else was coming over. Probably. Okay, there was a 5 percent chance that someone else would stop by. At least this way she'd hear them unlock the front door and could stash him in her closet before whoever it was made it down the hall.

If she heard them.

She had some plans here that just might end up being kind of noisy.

Mitch sitting on the edge of her bed, his hot, hard, tanned body and black boxers against the multicolored quilt and pillows was about the sexiest thing she'd ever seen. He looked out of place on the squares covered with stitched flowers and swirls. Her pillows were encased in different pillowcases as well. Something that, for some reason, drove her mom crazy. They were a mismatched bunch from different sheet sets. A couple had come from childhood sets, a couple from her grandmother, and she had no idea where the purple one had come from. But why did everything always have to match? Why did things have to go a certain way all the time? Why did there have to be a *plan* for every damned thing including matching sheets?

She took a deep breath. That didn't matter. At least not at this moment. Mitch looked out of place and she *loved* that. He didn't match and that was awesome. He wasn't like the guys here. He wasn't from here. Her mother didn't know his mother and grandmother and every aunt and cousin. *She* didn't know his mother. Nor would she.

This was perfect.

She pulled the top off the fudge container and took a piece

out. Then she tossed the box on top of her dresser and walked toward Mitch.

He opened his knees, welcoming her between them, his hands going to her butt.

She lifted the fudge and took a bite, then offered it to him. He bit into it, his eyes locked on hers.

The candy was incredibly sweet. She didn't eat much white sugar and very, very few candies. But she was definitely happy to make an exception here. The chili powder kept it from being too much as the chocolate melted on her tongue and the spiciness gave her a little tingle.

Mitch's fingers curled into her butt as he let the fudge melt in his mouth as well. Paige shifted to put a knee on the mattress next to him, pressing her body against his. She lowered her mouth, meeting his lips in a chocolatey, sweet and spicy kiss. This was by far her favorite way to eat fudge.

Except...

The piece of candy had grown a little sticky as she held it. She put it in her other hand and lifted her chocolatey fingertips to her nipple. She coated it in chocolate and then lifted her head from the kiss.

Mitch's gaze immediately found her sticky nipple and his lips followed.

He took the tip in his mouth, swirling his tongue around it, then sucking.

Her fingers gripped his head as she sighed. God, this was so good. Sex had never been like this before. No one had ever turned her on like this man. No one had ever known how to touch her, how to talk to her, the way he did.

"My turn," she said breathlessly, pushing him back.

She went to her knees in front of him, pulling one side of his boxers down. She still held the piece of fudge in her other hand, so needed his help—which he gladly gave—to slide his boxers down. She shifted out of the way so he could get them off his feet, but her gaze and her hand, immediately went to the impressive cock he exposed.

"You have to tell me if this hurts you," she said, looking up at him from beneath her lashes as she moved the fudge from her fingertips to her full palm. She closed her fist around it, letting it get melty.

"Oh babe, give me some good hurt," he said, his hand going to her head.

She was so glad he wasn't going to try to talk her out of this or even say something like *you don't have to do this*. She *did* have to do this. She *needed* to. She wanted him to get hard as soon as he opened that box of fudge when he was home.

Paige reached for him with her sticky hand and ran it up and down his hard length, leaving a chocolatey mess behind.

He hissed out a breath as she touched him, rubbing and squeezing, his fingers tightened against her scalp.

Then she leaned in and put her tongue to work cleaning up the mess. She licked and sucked until he was gripping her hair and breathing raggedly.

"Paige. Fuck. God. Sweetheart."

He could only manage single words it seemed, and she felt a definite surge of power knowing she was making him lose the ability to speak.

She took him deep and felt his whole body stiffen.

"No. Not like this."

Suddenly she found herself hauled to her feet, swung around, and tossed onto the mattress.

He immediately crawled up her body. He took her mouth in a deep, searing kiss and she arched into him, seeking full-body contact and heat. She needed all of his hardness against all of her softness.

He drove his fingers into her hair, holding her head still as he kissed her, his tongue stroking deep and amazingly making her clit ache as if he were licking it. She gripped his shoulders, wrapping her legs around him.

His cock pressed against her, hot and heavy and she whimpered. "Please, Mitch."

"Anything you want."

"You. Just you. All of you. Please."

"I don't know if I can take you slow, sweetheart." He moved his mouth along her jaw. "I'm trying to get some control here."

"No. Not slow." She tried to shake her head, but he still held her. She looked up at him. "Hard. Please."

He blew out a breath. "The first time... we got a little wild. But this time, I've been thinking about you, *waiting* for you, for a long time now. This might be... really hard."

When he'd told her before that he hadn't been with anyone else it had sent a shot of adrenaline through her that had felt a lot like panic. This was too intense, too fast, too much. She didn't want to be totally absorbed in someone. She didn't want someone who would be totally absorbed in her.

But now when he said it, she felt a surge of a different kind. *Mine.*

She had *never* felt that way about another person. She didn't feel that way about a single possession, her apartment, or her hometown. She didn't even feel it when she looked at her yoga studio or thought about the business she'd created. She felt it about her cats in some cases. Technically they were all available for adoption, but she kept *her* cats, the ones she just felt needed *her* and no one else, in another room when people came to look to adopt.

But in that moment, with Mitch, with him telling her that he'd been *waiting* on her, she felt it.

Mine. She wanted him to be hers.

She was so screwed.

"Yes," she said softly. She pressed one heel into his ass, but she moved her hands to hold his face. "Hard. Deep. Take me, Mitch."

His jaw tensed as he stared into her eyes for a long moment. Then he gave her a nod. "Glad we're on that same page."

She had a feeling the page they were on was not the fuck-me-hard page. It was more than that. Deeper. More serious.

But it didn't make her stomach tighten with trepidation. It made her whole body tighten with anticipation.

"Condom," he said, shifting slightly. "Dammit. They're in the other room."

She shook her head and pointed at her bedside table. "In there."

She had condoms in her bedside table. She rarely used them in here. Mostly she just grabbed them and stuffed them in her purse if she was going out with someone that she might want to use one with. She, frustratingly, couldn't keep them in the bathroom where her mother might see them. Not that she was embarrassed that her mom knew she had sex. It was that her mom would want to know who the guy was and how serious it was and did he have a good job and did he like meatloaf.

She just couldn't handle all of that, so she hid her condoms. Like a teenager sneaking around. Ugh, she hated that.

But Mitch didn't seem too annoyed by the idea that she had, and had needed, condoms in her bedside table. He shifted and reached, grabbing them out of the drawer and tossing about five on the quilt next to them.

His eyes locked on hers as he pushed up to kneel between her thighs, and rolled a condom on.

Damn, that was hot.

Then he lowered himself on top of her again and kissed her.

It was the sexiest, sweetest kiss of her life.

She wasn't sure what was different about it. It was still lips and tongues. But there was more there now.

Lord, just please don't let him propose.

Then as he lifted her leg a little higher and pressed forward, sliding into her, and her neck arched, her head pressing back into the mattress with the sheer delicious bliss of it, she added, *And don't let* me *propose to* him.

Mitch slid in deep and then paused.

She tightened around him and he groaned.

"Hard," she whispered.

"Okay." He pulled in a breath. "Hang on."

She grinned. "You break my bed, you have to fix it."

"Can do."

She didn't know if he was referring to breaking her bed or fixing it, but she knew he could do both.

Mitch shifted to brace his arm on the mattress next to her ear. The other gripped her thigh, lifting it, and spreading her a little wider.

And then he went hard. Braced above her, he was able to thrust deep and hard, and her headboard began banging against the wall just slightly louder than her gasps and cries of, "Oh, Mitch!" and "Yes!" and his growls and, "Fuck, yeahs" and "God, you're amazing."

Her hand gripped his shoulder while the other grabbed on to the quilt under her. But she couldn't do much more than lay there and take it. And she loved every second of that.

She was not the submissive type. At all. But something about letting Mitch do any dirty thing he wanted to made her hot and needy.

And all his.

Did he ever think *mine* about her? Surely not. They barely knew one another. She had no idea why *she* was thinking those things. There was no way he was thinking them too.

"Paige. Baby. Honey." He was panting as he thrust.

She arched closer. "Yes. Yes. Yes."

And then she was coming. Hard. The waves of pleasure washing through her took her breath away, and for just a second she thought *I can't live without this.*

Mitch's pace picked up, his body tensing, and he was coming, her name a long groan as he let go.

He held himself up from her for several seconds as they both breathed hard. Then he leaned down and kissed her. This was soft, but still as hot as the hungry ones from before. His lips clung to hers for a moment, then he kissed his way along her jaw and down her neck to her shoulder, before rolling to his side and bringing her nearly boneless body up against his until she was half draped over him.

"Holy. Shit," he said, breathing out in a very satisfied way.

She smiled against his chest. "Ditto."

It had been good. So good. Better than the first time they'd been together last summer.

But, of course, she could live without it. That had been a crazy thought. It was just sex. *Really good* sex, but still. It wasn't like it was oxygen or water.

But as he shifted and settled more fully into her mattress, his hand possessively splayed over her ass, she had a twinge of *I don't want him to leave* that was very concerning.

A huge yawn hit her just then, and she stretched as she pulled in the long, deep breath before settling against him again.

She was definitely going to need to think about all of her crazy thoughts and feelings about this guy and figure out what the hell was wrong with her and how to get over it.

Mitch kissed the top of her head and she smiled and sighed.

She'd figure out how to get over it—*him*—tomorrow.

Or maybe the day after that.

CHAPTER 8

He woke her up twice during the night. Normally that alone would have been enough for her to put a lot of distance between them immediately. Not having anyone dictating or interrupting her routines and schedules was one very big pro of being single.

But Mitch really made the waking up worthwhile.

Until he started talking after the second wake-up call via orgasm.

It had been going so well too. His hot mouth. His hot hands. His hot... everything else. Who cared about sleep when you had a big, hot, dirty-talking, sexy, sweet Cajun in your bed?

No one, that was who.

But big, hot, dirty-talking, sexy, sweet, *chatty* Cajuns were another thing.

"I was thinkin'," he said, his drawl more pronounced in the dark, and after his second orgasm.

"Uh-oh," Paige said. Out loud. Sincerely.

He gave her butt a squeeze. "I'm serious."

"Exactly why I said *uh-oh*." She shifted and propped up on her elbow. The room wasn't pitch black. Lights from the street outside filtered in through the gauzy curtains, and she still had twinkle lights up around the window.

He definitely looked serious. Hot. Sexy as hell. And serious.

She sighed. "Is there any chance you've been thinking about asking how I feel about being tied up in bed or nipple clamps or something?"

He cleared his throat, and she felt his hand tighten on her butt. But he shook his head. Unfortunately.

"I'm pretty sure you're a solid don't-you-fucking-dare-tie-me-up girl," he said.

She nodded. "You wouldn't be wrong." She never wanted to give up that much control. To anyone.

But nipple clamps might be something else...

"I want to stay."

Four words. No preamble. No easing into it. Just *I want to stay.*

And her heart flipped over. Then plummeted.

"Stay? Like here in bed rather than going to the festival? Or for a couple extra days? Or..."

"For good."

Dammit. She sighed and shifted farther away. For a second his arm tightened around her as if wanting to hold her in place, but then he relaxed and let her slip out from his arm. She pushed herself up to sitting and leaned over to grab her sweatshirt off the floor. The first garment she touched, however, was his t-shirt. She pulled it on anyway. She just needed to be covered.

Then she faced him.

He had shifted so he was propped up against her headboard. The sheet covered him from the waist down, but not his shoulders, chest, or abs.

Dammit. *Willpower. You have to have willpower.*

"So," she started, folding her hands in her lap and resting her elbows on her thighs, "that's crazy."

He nodded. "I know it seems that way."

"It doesn't just *seem* that way, Mitch," she said. "It *is* crazy. People don't just spend a couple of days together and then move a thousand miles from home to be together."

"People in my family do stuff like that all the time," he said, lifting a shoulder.

"Even more reason to stay far away from you and your family," she muttered.

"Tori's doing it."

Paige shook her head. "She knew Josh longer than we've known each other."

"Not that much."

"Well, I'm not Tori." She frowned.

He chuckled. Actually *chuckled* at that.

But it was true. Tori was fine with falling in love and making a long-term commitment. Paige was... not.

"What?" she asked.

"So you like your life the way it is? Your family drives you crazy being in your business all the time. The town drives you crazy being in your business all the time. You're judged for everything you do from your work to how you spend your free time to what you eat."

Paige opened her mouth to reply. But then she snapped it shut. Well... fuck. He was right, of course. How did he know all of that? He'd just figured it all out?

"So the last thing I want," she said, grabbing on to her argument. "Is *another* person in my business."

"I don't want to tell you what to eat or what job you should do."

"But you want to change how I live."

"No... I..." He frowned. "That's not what I'm trying to do."

"But it's what would happen. *Any* relationship changes my life, brings one more person in that needs to be a part of decisions and choices from what I do in the evening after work to how I spend my birthday. I've been *considerate* of the men who want to date me by saying no to anything more than a casual fling or hookup."

He scowled at that. "It's been *considerate* of you to not spend their birthdays with them, to not want to hang out with them and go to the festival or movies together?"

She threw up her hands. "Yes! If I don't want to spend every moment with them or have their opinions or advice on how I'm living my life, then it's *nice* of me to not lead them on thinking that I *do* want those things."

"That's not—"

"And I'd *especially* feel obligated to share my life with someone who would have moved *his* entire life a thousand miles just to be with me. I couldn't just let you sit at home by yourself here without feeling guilty. You wouldn't know anyone else here or have anything else to do."

"I'm not asking..." He shoved his hand through his hair.

She lifted a brow. "Then what are you asking?"

"For you to give this a chance. A *real* chance. To honestly see if this could be something."

"Right. To date you. Seriously. Exclusively. To go to movies and spend my birthday with you."

"*Yes*," he finally said, exasperated. "Yes. I want to be with you. A lot. I want to see what this could be if I lived here, or close enough, to see you more often. I want to get to know you. So, yes, Paige, I want to move here and see you every single day and be a part of your life."

Her stomach flipped at his words. But she wasn't sure if it was dread... or temptation.

"I've been proposed to four times."

He paused, his hand partway through his hair again. It dropped as he stared at her. "What?"

She nodded. "I've been proposed to four times. Twice by the same guy, so three guys. But four proposals."

He looked completely confused. "You're twenty-two."

"Yeah. The first time was right after my high school graduation."

"Um... wow."

"And I said yes to that one."

He scowled. "You've been *engaged*? Already?"

"Yep. Guy I'd known my whole life. My mom's best friend's son." She shrugged, her chest aching the way it always did when she thought of Garrett. He had been such a great guy. Still was a great guy. And she'd not only broken his heart and ended their lifelong friendship, but she'd broken his mom's heart and the heart of everyone in her family.

They would have been a little frustrated or even mad if she hadn't dated him at all, but nothing like the hurt and disappointment after she'd ended the engagement.

Now she really tried with everything in her not to break hearts. Any hearts.

Her mom didn't like her yoga studio or cat collection, but Paige was upfront about those being what she wanted, so Dee was just frustrated... and worried... but not *heartbroken* about those choices.

"Jesus." Mitch blew out a breath. "What happened?"

She shrugged. "We turned sixteen and our moms had always said they wished we'd date. So we did. And then... it's how things go here. You date. You get engaged. You get married. You get jobs. You have kids."

"But..." Mitch frowned. "You didn't."

She shook her head. "I was trying on wedding dresses. My mom was all teary-eyed about it. Amanda was so excited. Everyone was so happy. Except the girl in the mirror. I realized I was doing it for them and that I didn't want to get married. Not at age nineteen for sure. But not to Garrett any time. So I took the dress off, told them it was over, walked out, broke up with him, and... they've never fully forgiven me."

Mitch was just staring at her. "And..." He shook his head. "The other two?"

"Adam was the next one. We had some chemistry—I mean, I didn't hate kissing him or anything. And neither of us were planning to go off to college so I guess he figured why not."

"That is..." Mitch shook his head. "Wow."

"He was the one that proposed twice. After his dad passed away and he took over the farm completely just last spring, he asked me again."

"Had you been dating then?"

"Nope."

Mitch shook his head again. "And the other one?"

"Similar thing. Guy I've known forever who settled down here and getting married is the next thing on his to-do list. He looked around, saw a girl who seemed to be in a similar place, took me out to dinner a couple times, had some not-terrible sex, and then popped the question."

"You slept with them?" he asked with a frown.

"Not Adam," she said. "The one who asked twice. Garrett, the one I said yes to, sure. And the other one..." She shrugged. "Yeah."

Mitch seemed to be gritting his teeth. "You didn't explain the hookup-only rule to him?"

"Actually, I did." She leaned in. "But he didn't listen. Because that's not what he wanted to hear."

Just like *he* wasn't listening. She knew that he got the point.

"Everyone here is just marriage crazy?" he asked.

She shrugged. "It's just... what you do. It's just the natural progression. Or a bad habit. Or a contagious disease. Or something."

He snorted.

"You think I'm kidding? My *three* best friends from high school are already married."

"And they're all your age?"

She nodded. "And they all married their prom dates."

His eyes widened. "Prom is like a giant mass engagement event here or something?"

"It's serious. No one here believes in just... fucking around. Having fun. Doing anything... temporary. Everything is long term and about futures." She sighed. "One of my friends married the only guy she ever *kissed*. They started 'dating' when they were ten. Another married the guy who asked her to prom. I mean, they had *a little bit* of an excuse. She got pregnant prom night."

Mitch snorted again. "Prom is trouble around here."

"Oh, for sure. But they're still together and have *two more* kids." She rolled her eyes. "And *another* friend, the one I had big hopes for, left her high school boyfriend behind to go off to college, but she only lasted a semester before she was back here, going to school in Dubuque, and planning their wedding."

"Wow." Mitch nodded. "Okay, so there's a lot of pressure."

"Oh, and that's not even my family," she said. "My grandparents eloped when they were seventeen. My parents were childhood sweethearts. My sister married her high school boyfriend and had two kids by the time she was twenty-four and she wants two more."

"Josie didn't marry her high school boyfriend," Mitch pointed out.

"Only because she didn't have one. Sure, she's marrying an outsider, but she's always been a romantic, wanting to settle down and the whole thing. And they're living in a house that's been in my family for five generations. She's working a job in a business that's been a staple in this town for fifty years. She's seeing the same people she always sees. She sees my family *all the time*."

"She must like it." Mitch was frowning.

"She does." Paige didn't doubt that for a minute, and she

didn't begrudge her sisters their happiness. It was just that their lives made *her* feel restless and itchy.

"So what do *you* want?" he asked.

She took a breath. "It's going to sound selfish." Her oldest sister had flat-out told her it was selfish as a matter of fact.

"Hit me," he said, making a *come on* motion.

"A Year of Aloneness."

He studied her, then one corner of his mouth curled. "A Year of Aloneness?"

She nodded. "I want to go to Colorado and have a Year of Aloneness. I want to live alone in a new place where it's not weird to be a yoga-doing, cat collecting, vegetarian. Where no one has known me for even six months not to mention since I was born. And where *no one* will propose to me."

Mitch didn't say anything for a long moment. "For a year, huh?"

"At least." She could go a hell of a lot longer than a year not being proposed to. Or even just not being considered a weird failure. But a year seemed like a great starting point.

"And when does this year begin?"

"When I have enough money saved up."

"Why Colorado?"

"Steamboat Springs is a gorgeous place with a happy, healthy population. They have hot springs and tourists. Seems like a good place to have a yoga studio. And while I save up money, I'm getting my massage therapy license too. Yoga and massages seem to go with hot springs and gorgeous walking trails with stunning mountain views, don't you think?"

"I guess I've never given hot springs and yoga a lot of thought," Mitch said. "But I'll take your word for it."

She shrugged. "I actually hope I can just work for someone else. That would be easier. No roots."

"You're against roots?"

"I've got so many roots right now that I can barely pick my feet up." She sighed. "I'd like to be rootless for a while."

"For a year."

She tipped her head. He was hung up on that it seemed. "*At least,*" she added.

"Right." He seemed to be thinking that over.

Paige frowned. "Told you that it sounded selfish."

"It doesn't," he denied. "You have... a lot here."

"I do."

He shifted, sitting up a little straighter. "So it's not marriage you're against. Just the importance your family has put on it."

She frowned, wondering why he cared so much how she felt about marriage. She swore to God, if he proposed to her, she'd throw him out in the snow. Without Max's coat.

Maybe without his pants.

"It's the idea that I'm weird or failing if I don't have the marriage and family and mortgage thing."

"So that's what you want to get away from. Their expectations and pressures."

"Yes."

He sat forward. "Come to Louisiana."

Her heart flipped in her chest. "What?"

He'd better not be proposing. Though asking her to come to Louisiana was *not* just a movie date.

"For the wedding. Josh and Tori's," he added.

She breathed out. But she couldn't deny there was a tiny twinge of disappointment. "Oh. Yeah, I could—"

"Then stay."

She felt her mouth drop open.

"Shake it up. Tell your family you're going to do your own thing. In Louisiana. They won't have a front row for your life there. They won't even know what you're doing, so they can't judge it."

That was crazy.

And it sounded nice.

"Just move to Louisiana?"

"Yep. I can give you a place to live. Free by the way." He gave her a little wink. "And a job. You can save up money there just as easy as you can here. Maybe easier. No rent. No paying business overhead."

She also sat forward. "I'm guessing the place to live would be with you?"

"In my house," he said with a nod. "But it's got four bedrooms. There's another guy living there too. Works for our family business. He's our veterinarian."

Her own bedroom. But in his house. Uh-huh. "What's the job?"

"Otter yoga."

Her eyebrows rose. "Um... what?"

He chuckled. "I mean, you can do more than that. But there are no yoga studios in Autre."

"Hmm..." She quirked an eyebrow. "Otters?"

He grinned. "We have otters. A whole family of them. We've decided to start an otter encounter as a part of the Boys of the Bayou business. People can come and interact with the otters, feed them, play with them. Seems like a girl who is used to doing yoga with cats, could figure something out with otters too."

That sounded fun, actually. Otters were adorable.

"We have alligators too. Turtles. Lizards."

"Yoga with *alligators*?"

"Maybe the babies?"

She laughed.

"And we're getting a llama. Tori is taking one back with us. Maybe two. Knowing Tori, actually, probably three."

"From Drew and Dallas Ryan?"

"Yep."

"They're alpacas, actually."

"Right. Alpacas."

Alpaca yoga. Otter yoga. Seeing Mitch every day. Hmmm...

"My family would assume that we'd run off and, of course, gotten married," she said.

"And when we don't, that will *really* make them wonder," Mitch said. "They'll just have to guess about what the hell is going on." He leaned closer. "Admit it, that could be kind of fun."

It could be.

A chance to have a relationship without any outside influences? To spend time with a guy and actually see what could happen without anyone else's hopes getting up? A chance to really date someone without worrying about breaking her mom's heart if it didn't work out?

"You *promise* you're not going to propose?" she asked.

"I think I can resist." He gave her a half grin.

That wasn't an *I promise*, but she smiled back.

"Living with you and some other guy isn't really *aloneness*," she pointed out.

"No." He nodded. "There's not a lot of space or alone time in my life, I'll admit."

Yeah, see that was a red flag. She didn't want to trade one crazy big family for another.

"But you're still saving up for the Year of Aloneness, right?" he asked.

"Right." She was probably six months away, honestly. She wanted to have enough to pay rent for at least part of the year in Colorado without worrying about her job situation.

"So come do that in Autre. Away from the proposals that keep happening up here." He actually frowned slightly at that.

She grinned. Was he jealous? She hated herself for liking that idea.

"You worried they might wear me down and I'll finally say yes to one just to shut everyone up?"

His frowned deepened. "Let's just say I don't hate the idea of you being away from all the marriage-minded guys that seem to populate this little town."

Paige laughed lightly. "That should be a huge reason *not* to come to Louisiana, you know."

He reached out and snagged her wrist, tugging her up the bed.

She went. Willingly.

He rolled her under him and kissed her long and deep. When he lifted his head, he said, "Come to Louisiana and be my friend with benefits for a few months."

"That's it? That's all you want?"

"I want you to have what *you* want," he said, his eyes sincere.

A little bit of her resolve melted. She actually felt it turn to liquid and slip away.

"And I do want men to stop proposing to you," he added. "Louisiana seems like a good place for you to land temporarily."

She smiled and ran a hand up the side of his face. "You're very tempting."

He pressed his cock against her hip and she felt her body heat instantly. "I promise the benefits will be nice."

"Your other roommate is a heavy sleeper?" she teased.

"He can get his ass out if he doesn't like it," Mitch said gruffly, dragging his jaw along hers.

She shivered and arched closer.

A place to land temporarily. A little adventure. A chance to save up the money she needed but be out from under the magnifying glass of Appleby. Well, her family in particular. The whole town seemed to think that marriage and family were the ultimate goals, but her family was particularly obsessed.

Her Year of Aloneness was still the plan, but she couldn't

afford to do it yet, and the idea of spending another six months here did give her a little *ugh* feeling.

And otter yoga? Come on. That sounded really cool.

"How about I come for Tori and Josh's wedding and we see how it goes?" she asked.

He shook his head, but he was smiling. "Can't even commit to six months?"

"Six months is a *long* time."

"Okay... six days. Promise six days when you come to the wedding. I want to really show you the bayou." He lowered his head and kissed her neck, then dragged his mouth up the sensitive skin to her ear. "And everything you can have if you stay there."

She arched into him, unable to help it. The *stay there* gave her pause. But he meant for six months. That wasn't too long. Not long enough to mess up any plans, anyway. Probably.

Then he dragged his mouth down her neck, past her shoulder, to her breast. He pushed his shirt up and took her nipple in his mouth, and all she could think was *I'll give you six of whatever you want, Mitch Landry.*

CHAPTER 9

Paige rolled over and eyed her clock. Then sat straight upright. Nine a.m.?

Nine? How had she slept till nine? She had yoga...

Wait, no, she didn't. It was the first day of the festival and everything else in town shut down.

She started to lay back down. Why was she so tired though?

Then sat straight up again.

Mitch.

She was tired because of Mitch. The sex. The *talking*. The sex. And geez, the *talking*.

She looked around. Where was he? His side of the bed was still rumpled, but it was cold when she touched the sheets, and there wasn't a sound in her apartment.

Had he actually snuck out and *left*?

Had he realized that everything he said last night about her going to Louisiana for a few months was batshit crazy and gotten out before she woke up and he found himself with a live-in girlfriend he barely knew? And her twenty-three cats?

Hmm... the cats. She was going to have to figure something out with the cats. She'd thought she had a few months before she moved to Colorado and had been figuring out a way to take them with her...

She shook her head. She needed to focus. She didn't need to figure out what to do with her cats when she went to Louisiana if Mitch had snuck out and taken off for Louisiana without her.

That would be such a good thing.

So why did she feel really disappointed?

Paige threw back the sheets and got out of bed. She was *not* disappointed. The whole conversation had come on the heels of major orgasm endorphins in the middle of the night. No rational life decisions should be made in that circumstance.

But two minutes later, she did at least admit to herself that she was looking for a note from him.

He couldn't even leave a note?

She reached for her phone, thinking maybe there was at least a text. Maybe he'd waited until he was safely driving through Oklahoma...

Her phone rang just then.

It was her sister's number.

"Hello?"

"Good morning," Josie greeted brightly.

Paige leaned back against her counter. Josie was a morning person. Paige was not. Paige got up early. But she liked quiet and meditation and slow, gentle stretching first thing. Josie was bright and bubbly and thought the day should be started with caffeine and sugar.

It made the fact that she worked in the local bakery very convenient.

"Morning," Paige said.

Josie was calling her to come help at the bakery. Paige could feel it. She often filled in at Buttered Up. It was a block away and sometimes they needed extra hands. She was happy to do it. Usually. Right now she was feeling very *unbubbly* and sweet this morning.

Which was so stupid. Mitch realizing his suggestion was crazy and getting out of town, thereby keeping her from having to tell him it was crazy and say no in the morning light when she wasn't hopped up on endorphins was a *good* thing.

"You should stop by the bakery this morning," Josie said.

She knew it. "You guys swamped?"

The bakery didn't close completely on festival day, just early. But they opened so people could get breakfast and coffee before hitting the chilly town square. In fact, it was a big business day.

"We are," Josie said. "You should stop by."

"I'm not really hungry." She was grumpy. About a guy. Wow, she needed... something.

"You don't have to eat."

"So what would I do?" Help at the register, probably. Which would at least take her mind off Mitch. Maybe that was good.

"You could just talk."

"Talk?" Paige frowned. "We can talk later."

"I mean to Tori."

Paige froze. Then straightened away from the counter. "Tori?"

"Tori Kramer. She's here with her fiancé. And his cousin. Who is *hot*. You should totally come down here and meet him."

Tori was at Buttered Up? With Josh? And... Mitch?

Paige's heart *thunked* so hard in her chest she actually lifted her hand and pressed it over the spot.

Wow. She was in so much trouble here.

But... *fuck.*

If Tori was there with Josh, then it would be clear that *Mitch* was not her fiancé, and if anyone walked in who thought he was—and that was *very* possible—they were screwed. Linda,

Carol, Melanie, Mike, Larry... hell, the whole town...were regulars at the bakery.

As was Paige's mother.

Ugh.

"I'll be right there," she said quickly, heading for her bedroom.

"Awesome," Josie said happily.

Paige stopped. Crap. She'd sounded enthusiastic about getting down there to meet Tori's hot cousin. But... she couldn't deal with her romance-loving sister right now. "See you soon." She disconnected and tossed the phone on the bed and headed for the shower.

Fifteen minutes later, Paige let herself in through the back door of the bakery. That was a friends-with-the-owner privilege that Paige happily used this morning. She couldn't just walk in through the front without checking things out.

She came up short when she found the kitchen full.

"What are you all doing here?"

Whitney and Jane both grinned.

"Packing apple pies up for the booth at the festival."

Every business in town had a booth in the square, including the bakery. Even though everyone had spent the holidays overeating and most of the town stopped in here this morning on their way over there. The stuff at the booth was taken home and saved for when people were in the mood for sweets again. Like in a couple of days.

Jane and Whitney didn't work at the bakery but they were Zoe and Josie's best friends. They had big boxes and tons of packing peanuts in front of them and were filling the boxes with little mason jars. Zoe had started doing cakes and pies in jars and they'd been a big hit. They were especially great for expos and fairs.

Paige focused on Whitney. She and Whitney had also become friends over the past few months. Whitney had been a regular at yoga and a few months back had reached out for a girls' night out. Paige had turned her down the first time but since then they'd gone out a few times.

That first time, she'd had to decline because Tori was in town. With her fiancé. And his hot cousin.

Paige had also spilled about that hot cousin to Whitney over hard ciders at Granny Smith's, the local bar.

She crossed the room, braced her hands on the worktable across from Whitney and narrowed her eyes. "What did you do?"

Whitney's eyes widened. "About what?"

"What did you tell my sister about Tori's fiancé and his hot cousin?" she asked, shooting a glance at Jane.

Jane kept packing her box. But she was clearly fighting a smile.

Shit. They all knew. Paige could tell.

Whitney shrugged. "I just..." Then she blew out a breath. "You should have told me it was a secret."

"You told Josie who Mitch is?"

"I just said that you had a hot night with a guy with a sexy Louisiana accent."

Okay, so that would...

"And I might have said the name Mitch." Whitney bit her bottom lip.

"You totally said the name Mitch," Jane said with a snort.

Paige groaned. "Whit."

"I'm sorry."

"Why are you trying to hide this?" Jane asked.

"Oh, hey!" Josie swept into the kitchen just then from the front of the bakery. She gave Paige a big grin. "They're right out front. He's *very* cute."

Paige shot Jane a glance. Jane met her eyes and gave a nod. Yeah, she got it. She knew Paige's family. She knew Josie best, of course, and Josie's romantic streak was just an adorable part of

Josie's adorable personality. When that romantic streak was about her own life. But when it was turned on the people around her and she wanted everyone to fall in love, it wasn't quite as cute.

Jane had experienced that too.

"Have you talked to them?" Paige asked her sister.

"I waited on them," Josie said with a nod. "But it's crazy out there, so we didn't really *talk*."

"Oh, do you guys need help?" Paige asked. Hey, she was here now. She could pitch in. And avoid the table with Tori and Josh and Mitch and whatever they had told everyone about... whatever.

"Nope. Maggie and Cam both came in to help bake this morning," Josie said of Zoe's mom and brother—Whitney's boyfriend. "And Grant and Aiden are out there helping Zoe wait on everyone." Her smile was soft and affectionate as she mentioned her fiancé, Grant, and Zoe's, Aiden.

Well, they really were covered. With all of those people, two of them big guys, there probably wasn't room behind the counter anyway.

And, really, she probably did need to go find out what Mitch had told Tori and Josh about their little lie about Mitch and Tori being engaged. Paige's cover wasn't entirely blown because Josie still, apparently, thought Mitch was Tori's fiancé.

Plus she wanted to see Mitch. She wasn't able to forget the disappointment she'd felt thinking he'd hightailed it back to Louisiana. She liked him more than she'd wanted to admit.

"Go introduce yourself to the cousin," Josie urged. "You and Tori are friends. Just go out and join them."

Okay, so apparently Whitney had slipped about Mitch in front of Jane but not Josie? That was fortunate. She supposed.

And Josie was reading Paige's hesitation as nerves about meeting a new guy. Well, that was better than her guessing that

Paige was nervous that Mitch was going to upend all of her carefully laid plans.

"Oh my gosh!"

Paige had to jump back as the swinging door that led to the front of the bakery suddenly swung in, almost whacking her in the face.

"Hey, Kelsey!" Josie greeted Jane's younger sister.

"Hi," she said to everyone collectively. Then she focused on Jane. "Guess what?"

Jane turned and faced her. "What?"

"Look what Matt gave me for my birthday!" Kelsey held up the little heart-shaped charm hanging from the chain around her neck.

"Oh wow," Josie said, moving in before Jane could. "That's so pretty!"

Kelsey nodded, nearly squealing. "He said that now I can *actually* take his heart with me wherever I go."

Paige caught herself before she rolled her eyes.

Josie, on the other hand, audibly sighed. "That's so romantic."

"Oh wow, Kels, that's awesome," Jane said.

Was it? Maybe. What did Paige know?

"That really is," Whitney agreed.

Okay, so all of the women who were in *actual* relationships thought Matt had done something good here. Fine. The kid was a senior in high school giving another senior in high school a birthday gift after dating for about six months. He was Kelsey's first serious boyfriend. There had probably been some pressure to make it meaningful. Paige probably needed to lighten up.

"His birthday is two days after mine," Kelsey said.

"No way," Whitney said.

Kelsey nodded. "Cute, right?"

They all laughed. "Very cute," Josie agreed. "What did you get him?"

"It's not as good as this," Kelsey said, shaking her head. "I told him I'd play *Warriors of Easton* with him for an entire weekend."

"That *is* good," Jane said. "He loves *Warriors* and always wants you to play but knows you don't really like it. That's sweet. You're putting him first and willing to do something that matters to him."

"You think so?" Kelsey asked. "I mean, I'm going to suck at it."

"How did he react?" Paige heard herself ask.

Kelsey looked over and shrugged. "He was thrilled, actually." She looked back at her sister. "But it's not something he can *keep*, like this."

"It will be a memory." Paige frowned. Why did she keep talking? But when they all looked at her, she tipped her head. "It will. You show up with all his favorite snacks and a *Warriors of Easton* sweatshirt and hat on to show him that you're really committed to doing it right and truly settle in for the whole weekend, no interruptions. He'll think that's super hot."

Then she winced. Oops, maybe she shouldn't tell teenagers how to be hot.

But Whitney, Josie, and Jane were nodding.

"It's true," Josie said. "Our parents were all about making the little things sweet and romantic." She shot Paige a smile. "Memories really matter. They *do* stay with you."

Oh crap, Paige thought as Josie looked at her with what could have easily been described as pride. She was right. And her sappy, romance-crazy parents had rubbed off on her after all.

Dammit.

"I need to go." She looked around. "Up front."

At least up front she wouldn't be opening her mouth in front of Josie and acting like she actually thought about romantic weekends and knew how to make things special and meaningful.

Paige took a deep breath and pushed through the swinging door to the front of the bakery. She immediately found Mitch in spite of the crowd of people.

I'd play stupid video games with him all weekend. For sure. Or go out on fishing boats on the swamp.

Dammit.

It seemed that he sensed her as well. He was sitting closest to the window at their table, not facing the kitchen door, but he looked over as soon as she stepped out. Their eyes met, and his mouth curled in a grin that sent heat skittering through her body. It was a knowing smile. A smile that said he knew her. Knew her body. Knew her thoughts. Knew that she would be here.

That idea made trepidation slip down her spine.

Turn around and go right back out of here. That was her first thought. Her first instinct.

But then he gave her a wink and leaned over, draping his arm across the back of the chair where Tori sat.

For some reason, that made Paige relax. So Josh and Tori were playing along? That was nice. And awkward. She felt bad. Her crazy family, and her own crazy commitment issues were causing Tori and Josh and Mitch to have to lie.

She sighed and made her way from behind the counter over to their table.

"Good morning."

"Paige!" Tori bounced up from her chair and hugged Paige. "Hi!"

Paige squeezed her back with a huge smile. Tori Kramer, soon-to-be-Landry, was impossible not to like. She was sweet and kind and genuine and slightly awkward in a very adorable I-just-want-to-take-care-of-her way.

Over Tori's shoulder, Paige noticed Josh watching them. He was smiling with an affectionate look that, if anyone had been looking, would have *clearly* said he was madly in love with Tori.

Paige let Tori go and grinned at her. "It's so good to see you. But I didn't know you were going to come over for the festival."

"Oh, it's the perfect reason to come see you," Tori said, taking her seat again. "When Mitch said that he was—"

"When he said how much he missed her but that he needed to stay to make sure all the electrical worked once things kicked off, Tori wanted to head right over," Josh interrupted, sitting forward.

Tori pressed her lips together and nodded, glancing at Mitch. "Right," she said. Then giggled. "I couldn't stay away from him another day though."

"Aw, love you, Tori," Mitch said. Then he pulled her in and kissed her.

It was just a quick peck on the lips, and his grin was full of mischief, but Josh's grin fell away and his body tensed.

Tori blushed.

Paige thought about knocking the rest of Mitch's coffee into his lap.

CHAPTER 10

O f course, *all* of those reactions were what Mitch was going for.

"Dammit, Mitch," Josh muttered, too low for anyone else to hear.

But Mitch was focused on Paige. And she realized that he was trying to see how she'd react.

With jealousy. That's how she was reacting.

With stupid, makes-no-sense-because-she-knew-it-was-a-lie jealousy. Even more, she couldn't feel jealous over a guy that she didn't want anything long-term with. That was her call. That was her rule. That was her decision. She couldn't be jealous over other women or how he spent his time or if he didn't text or call her every day.

Even *more*, she *never* felt jealous. That was the truth. She had never met, dated, kissed, or even had a hookup with a guy she felt jealous about over anything.

She was going to have to get a handle on her emotions about *this* guy.

And it was definitely a red flag that her emotions were not handled even when she knew that he was just messing around.

Paige made herself sit back in her chair, cross her legs, and smile.

"Got to sell it," Mitch said to his cousin.

"I'm keepin' track," Josh told him. "I'm going to make you pay for *every* one of those."

"I'm so sorry," Paige said. She kept her voice low too. The bakery was busy and there was a lot of noise, but this was Appleby. It sometimes felt like the walls and trees even had ears. "He's helping me out and I realize it's ridiculous."

"It's fine," Tori said. "We've all got each other's backs. Mitch told us what was up before we even headed over here." She gave Josh a look. "You have nothing to worry about."

Josh nodded and gave her a wink. Then he leaned in and took Paige's hand in his on top of the table. "So, how are things at the yoga-cat café?"

Paige was surprised by the hand holding but she slid a glance at Mitch, knowing immediately what was going on. Mitch was looking at his cousin with his eyebrow arched.

Paige leaned in, closer to Josh too, feeling a touch of that same mischief that was in the air. "It's good. Very... relaxing."

Josh grinned and Paige completely understood what Tori saw in him. He was very good looking, but even more, he had a confident, laid-back charm about him that was definitely appealing.

"I mentioned she should look into otter yoga," Mitch said from across the table.

Josh's brows both arched. "You have otters?"

She laughed. "No."

"But *we* do," Mitch said.

Josh nodded. "Ah. Got it. Is that something you could do?" he asked Paige.

She shrugged. "I'd have to learn a lot about otters."

"Otters are not going to lie still and just stretch out like the cats," Tori said. "They're pretty active. If your yoga class is distracted by the otters, they won't be getting much meditation done."

Paige laughed. "Noted."

"Now, now," Mitch said. He moved his hand to rest it across Tori's shoulders rather than on the chair.

His big hand resting on the other woman made Paige's eyes narrow and she had to tell herself to relax.

"Let's not talk her out of things before we give it a fair try. I told her about the otter encounter and just said there wasn't a yoga studio in Autre. Let's not get excited about what *won't* work."

Josh looked interested in his cousin's interest in yoga. He slid his chair closer to Paige's.

Mitch's eyes followed the movement and he did the same, sliding closer to Tori.

Paige almost grinned. Tori laughed lightly.

"Well, how do you feel about alpacas?" she asked. "We're taking four back with us."

Paige did laugh then, sharing a look with Mitch. "Four?"

Tori grinned. "We went to talk to Drew. The one he thought I should take back with me is just a baby. An orphan. His mom died about a month ago. They've been bottle-feeding him but they don't really have the time to give him."

Drew and his brother Dallas were young bachelor farmers. They raised the alpacas for their wool. They weren't doing it because they wanted to spend all their time being fill-in moms, she was sure. They were nice guys but they had a huge farm to run, and whenever they had a runt kitten or found a stray, they called Paige rather than caring for it themselves.

"So, of course, they thought of you," Paige teased.

She and Tori had absolutely bonded over their love of animals, especially cats. Tori had told her that she'd been called Cinderella in elementary school after her classmates found out she'd had a pet racoon, rabbits, even mice. All animals liked her. And vice versa. When she'd lived in Iowa, she'd collected "special needs" animals, including a pig that was afraid of thunder, an English bulldog that had been born with a cleft palate and had needed to be fed by hand, and a mountain lion she'd saved after it had been shot as a cub, along with a few "regular" animals like goats and dogs and a whole bunch of cats. She'd even had an alpaca that loved it when she sang to him. Paige had no reason to believe that the sweet veterinarian was any different now just because she lived in Louisiana. And clearly Josh was very willing to indulge her.

"So what about the other three alpacas?" Paige asked.

"Well, I said..." Tori's cheeks got pink and she looked at Josh.

Paige looked at Josh too. The guy who was holding *her* hand. He was looking at Tori like he thought she was fucking adorable and hot as hell all at once.

"One of them came up and kissed her on the cheek," Josh said.

"Come on," Paige said with a laugh.

"Well, pretty much," Josh said. "Saw her across the pen and came straight over and put his mouth on her cheek. She, of course, was smitten. Then *his* girlfriend had to come. And their baby girl. Which, if things go well, will maybe be the other little llama's girlfriend someday, right?" he asked Tori.

Tori smiled at him like she thought *he* was adorable and hot as well.

Paige rolled her eyes. She hoped no one in the bakery was *really* paying attention because no way would they not realize these two wanted to tear each other's clothes off and sit on the porch in their rocking chairs at age ninety together.

Paige looked at Mitch. He was watching *her*. It made her feel warm and she smiled at him. Even though she knew that her smile didn't look casual to anyone looking on either. It was mostly tear-his-clothes-off. But there might have been a touch of rocking chair in there.

Dammit.

"Tell her about the whole plan," Mitch said to Tori. He picked up a strand of her hair and twirled it around his finger.

Josh shifted to put his arm around Paige.

"Well," Tori said, her eyes on Josh's arm. "We're starting a whole petting zoo and animal encounter as an offshoot of Boys of the Bayou."

"We're calling it Boys of the Bayou Gone Wild," Josh said. He grinned. "Totally tongue-in-cheek since otters and alpacas aren't very wild."

Paige laughed. "I love it." She looked at Tori. "That sounds like your kind of thing, for sure."

"Yeah, otters and alpacas and goats and my pot-bellied pig and who knows what else." Tori said with a smile. "But I'm not doing it. I mean, most of the petting zoo animals are mine and I'll help out, but a friend of mine from vet school has joined me in my practice and Gone Wild will be his thing. And we still need someone to run that part of the business. Josh and Owen and Sawyer don't have time. That's where Mitch comes in."

Paige looked at Mitch. He shook his head.

"I'm just building pens and things."

"No you're not. You're going to be great managing it," Tori said, pivoting on her chair to look at him more fully. "You're going to do what Josh and Owen do on the boats."

Mitch grinned and looked at his cousin. "I don't know what you're talkin' about."

Tori rolled her eyes. "Uh-huh." She looked at Paige. "The Boys of the Bayou is a fantastic tour of the bayou with a lot of information and great experiences built in. They talk about the plants and animals of the bayou as well as the history and legends of the area. They make sure the tourists see alligators and other animals in the wild, and they take them to see some of the old cabins and talk about the people who settled the area. It's a great tour. But..." She cast another affectionate glance at her fiancé.

"But?" Paige asked, looking from Josh to Tori.

"But the *boys* of the bayou are a huge draw. Josh and Owen and even Sawyer are a part of the fabulous reviews. They flirt. They talk hunting and fishing. They turn on the Southern charm and those drawls."

Paige nodded, but she was looking at Mitch now. "I know exactly what you're talking about."

Tori laughed. "Yep. The women think they're hot and charming when they're teasing and flirting, and it's really weird how often the guys end up shirtless and wet."

"Hmm, that is really *weird*," Paige said sarcastically to Josh.

He just grinned.

"And the men think they're cool. They drive airboats and hunt alligators and all kinds of manly man stuff." Tori rolled her eyes again, but she was still smiling.

Paige shook her head, fighting her own smile. "That does sound pretty cool."

Josh nodded. "And then there's how great we are with kids." He looked at his fiancé. "Admit it. That makes your panties melt, Iowa."

Tori didn't answer right away, but she didn't deny it either.

Paige knew that guys interacting well with children were a lust button for a lot of women. A lot of her friends, for that matter.

"So you're going to manage the petting zoo and otter encounter?" she asked Mitch. She wasn't going to think about him with kids. That didn't work with her. She had nieces and nephews. She liked kids fine, but she wasn't ga-ga over babies or little kids, and her biological clock wasn't even wound up not to mention ticking.

"No. I'm building the pens and enclosures," he said again. He gave Tori a look.

She sighed. "You'd be so good."

"You want me puttin' up fences with my shirt off?" he asked, giving her a small smile. "I can do that."

He should *absolutely* do that. And charge admission, for sure, Paige thought.

But she noted his smile seemed forced.

Interesting. He didn't want to be more involved with the animal portion of the business? Why not?

"Well, *at least* that," Tori teased. "You'd just be so good talking about the animals. You love them. And you're as charming and sweet and funny as Josh and Owen."

"Hey, now," Josh said. But his tone was light.

Tori shot him a smile. "You know what I mean. All the charm you turn on for the tourists. Mitch can do that. I'm not talking about the you-and-me charm."

The way she said *charm* made Paige's eyes widen. It looked like the sweet, small-town farmgirl had been a little corrupted by the Louisiana boy who was now giving her hot looks over sweet, small-town muffins and coffee.

Paige glanced at Mitch. She understood that. She really did. She wanted to be a little corrupted herself.

"There's no other charm like that, babe," Josh said, his voice dropping low.

"Okay," Paige said, squeezing Josh's hand to remind him not to eye-fuck Tori across the table in the bakery.

Tori fanned her face and gave Josh a wink, but she said to Mitch, "And you love the otters. Admit it."

"Otters are cute." Mitch shrugged. "Everyone likes otters."

Tori blew out a breath.

"I've got Fletcher and Zeke helping me," Mitch said. "They can take care of the tourists."

"His mom specifically told me we're supposed to call him Ezekiel," Tori said with a grin.

Mitch and Josh both laughed. Mitch looked at Paige. "Zeke's one of my cousins. Fletcher too. But Zeke and Zander are twins. Their mom hates that we shorten Ezekiel and Alexander."

"But the family's been doing it all their lives and they're twenty-six," Josh said. "You'd think she'd be used to it by now."

Tori shook her head. "I think she was hoping that since I'm kind of new, she could at least get me to do it right." She looked at Paige. "In the Landry family, the *more* something bugs you, the more likely it's going to continue. You have to learn to roll with things on the bayou."

Paige couldn't deny she was fascinated.

The conversation about Mitch's role with the tourists had gotten sidetracked. She was pretty sure he'd intended that, but the whole topic seemed to be an ongoing discussion. Paige wanted to ask him more about it later. Then realized that it was none of her business what Mitch did with his job and his family's business. If he didn't want to do more, that was his choice. She didn't know what that was about and it didn't matter.

Paige opened her mouth to ask a question when suddenly there was a murmuring in the crowd and the sound of chairs scraping and people started to pivot in the same direction.

Paige frowned and looked as well.

"I know we haven't known each other very long, but I'm absolutely crazy about you."

Elliot, one of the programmers who worked for Aiden, Grant, Cam, and Oliver, the guys who had bought the Hot Cakes factory, was standing in front of the bakery case. He was facing his boyfriend, Max, one of the factory workers, who everyone in town adored.

Max's eyes were wide and his mouth was hanging open.

"When I bid on you at the bachelor auction, I knew we were going to have fun," Elliot said. "But I had no idea what I was *actually* winning." He dropped to one knee in front of Max. "A chance at everything I've always wanted." He was holding a red velvet cupcake in one hand and a gold band in the other. "Max, will you marry me?"

The entire bakery sucked in a breath all at once and not a single person moved.

Including Max.

He just stood staring down at his boyfriend.

Paige felt herself leaning forward. Holy shit, was Max going to turn him down in front of everyone?

But Elliot didn't look nervous. He just waited.

Finally Jane coughed from behind the counter. Her cough sounded like, "*Max.*"

Max shook his head. "Elliot."

Elliot just kept the ring extended.

"Fuck, yes," Max said, shaking his head slowly. "Damn."

Elliot gave him a huge smile and got to his feet.

The big, burly man grabbed Elliot and pulled him into his arms, hugging him tightly.

The whole bakery cheered, and Jane came rushing around the bakery case to throw her arms around both men.

Paige tried to swallow and found that her throat was tight. She blinked fast. What the hell? Were her eyes a little watery?

She sat back in her chair and glanced over at Mitch. He was watching her with a smile. She rolled her eyes at him. He laughed.

"Oh my gosh!" Tori said, then gave a happy sigh. "That was amazing. Do you know them?" she asked Paige.

"I know Max," Paige said. "Elliot is from Chicago. They just met this past summer."

"When you know, you know," Mitch said simply.

She frowned at him. "Watch yourself, Bayou."

Josh laughed at that. "He can't help it. He's a Landry."

"What's that mean?" Paige asked, not sure she really wanted to know.

"The Landrys have a long, proud history of big romance," Josh said, almost smugly.

Paige groaned.

Josh chuckled. "That's a bad thing?"

"Don't scare her off before I get her down there and can seduce her with beignets," Mitch said.

"Romance scares you off?" Tori asked.

Paige glanced over to where Max and Elliot were accepting congratulations and she couldn't help but smile.

"I'm not sure scared is the right word," she admitted.

"That's my girl," Mitch said gruffly from across the table.

"Maybe you just haven't—" Tori started but she gave a little, "*Eek*," and then pressed her lips together.

Paige assumed Mitch had pinched her or something.

Well, good. At least he was getting the message not to *talk about it* all the damned time, no matter how he felt.

"Paige is gonna be my 'plus one' at your wedding," Mitch told Tori, his eyes on Paige.

She should say no.

If she went to Louisiana she might not make it to Colorado.

"Oh *yes*," Tori exclaimed, her eyes bright. "I was going to invite you anyway. Please come. Mitch will make sure you have fun." Then she giggled. "I didn't mean it like that but..."

"Okay, Tor," Mitch said with a grin. "Paige knows what you meant."

Paige didn't care what Tori meant. She was concerned about what *Mitch* meant.

"It will be a ton of fun. You'll love Autre and everyone," Josh said. "Please come."

Everyone. She was going to meet everyone.

The big, romantic everyone.

Ugh.

Paige looked back and forth between Tori and Josh. They were such nice people. Then she looked at Mitch. Then over at Max and Elliot and then at Kelsey who was standing with Josie and Grant and Zoe and Aiden wearing her new heart necklace.

Everyone was freaking in love.

There was romance and wedding stuff everywhere she looked.

She blew out a breath. Escaping sounded great, but escaping by going to a *wedding* in another little town with a whole bunch of people who loved love seemed like kind of the opposite thing she should do.

But then she looked at Mitch.

She wasn't ready to say goodbye to him yet.

Crap.

She felt herself nodding. "Yeah, okay, I'll come to the wedding."

Mitch's smile was definitely pleased. But also a little knowing.

She was going to have to limit the texting and calls between now and the wedding. She didn't want him to get the idea that they were *dating* or had a serious relationship going into that romantic weekend.

And she was only staying for a couple of days. Tops.

Twenty minutes later, they were wandering through the town square, stopping at every single booth.

They sampled hot cider—that was very hot thanks to the electricity flowing into the booth—and caramel apples and mini apple pies from Buttered Up and apple cookies and applesauce and even apple wine. It was all homemade and, frankly, delicious.

Most people claimed they wouldn't touch another apple

recipe for weeks after leaving the square but that never ended up being true.

They also checked out the craft stations where you could paint with apple cores and get a temporary apple tattoo along with the booths where people were selling everything from wooden apples to ceramic apples to towels embroidered with apples.

"Wow," Mitch said when they were through the square and on their way to the yoga studio so Tori could take a look at the cats. "I mean, when you people adopt a theme, you go all in."

Paige laughed. "For sure."

"Oh, you bayou boys can't talk," Tori said. "There are alligators on everything in Autre."

"The bayou is a way of life," Josh told her. "We have to celebrate it."

Mitch nodded his agreement.

After Tori checked over all the cats, which took a while considering all the ooh-ing and ahh-ing and cuddling that went on while she examined them, Mitch finally got to his feet.

"Guess we're heading out," he said.

Paige looked up, then scrambled to her feet. "Oh. Really? Today?"

Today was the day they were supposed to *arrive*.

But it was fine they were leaving. This was the amount of time she'd expected to spend with Mitch. Short and sweet. No big deal.

So why did it feel like so much had happened and that his visit had been a very big deal?

"Yeah, we need to get back," he said, shooting a glance at Tori.

"I'm sorry," Tori said. "It's my fault."

"It's *my* fault," Josh said. "I should have known taking her over to the Ryan farm was the wrong move."

"But I wanted to meet everybody," Tori said.

"Everybody being the alpaca—the *one* alpaca—that she was supposed to be taking back to Louisiana," Mitch added.

"And now it's four alpacas," Paige said with a smile.

Tori nodded.

"And…" Mitch said.

Paige looked at her with wide eyes. "There's more?"

"There was a donkey," Tori said, lifting her shoulder.

"Who now belongs to us too," Josh said.

Paige shook her head. "Wow."

Tori said, lifting a shoulder. "Drew asked if I wanted him."

Mitch laughed. "And Tori's never met an animal she *doesn't* want."

"Anyway," Josh said, "now that she's met her new babies, she wants to get them home and settled."

Paige wondered if Josh *ever* said no to Tori. But she couldn't help smiling. Clearly they were both incredibly happy.

She looked up at Mitch. And now she was going to get rid of him sooner. Before she started liking him any more than she already did.

"I am sorry to be taking Mitch back to Louisiana so soon though," Tori said, truly looking regretful. "But we do need his help with the trailers and driving that far straight through and everything."

"It's fine," Paige assured her.

Mitch lifted a brow as if to ask *it is, huh?*

Well, it *should* be. He was just some guy she'd met and had some sexy fun with. Hell, he already knew more about her life than the last three guys she'd "dated". It was time for him to go.

But she was going to miss him.

She wasn't able to quite avoid that thought entirely.

"I need to grab my stuff from upstairs," he said to her. "Come with me."

There was not a question mark at the end of that sentence. Still, she nodded.

"I didn't realize you'd left your stuff up there," she said as she led him up the stairs.

"You thought I took it all to the bakery with me?" he asked.

"I didn't know you went to the bakery."

"Where did you think I went?"

"Louisiana."

She pushed the door open and stepped inside.

He grabbed her wrist and swung her around. He wrapped an arm around her waist and brought her in for a deep kiss.

Her hands slid into his hair, and she went up on tiptoe to get closer.

This is what I'm going to miss she told herself. *All I'm going to miss.*

You're a freaking liar herself said right back.

When he let her go she was breathing hard.

"I've been dying to do that all morning," he said.

She nodded. Hanging out at the bakery and watching him pretend to be with Tori—and being stupidly jealous of it—had been bad enough, but walking through the square and watching him hold Tori's hand and feed her bites of cookie and brush glitter out of her hair had been irritating. Even though it was all fake. And she didn't want any of that herself.

It was definitely good he was leaving.

He was cupping her cheek and watching her. "I'll see you in thirty-eight days," he said.

Her eyes widened. "Thirty-eight days? That's not even two months."

He grinned. "Exactly."

"Are you coming back here for some reason?" Her heart thumped. She tried to tell herself it was because that idea made her nervous. But she was starting to think that she was not only a liar, but a pretty bad one.

"Do you want me to come back before then? I'll be here. Just say the word," he told her gruffly.

She wanted to say that word. Kind of. More than she did with anyone else anyway.

"Though you'll have to somehow explain that to your mom."

That would be interesting.

"I just... I mean..."

He finally chuckled. "Relax. I'm just giving you shit, you gorgeous commitment-phobe. The wedding is in thirty-eight days."

She pulled back. "What? That means they're getting married in February."

She'd assumed the wedding would be in the spring. Or June. Like a normal wedding time. Several months in the future.

Why was nothing with this guy going according to plan?

"They're getting married on Mardi Gras," he said. "That's when they met and when they got back together. So they almost have to." He shrugged.

"Mardi Gras is in *February*?"

Why didn't she know that? Why did Mardi Gras seem like a warm-weather event? Probably all the naked boobs associated with the holiday. Then again, it *was* a warm-weather event since it was mostly celebrated in the South. February in Louisiana was definitely warmer than February in Iowa.

Which was a major draw to this wedding for this Iowa girl.

As if the big guy who was dragging his hand down the side of her body and settling it on her hip wasn't enough.

He is. He so is. And don't even try to lie about it.

Yeah, yeah.

"Well, I guess I'll see you soon, then," she said.

He laughed and leaned in and kissed her before letting her go. "You need to work on acting enthusiastic about that before you get there, okay? My ego can only take so much."

She grinned a genuine grin. "I'm not worried about your ego."

It was probably a good thing he was sure of himself and cocky. He could handle her less-than-enthusiastic quirks about intimacy and commitment better than most men. The guys around here got their feelings hurt pretty easily. It was another reason she rarely said yes to dates with guys from Appleby. She mostly dated guys from other towns... the bigger and farther away, the better.

Mitch would be the farthest away of any guy she'd dated though—if that's what they were going to call it—and that didn't feel like a perk, exactly.

He pulled her in close again and put his mouth against her ear. "I can't wait to see you and have you for six months straight."

She felt tingles racing through her body and she had to focus on what he'd said. "You said six *days* last night," she reminded him. And she hadn't agreed to that. Yet.

"Okay, fine, we'll compromise at six weeks."

"I can't." Well, she *shouldn't*. She *could*. Technically, she supposed.

He kissed her, then lifted his head. "We'll see."

"That should sound creepy. Like you're going to lock me up or something."

He didn't grin. He cupped her face again. "*Does* it sound creepy?"

She wet her lips and then said honestly, "No."

"We'll take it... six days at a time," he said.

She smiled. "You don't take no for an answer very easily."

"Actually, I'm pretty easy going about most things. Usually. But I've never wanted something this much." His gaze was still serious and she felt her stomach flip. He dragged his thumb over her bottom lip. "But I won't push you."

"You'll just *tempt* me?" she asked.

"Oh yes. That. For sure." Now the slow, sexy smile curled his mouth.

"Thanks for the warning."

He stepped back after another long look. Then he grabbed his bag from beside the door.

How had she not noticed that before? Well, she'd been on the phone with her sister, panicking about Tori and Josh and Mitch being at Buttered Up.

Mitch pulled the door open and looked back. "See ya soon."

She nodded. "Yeah."

He smiled and then left.

As the door shut behind him, only one thought went through her head.

I already miss him.

Well, fu... fudge.

CHAPTER 11

One week later...

J osie and Grant's wedding was easily the most romantic thing Paige had ever witnessed.

Of course it was. It was Josie. The most in-love-with-love person Paige had ever met. And that included their own parents and grandparents.

Josie looked gorgeous, even with tears—happy tears, of course—streaming down her face. Grant had even choked up during his vows.

The flowers were gorgeous. The music was gorgeous. Josie's dress was gorgeous. Hell, even the bridesmaids' dresses—Paige, Zoe, Jane, and Amanda wore—were gorgeous. And when did that ever happen?

The cake was, of course, *gorgeous*. Zoe and Josie had made it themselves, and Paige had to admit, it was a work of art.

Paige tipped back her glass of champagne. Her first, but she intended to keep the free booze flowing. They were at the reception now, and she didn't have to make a speech—that was

Zoe's job as maid of honor—so Paige could definitely get drunk.

She really wanted to get drunk.

She was surrounded by in-love people. Her sister and Grant. Zoe and Aiden. Jane and Dax. Whitney and Cam. Max and Elliot. Even Kelsey was here with Matt, freaking *glowing* as they danced.

The worst part though, was that her and Josie's parents and grandparents and aunts and uncles and, well, *everyone*, were so, so happy. No, it wasn't bad that they were happy. She didn't begrudge them that. But it did remind her that they were still sad about the Wedding Reception That Never Was.

Aka, Paige's fuckup.

They were learning though, because only two people—and neither relatives of hers—had commented that it was her turn next. So she only needed to add two cats to her collection.

Of course, part of being around her extended family at a *wedding,* of all things, was she knew they were all whispering to one another about how "too bad" it was that the handsome, charming man she'd been holding hands with in the bakery last week lived so far away. What they really meant was that it was typical that Paige would finally show some interest in someone and he'd be out of reach. But Josie telling them all that Josh was from Louisiana and he owned his own business there, and, no, there was no way he could move to Iowa, did keep them from bugging Paige about holding his hand in public.

Paige set the champagne glass down and sighed.

And admitted the *actual* worst part.

She wished that Mitch were here.

And not just because then her Aunt Vivian would stop giving her pitying looks as she sat at the head table alone, the only single bridesmaid. She and Oliver, one of Grant's best friends, were the only two single members of the bridal party, period, and everyone knew Ollie was in love with Piper.

Well, everyone except Ollie himself.

Ollie and Piper were dancing now too.

Paige wished Mitch were here because she'd love to dance with him. And drink champagne. And flirt and laugh and tease and just have fun.

Mitch would be fun to be with.

At the dance. At the *wedding dance*.

She wouldn't even mind that her mother would be pleased and hopeful-watching her and Mitch together. She might even smile and say, "We'll see" when her mother asked if he could be The One. Instead of her usual, "You just added another year of spinsterhood to my calendar. At this rate, I won't be married until I'm fifty."

Her mother would always roll her eyes and mutter something under her breath, and Paige couldn't quite hear but assumed was along the lines of "Where did I go wrong?" or "I need to stop for wine on the way home."

"Hi, Paige."

She looked up and blinked, pulling her attention away from her thoughts. "Oh, hi, Carter."

"Would you like to dance?"

She looked from Carter Rogers to the dance floor then back.

No, not really. Not unless Mitch was here.

But Mitch wasn't here, and it was her sister's wedding dance, and, as much as she hated to do it, it would make her mom happy.

She sighed. She didn't hate making her mom happy. She loved her mom. She just wished that making her happy didn't involve her getting hitched. She'd given her mother *plenty* of grandkids to spoil. They had fur and couldn't talk, but they also potty trained *really* easily and could be left alone when she went out, like to a wedding, without her having to pay a sitter.

"Paige?"

"Oh right." She smiled at Carter. Carter had been a class-mate of hers and she'd always liked him. He was one of the smartest guys in their class and he'd gone off to college on a full scholarship. He'd just moved back and started his business. Something about bringing up-and-coming tech to rural areas of the Midwest. She was sure he was going to be successful. And in Appleby for the rest of his life.

"Sure," she finally said. They could *dance* though.

He led her to the dance floor and she let him pull her close. It wasn't her fault that she instantly began comparing being against him to being against Mitch.

But as they danced she relaxed.

They talked and laughed. She'd forgotten Carter was funny. She hadn't forgotten that he was cute and they got along well though. She was glad he'd asked her to dance.

She participated in the bouquet toss—dodging the stupid thing when her sister practically threw it right to her. Carter took part in the garter toss. They did the "Hokey Pokey" and line danced to "Achy Breaky Heart".

And when the dance was over, she let him walk her out to her car. She would have walked all the way home if it weren't for her heels and fancy dress and the sixteen-degree wind chill. Why her sister had wanted to get married in January was beyond her.

"This was fun," Carter said, pulling her door open.

"It was," Paige agreed. See? Why couldn't people just hang out and have fun without it meaning more?

"I've been thinking about you since I moved back," Carter said.

Paige froze. *No.* No, no, no.

"What do you mean?"

He smiled. And it did *nothing* to her stomach.

"I was really glad you were still single when I got back," he said.

Paige tossed her purse onto the passenger seat with a sigh. Well, dammit.

"I'm not looking for a boyfriend, Carter," she said.

He moved in closer. "Well, good. Because I don't want to be your boyfriend."

Paige narrowed her eyes. Was he thinking about a fling? She *might* have considered that, but... Mitch had happened. And now she wasn't attracted to Carter at all.

"Then what do you want?" she asked, not wanting to assume anything here.

"We're both living and working here, settling down," Carter said. "We're at the same place in our lives. I think we should get married."

Paige wondered for a moment if she'd had more champagne than she'd thought. But no. This was happening.

"You're not even going to take me out to dinner?" she asked with an eye roll. "Pretend to work up to this?"

In one way, in the back part of her brain, she kind of appreciated the no-nonsense, skip-the-romantic-bullshit approach.

That didn't, however, make her appreciate that she was being *proposed to*. *Again*. For fuck's sake.

Did she have a sign on her forehead? Had her mother signed her up on an online dating site with a description that read "Ready to marry immediately. Serious offers only"?

Actually, that last one made a little sense, and Paige made a mental note to check those sites tomorrow.

"Of course I'll take you to dinner," Carter said. "Anything you want. But I just don't think we should beat around the bush. I want you to know that I'm serious about this. I'm ready to make a commitment."

Otter yoga.

Those were the two words that went through her head.

She had to get out of here.

And there was really only one place she could even consider going.

"Well, that's not really going to work for me," she said, pushing Carter back and getting into the car.

"What? Why not? I've asked around. You've dated pretty much everyone here. If something was going to happen with someone here, it would have, don't you think?"

She nodded. "Absolutely."

"So what's the problem?"

"Well, gosh, for one... I don't want to marry you." She reached for the door and pulled it partially shut. Then she added. "For another, I'm leaving in the morning." Sure, it was a month early, but the idea of showing up in Autre, Louisiana and surprising Mitch made her heart pound.

"Leaving?" Carter asked, clearly confused.

"Yeah. I'm moving." She sounded completely confident. And happy. And she maybe *felt* both of those things too. "Away from Appleby."

"Where are you going? My grandma didn't say anything about that," Carter said with a frown.

It was actually fair, sadly, for Carter to assume his grandmother would know all about any plans like that.

Paige smiled at her fifth proposal and said with relief and a sense of anticipation that she hadn't felt in... ever, "South. I need a break and a little... heat."

"Just south? That's all you know?"

"That's all *you* need to know."

"Is it a guy?" he asked with a frown.

She didn't answer right away. That would definitely get back to his grandmother, then to her grandmother, then to her mother...

But would that be so bad? She'd be out of state, away from here, away from the drop-ins to try to get information.

"Yeah, it is," she finally said.

"Wow," Carter said. "You must be in love."

"No," she said quickly. "It's not that."

"Paige," Carter said. "You've never so much as changed your pizza order for a guy. But now you're *moving* for one? If it's not love, what is it?"

Well, she... couldn't say for sure. But it *wasn't* love.

Was it?

Was this what falling in love felt like?

Oh... fu... *fuck*.

Thank you so much for reading **Oh, Fudge!**

Want to know what happens once Paige gets to Louisiana? Yes, there's more to their story!

You can see it *all* in Mitch and Paige's book, the happily-ever-after, full-length novel **Four Weddings and a Swamp Boat Tour!**

You do not have to read the rest of the series to enjoy the book! They are all stand alone, full HEAs, featuring a different couple in each book!

But if you want to start at book one of the Boys of the Bayou series, you can grab it now everywhere!

My Best Friend's Mardi Gras Wedding
She needs a date to her best friend's wedding ASAP. Even if he's just faking it.

Spoiler alert: he's not just faking it.

And join in on all the FAN FUN!

Join my **email list!**
http://bit.ly/ErinNicholasEmails

And be the first to hear about my news, sales, freebies, behind-the-scenes, and more!

Or for even more fun, join my **Super Fan page** on Facebook and chat with me and other super fans every day! Just search Facebook for Erin Nicholas Super Fans!

Find all my books, including a printable book list, at
www.ErinNicholas.com

IF YOU LOVE AUTRE AND THE LANDRYS...

Don't miss anything from Autre!

Boys of the Bayou-Gone Wild

Things are going to get wild when the next batch of bayou boys falls in love!

Otterly Irresistible (Griffin & Charlie)

Heavy Petting (Fletcher & Jordan)

Flipping Love You (Zeke & Jill)

Sealed With A Kiss (Donovan & Naomi)

Head Over Hooves (Drew & Rory)

Say It Like You Mane It (Zander & Caroline)

If you love the **Boys of the Bayou Gone Wild**, you can't miss the **Boys of the Bayou series!** *All available now!*

My Best Friend's Mardi Gras Wedding (Josh & Tori)

Sweet Home Louisiana (Owen & Maddie)

Beauty and the Bayou (Sawyer & Juliet)

Crazy Rich Cajuns (Bennett & Kennedy)

Must Love Alligators (Chase & Bailey)

Four Weddings and a Swamp Boat Tour (Mitch & Paige)

The Hot Cakes Series

One small Iowa town.

Two rival baking companies.

A three-generation old family feud.

And six guys who are going to be heating up a lot more than the kitchen.

Sugar Rush (prequel)

Sugarcoated

Forking Around

Making Whoopie

Semi-Sweet On You

Oh, Fudge

Gimme S'more

And much more—

including my printable booklist— at

ErinNicholas.com

ABOUT ERIN

Erin Nicholas is the New York Times and USA Today bestselling author of over forty sexy contemporary romances. Her stories have been described as toe-curling, enchanting, steamy and fun. She loves to write about reluctant heroes, imperfect heroines and happily ever afters. She lives in the Midwest with her husband who only wants to read the sex scenes in her books, her kids who will never read the sex scenes in her books, and family and friends who say they're shocked by the sex scenes in her books (yeah, right!).

Find her and all her books at
www.ErinNicholas.com

And find her on Facebook, Goodreads, BookBub, and Instagram!

CPSIA information can be obtained
at www.ICGtesting.com
Printed in the USA
BVHW071010141221
624005BV00009B/274

9 781952 280269